The Spellmaster of Tutting-on-Cress

A Queer Fantasy Romance

By

Sarah Wallace

The Spellmaster of Tutting-on-Cress

For those who took a while to figure themselves out, this book is for you.

Contents

Content Warning

My books will always be about the power of kindness and hope and will always have a HEA, but please note that this book does contain the death of a parent and deals with the subsequent grief.

Family Record.

BIRTHS.

Basil Thorne.
Born 31 March, 1786

Sophia Thorne,
Born 1 September, 1800

Levinia Thorne,
Born 28 February, 1802

Elias Thorne.
Born 20 June, 1805

Arabella Thorne,
Born 21 June, 1805

Grace Thorne.
Born 23 December, 1807

Martin Thorne.
Born 9 May, 1810

Lucy Thorne.
Born 16 October, 1815

Chapter 1
Gerry

Geraldine Hartford was, at six and twenty, very ready for romance.

One might wonder how a nextborn of genteel birth, pretty face, friendly temperament, and quick wit could have reached such an age and remain unattached. As it happened, many people did wonder that, including her closest friends who came to visit her one chilly Sunday afternoon in December 1817.

There was her cousin, Rose Hearst, a nosy and impetuous woman who tended to get into scrapes. Her wife, Julia—a lovely and even-tempered woman—tended to get her out of them. Along with the Hearsts, Gerry's best friends included the Ladies Windham and Lizzy Canterbury, who all sat together in the small sitting room.

"How is business?" Julia asked, accepting a cup of tea.

"Capital," Gerry replied. Julia smiled, her cheek dimpling.

"Of course business is good," Lady Caroline Windham said.

Where Caro was flirtatious and bold, her wife Maria was calm and good-natured. Lizzy Canterbury had a cheerful and chatty disposition.

"Half the town is in love with you," Caro continued, "And the other half isn't of the feminine persuasion."

Gerry laughed. "Very kind of you to say."

"I know you think I'm just flirting," Caro said, tapping Gerry on the nose. "But it's the truth."

"We know you're flirting," Rose said, her eyes narrowed. Maria Windham ducked her head to hide her grin.

Caro smirked. "Well, perhaps I am. But that doesn't mean I'm any less earnest. Everyone adores you, pet."

Rose turned a beady eye to her cousin. "I rather think it's time you settled down."

"You sound like Veronica," Gerry said, wrinkling her nose at the thought of her sister-in-law.

Rose grimaced. "Nothing of the sort. You know I don't mean anything cutting. I mean to say that you're far too pretty, too clever, and too nice to be single. I think it's past time we rectified it."

Gerry took a sip of tea and didn't reply. She had gone through two London Seasons. She had learned that as much as she enjoyed dancing, pretty dresses, and being sought after by handsome gentlemen, the prospect of marriage paled in comparison to that of a career in magic.

"I'm not sure Gerry needs marriage to be happy," Maria commented. "She's doing very well as she is."

Caro tutted. "Don't be silly, my love. Of course she wants to be married. Rose is perfectly right. We ought to rectify it."

Rose, who was not overly fond of Caro, looked disgruntled to have the lady agree with her. Julia grinned at her wife knowingly and said, "It's all very well for us to scheme on our friend's behalf. But perhaps Gerry ought to be the one to decide what she wants in this matter."

"Thank you, Julia," Gerry said.

"That doesn't mean we can't help her along," Lizzy chimed in. "Why, I'm sure I wouldn't be married if Julia hadn't made sure Roger and I were invited to the same functions. Come to think on it, Gerry was part of that scheme as well."

"That's different," Gerry said. "You two are perfect for each other. Anybody could see that."

"It was simply a matter of putting you two together so you could see it too," Julia added.

Rose huffed. "There must be some eligible men in town who might suit."

"The vicar is very nice," Lizzy put in helpfully.

"Does it have to be a man, pet?" Caro said. "You are surrounded by men, you know. Perhaps you need a change of scenery."

Gerry laughed. "I'm afraid I am quite certainly of the masculine persuasion."

Caro sipped her tea and muttered, "You never know."

"Mr. Bowden is supposed to be very attractive for a man. Isn't he?" Maria supplied.

Both Rose and Lizzy grimaced.

11

"Certainly not," Rose said. "He's a cad."

"He *is* attractive," Lizzy said. "He was the most attractive man in town before, well, your family moved here," she added with a grin at Gerry. "Of course, it's hard to compete with the likes of Mr. and Mr. Kentworthy or Mr. Standish or Lord Finlington."

"I beg you not include my brother in any sort of ranking of the most attractive men in town," Gerry said.

Julia smiled.

"I am, as Maria correctly pointed out, perfectly contented," Gerry said.

"You mean you really don't wish to be married?" Lizzy asked, looking disappointed.

"As I said, I am perfectly contented."

"So you *would* like to be married," Caro said.

Gerry shrugged. "He would have to be a man who lives here or is willing to live here and will be supportive of a nextborn wife who works. I am not at all sure that is likely to happen." She glanced at Caro. "I am telling you now in case you take it into your head to parade a bunch of single gentlemen in front of me. I might enjoy the spectacle, but I fear you will be disappointed when I don't accept them."

"We have your blessing then?" Rose said, leaning forward. "To try to find you a suitable match?"

"Do stop putting words in my mouth, dear," Gerry said.

"That wasn't a no," Rose murmured.

Gerry sighed. "I am sure I will pose far too great a challenge. I don't wish you to get your hopes up."

"Well, that is certainly the wrong way to discourage them," Julia said cheerfully.

Chapter 2
Charles

Charles Kentworthy stepped into the sitting room where the ladies were having tea. He had a standing invitation to join all of Gerry's social calls and he always enjoyed the opportunity to catch up with her friends. "And how are we all doing today?" he said.

As he might have predicted, he was greeted cheerfully by Julia, Rose, Maria, and Lizzy, and greeted indifferently by Caro. To his surprise, Gerry looked flushed. He wondered what had made her blush so. While the entire Hartford family was adorably prone to blushing, Gerry was usually not easily embarrassed.

Intrigued, Charles took a seat and exchanged polite pleasantries with the assembled ladies. The conversation was frivolous and largely inconsequential. By the time the visitors left, Charles was still completely in the dark as to why his sister-in-law seemed ever-so-slightly disconcerted.

Not one to avoid a difficult conversation, he waited

until the room was empty of guests and turned to Gerry. "Everything all right, darling?"

"Oh yes," Gerry said in an airy tone. "Everything is quite all right, Charles."

"Gerry," Charles said. "What is it?"

She raised an eyebrow, impertinent girl.

He cocked his head, waiting.

Finally she sighed. "It is nothing, Charles. My friends have all taken it into their heads that I need to be matched with someone. That's all."

"And you don't want this?"

She shrugged. "I'm not sure I'm in the mood to have a procession of suitors who won't suit."

Charles's mind was already whirring. He had long been worried about Gerry remaining unattached, so he not only hoped her friends would succeed in their matchmaking, but was trying to come up with ways he could help. He knew her well, so he said none of this and instead gave her a charming smile and said, "But, darling, think of the entertainment. Think of the beauty. You must allow me to join you. We can exchange notes."

She giggled. "I can't imagine you'll find much beauty in the few prospects there are to be had in this vicinity. But you're welcome to join. I'm sure I would love to exchange notes." Then her eyes narrowed. "But don't take it into your head to meddle too."

"I wouldn't dream of it," he lied blithely.

Judging by her expression, Gerry didn't believe him for a second.

Chapter 3
Basil

Truth be told, Basil Thorne had enjoyed better Christmases than the Christmas of 1817. For on the 25th of December of that year, he received a letter from his stepmother detailing how his father had fallen ill, and requesting that he return to Tutting-on-Cress immediately.

As a result, Basil was much subdued over the course of the holiday. His closest friend, Modesty Munro, did her best to console him. She offered to go with him, but he rejected her offer, much as he wanted to accept. It hardly seemed fair to have her join him during such a forlorn event, and he was quite sure he would not be an enjoyable companion.

So she ordered a dinner with his favorite dishes and reminded him that it had been an age since he had visited home, and wouldn't it be nice to see his siblings again? She attempted to distract him by asking all about his siblings, but Basil was embarrassed to admit that he had little to say about them; it really had been a frightfully long time since he'd gone to visit.

"They're more along the lines of half-siblings," he explained.

"What does 'along the lines of' mean?"

"Well, in this instance, it means they are, in fact, my half-siblings."

She tutted and said they were no less family. Ashamed, Basil agreed.

Modesty sent him off, making him promise to write with any news, and assuring she would come at a moment's notice if he needed her. It was late at night by the time Basil returned to his lodgings. It would have been mad to attempt to travel at such a late hour on a holiday, so he spent the evening preparing for the trip instead. He oversaw the packing of his things and ensured he was leaving nothing behind in the hotel. If his father's health was truly failing, it was better to be prepared for the worst. In which case, he was unlikely to take a pleasure jaunt to Bath in the near future.

Basil went to bed, slept fitfully, and then travelled by hired carriage to his father's estate in Tutting-on-Cress. It was not a pleasant journey. Basil had little talent for working magic, so speed spells were quite out of the question, as were warming spells. Thus, the journey was cold and long. It took him nearly three days, even though he paid to change horses. By the time he arrived in Bedfordshire, he was exhausted and anxious.

His stepmother, Mary, came out to greet him, looking tired and drawn.

"I'm so glad you came," she said, clasping his hands.

"I would have come sooner had it not been for the holiday," he said, unsure whether to kiss her cheek or not. He settled for squeezing her hands instead. "How is he?"

"He is alive, but doing poorly. You'll find him...much altered."

He could readily believe it, considering how long it had been since his last visit. She led him into the house and up the large staircase to his father's bedroom. Along the way, she shooed some of her children back to their rooms, so Basil saw them only briefly before they disappeared behind closed doors. He didn't entirely mind; he was too concerned to be able to properly greet his half-siblings anyway.

One of the girls was sitting by his father's bed— Levinia, he thought her name was. She looked very mournful and tragic and she wrapped Basil in a startlingly tight hug, despite being much shorter and smaller than he was. He was a little stunned, as he was unaccustomed to embraces, much less embraces from young girls.

Mary pried her off. "You know better than to embrace people without warning," she scolded gently.

Levinia sniffed. "It is so good of you to come to us in our hour of need."

Basil grappled for a sufficient response. "To be sure."

"Let's give them some privacy," Mary said. She walked her daughter out of the room, leaving Basil alone with his father.

Basil approached the bed, feeling very unsure of himself. The fact of the matter was, he barely knew his father, barely knew his whole family, really. His mother had died when he was very young and his father, filled with grief, deemed himself unable to properly care for his son on his own. Consequently, Basil spent most of his life at Eton and Cambridge, surrounded by peers. It was a wonder of this age, really, that he turned out to be as responsible and practical as he did. He considered himself to be a man somewhat aloof in temperament. He wasn't cold by any means, but he believed he tended to come at life from the practical side.

When Basil was still at Eton, his father remarried and started to have a great many children. Basil quite liked his stepmother, but he also felt as though his father's new family was something separate from himself. As a result, he stayed away to avoid reminding his father of his earlier grief and to allow his family to live their own lives in peace. It had been a lonely existence, being adjacent to domestic bliss without partaking in it, but he had stood firm in his resolve to look to his family's happiness rather than his own. For years, he contented himself that the sacrifice had been to his family's benefit, but as he approached his father's bed, Basil wondered, not for the first time, if that had actually been a poor choice.

Nevertheless, his father did not seem to hold it against him. He held his hand out for Basil, who took it, uncomfortable with the show of affection.

"I'm here, Father," he said, feeling a bit silly saying it. He had meant to sound reassuring, but now it just seemed like he was stating an obvious fact.

"Basil, my boy," his father said, sounding weak and

tired. "I'm so glad you've come. My one regret in life is that I have failed to know you as I ought. Can you ever forgive me?"

"To be sure, sir," he replied, a bit at sea. "I should not have stayed away so long."

Mr. Thorne shook his head. "I should have sent for you sooner." He sighed. "But what's done is done. I'm sure you are aware that the estate and property are all going to you."

"Is this really the right time to discuss this, Father? I'm not—"

"Yes," Mr. Thorne insisted, squeezing Basil's hand tightly. "It is all going to you. The house in London and this one as well. That is how it is meant to be. I'm sure you deserve it and I'm sure you will take good care of it. I was not a very good father to you, but I am comforted that in this, at least, you may have some security and happiness."

Basil sighed. This was not a particularly cheerful conversation. But he supposed he had to inherit practicality from someone, so he gave his father his full attention. "Thank you, Father."

"But Mary...and the children...there is so little for them. Basil, son, I beg you to look after them. Please see to it that they live in comfort."

Basil was struck by the request. Did his father think him a monster? He wrapped his other hand around his father's and said, "Please do not fret about it. I promise you they will be well looked after. And they shall be welcome to stay here for as long as they have the need or the desire to do so."

Mr. Thorne smiled—the first smile Basil had received from his father in many years. "Thank you," he whispered.

Wishing to give his father time to rest, and needing rest himself, Basil excused himself. He fetched his stepmother and then went to bed.

The following evening, Mr. Thorne died, surrounded by all of his children and his wife. Basil decided, as somber an event as it was, that it was not an altogether unpleasant way to die, if one had to do such a thing.

Later, he offered his stepmother his arm as they walked to the funeral, and he didn't complain when Levinia cried against his chest and got his coat dirty. He scooped up the littlest one and carried her in his arms, surprising himself as well as everyone else.

When all was said and done, he sat down with his stepmother, Mary, and assured her what he had assured his father. "Please know that even though the estate has been passed down to me, I have no intention of turning you out. This house is yours for as long as you have need of it. If I am to assist with guardianship of the children, we can talk about their dowries and whatnot as they get older. I have no desire to see my own family be destitute."

Mary embraced him, which came as a bit of a shock. Although, he reasoned, it shouldn't have. After all, she was a very emotional sort of person. Then she opened the door of the sitting room where the children had been crowding to eavesdrop. Mary seemed thoroughly unsurprised to find them there.

"We have some good news at last," she told them. "Your brother is allowing us to stay at Verdimere Hall."

The children gasped as if they hadn't overheard the conversation.

Levinia clasped her hands together, her eyes watery. "At our darkest hour, a hero emerges."

Basil thought he saw one of the twins roll her eyes at this.

"And even better," Mary continued as if Levinia hadn't spoken, "he is going to stay with us."

"Oh, I say," Basil tried to interject. Had he said he would stay? He honestly couldn't remember anymore. But he supposed it wouldn't really do for him to leave his stepmother and half-siblings without a firstborn in the house.

No one noticed his interjection and Basil was suddenly surrounded by a great many arms and smiles and tears and embraces and it was all, frankly, a bit overwhelming. He could barely keep all of the children straight, let alone countenance being embraced by all of them at once.

Later, he snuck away to the library and found the family Bible. Sophia was the oldest, seventeen, which alarmed him because it meant that he would have to think about dowries and spouses sooner rather than later. Then came Levinia, who was fifteen, and the twins, Arabella and Elias, both twelve. Grace was ten, Martin was seven, and little Lucy was two. Seven siblings. What on earth possessed his father to sire eight children in his lifetime?

Basil sighed and began committing the names and

ages to memory. Sophia came in while he was attempting this. He was a bit embarrassed to be caught in the act but she gave him a brief, small smile.

"There really are a frightful lot of us," she remarked.

"Yes," he said.

"Clever of you to use the Bible."

"Thank you. I thought I'd better know ages if I'm to be in charge of dowries. Good to know how much time I have."

"Are you really going to stay here?"

"Your mother certainly seemed to think so."

She frowned. "Oh. Are you not staying then?"

"I suppose I should," he said. "It wouldn't do to leave you all unprotected. I believe you are all under my care now. Besides, I feel as though I have stayed away for too long as it is. I really ought to have tried harder to get to know my father. And my family."

She took a seat next to him at the table. "That will be nice. I've always wanted to have an older sibling."

"Why? Don't you have enough siblings as it is?"

She smiled her small smile again and it occurred to Basil that his oldest half-sister was a fairly serious sort of person. She leaned forward and pointed to one of the names. "Levinia is very romantic and very ready to fall in love. She tends to think everyone is beautiful. She likes poetry and paints very well. The twins are inseparable. They want to sail the world for King and country when they grow up. Bel will be the captain of their ship and Eli will be the first mate. Mind you don't mix that up."

Basil frowned. Was she joking? He couldn't tell.

She went on. "Grace is quiet. Plays the pianoforte beautifully. She'll be brilliant at it someday. She is shy but very sweet. Martin is the most athletic. He is always running around and getting his clothing dirty. Lucy asks a great many questions, her favorite color is blue, and she is the most affectionate of all of us."

She sat back as if that was the end to the matter.

"What about you?"

She blinked at him. "Well," she said. "I'm the oldest. I like to read. I like to write. For a long time I've wanted to become a writer, although I daresay that is not a practical decision."

"Well," Basil said, "Pen and paper cost very little these days. Not a bad choice, all things considered."

"At any rate," she said. "That should give you a fair enough idea of what I'm like."

"Enough to be going on with, at least," he agreed.

"And what about you?"

"Well, let me think. I am the oldest by a good many years—"

"How many?"

"It is not strictly polite to ask that, you know."

"Yes, but you're family."

"I was fifteen when you were born."

Her eyes widened. "Goodness," she said. "You're rather more like an uncle than a brother."

"Rather, yes. What else? I too like to read. I like to ride. I do not like sugar in my tea."

"Are you married?"

"No."

"Why not?"

"Haven't found the right person yet, I suppose."

Sophia looked interested. "Person?"

Basil waved a hand dismissively. "I have no preference. Perhaps I'm like Levinia in that way."

Sophia didn't seem to have anything to say to that, but later, Levinia herself came and found Basil and proclaimed herself delighted to find another person in the family who appreciated beauty. Basil was confused by the compliment.

"Sophia keeps her opinions to herself," Levinia explained. "Bel doesn't seem interested in anybody. And Eli, bless him, does try, but he is a little young, you understand."

"A little young to appreciate beauty?"

She nodded. "It is very tiresome. I have long wondered how I came to be the only one of my siblings to find practically everybody I meet beautiful." She clasped his hand. "But now I know that you think so too and it is too, too wonderful."

"I'm glad my persuasion pleases you," he said.

"Will you tell me about the most beautiful person you've ever met?"

"I'm...not sure I can think of anyone at the moment," he admitted. "Well..."

"Yes?" she said, leaning forward.

"There was a young lady—is, I should say. She is very beautiful."

"What's she like?"

"Her name is Modesty Munro. She's...she's my best friend. I proposed to her, actually and—"

But then Martin ran in because he was trying to avoid

bath time and Basil forgot to explain to his sister that his proposal to Modesty had been rejected.

From Basil Thorne
Verdimere Hall, Tutting-on-Cress

To Modesty Munro
23 Royal Crescent, Bath

12 January 1818

Dear Modesty,

It would appear I am staying in Tutting-on-Cress indefinitely. The more I've thought about it, the more it makes sense for me to stay, at least for a while. Particularly as I am now taking responsibility for them all. Well, I'm not exactly taking responsibility for Mary. You know what I mean.

At any rate, I am sorry that it will likely be some time before I see you again. I would invite you to come visit, but everything is in such a state, I do not believe I would be a very good host. Besides, I'm not certain if we can have visitors with Mary in mourning. I'm sure I should know these things, but I was quite young when my mother died. And I believe it is somewhat different with widows. At any rate, I shall learn more and invite you when I can.

The countryside is quite nice and the house is lovely. The children are all remarkable, although we are still barely acquainted, so I shall have to give you a more thorough report when I get to know them better. One thing I can tell you is that we all look decidedly related, which is rather nice. It is also unsettling considering the fact that we're virtually strangers. But our skin is all the same shade of golden brown, our eyes are all dark brown, and some of us even have the same shape of nose! Well, I suppose we have our father's nose, which isn't all that extraordinary. But it feels extraordinary; it has been so long since I've found myself in the company of those who resemble me. I am sure I have painted the most egregiously inadequate picture for you, but I promise to do better later.

Hope you are well.

Affectionately,

Basil

Chapter 4
Sophia

For most of her seventeen years, Sophia Thorne had lived the life of an oldest child.

She always knew she had a half-brother who was significantly older from her father's first marriage. But Basil had been so separate from their lives that it was easy to forget about him. If he was remembered, he was thought of as more of a distant relation. But by the end of January, whether Basil knew it or not, he had been accepted as one of them. The Thorne family had adopted their brother with the same care with which he had chosen to take care of them.

"I hope his fiancée is as nice as he is," Eli said one afternoon. Levinia had recounted Basil's proposal to her siblings.

"He hasn't mentioned her recently," she said. "Do you think she cried off?"

"I think he's trying to be respectful," Sophia said. "After all, when they get married, she'll be the lady of the house."

"What if she's horrid?" Grace said.

"Then we'll dispose of her," Bel said casually.

"Then we'll find him someone more romantic," Levinia said.

Bel rolled her eyes.

"There are plenty of eligible young people nearby," Sophia said. "I don't think we'd have a problem finding him an alternative if it came to it."

"And he's so agreeable," Eli said. "Not to mention a wealthy and handsome firstborn. He's sure to be a catch."

"Exactly," Sophia said. "And his fiancée might be wonderful. But we can keep our eyes open for any viable options just in case."

Levinia and the twins nodded in agreement. Grace looked dubious, but she shrugged, content to let Sophia handle things. After all, Sophia usually did.

Chapter 5
Gerry

Gerry was relieved when Christmas came and went with no signs of her friends or brother-in-law interfering. By the end of January, she was hopeful that everyone had forgotten their schemes. When Rose and Julia called on her for tea, she discovered that this assumption was decidedly incorrect.

"It really isn't fair," Rose said in a forced casual tone, "for you to forever be hosting our teatime visits."

Gerry frowned in confusion. "I don't mind."

"Of course you don't," Julia said. "But we would be happy to have you over some time. Mrs. Bailey, our cook, makes the most divine shortbread."

"Oh, yes!" Rose said, enthusiastic. "You really must call on us. Won't you, Gerry?"

"Well, of course, if you really want me to," Gerry said.

"Unless you're too tired to leave the house on your day off," Julia said.

"Oh, well," Rose said in an annoyed way. "If that's the issue, then I suppose we can keep coming here."

"No," Gerry said. "I wouldn't be too tired. I'd be happy to come visit you. I'm sorry, I didn't realize I was offending you by forever hosting."

Rose grinned, making Gerry immediately suspicious. "Oh, we don't mind!" Rose said cheerfully.

"Would next Sunday do?" Julia said.

Gerry saw that she had fallen into a trap. Rose and Julia were up to something and she was now neatly caught prey. "I would be delighted," she said politely.

"Wonderful!" Rose said. "Maybe we can invite Lizzy too. A-and maybe the Ladies Windham?" she added doubtfully.

Gerry tried not to laugh. "It's your house, dear."

Rose glanced at Julia and then said, "No, of course we should invite them too."

Julia deftly changed the subject and the two ladies left an hour later.

Gerry sat alone in the sitting room feeling vaguely annoyed. It wasn't that she opposed the idea of marriage; on the contrary, she was quite enthusiastic about it. But she wanted to find someone on her own terms and in her own time.

Charles walked in while she was still mulling through her thoughts.

"How was tea?" he said.

She smiled at him. "It was lovely, thank you. The Hearsts have invited me to call on them next week."

Charles looked amused. "Indeed? Well, I'm sure that will be pleasant. They have a lovely cottage."

She gave him an arch look. "Yes, it has been far too long since I've gone to see them."

He nodded soberly. "Quite negligent on your part, darling. Would you like me to accompany you?"

She resisted the temptation to roll her eyes. "No, thank you, Charles."

"If you're sure—"

"Yes, Charles, I'm quite sure I can handle whatever suitor Rose, Julia, Lizzy, Caro, and Maria see fit to show me."

He laughed. "Caro too? I wouldn't have thought Rose would ever ally herself with her nemesis."

Gerry chuckled. "Rose is very dramatic sometimes."

"Hmm," Charles said. "It would seem alliances can be made for a common goal."

"Yes," Gerry agreed. "Especially in such desperate times as these." She stood to go, tired of the conversation.

"Are you in desperate times, darling?"

She forced a smile. "Not at all. I was only joking."

He raised an eyebrow.

She sighed. "I don't want people to throw suitors my way. It was exhausting in London and I'm far too busy now."

Charles gave her a careful look. "That is perfectly understandable. Although I regret to tell you that suitors are a necessary prerequisite to marriage."

"Yes, well, I rather wish I could simply chance upon someone who becomes a friend, like Gavin did with you. There is nothing romantic about being forced to make small talk on the basis of mutual single status." She hadn't meant to say that much and seeing Charles's thoughtful expression, instantly regretted it. She gave him another cheery smile and said, "Ah, well. You know how Rose and Julia are. I daresay it's a taste of my own medicine after I helped Lizzy find her Mr. Canterbury."

She hurried out of the room without waiting for Charles to respond.

Chapter 6
Charles

Charles watched Gerry leave. Clearly it was time to take action. To do that, he needed to talk to a very particular person. He sent for the carriage and went in search of his husband, Gavin, and found him in the library.

"Charles," Gavin said as he walked in. "Do you know if we have a copy of Randolph's poems?"

"Randolph?" Charles said.

"Yes, Cynthia Lacey Randolph. She's been doing some exciting new things in poetry."

Charles hid a smile. Only Gavin would say such a thing. "Really? I've never heard of her."

Gavin made an impatient noise. "Well, she's mixing poetry and magic or something. I don't understand it. But I'd hoped we might have purchased a copy at some point." He glanced at Charles. "You keep buying me new books and I wasn't sure if you might have come across it."

Charles grinned and stepped forward to wrap an arm

around Gavin's chest. "Yes, that does sound like me," he said. "But if she's combining poetry and magic, perhaps Bertie will know more about her."

"Oh," Gavin said. "That's a good thought. Should I write to him?"

"Well," Charles said, pulling Gavin against him. "I was just thinking how nice it would be to go and visit him. Care to join?" He leaned down to kiss Gavin's cheek.

Gavin frowned. "In the middle of the afternoon? That's very unusual, isn't it?"

"Well, I have something I want to discuss with him. I'd like to do it while it's on my mind."

"Are you sure you want me there?"

Charles chuckled. "I always want you around, my heart. But even if Bertie and I need to talk in private, I expect you'll be busy in his library."

Gavin tilted his head thoughtfully. "Yes, that's true."

Charles took advantage of the opportunity to kiss Gavin's neck.

Gavin cleared his throat. "Well, should we be going then?"

Charles hummed in agreement and pressed another kiss. Then he pulled away, took Gavin's hand, and led him to the door.

Once they were settled in the carriage, Charles pulled Gavin against his shoulder.

"Is everything all right?" Gavin said quietly.

"Of course," Charles said, surprised. "Why shouldn't it be?"

"Well, you don't usually need Bertie in the middle of

the day. Nor do you usually need to go visit him personally. I feel as though you two write letters practically daily. Is there an emergency I should know about?"

Charles smiled and kissed the top of Gavin's head. "No emergency," he said. "I just want his advice on something."

"Then I suppose it's just as well we didn't invite Gerry or Pip to join us."

"Yes," Charles agreed. "It is just as well."

Gavin sat up suddenly. "Is this about one of them?"

Charles cupped Gavin's chin and leaned forward for a kiss.

After a moment, Gavin pulled away and gave him an arch look. "You did not answer my question."

"Yes, it's about one of them."

"Should I be concerned?"

"No."

Gavin narrowed his eyes. "Is there a reason you're not telling me about it?"

"I certainly can, but I don't think you will approve."

"Are you meddling again?"

"Everyone needs a hobby, darling."

Gavin groaned. "You're right. Don't tell me."

When they reached Bertie's house, they were let inside without introduction and informed that his lordship was in his study. Charles offered Gavin his arm and led the way through the large house.

Viscount Bertie Finlington was a gentleman of sophisticated taste, sharp wit, and good humor. He also happened to be one of the most powerful spellcasters in the country, but this last bit was less generally known. Charles had known Bertie since they were children and had practically grown up with him. Bertie was unendingly loyal and a great source for advice. Charles was not ashamed to admit that he often went to his friend for guidance.

He and Gavin found Bertie kneeling on the floor of his study and leaning forward on his elbow as he chalked a sigil into the wood.

Bertie glanced at them over his shoulder and said, "Why, darlings! What a delightful surprise! Give me a moment, will you?"

"Of course," Charles said.

Bertie finished what he was doing and sat back on his heels. He gave the sigil another long look then nodded as if satisfied. "Good a place to stop as any," he said as he stood. "To what do I owe the honor?" He strode up and kissed Charles on the cheek and then did the same for Gavin.

Gavin blushed, as he usually did with this greeting.

"Gavin and I were wondering if you might have a certain book in your library. What was the name of it, dearest?"

Gavin looked up at him in surprise. "But what about—"

Bertie put a hand on Gavin's shoulder. "I'm happy to help, my sweet. Although I confess my poetry collection is rather slim in comparison to yours."

Gavin turned back to Bertie, still blushing. "Cynthia Lacey Randolph?"

"Ah, wonderful timing, m'dear. I just received a copy of her work last week."

Gavin brightened. "You did?"

"Yes. I haven't had a chance to look through it yet, so this is quite fortuitous. Perhaps you can tell me if there is any spellwork worth trying."

"Oh," Gavin said. "I can certainly try. Although I'm sure you will be a much better judge of that."

"Well, in all honesty," Bertie said in a confiding tone, "I'm not sure how I shall parse through her poems to get to the spells. I do not possess your keen understanding when it comes to poetry. So I would consider it a great kindness if you were to read it and tell me your thoughts."

"Thank you," Gavin said shyly.

Bertie smiled at him. "You sweet thing. Let's go to the library then, shall we?" He cut a glance at Charles and then led Gavin out of the room.

Charles knew the look and stayed in the study. He didn't move from his spot as he had no idea what spell Bertie was casting and didn't wish to mess it up.

Bertie returned a few minutes later. "You know your husband is quite adorable," he said as he shut the door. He gave Charles an assessing look. "Very convenient that Gavin had a poetry emergency right when you needed to talk to me."

"Yes, I was very pleased."

Bertie led the way around the spell on the floor to a sofa by the window. "I expect he'll be busy for some time. Now, what is this visit really about?"

Charles smiled. "It is time to find Gerry a husband."

Bertie looked amused. "Is she aware of that?"

"Well, it would appear all of her friends have taken it into their heads to start matchmaking. So I expect she's painfully aware."

"Julia?"

"And Rose, Lizzy, Caro, and Maria."

Bertie raised an eyebrow. "Rose and Caro together? My, how unprecedented. I take it, however, that you do not intend to join them?"

Charles shrugged. "I am not sure our scheming styles are quite the same. Besides, I rather think Caro would not appreciate my assistance. She is not overly fond of male intervention. I won't get in their way, of course, as it will be very convenient if they do the initial search for suitors. They intend to invite Gerry over for tea, along with whatever eligible gentlemen live nearby. I confess I don't think there is anyone suitable in the vicinity. At least no one I've met."

"Poor Gerry," Bertie remarked. "She's in for a great many tea parties with a great many unsuitable gentlemen."

"She might be grateful for the distraction when the John Hartfords come to visit. At the very least, it will save her from some of their inevitable lectures."

"I forgot about that. When is the dreaded oldest Hartford sibling coming?"

"In a month or so, I think."

"Remind me again why he's coming?"

"He wants to make amends, I think."

"From what I've heard, that might be difficult to do with his wife along."

Charles chuckled. "Yes, it certainly will be. But I can't deny that I appreciate him making the effort. Now to the matter with Gerry..."

Bertie leaned back against the sofa. "You know I'm always delighted to see you, darling, but I confess to being thoroughly baffled as to how I can help."

"Gerry is a romantic, but she is convinced she will not find love in a conversation organized by others."

"Not an altogether incorrect assumption."

"She let slip that she wants to meet someone accidentally and become friends with them, much like Gavin did with me."

Bertie barked out a laugh. "Poor darling. She doesn't realize that you orchestrated that entire introduction?"

"It would appear not."

Bertie looked thoughtful. "I suppose if a gentleman did something similar for her, it would feel more romantic than a drawing room suitor."

"Here's hoping we find someone who will."

"I'm still mystified by my role in this."

"Gerry's friends are going to be setting her up with suitors. We need to be on the lookout for someone who will suit Gerry and then see that they are thrown together in more organic ways."

"So when this paragon of romance is identified, I am to coincidentally invite them both to the same events, recommend the fellow go to Gerry's shop, and give directions to places that will happen to cross her path?"

"Yes! Just like that. If you invite them both over for tea, it won't be nearly as obvious. And anything else you might happen to think of. I trust your judgment. And I

45

thought you might throw a ball when we need to give them a final push."

"Sounds like an enjoyable challenge."

"I was hoping you'd say that."

"What do you have planned?"

"Nothing yet, but I wanted to be sure of your involvement first."

"You don't even have to ask, m'dear. You will keep me informed?"

"Oh, darling, you will most certainly be my first co-conspirator."

Bertie laughed. "Splendid. Who else do you have in mind?"

"Laury and Seb are due to come back in a month or two." Charles was fairly certain Seb, the youngest Hartford sibling, would be delighted by the opportunity for meddling; the young man had an uncanny talent for mischief. His betrothed, Laurence Ayles, was significantly less puckish, but Charles suspected he would be pleased to be a part of the scheme.

"Poor Gerry. She doesn't stand a chance, does she?"

"We'll find someone who will make her happy and then she'll forgive us. Don't worry."

"Do we need to send for Julian?"

Bertie's cousin, the Dukex of Molbury, was known to be an adroit matchmaker, but Charles was less than keen to ask for help. "We'll keep them in reserve for now," he hedged.

Bertie nodded, satisfied. "Shall we go extract your husband from his poetry or give him more time?"

"As long as he knows he's not disturbing us when he

returns, I think he'll be happy reading for a while longer. Besides, we haven't talked in an age."

Bertie pulled something out of his pocket and flicked his wrist in the direction of the door. The door opened. "It's been about three days, in point of fact. But, yes, I agree, we're quite overdue."

Chapter 7
Basil

After he had been at the estate about a month and a half, Basil began to assess his situation. He had prepared as well as he could for a long stay in Tutting-on-Cress, but it occurred to him that more country-appropriate attire might be agreeable. He waited another week before saying as much to his stepmother. She had been so grief-stricken, poor thing, he was doing his best to leave her in peace.

She replied with far more enthusiasm than he anticipated, saying, "Oh, wonderful. When you go to the village, would you be so kind as to take Elias? He has gotten so gangly, you know, he has outgrown most of his clothes. And of course, Arabella will want to go too. If you bring Sophia along, she can help keep an eye on them."

Basil had no idea how the minor shopping trip had gotten so out of hand, but he knew better than to argue. Besides, he was tolerably sure that bringing some of the children would give his stepmother some time to herself. He called for the carriage and loaded up five of his half-siblings (somehow, Levinia and Grace joined them as well, although he couldn't figure out how that had happened). Elias and Arabella climbed up to sit with the driver, so he didn't have to worry about space. Although he was worried about the two children sitting up top. What if one of them fell off? Was that liable to happen? He really had no knowledge of what children were apt to do.

What ought to have been a quiet and uneventful stroll alone in the village turned into a bit of a scramble. The children were all well-behaved, but they had a great many questions and wanted to go to all of the shops. Grace eschewed Sophia's hand in favor of Basil's and Levinia tucked her hand around his other arm. Sophia took charge of the twins.

"Basil," Elias said, skipping sideways next to Levinia, "are you going to get another coat like the one you're wearing now? I think it's very fine."

Levinia gasped. "Is that not the most beautiful gown?"

"You mustn't point," Sophia muttered.

Levinia dropped her hand, looking thoroughly unrepentant.

"Can I have a coat like yours to match?" Elias asked.

"Exactly how much are you going to buy for Eli?" Arabella chimed in. "He doesn't go anywhere, so I don't think he needs so very much."

"Will you be getting riding boots?" Elias asked, ignoring his sister. "Do you like riding, Basil?"

Levinia squealed. "That is the most beautiful bonnet I have ever seen! Don't you think so, Basil?"

"The shop is just around the corner," Sophia said.

"What are the tailors in Bath like?" Elias asked.

"What do you know of tailors?" Arabella asked her twin. "You are hardly a sartorial expert."

"I'm hardly a sartorial expert either," Basil said.

"But you wear such fine hats!" Elias said.

"The brim on your hat is most distinguished," Levinia agreed.

"Can I get a fine hat too?" Elias asked.

Basil glanced around, feeling hard-pressed to respond to all of the questions. Grace did not say anything. Basil was, truthfully, grateful that at least one of the children was shy and quiet. Although he had to admit that Sophia was quiet too, in her way. When he considered further, he was of a quiet nature too. The thought warmed him suddenly, to see a similarity between himself and his siblings—well, two of them anyway. Thus cheered, he took Elias to get measured and fitted, and Sophia and Levinia took charge of the other two girls to wander in the shops.

He was worried about finding them again, but no one else seemed to think this might be a problem. When he strolled out an hour later with Elias, he realized why: Arabella was standing sentry in front of one of the shops, looking very dignified and important. As Basil approached the building, he saw the rest of the children through the shop window, and he hurried inside to see what havoc they may have wreaked in his absence.

Chapter 8
Gerry

When the extraordinarily attractive stranger with skin
the color of bronze and dark brown eyes was led into
the shop by the Thorne twins, Gerry wondered briefly if
marriage was more possible than she'd previously
supposed. The gentleman had the same complexion as
the Thorne children, which led Gerry to believe he was a
relation of some kind. He was one of the handsomest
men she'd ever seen, and, as her friends had pointed
out, she knew a lot of handsome people. He seemed
very bewildered to be dragged about by two children,
and she was instantly charmed.

Thankfully, Sophia Thorne stepped forward and
quickly provided explanation: "Miss Hartford, please
allow me to introduce my brother, Mr. Basil Thorne."

Gerry curtsied. "A pleasure, Mr. Thorne. I did not
know the Thornes had an older brother."

The gentleman bowed and said, "Well, technically, I'm
their brother by my father's first marriage. So really, I'm
more of a..." He tapered off after a glance at Sophia.

"Well, that is. Yes. I am. Their older brother. Sorry. I have a tendency toward pedantry. Been out of town, though. Just moved back in December when my father... well...you understand."

"My sincere condolences, sir," Gerry said.

He gave a brief little smile that reminded Gerry very strongly of Sophia's brief little smiles. "I daresay he was happy...at the end. To have all of his family about him, you know. Couldn't ask for a better way, I should think."

"No, I don't think you could," Gerry said, smiling warmly at him.

"Basil just bought me loads of new clothes," Elias put in.

"Can I have new clothes, Basil?" Arabella said. "It isn't fair that Eli should get new things just because he's a mite older."

"It isn't because he's older," Mr. Thorne said. "It's because he was growing out of his clothes."

"Well, whenever I grow out of my clothes, I get Levinia's cast offs. And that's not entirely fair."

"I suppose it isn't," he agreed. "But I believe that is more a matter for your mother than for me, isn't it?"

"Yes, but you might actually buy me something," Arabella said.

Mr. Thorne looked flummoxed by this logic.

"Enough, Bel," Sophia put in. "Sorry, Basil," she added. She ushered the twins away, following them to ensure they didn't continue to interrupt.

He watched them walk away and then seemed to look about himself for the first time. "This is a charming shop."

"Thank you."

He blinked at her. "Er...?"

She smiled. "I'm the spellmaster."

"Oh!" He didn't seem bothered by this, only surprised. "Well, then my compliments, Miss Hartford. Very charming."

"Mr. Fenshaw, the former spellmaster, left it to me when he retired. I've been running it ever since."

"Ah." He waved a hand in his siblings' direction. "I didn't realize a spell shop would prove so entertaining to them. Although I'm sure magic is a good science for them to explore."

Gerry grinned at him. "Sophia is very talented with magic, as I understand. Perhaps magical talents run in your family?"

"Good God, no," he said. "At least not with me. I'm hopelessly terrible at magic, I'm afraid."

"Oh, not hopeless, surely," she said with a wide smile.

He looked a bit dazed for a moment, then murmured, "Well, we can't all be gifted."

The compliment did much to endear the gentleman to her. "What are you good at, then?"

He gave an embarrassed but amused huff. "I'm not sure I've ever considered myself particularly good at anything, really. I was tolerable in school. But that was mostly because I was diligent rather than naturally clever."

"I'm sure you don't give yourself enough credit, sir."

"I'm not attempting any sort of false modesty," he said, a bit hastily. "I believe myself to be passably good at many things, but exceptional at none of them." He smiled briefly again and Gerry was distracted by noting his very nice teeth.

In an apparent effort to divert the conversation, he glanced at a few of his siblings roaming around the shop. "My siblings all seem to be terribly clever, though. And very talented. Did you know the twins are going to command ships some day?"

Gerry laughed. "I do! We've discussed it when they've come in. They want me to design a spell for them to assist with navigation."

He gave another small smile. "Very practical of them. I hope you will let me know when you need to be paid your commission."

"You will be funding their adventures, then?"

He shrugged. "Someone has to, haven't they? That is, I think they're my responsibility now. Of a sort."

Gerry decided he was adorable.

"Basil?" Levinia Thorne tucked her hand around the gentleman's arm. "Might we go to the bookshop after?"

"Levinia wants to see if you'll buy her poetry by Lord Byron," Grace put in. "Mama won't let her."

Gerry stifled a laugh. Mr. Thorne looked at a loss. "Well, if your mother won't permit, Levinia, I'm sure I couldn't—"

"But he's so impossibly romantic, Basil!"

He glanced around, probably hoping for Sophia, but she was still busy entertaining the twins. "Perhaps something else, Levinia?"

She sighed and wandered away.

"Are you a lover of poetry, Mr. Thorne?" Gerry said.

He cleared his throat. "Well, I do not think I appreciate it quite as much as I ought to."

Relieved to hear this, she said, "Neither do I. But there is a nice pocket volume of Shakespeare's sonnets in the bookshop. Very pretty and set at a decent price."

"In this bookshop?" he said, gesturing behind him.

She nodded.

He let out a relieved breath. "Thank you, Miss Hartford. I'm sure that will do nicely."

Grace was still standing nearby. "If you get her a book, everyone else will expect a gift too," she said solemnly.

"Oh, dear," he said, looking down at her. "Will they really?"

She nodded.

He looked apprehensive. "What would you like?"

Grace seemed pleased by the question. "I believe the bookshop has some sheet music."

"All right then."

"Sophia will ask for a spell," she added.

"Oh," he said, looking back up at Gerry. "Well, I don't mind that. We've spent such a long time in your shop. We ought to pay you something for it. I daresay they've all been quite entertained here. I would hate to disrupt your business and then not properly thank you for it."

Gerry chuckled. "Not a disruption, Mr. Thorne, I assure you. Your family has been visiting my shop regularly for quite some time. I always enjoy it." She beamed at Grace, who smiled shyly back.

Gerry's assistant, Pip Standish, put a light hand on

her arm. "Forgive me for interrupting you. I believe we may be out of levitation spells."

"Oh, of course," she said. "Pip, have you met Mr. Thorne? Mr. Thorne, this is my assistant, Mr. Standish."

The two gentlemen bowed.

"Mr. Thorne, please excuse me. It would appear I have to put together some spells. Levitation is very popular, you see. But it was a pleasure to meet you. I hope we might see you again soon."

Mr. Thorne stammered that he would be delighted.

Gerry strolled to the back of the shop, feeling pleased.

By the time she came back out, the Thornes had left. She wasn't surprised; it would have been difficult to keep that many children excited about a spell shop for a long time, but she was a trifle disappointed. After all, Mr. Thorne had been very attractive and charming. The challenge was going to be in keeping the gentleman a secret from Charles and her friends. She had no interest in being matched with him. If such an attempt was made, Gerry felt sure the lovely Mr. Thorne would lose all appeal.

Chapter 9
Basil

Basil felt winded when he finally reached home. This was partly due to the large party that had been deemed necessary for the shopping trip and partly due to his mind still reeling from his interaction with the spellmaster. She had been so very pretty and friendly, Basil had felt a little tongue-tied in front of her.

"How was the shopping trip, dears?" Mary said, coming out to greet them.

Lucy and Martin came scampering down the stairs, as if Basil and his charges had returned from a long journey instead of a few hours in the village. Lucy tugged on Basil's pant leg until he picked her up.

"Really," Mary tutted. "You're much too big to be carried about like that, Luce."

Lucy leaned her head on Basil's shoulder and didn't respond.

"It was wonderful," Levinia said. "Basil bought me the most *divine* book of sonnets. Isn't it too beautiful, Mama?"

"Very nice," Mary said appreciatively.

"And wait until you see the clothes Basil got me,"
Elias put in. "They're positively smashing!"

Mary ushered everyone into the sitting room and rang
for tea. Basil was grateful. He was pretty sure he needed
tea. As soon as he sat down, Lucy clambered onto his
lap and Grace nestled onto the sofa next to him.

"And he bought me a new atlas!" Arabella said.

"It's our atlas," Elias protested.

"No, you got new clothes. The atlas is mine. But you
can use it," she added kindly. "Sometimes."

"What did you get for me?" Martin said, looking
impossibly unkempt for the early afternoon. Frankly,
Basil had no idea how the child managed to always be
covered in dirt. He almost said soap, but that would have
been unkind. Besides, Sophia had encouraged him to get
the little ones sweets, so he handed one to Martin and
the other to Lucy.

Martin took his, pleased, and ran outside.

"I see you went to the spell shop too," Mary said,
gesturing at Sophia's spell bag. "Really, Basil dear, you
don't need to spoil them."

He tugged at his collar. "Well, it was not exactly
intentional, ma'am. But I did wish to be fair, considering
the expense put forth for Elias's wardrobe."

"You are too kind to us, dear boy."

Grace leaned her head against his arm and Basil
realized he would likely need that arm for tea. He raised
it and she accommodatingly leaned into his side.

"We introduced him to Miss Hartford," Sophia said.

"Oh, she's such a dear girl," Mary said. "So pretty."

Luckily, Basil was spared from responding to this observation by Levinia saying, "And he met Mr. Standish. Isn't Mr. Standish the most beautiful man you've ever seen, Basil?"

"Er..." Basil said, trying to remember if he had even noticed Mr. Standish. He had been so distracted by Miss Hartford, he'd barely seen anyone else in the shop.

"I don't think he'll go for you," Elias said suddenly.

"And why not?" Levinia said, affronted.

Her younger brother shrugged. "I don't think he likes girls."

Levinia sighed. "But he smiles so prettily."

"You can't marry him either," Arabella said, pointing an accusatory finger at her brother. "No husbands allowed on ship."

Elias ducked his head. Basil couldn't read the emotion behind it—was it embarrassment? Disappointment? Then he realized he had no idea what to do with that emotion even if he did figure out what it was. He supposed he was the closest thing his siblings had to a father now. Would Elias be looking to him for relationship advice? That thought made Basil feel dreadfully uncomfortable. He didn't have much experience in romance. His proposal to Modesty had been one made of fondness rather than romantic attachment.

He was so caught up in these swirling thoughts that he barely noticed when Mary handed him a cup of tea.

Chapter 10
Sophia

Sophia called for an emergency family meeting that evening.

Family meetings were taken very seriously in the Thorne household. The signal was turning the porcelain shepherdess in the dining room to face the fireplace instead of the window. It was the easiest signal that the adults in the house would disregard, but the children would all notice. Anyone could request one as it was easily reachable even by Lucy. Furthermore, Mrs. Thorne had never cared for the shepherdess statuette, saying the facial expression had been painted to look too simpering, so she didn't seem to mind when Martin and Lucy moved it about. Sophia suspected her mother secretly hoped someone would break it.

Family meetings were always held in the same place. At the end of the gallery was a large bay window with a round window seat. It was just large enough for everyone to sit.

So, after their mother and older brother had gone to

bed, the Thorne children crept from their rooms and tiptoed down the stairs to the gallery. They set their candles on the floor, as if they were seated around a campfire. Levinia put Luce on her lap and Bel hung off the side of the bench to be a better lookout. Eli was in charge of making sure Martin didn't get too rowdy. Grace sat on Martin's other side, as she tended to have a quieting influence.

"I'm sure you're all wondering why I've called this meeting," Sophia began.

"I thought Levinia called it," Eli said.

"Well, I did find the most perfect poem that aptly describes my current despondent state—"

"No, it was me."

"Oh, thank goodness," Bel said. "I don't think I could stomach poetry tonight."

Levinia stuck her nose in the air.

Sophia soldiered on. "I think Basil needs our help."

Her siblings stared at her, baffled.

"I agree," said Eli.

Everyone swiveled to look at him.

He blinked at them. "Well, he's never really had a family before, has he? I don't think he knows how to be a part of one. I think we need to teach him."

Sophia hadn't noticed this, but she trusted Eli's instincts. "You're right. But that's not what I meant. I think we need to find him a spouse."

"But he's already betrothed, isn't he? Didn't we already discuss this?" Grace asked.

Levinia rolled her eyes. "She's clearly not in love with him, though. There's no depth of passion."

"How do you know?" Eli asked.

"If there were, she would already be here," Levinia said, as if it were obvious. "Mere distance would not keep them apart. And if it did, she would write him letters every day. I know I would if I were in love with someone."

"She does write to him though," Grace said. "I've seen the letters addressed to him."

"It's not often enough," Levinia pressed.

Eli did not look convinced, nor did Grace, which was not helpful to the schemes Sophia was devising.

"At any rate," Sophia said. "We need to find someone who feels the depth of passion."

Bel narrowed her eyes. "I suspect you already have someone in mind."

"Miss Hartford."

"Oh, wouldn't they make the most gorgeous couple?" Levinia said, clasping her hands together.

"I like Miss Hartford," Grace said.

"I thought you liked Miss Hartford," Eli said, looking at Sophia.

"Well, I do...but I don't think she likes women. In that way."

"No," he said. "I think you're right."

"So we're getting Basil to marry her?" Martin said.

Sophia nodded. "It will take all of us, I expect."

"What are we going to do about his fiancée?" Grace said.

"I have ideas," Bel said.

"Nothing too horrible," Sophia said. "At least, not until we've met her. She might be quite nice. We don't want to scare her or anything. Just discourage her from wanting to live here."

"But what if Basil still marries her and leaves?" Grace said.

"We'll have to be strategic," Sophia said. "For now, we'll just watch and listen. But start thinking of ideas."

Everyone nodded except Luce; she had fallen asleep.

Chapter 11
Charles

"I forgot to ask you how business was yesterday," Charles said to Gerry the next morning at breakfast.

"Very good," she said, smiling. "We had a busy day."

"Any exciting gossip?" Charles asked, looking at Pip.

Pip considered the question. "Did you know that the late Mr. Thorne had a son by another marriage?"

"I did not," Charles said. "Although I only met the late Mr. Thorne once or twice."

"The son is much older than the rest of the siblings," Pip explained. "He came into the shop yesterday. Very pleasant gentleman."

"Is he to inherit then? I wonder where the rest of the family will go?"

Gerry took a sip of tea and said, "According to Miss Sophia, he did inherit but invited the family to stay. I think he has taken over some guardianship responsibilities for his siblings as well."

Charles noticed, with delight, that she was blushing.

"Indeed? Well, that is remarkable. He must be a very good sort of man."

"I think he might be. He seemed very kind," Pip said. Gerry nodded.

Charles wanted dearly to ask what the gentleman looked like, but had a strong suspicion that he looked very well indeed for Gerry to blush at the thought of him. He tactfully changed the subject. After Gerry and Pip left for the shop, he sent a letter to the Thorne residence, inviting Mr. Thorne and the rest of the family to tea the following Sunday. He knew Gerry wouldn't be present, which was perfect. He was pleased by the notion of getting an idea of the gentleman's character first. After setting the invitation in the hall to be sent out, he started composing a letter to Bertie, to keep him abreast of the new information.

"Charles, what is the letter in the hall for?" Gavin said, stepping into Charles's study.

Charles set aside the letter he was writing. "It's an invitation to tea, dearest."

Gavin frowned and squared his shoulders.

Charles fought to hide a grin. Before Gavin could say anything, Charles said, "Would you mind closing the door, darling?"

Gavin blinked at him. "But we're not having that sort of conversation...er...are we?"

"Well, I do like to keep the option available."

Gavin hesitated, then closed the door and walked to the desk. "Charles," he said, his voice stern. "What are you scheming?"

Charles adored when Gavin attempted to be stern. It

was high on his list of favorite things about his husband. Admittedly, it was a long list, but he would have ranked it at least at item number 23. Hoping to encourage this behavior, Charles widened his eyes in an innocent expression and said, "Me? Scheming?"

Gavin narrowed his eyes. "Yes. I know perfectly well that you're inviting that Thorne fellow in an attempt to set him up with Gerry. Now, it won't do. You really must stop meddling."

"Must I?"

"Yes! It is getting quite out of hand, you know. First Seb, now Gerry." Gavin jabbed his finger at the desk. "Gerry has shown no interest in marrying. I think we ought to respect that."

Charles laid his hand on the desk, palm up in invitation. Gavin sighed and placed his hand over Charles's. "My heart," Charles said, "I hope you know I would never do anything to make Gerry unhappy."

"But?" Gavin said, arching an eyebrow.

Charles grinned and clasped Gavin's hand and held it to his lips. He pressed a kiss to the knuckles and said, "It is true that there are people who are not romantic by nature. And plenty more who are, but are happy to be unmarried."

"Yes, and I do believe Gerry to be one of them."

Charles slipped his hand in Gavin's grasp so he could kiss the inside of his husband's wrist.

Gavin, predictably, melted a bit at the touch. Then he grumbled, "You're not playing fairly and you know it."

Charles chuckled and gently tugged Gavin closer.

Gavin, knowing perfectly well what Charles was

after, obligingly sat in his lap. "This conversation is not over," he said.

"No," Charles agreed. "But this is a more comfortable position to have it in, don't you think?"

"And here I thought you were going to try to distract me."

"Not yet."

Gavin huffed in amusement.

"You Hartfords have some very strong family traits. You're all very intelligent—"

"Even John?"

Charles laughed. "Yes, even John. And you're all very talented in magic, from what Bertie tells me. You're all exceptionally good-looking. And..."

Gavin sighed. "Yes, I know. We're all frightfully stubborn."

Charles kissed his cheek. "Precisely. You all have a tendency to get in the way of your own happiness. It's a very bad habit, darling."

"Yes, I know, but Gerry isn't like that. I always thought she was smarter than the rest of us."

Charles smiled. "Yes, she usually is. But I think she's beginning to exhibit the trait nevertheless."

"What do you mean?"

"I mean that Gerry is unlikely to want any gentleman who is foisted upon her."

"Agreed."

"Even if the gentleman being foisted is perfect for her."

"How do you know he will be?"

"I don't. But I would like to form an opinion of the

gentleman in advance. If I think he will suit, it will take some maneuvering, but I have faith in our collective abilities."

"But she would be expected to keep house," Gavin protested. "I'm sure I couldn't work all day as Gerry does and still run the house."

"True. That would be a challenge. But if she were to meet a young man who lived with someone who already kept house, his mother, for instance—"

"Or stepmother?"

"Exactly! Someone who could have sent his family packing, but instead chose to take responsibility for them must be a very kind and generous person. Furthermore, a man living with a number of younger siblings might be more inclined to respect nextborns in general. He could quite possibly be the sort of person who would marry a nextborn and respect her desire to work in trade. As his family is already staying with him, Gerry would have no need to run the house. And she adores children, so she will probably get along famously with all of them."

"Bravo," Gavin said drily. "Have you announced the wedding yet?"

Charles grinned and deftly untied Gavin's cravat knot. "Of course, we still have to meet the man."

"Small detail, I suppose."

"A necessary first step nonetheless. But if he is the sort of man I think he is..."

"You seem to already be sure of that."

Charles slid the cravat off Gavin's neck and began unbuttoning his waistcoat. "So in answer to your question, darling, that is why I am inviting them to tea."

"But did you have to invite the children?"

Charles laughed. "I suspect where Mr. Thorne goes, the Thorne children go, at least for some time. Particularly if the mother is still in mourning."

"Well, I will likely be busy," Gavin said. "You know there's so much to—"

"You mean you don't want to meet Gerry's young man?"

Gavin huffed. "You really are sure of yourself, aren't you? I'm sure I wouldn't mind meeting *him*. But really, Charles. Seven children!"

"Well, just think of it as meeting Gerry's future in-laws."

"That does not make me feel better. And is not at all the right strategy to get me to help you."

"Oh, are you helping me, darling?" Charles said as he slipped Gavin's waistcoat off and began unbuttoning his shirt. "That is a nice surprise."

"Impossible man," Gavin muttered. "I most certainly will not help you with that attitude. If you were a kind husband, you'd spare some pity. I already have to host John and Veronica for God knows how long."

"Ah yes. I rather thought you'd forgotten they were coming to visit."

"I wish I could forget."

"When are they coming again?" Charles asked.

Gavin sighed. "Soon, I think. Next week perhaps? I'd better read over John's letter." He paused. "Maybe you'd better read over John's letter. I'll just get angry again."

"What did John say?"

Gavin rolled his eyes. "Oh, you know. The usual nonsense—lectures about how I need to be a proper host and how he hopes married life has taught me to be responsible. All that rot. I am positively dreading their visit."

Charles reached up to brush Gavin's cheek with the back of his fingers. "I'll gladly read it for you, darling. And I promise to keep you from your brother's lectures as much as possible. And Gerry will be here too," he continued. "You're not alone with him this time."

"I know," Gavin said. "But this time he'll have Veronica with him and she's even worse. And she makes him worse."

"Then perhaps it's just as well that I'm preparing to launch my campaign on Gerry's behalf now. We shall all be properly distracted when our visitors arrive."

Gavin narrowed his eyes. "When are the Thornes coming to visit?"

"Sunday."

"Gerry probably won't be here, you know. She's going to have tea with the Hearsts."

"I know, but I want to get my own assessment of the gentleman first. I'm also keen to see how he is with the children, so having them present will suit my purposes."

"You seem to have thought of everything."

Charles slid his hand under Gavin's now open shirt and nuzzled Gavin's neck. "I have my talents."

Gavin looked down at his revealed chest. "Are you undressing me?"

Chapter 12
Basil

The day after his trip to the village, Basil found himself returning to it. He told himself he was going to get a better lay of the land. After all, he reasoned, he had not been at leisure to walk or ride there the previous time, and had been too busy keeping an eye on the children to attend to his surroundings. So he left the house without telling anyone he was going, had his horse saddled, and rode to Tutting-on-Cress at a leisurely pace.

To convince himself that he was not taking the trip to catch another glimpse of the lovely Miss Hartford, Basil went to the spell shop last. He explored the market, the bookshop, the haberdashery, and looked through the fabrics at the tailor's, even though he no longer needed any additional clothes. He took tea at a teashop. Finally, trying to ignore the niggling feeling of excitement, he walked into the spell shop.

Miss Hartford was busy talking to customers when he walked in, so he began browsing through the shop wares, realizing he hadn't really looked the last time he had been there.

"What a pleasure to see you again, Mr. Thorne," said a quiet voice behind him.

Basil turned to see Miss Hartford's shop assistant, Mr. Standish. He bowed to the younger gentleman. "A pleasure, Mr. Standish."

"Are you looking for anything particular today?"

He remembered Levinia's praise of the gentleman and discovered, now that he was not thoroughly distracted by chatting children and lovely ladies, that her assessment had been correct: Mr. Standish was very beautiful, with faun-colored skin, large dark eyes framed with long lashes, and dark curly hair.

"Not at all," Basil said. "I'm just exploring the village a bit. Didn't really get a chance to see much of it the last time I came."

Mr. Standish flashed him a smile. "I can certainly understand that. I imagine your siblings have a way of taking over things."

"Yes," Basil said. "Not that I mind," he added hurriedly. "I'm just getting accustomed to it. I'm not used to being surrounded by people, really."

Mr. Standish nodded his understanding. "Well, I'll leave you to peruse. But I hope you'll let me know if you have any questions."

Basil thanked him and turned back to the rows of bags that lined the walls. He found himself intrigued by the spell bags, even though he knew he was unlikely to be good at casting them. Since Mr. Standish had encouraged him to peruse, Basil began plucking down spells that interested him and peeking into the bags. He had a solid enough grounding in magical theory to understand some of the ingredients and recognize some of the spells, but Miss Hartford's shop had a number of spells Basil had never heard of. He noticed one labeled *Personal Quick-Dry Spell* and picked it up.

"That one is very popular," Miss Hartford said, coming up next to him. "One of my earlier inventions."

"You invented this?" he said, surprised.

She grinned. "Oh, yes. I sell a good number of spells that are of my own design."

"Extraordinary," he said, looking into the bag. "How does this one differ from a normal Quick-Dry Spell?"

"It is safe to use upon your person. There aren't any dangerous ingredients or anything."

"Good heavens. Do you often work with dangerous ingredients?"

She gave him a broad smile. "Quite often."

"You don't seem to be concerned by it."

"I've been experimenting with spell-building for years now. My family did have concerns initially."

"But not now?"

"Most of them have come around."

He closed the bag but did not put it back. "Not all?"

"I think my parents are cautiously approving of my choice. My oldest brother decidedly does not approve."

"Whyever not?" he said before he could stop himself.

She seemed to hesitate for a moment and then said, "Well, it was a bit of a step down, you see, my going into trade."

"Are you happy with the choice?" he asked, surprising himself with his own daring.

"I am, yes."

"Then I can't see why anyone should disapprove," he said matter-of-factly. "I am sure I wouldn't mind if any of my siblings decided to take a step down socially, provided they were still safe and happy with the decision."

"My brother Gavin has been very supportive. I live with him and his husband, Mr. Charles Kentworthy. They actually moved here in order to help me take over the shop."

"Well, I'm glad to hear you have some supportive relations."

She gave him a twinkling smile and he felt just as dazzled as he had the previous day. He had no idea what moved him to be so honest with her, not to mention so curious. He would never have dreamed of asking her so many personal questions. He wondered if it was the influence of being around so many inquisitive children, that questions now felt more ordinary than impertinent. He hoped she didn't think him impertinent.

He cast about for a change of topic and then held up the bag in his hand. "Is this one difficult?"

The lady smiled again. "I'm confident you can handle it, sir."

"I wouldn't be, if I were you," he said. "I really do have a shocking lack of talent where magic is concerned."

She laughed. "Here, come over to the counter for a moment."

She walked him to a large counter at the front of the shop and gently took the bag out of his hands. She removed each ingredient from the bag and laid it in front of them, along with a small slip of paper. Then she explained what each ingredient was for and showed Basil how it would be placed for the spell. She did all of this without any condescension, explaining things patiently and thoroughly but with the manner of a person who trusted him to understand.

"The instructions are included," she said, tapping the paper. "So, if you should forget before the casting, you needn't worry."

Then she showed him the hand motion. Basil was embarrassed when she encouraged him to imitate her, but she was so cheerful about it that he wasn't as self-conscious as he might have been. And she was much kinder than his professors. She made him repeat the incantation a couple of times before pronouncing herself satisfied. Then she placed all of the items back into the bag.

"I think you'll do just fine, Mr. Thorne," she said, handing the bag back to him.

"Very kind of you to say. And it was good of you to show me."

She waved a hand dismissively. "I do this with all of my customers."

"Do you really?"

"Well, I do it with customers who do not seem confident or are picking out spells that are new to them. I am of the opinion that everyone can do magic as long as they have the tools, information, and encouragement they need. Some people might need more practice than others, but that is no different than any other skill."

Basil tilted his head in acknowledgement. "I suppose you are correct. Although I would argue that some talents are innate. For instance, I have no eye for art. I'm sure I couldn't paint like my sister Levinia does. And I have no ear for music. I'm sure I couldn't play like Grace does."

Her smile widened. "It is true that some talents are stronger in others. I come from a family of strong spellcasters. But I rather think you do as well."

He blinked at her. "I do?"

"Certainly. Your father was a regular customer of mine and he did not limit himself to the easiest spells in my shop. I daresay Sophia may well be on her way to following him in that regard. The others are a bit too young to gauge their talents, but I wouldn't be the least bit surprised if more of your siblings showed aptitude."

Basil twisted the drawstring of the bag between his thumb and forefinger. "I didn't know that about my father," he said softly. "I suppose I hardly know what talents I may have inherited from him."

"I'm sure your family would be only too happy to tell you about him," Miss Hartford said, matching his tone.

He nodded. "I shall have to ask them sometime." He took a deep breath. "How much is the spell?"

The lady brightened. "You wish to buy it?"

"I can't say I'll be any good at it. It may well sit on my desk for months before I work up the nerve to attempt it. But I'm intrigued. And you were so kind to show it to me."

"You're welcome to come any time if you'd like a review," she said with a grin. "And this is a good one to practice with. It has recastability. So you can use it multiple times before it loses efficacy."

Basil thanked her, paid, and then left the shop. He placed the bag carefully into his coat pocket. He wasn't entirely sure what had possessed him to purchase a spell. He hadn't been exaggerating in describing his lack of talent. But Miss Hartford made him feel so comfortable as to make even daunting tasks seem worth the challenge. He gave his pocket a little pat and then headed home.

When he arrived, he learned that he had received an invitation to have tea with Mr. Charles Kentworthy.

"I cannot go," Mary said, "as I am still in mourning, but I think the children could do with a social outing."

Basil was anxious about the prospect of taking care of the children again, but he didn't say so. "Of course," he said instead. "The invitation is for the entire...that is, it is an invitation for the Thornes."

Mary smiled, but Basil could only manage a grimace in response and hoped she didn't notice. He also hoped she didn't notice the way he'd been unable to count himself as one of the family in anything other than name.

Chapter 13
Gerry

Later, when Gerry and Pip were cleaning up the shop at the end of the day, Pip surprised her by bringing up the topic. "I quite like Mr. Thorne," he said as he swept the empty shop. "He's very unlike his father in terms of his interests, I think. But he seems just as kind and understanding."

Gerry nodded. "Yes. He seems very nice."

Pip seemed to hesitate for a moment and then said, "I hope you are not angry with me for bringing him up in conversation at breakfast."

"Of course I'm not angry," she said, surprised. "I could never be angry with you. Why should I be?"

He gave a small smile. "Thank you. It's just that you didn't really pursue the topic. I thought you had liked him, so I was surprised. Then it occurred to me that you might not want to have him discussed because you liked him."

She sighed. "I didn't want Charles to take it into his head to meddle," she admitted. "But I can't really stop him from doing it. I do like Mr. Thorne, but I'm not interested in being pushed together constantly."

Pip looked like he was going to say something else and then thought better of it. "I understand." He gave a knowing little smile. "So I suppose we are not telling Charles that Mr. Thorne could barely keep his eyes off you when you were teaching him the spell?"

She laughed. "That's because he was a good listener."

Pip raised an eyebrow but didn't comment.

"And no," Gerry said, "we are not telling Charles that."

Pip chuckled. "Understood," he said, and went back to sweeping the shop.

Gerry walked to the back of the shop and began putting together the spells to replenish what they had sold. Had Mr. Thorne really been looking at her in the way Pip said? And did she want him to do that? She was glad Pip had essentially offered to keep the gentleman's visit a secret, although she felt guilty and conflicted about that too. Nothing had changed, she concluded, except that a charming, attractive, and eligible man had moved into the neighborhood. It need not impact her life at all. Although perhaps, she considered, it might be nice to make a new friend.

She thought too about how impressed Mr. Thorne had been in learning that she invented spells. It occurred to her that she hadn't invented any new ones in quite some time. This realization troubled her more than she cared to admit. She began thinking about the problem in her usual way: trying to remember if she'd cast any spells recently that didn't satisfy her. She typically came at spell design from the perspective of disassembling and reassembling spells that had already been created. But nothing came immediately to mind. She considered the matter for days, and by the time she went to the Hearsts' cottage on Sunday, she still had no new ideas.

Chapter 14
Sophia

Sophia was sitting in her room, looking over the spell Basil had purchased for her on their trip to the village when Levinia burst in.

"It is too, too exciting!" her sister said.

"What is?" Sophia said, packing everything back into the drawstring bag. Levinia was never one for brevity, so it was a sure thing the interruption would be a long one.

"We have been invited to tea!"

"By whom?"

"By Mr. Charles Kentworthy," Levinia said dramatically.

"We're going to the Kentworthy place? That will be nice. We've never been there before."

"Do you know what I think? I think Miss Hartford went home and told them all about Basil and how wonderful he is and now Mr. Kentworthy is inviting him to see if they're a suitable match. I wonder what Miss Hartford said about him. Do you think she's been thinking about him? She must have. I can just imagine the sleepless nights she's been having, dreaming about him."

"Wouldn't that be perfect? Not the sleepless nights. I mean if she really did like Basil."

"We've been invited to—" Bel said, poking her head in the door. "Oh, never mind. I'm guessing Levinia told you."

"Tea at the Kentworthy place?"

Bel nodded. "Is there a plan?"

Sophia considered. "We should try to get him alone with Miss Hartford."

"Isn't that technically inappropriate?" Eli said, coming to stand next to Bel in the doorway.

"I'm sure we can find a way," Sophia said.

"And then Basil can declare his love!" Levinia said.

Bel rolled her eyes. "They've only met once, you ninny."

"Basil went out riding earlier," Eli said. "They may have met more than once."

"How do you know that?" Sophia asked.

He shrugged. "I went into the stables when the groom was brushing down his horse."

"Secret liaisons," Levinia gushed.

Bel let out a long sigh. "So, we're leaving them alone. Any other instructions?"

"I think it might be best if she doesn't know Basil is engaged," Sophia said thoughtfully.

"Basil's so honorable, though," Eli said. "He's sure to bring it up."

"Then we can interrupt him," Sophia said. "Not particularly polite, of course, but no one will think anything of it. Everyone have interruptions prepared if Basil appears to be about to talk about Miss What's-Her-Name."

Her siblings nodded.

"Do we need to tell the other three?" Bel said.

"No..." Sophia said slowly. "Grace perhaps. But Martin and Luce might just talk about it if we mention it."

"And those two are just as likely to interrupt for no reason at all anyway," Eli said.

"Exactly."

"Right," Bel said. "We shall be on alert." She gave a salute.

Levinia sighed. "So romantic. Falling in love over tea and cake."

Bel and Eli left before Levinia could become over poetic. Sophia resigned herself to a long soliloquy about romance.

From Basil Thorne
   Verdimere Hall, Tutting-on-Cress

To Modesty Munro
   23 Royal Crescent, Bath

                              20 February 1818

   Dear Modesty,
   It is kind of you to offer help, but I hardly know what
I need help with at this point. I shall certainly tell you
when I am ready for your assistance.
   I rather think you ought to wear that powder-blue
concoction to the ball. I've always said you look very
fetching in blue. Then again, if Mr. Brummerton is there,
it might do for you to look a bit less fetching. No sense
in encouraging the cad.
   I've received my first invitation to tea. A Mr. Charles
Kentworthy invited me to join him and his husband on
Sunday next. He encouraged me to bring the children,
which was very hospitable of him. Let's hope he doesn't
regret that decision. Not that the children are poorly
behaved, of course. But I'm not sure if he realizes there
are seven of them. Thankfully Sophia and Levinia are
very good at corralling the younger ones. The twins are
too, when asked, but they're a bit more independent in
spirit, I think. They often wander off on their own. Which
means that I then have to keep an eye on them too.
Although unlike the little ones, the twins are old enough
to not be too rowdy and break things. Grace is one of

the younger ones, but is so quiet and mild-mannered that I tend to see her as older than she really is. So it is really Martin and Lucy I am worried about. Let us hope we all come out of this visit in one piece. And that the Kentworthys don't end the association before it has even begun.

From my understanding, Mr. Charles Kentworthy is the brother-in-law of Miss Hartford, the spellmaster I wrote about in my earlier letter. The one with the...well, I think I went into embarrassing detail about the color of her hair and other...qualities so I can imagine you will recall the description. At any rate, I am very curious about her family.

Levinia tells me that Mr. Standish, the spellmaster's assistant, also lives with them, which I find rather odd. But I suppose it does make sense since they work together. From what I've seen of him, he does not seem like the sort of person who would be burdensome to have around. He has a very quiet and gentle spirit. Levinia also proceeded to talk about how very attractive the man is and, while I can certainly agree with her, I do worry about her falling in love with someone so much older. Should I be worried, do you think?

Of course, one never knows with Levinia. She might not actually be in love but rather taken with his beauty in a more general sense. She is as prone to swooning over a person as she is to asking them to pose for a portrait. So if Mr. Standish is present I daresay that will add an interesting element to the proceedings. I suppose I shall have to keep an eye on Levinia to see if she is near the swooning point. I should also probably interfere if she asks him to pose, for I do not think that can be a proper request for a young nextborn to make. But this is a small village, so maybe everyone is used to it. Then again, I believe this is the family's first time being invited to the Kentworthys' house.

Oh, dear, I'm getting myself quite agitated. I'd better go take a walk around the house.

Affectionately,

Basil

Chapter 15
Basil

On Sunday afternoon, Basil led his siblings into the carriage and to the Kentworthys' for tea.

Basil wondered what Miss Hartford's brother would be like and whether her cheerfulness was a family trait. As it turned out, it was not. Mr. Gavin Kentworthy looked very much like his sister—the same strong cheekbones, the same dark eyes, the same pale skin that blushed prettily, the same small mouth—overall, a very attractive person as well. But Basil could tell within moments of meeting the young gentleman that he was of a decidedly serious disposition. He remembered what Miss Hartford had told him, that her brother and brother-in-law had moved to Tutting-on-Cress in order to support her while she worked. He reasoned that beneath the young man's shyness must be a generous and kind soul.

His husband's generous soul, on the other hand, was not hidden at all. He was very friendly and seemed particularly pleased to meet Basil. Mr. Charles

Kentworthy was tall and had broad shoulders and tan skin a few shades lighter than Basil's. He was also impossibly good-looking with dark angular eyes, black hair, and a wide smile. Basil wondered idly how Levinia was handling the massive amount of beauty in the room, particularly since Mr. Standish was present as well, as quiet and shy as he had been at the shop.

Miss Hartford was conspicuously absent, and Basil tried not to be too disappointed. Mr. Charles Kentworthy explained that she had gone to have tea with her cousin.

The children were, in a word, everywhere. Not that they were misbehaving. Basil was pleased to note that there was no roughness or naughtiness to their actions. But they were curious and talkative. Grace was admiring the pianoforte (which is to say, she was playing it), Levinia was in raptures about a painting, Lucy was pulling at Basil's coat to encourage him to pick her up, Elias and Arabella were examining a statue of a bullfighter and discussing bullfighting in general quite loudly, Martin was attempting to get into the teacakes but Sophia was keeping a firm grip on his hand as she talked to Mr. Standish. Basil hoisted Lucy up onto his hip to stop her from fussing.

Charles Kentworthy offered Basil a seat, looking amused. "I take it you have recently arrived in town, Mr. Thorne."

"Yes," Basil replied. "Arrived right before the new year." Sophia ordered her siblings to sit and take their tea nicely, which Basil was incredibly grateful for. He accepted a cup of tea from Mr. Gavin Kentworthy.

"So you will be living in Tutting-on-Cress then?" Mr. Charles Kentworthy asked.

"For the time being. It felt...right to stay here, for a little while." Basil carefully lifted the teacup around Lucy so as not to spill, and took a sip. "It may depend on what my—"

"Isn't that painting simply stunning?" Levinia said, apropos of nothing. "The waves are so vibrant! So lifelike! So exciting! Did you pick out the painting, Mr. Kentworthy? It is magnificent."

Mr. Charles Kentworthy smiled. "It is lovely, isn't it? But I'm afraid I cannot take credit for the choice, my dear. It came with the house."

"I hope you keep it forever," she said.

"What were you saying, Mr. Thorne?" Mr. Gavin Kentworthy asked politely.

Basil tried to remember what he was even talking about.

"You were saying that your stay depended on something," Mr. Charles Kentworthy said helpfully.

"Ah, yes, thank you. Well, it rather depends on what my—"

"Is it true you plan to go on living here, Mr. Kentworthy?" Elias said.

Sophia sighed. "I am sorry. They are terrible about interrupting."

Mr. Charles Kentworthy chuckled. "It is understandable. I don't think we've ever had you to visit before. New places are always exciting. And yes, darling," he said, smiling at Elias, who looked shy from the attention. "It is true. I was leasing the house before we got married. I have since purchased it. I quite like it, you know. And we both love to see Gerry and Pip every day. My brother-in-law, Mr. Sebastian Hartford, will be settling down in the vicinity as well, actually. He is engaged to a local gentleman, Mr. Laurence Ayles. Are you familiar with the Ayles family, Miss Sophia?"

"Oh, yes, we're very close. Although we haven't met Mr. Sebastian Hartford."

"He is out of town at the moment. They are making it a long engagement, much like Gavin and I did. I have always been in favor of long engagements. It allows a couple to get to know one another before marriage."

"That does not sound very exciting," Levinia said. "I should like to fall in love immediately."

"Well," Mr. Charles Kentworthy said with a side-long glance at his husband. "I confess that I was quite smitten before we'd even met."

Levinia clasped her hands together and sighed. "How romantic!"

Mr. Gavin Kentworthy was blushing profusely.

"But it is still wise to not rush into things," Mr. Charles Kentworthy added.

"Very practical," Sophia commented.

"Thank you, Miss Sophia," Mr. Charles Kentworthy said.

"Does your garden have a maze?" Arabella said. "I've always wanted to see a garden with a maze."

"We do not, sadly, have a maze. But we do have some very nice hedgerows." He looked around the room. "Perhaps the children would enjoy a visit to the garden."

With that, Mr. Charles Kentworthy stood and held one

arm out for each twin. Lucy hopped down from Basil's lap and took Sophia's hand. Levinia and Grace took charge of Martin. Basil was surprised when Mr. Standish strolled quietly after them. He glanced at Mr. Gavin Kentworthy, who was still holding a cup of tea and looking thoroughly confused as to why everyone had left so suddenly. Basil understood the feeling. He wasn't sure if he ought to follow the departing party or stay with his host.

Mr. Gavin Kentworthy turned back to him, blushing. "Charles has a way of taking over."

Basil smiled. "My siblings have the same knack, I think."

Mr. Kentworthy seemed to think for a long moment. Then he said, "How do you like Tutting-on-Cress?"

"I confess I've seen little of it. I've been to the village a couple of times and it's very pleasant there. I've been to your sister's shop," Basil added. "I can barely manage to cast spells; I can only imagine the ingenuity it would take to create them."

Mr. Kentworthy's smile was fond. "Yes, Gerry is something of a genius, I think."

Basil noted the nickname, remembering how Mr. Charles Kentowrthy had used it as well. He found it suited the young lady perfectly. "I visited the shop yesterday and she told me how you and your husband had moved here to help her. That was remarkably generous of you. You must be very proud of her."

"Yes, I am. Gerry's always been a person of decisive nature. I wish I were more like her in that respect. She knows what she wants and she goes after it. She is so talented, it would have been a shame for her to miss the opportunity to run her own shop. So moving here to help her took little generosity on my part, as I was only too happy to do it. Besides," he added, "it was all Charles's idea anyway. I've done precious little."

"That's not the way she talks about it," Basil said. "I think your support means more than you realize."

Mr. Kentworthy's mouth twitched. "I imagine the same could be said of you, opting not to send your family away and instead moving in to take care of them."

Basil shrugged. "I'm not sure why that surprises people. I'm not a monster."

Mr. Kentworthy's mouth quirked again. "Indeed not, Mr. Thorne." He glanced at the doors the rest of the party had walked through. "I confess I find myself daunted in the presence of children. I'm not at all sure how you manage it."

"I'm not at all sure I am managing it," Basil said. "But they seem to like me as I am, which is something of a wonder."

Mr. Kentworthy sighed.

"Is something the matter?" Basil asked.

"No, forgive me," he said hurriedly. He blushed again and said, "Only I hate it when my husband is right. It's a damned nuisance. Would you like to join them in the garden?"

"I'd be glad to," Basil said. "But if you are uncomfortable with the children, I'm happy to keep you company here."

Mr. Kentworthy gave the tea set a longing sort of look. "I appreciate the offer," he said. "But I probably ought to get to know them better, considering."

Basil didn't know what Mr. Kentworthy was alluding to, but he obligingly followed the young man out of the house and into the garden.

Chapter 16
Charles

Charles considered the Thornes' visit to be very successful. The children were delightful and he was immensely pleased by Mr. Thorne. The young man turned out to be polite, soft-spoken, patient, and seemed to be of an affectionate nature, even if he was not fully aware of it. Charles had found it endlessly amusing how surprised Mr. Thorne had been every time the youngest Thorne child had climbed into his lap or taken his hand. He had never been irritated by the children interrupting him, which was a very good mark in his favor. Indeed, he had the makings of a very fine father, which was just as well, as Charles suspected Gerry wanted children of her own.

Gavin had seemed to like Mr. Thorne, which said a great deal for the gentleman's character. Charles had also been able to satisfy his curiosity as to Mr. Thorne's looks: he was very attractive. No wonder Gerry had blushed at the thought of him.

He had encouraged the party to go to the garden for

several reasons: he thought the children would enjoy it and he suspected it would break their party into groups, which would allow him to gauge everyone's different characters and interactions. As such, he was pleased when Gavin and Mr. Thorne remained behind while he and Pip escorted the rest of the family outside. As soon as the garden was in view, the twins left his side and ran. The youngest boy broke free of his sister's hold and tore off after the twins, with the youngest girl toddling behind.

"Ah," Charles said. "I take it our lack of maze was not a disappointment."

"The hedges are tall enough to feel like one," Miss Sophia said. "At least for them."

"You have a beautiful garden," Miss Levinia said. "'And 'tis my faith that every flower enjoys the air it breathes!'"

Charles smiled at her. "Fond of poetry, I take it, Miss Levinia?"

"I adore it!"

"I shall mention it to my husband. Gavin is particularly fond of poetry. He always enjoys meeting a fellow enthusiast. We have quite a nice collection, thanks to him. You are welcome to borrow anything you like."

Miss Levinia looked as though she might hug him. Charles privately amused himself with imagining eventual conversations between Miss Levinia and Gavin; the young lady was so excitable, she was sure to unsettle his quiet husband. He suspected Gavin would be too fascinated by her love of poetry to avoid friendship for long.

Charles fell into step with the other three girls. "If you don't mind my asking," he said in a low voice. "What was it you were attempting to keep Mr. Thorne from talking about?"

"Oh, dear. You noticed?" Miss Sophia said.

He chuckled. "It was an impressively orchestrated attempt."

She looked adorably embarrassed and proud of the compliment.

"We didn't want Basil to talk about his fiancée," Miss Levinia said.

"He's engaged?" Charles said, his eyebrows raised.

"Unfortunately," Miss Grace said.

"We would much prefer it if he married Miss Hartford," Miss Sophia said.

"Is his fiancée so terrible?"

"We've never met her," Miss Levinia admitted. "We keep hoping she'll cry off or something."

Charles cleared his throat, trying not to laugh. "How interesting. Well, as a married man myself, you know I cannot condone—"

"Yes, but you're different," Miss Levinia said. "You're definitely in love."

"If she isn't terrible, then it might be all right," Miss Sophia added.

"Very good of you to give her the benefit of the doubt," he said somberly. "Do you happen to know when she is coming to visit?"

Miss Sophia shook her head. "I don't think *he* knows."

Charles hummed thoughtfully.

When Mr. Thorne and Gavin exited the house to join

them, the three girls walked away. Charles wondered if they were trying to give him time to meet Mr. Thorne himself. He was grateful for it, as he was full of curiosity. He held out his arm for Gavin as they approached. Gavin blushed and accepted it.

"I'm so glad you two came out to join us," he said, smiling at both of them.

Gavin raised an eyebrow expressively.

Mr. Thorne said, "Mr. Kentworthy said he'd like to get to know my siblings better."

Charles looked at his husband in some surprise. Gavin's blush deepened. Perhaps this was Gavin's way of consenting to Charles's schemes. "How wonderful, darling," Charles said. "I'm sure they will adore you. Although you may have difficulty catching some of them at the moment; they are tearing through our garden at an alarming rate. Perhaps if you joined Pip where he's sitting in the shade?"

Gavin looked relieved and left without another word.

Mr. Thorne hung back and looked at his siblings as they wound their way through the hedgerows. "It was very kind of you to let them explore."

Charles beamed. "Glad to do it, my dear. I do hope we can have you all over more often. Your family is delightful."

Mr. Thorne gave a small smile of his own. "Thank you. I'm sure we would all like that. I confess I've met precious few people since I arrived." He paused. "Unless you count my trips to the village. I've met a few of the shop owners there, including Miss Hartford and Mr. Standish."

"That's to be expected," Charles said. "I'm sure you'll get to know everyone once you've been here for a while."

Mr. Thorne nodded.

Charles hesitated, unsure if he should broach the subject. He decided hesitation was not his style and said, "Your sisters told me they expect your fiancée to come visit sometime soon. May I offer my congratulations?"

Mr. Thorne looked at him in surprise. "Fiancée? What fiancée?"

"Are you not engaged?"

Mr. Thorne shook his head. "Not at all. I wonder where they got the notion. I suppose I mentioned to Levinia that I had proposed to someone once. But I also thought I told her that Modesty rejected my suit. Maybe I didn't. It's hard to remember what all I've said to them sometimes."

"Perhaps they are reading more into the situation," Charles offered.

Mr. Thorne chuckled. "They must be because there isn't much to read into. Modesty is my best friend— practically my only friend, really. She lives in Bath. I did propose to her once for she's very dear to me. And she did offer to visit if I needed any help, which I may accept. But that is the extent of it."

Charles did his best to hide his relief. "Well, I'm sure we would all love to meet her when she does come."

"Thank you," Mr. Thorne said with a smile. "I'm sure she will like all of you. Although I should probably tell the girls not to pass the word around that I'm engaged."

Charles shrugged. "Probably. Particularly if you are interested in finding a spouse."

"I don't know that it's a good time for me to be looking for a spouse. I have quite a lot on my plate all of a sudden."

Charles laughed. "Well, there's certainly no rush, darling. But I can tell you we have a number of charming people in town."

"Thank you," Mr. Thorne said, looking amused. "I will keep that in mind."

After the Thornes left, Pip went away to visit Bertie, and Charles pulled Gavin to a sofa and onto his lap.

"Well?" he said, running a hand through Gavin's hair.

Gavin arched an eyebrow. "You are impossible."

Charles smiled, waiting.

Gavin heaved a sigh. "Oh, all right. He seems very nice, he's perfectly charming, he was easy to talk to, and he's probably perfect for her. Must you be so smug?"

By way of answer, Charles pulled him into a kiss.

When they broke off, Gavin caught his breath and then said, "You do realize I'm not the one you need to convince, don't you? You'll have a devil of a time changing Gerry's mind."

Charles hummed thoughtfully. "I seem to recall you proved very stubborn as well."

"Oh, I see. We're going to list all of your accomplishments now, are we?"

"Do you recall how mischievous Seb was when he arrived? All those pranks and silly behavior until I gave him a proper regimen and he started to settle down and—"

Gavin groaned. "All right, all right. Although I won't admit to your victory until they are betrothed, understood?"

Charles grinned. "What a delightful challenge, darling. Do I get any particular prize when I'm victorious?"

Gavin blushed. "Er...did you have something in mind?"

"Oh, yes. I am full of ideas."

Gavin gave him a wary look. "I really ought to extract details from you before I promise anything." He considered for a moment, looking adorably focused. "But I daresay I've enjoyed everything you've done so far, so I suppose I can safely agree to whatever it is you have in mind."

"Excellent. Thank you, my darling. I am very much looking forward to that prize." He pulled Gavin into another deep kiss.

After several moments, they broke apart and Gavin leaned his head against Charles's. "You know you're quite terrible," he said. "Impossibly smug."

Charles grinned and ran a hand through Gavin's hair again. "And did you know that I was very proud of you for going out to meet the children? I know how daunted you were by the prospect. You were a perfect host today. Have I mentioned that?"

Gavin squirmed. "Thank you."

"Did you have a chance to meet Miss Levinia? She is mad for poetry, you know. I told her she could come borrow some of our volumes."

"You didn't?" Gavin said, sitting up and looking at him in horror.

"I'm sure she would love to discuss poetry with you, my darling."

"Which one was Levinia?"

"The second oldest. Well, I suppose I should say third oldest, after Mr. Thorne. The one who loved the painting."

"Oh," Gavin said, leaning back against Charles's shoulder. "Old enough to take care of the books, at least, I hope. Very excitable little thing, I fancy."

"To be sure," Charles said. "Don't worry, dearest. You'll have plenty of opportunities to learn all about them, I expect."

Gavin groaned and buried his face against Charles's neck. Charles laughed and wrapped his arms around Gavin to tug him closer.

"I quite adore you, you know," he murmured.

Gavin sighed. "Yes. It's the only reason you get away with being right all the time."

Charles tilted Gavin's face up and pressed a soft kiss to his lips.

Then Gavin frowned and said, "I wonder how Gerry's tea is going."

Charles burst into laughter. "If I were to guess, I'd say it was going terribly. Poor Gerry. But don't worry, darling. We'll make it up to her."

Gavin arched an eyebrow. "I suppose you mean Mr. Thorne will make it up to her."

Charles smiled and kissed the corner of Gavin's mouth. "I certainly hope so."

Chapter 17
Gerry

The first tea hosted by the Hearsts was exactly as dreadful as Gerry feared. Mr. Milton Weatherbee was a farmer who was handsome, plainspoken, unassuming and, as it turned out, rather terrified of Gerry. Every time she inquired politely into the man's family or farm, he would cringe and mutter some incomprehensible answer. In the end, he only stayed about twenty minutes before saying something about seeing to his dogs and hurrying out as if being chased.

"Well, pet," Caro said. "What do you think?"

Gerry raised an eyebrow and took a sip of tea. "I think you're well on your way to making me a confirmed spinster."

"But he likes dogs," Lizzy said. "He can't be all that bad, can he? No one who likes dogs can be terrible."

"I can certainly appreciate someone who likes dogs," Gerry said in a patient tone. "But I think I would need my husband to like people a bit more than Mr. Weatherbee does. Or at the very least to not be so very afraid of them. Did you see the way he cringed when I talked to him?" She patted her hair. "It made me rather wonder at how I looked."

"You look lovely," Caro said, bopping Gerry on the nose. "Don't be silly."

"Shyness can be very appealing," Maria said.

"Sometimes, yes," Gerry said.

"Mr. Weatherbee has very nice hair," Lizzy said. "Didn't you think his hair was lovely?"

"Very lovely," Gerry said, sighing. "But I do not think I could marry someone for their hair alone."

Julia hummed thoughtfully. "He has a well-shaped calf, I think. That could certainly help."

"I'm sorry, dear," Gerry said. "Were you referring to his leg or his livestock?"

"Both?" Julia said with a grin.

Gerry laughed. "All right, all right. This was all very entertaining. But please tell me you are not about to make me suffer through a half dozen teas with entirely unsuitable gentlemen."

Rose said, "Not a half dozen."

Gerry rolled her eyes. "Incorrigible lot. For this, you'd better keep the shortbread in good supply because I will need it." She picked up another piece of shortbread for emphasis.

"We can certainly add some diversity to the offerings," Julia said, "if you have any gentlemen you'd like to suggest."

Gerry quickly took a sip of tea to hide the way her cheeks heated at the thought of Mr. Thorne. "No, I have no suggestions. Although I may have to start inviting

Charles. He offered to compare notes and I think that is about the only way I shall suffer through such tribulations."

"Charles is welcome any time," Rose said cheerfully.

Caro gave a delicate sniff. "I rather prefer it when there are no men present."

Gerry turned to her with a mischievous grin. "Excellent, then you are in a perfect position to stop inviting prospective suitors."

Caro chuckled. "We can continue with these parties after you are married, pet."

Gerry rolled her eyes. "There is no dissuading you?" she said, looking around the room. She gave a dramatic sigh. "Ah well. If I must, I must. But I warn you: I'm inviting Charles next time because I shall need the entertainment." She took another fortifying bite of shortbread.

By the time she left, she had managed to extract a promise that the next time they wanted to offer up a suitor on a silver platter, they would do so while she was in the comfort of her own home. She argued that it would be easier for Charles and that it might not be a bad thing for Gavin to meet potential suitors as well. She didn't mention that she would also be relieved to have Pip around; Pip was a very soothing presence.

As it was, she walked home in high dudgeon and began wondering if she made the right decision about the location of the teatime visits. She was walking off her irritation quite effectively. It gave her time to think. She couldn't entirely identify why she was so angry about the situation. She had gone through two London

Seasons and was well acquainted with the Marriage Mart. She even enjoyed her time, to a certain degree. She loved dancing and she loved meeting new people. Why could she not enjoy herself now?

She supposed that now the interactions were too pointed to be enjoyable. There was a definite expectation that Gerry would eventually like one of the suitors. Even if she did happen to like one of them, she suspected her friends would jump at the slightest hint of regard and start planning a wedding. But Gerry was sure romance and love should happen naturally. She wanted friendship and companionship, not a practically arranged marriage.

She was pulled out of her musings by someone calling her name. She looked up to see Pip walking across the field to meet her. "How lucky that I ran into you," he said, giving her a dimpled smile.

"Are you walking back with me?" she said.

He shook his head. "I'm off to see Bertie. How was tea?"

She grimaced. "Dreadful."

He offered his arm. "Why don't we walk together a ways and you can tell me about it?"

She took him up on the offer and described the visit in detail, ending with her friends agreeing to let her host the visits moving forward. "Then you all can suffer through them with me."

"I shall do my best. And I'm sure Charles will be only too happy to join."

She sighed. "I know. He offered to compare notes."

Pip smiled. Then he looked uncertain.

"What's the matter?" she said.

"You ought to know," he said quietly. "The Thornes came to visit. They called on us for tea while you were out. I didn't tell Charles anything," he added hurriedly. "But I think he figured out that you found Mr. Thorne appealing, somehow."

"Bother. Are you sure they did it for my benefit? I wasn't even there. Charles knew I would be out."

Pip inclined his head. "I suspect he invited them because you were going to be out. If it helps, they both liked Mr. Thorne."

"Even Gavin?"

He smiled. "Yes, even Gavin." He patted her hand. "I'd better go to Bertie's now. I thought you'd like to know about our visitors, in any case."

"Thank you. I'm glad to not be caught off guard with it."

"I hope you don't mind me saying that if you are fond of Mr. Thorne, I think Charles and Gavin would approve of the match."

"Thank you." She leaned forward and kissed Pip's cheek. He gave her a nod and set off in the direction of Bertie's estate.

Gerry heaved a sigh. What nosy company she kept. First her friends and now Charles. She continued on her walk, muddling through the information Pip had given her. She began to wonder, despite herself, how Gavin had weathered the storm of the Thorne siblings. Thus cheered by this thought, she ended her walk in higher spirits than when she had started.

Charles greeted her in the sitting room. "How was tea, darling?"

She gave him a meaningful look and dropped onto the sofa opposite him. "Just about what you'd expect. Only I've persuaded them to have future such meetings here instead."

He looked amused. "Indeed? Well, that was thoughtful of you. I do like my entertainment brought directly to me."

"Yes, I was primarily thinking of your convenience."

Charles's amusement grew. "Who was first in the parade?"

"Milton Weatherbee."

Charles attempted—and failed—to hide a smile. "Ah. A very sturdy lad, Weatherbee."

"Yes, it was brought to my attention that he has very nice hair. And well-shaped calves."

Charles choked back a laugh. "Sterling qualities, to be sure."

She put on an affected air of deep thoughtfulness. "Although, I think I would prefer it if my husband did not cringe at the sight of me."

"Did he do that? I'm sorry, my dear. I hope you did not take it personally."

"I was mostly annoyed by how difficult it made conversation."

"Good. You look very fetching, by the way. I've always liked that shade of green on you."

"I wish you'd said as much before I left."

He gave her a sympathetic smile. "That bad?"

112

"I'm not sure how I shall put up with more of them."
She paused and then said, "Charles?"

"Hm?"

"Is there a reason you invited the Thornes to tea
today?"

He gave her a thoroughly unconvincingly innocent
look. "Should I not have?"

She glared at him.

He chuckled. "Have I ever told you that one of my
favorite Hartford family traits is your tendency to
blush?"

She groaned and covered her face with her hands.

"He's very lovely, Gerry."

She dropped her hands and continued to glare at him.

"I fully concur with your assessment of his beauty.
Those dark eyes. And that mouth. My word, but he is
beautiful. And so charming. Do you know that Gavin
liked him? And have you seen how he is with the
children? So patient and sweet."

"You are impossible."

"So Gavin tells me."

"I'm beginning to see what he means. Why don't you
meddle with someone else? Pip or Bertie?"

He smirked. "Oh, don't worry, my dear. They're next.
You're my priority at the moment."

She was saved from further argument by Gavin
walking into the room. "Oh, you're back," he said, by way
of greeting. "How was tea?"

"It was horrid. But you get to witness it next time. I'm
hosting from here on out."

Gavin grimaced. "Why the blazes did you agree to that?"

He strode forward as if he was about to sit on the sofa next to his husband, but Charles quickly stood and pulled Gavin close. "She wants us to be here to support her," Charles said, wrapping his arms around Gavin's chest.

"I'm beginning to regret that," Gerry remarked.

Charles grinned at her over Gavin's shoulder. "And since I imagine John and Veronica will wish to be present for these teatime visits, I am sure our company will be most appreciated."

Gerry covered her mouth in horror.

"Exactly," Gavin said.

"I forgot they were coming. When are they coming? And why?"

"Charles can better answer the first question. He's taken over correspondence in the situation. I could only stomach John's letters for so long. And God only knows why. Because they wish to make us all miserable?"

Charles chuckled. "In about a fortnight. And because John wishes to become better acquainted with me." He rested his chin on Gavin's shoulder. "Although between you and me, darlings, I suspect he hopes to make up for his first impression in London."

Gavin rolled his eyes. "He has a lot to make up for. He was horrid."

Charles tilted his head in agreement. "He was. But he was rather young, you know."

"It was only two years ago. Seven and twenty is not that young," Gavin said.

"And he was very worried about you."

"It's no excuse."

Charles smiled. "Well, I confess that I'm relieved he wishes to improve our acquaintance."

"I'm not sure you'll think that once you've met Veronica," Gerry said. "How long are they staying?"

Gavin turned his head a little, waiting for Charles to answer.

"A few months, probably."

Gerry and Gavin both groaned.

"I am hopeful that John, at least, will learn to be more pleasant by the time he leaves."

"That's quite a generous expectation," Gerry said. "Even for you."

Gavin leaned back against Charles's chest. "It really is. But if you manage it, I daresay I'll owe you another victory prize."

Charles's smile was positively wicked. "That, my darling, is the best possible way to inspire me."

Gavin blushed.

Gerry had no doubt what sort of prize they were discussing, although she did wonder what the first victory prize was for.

Chapter 18
Sophia

Sophia called another family meeting that very night. When she and her siblings were gathered in the hall, she said, "I think we can consider today a success."

"Do you think they'll invite us back?" Bel said. "That garden was cracking."

"I hope so," Eli said.

"But next time," Levinia said, "please try to act with more decorum."

Bel straightened. "Decorum was not on the list of instructions. And we carried out our instructions perfectly, thank you very much."

"Yes, you did," Sophia said before an argument could ensue. "Everyone was perfect."

"We had instructions?" Martin said.

"Yes," Grace said soothingly. "You were meant to have fun and you did a very good job."

Martin looked pleased.

"I'm glad we were able to talk to Mr. Kentworthy about Basil's fiancée," Sophia said. "It seems like he's on our side. He knows we want Miss Hartford to marry Basil and he didn't seem bothered by the idea."

"You told him?" Bel said, incredulous.

"He's very dashing," Levinia said, by way of explanation.

Bel rolled her eyes. "Heaven save me from speedy surrenders." She turned and glared at Eli. "Don't try saying you wouldn't have cracked under the slightest bit of pressure. I saw how you looked at him."

Eli raised an eyebrow. "Thankfully pressure does not seem to be Mr. Kentworthy's style. He just charms people."

"Well, you're too easily charmed then."

He shrugged. "No one's ever called me 'darling' before. I liked it."

Bel groaned.

"Even if he hadn't been charming," Eli pressed, "I think he's trustworthy."

"I'm with Eli on this one," Levinia said. "I think Mr. Kentworthy is perfectly dashing and I find him heroic for taking our side of things."

"His smiles didn't work on me either, Bel," Sophia said. "But I do think we can trust him."

Bel heaved a sigh. "Oh, all right. So what's the next plan of attack?"

They all waited as Sophia considered. "I think we should wait to do anything definite until we get another invitation from Mr. Kentworthy or if Basil's fiancée comes. In the meantime, we can encourage Basil to go to the village as much as possible so he can see Miss Hartford."

"Allow the tender sprig of friendship to grow into the sweet blossom of love," Levinia breathed.

Bel snorted.

"Sounds like a good plan to me," Eli said. "Don't you agree?" he added, turning to his twin.

Bel saluted.

From Basil Thorne
Verdimere Hall, Tutting-on-Cress

To Modesty Munro
23 Royal Crescent, Bath

3 March 1818

Dear Modesty,

You have asked for more descriptions of people I've met since I came here. Thankfully, I do have a report to give: going to tea with the Kentworthys apparently signaled to the community that I was available for socialization. As such, I have suddenly found myself with a large number of visitors. Many came with the supposed intention of checking on Mary, although she is not receiving visitors yet. Others came expressly to welcome me.

The first couple who came to call were Miss Hartford's cousin, Mrs. Rose Hearst and her wife, Mrs. Julia Hearst. Both women were incredibly lovely. Mrs. Rose Hearst has dark eyes, a small mouth, pronounced cheekbones, and dark hair. She rather looks like a combination of Miss Hartford and Mr. Gavin Kentworthy. Mrs. Julia Hearst has an olive complexion and honey-colored hair. She is round where her wife is slender. Mrs. Rose Hearst has a forthright nature that struck me as similar to Miss Hartford, and she spoke her mind with little filter. Mrs. Julia Hearst has a calm, quiet demeanor that made me feel instantly at ease. She talked to the children like a doting aunt might and I gathered that she has long been a close friend of the family.

Mrs. Julia Hearst asked me if I had the opportunity to meet anyone else in town, so I told her about my visit to the Kentworthys' house.

"Oh," she said. "We are very fond of everyone there. It is unfortunate that you did not have a chance to meet Rose's cousin, Miss Hartford."

"I had the pleasure of meeting Miss Hartford when I went shopping." I confess I was relieved to be able to offer that account of myself.

Mrs. Hearst's eyebrows rose at this statement. "She has a lovely shop, does she not?"

"Very impressive," I said. "Her brother said she is something of a genius and I daresay I believe it."

Mrs. Hearst gave me a warm smile in response.

Her wife seemed to become aware of the topic of conversation and asked if I thought Miss Hartford was pretty. "She's considered one of the local beauties, you know," she added.

"Indeed," I said. "She's very beautiful."

The next person I met was the vicar, Mr. Applebough, a very amiable and quiet sort of man who pronounced himself pleased to see more young people come into the neighborhood. I politely did not point out that the vicar was, himself, a rather young man.

An older gentleman, Mr. Robert Ayles, came by to call a few days later. Mr. Ayles, as it turned out, is something of a popular figure among the children. I was a bit surprised by this as I had assumed the gentleman to be of a serious disposition.

"I have a farm," Mr. Ayles explained. "Animals and gardens are always an excellent diversion for young people. And my husband and I adore children, as does my son, Laurence. He's a bit younger than you, about twelve years the senior of young Sophia, I think, yes?" he said, with a glance at Sophia, who nodded.

"Laury has always gotten along famously with your family. He's been in London for the past few months. He quite likes it there. Found some good, comfortable rooms, and set himself up nicely. He was recently appointed to the position of Royal Spellcaster to the Crown."

"My goodness," I said. "That must be quite an honor."

Mr. Ayles smiled. "It is a great honor. The position is primarily in London, at least for the time being, so he has been away the past few months to train for it."

"Has he moved there then?" I said.

"I believe he will be able to conduct most of his business from here, eventually. But I'm not sure when that will be. He did say his training is complete. He left London earlier this month to visit his fiancé and his family."

"Oh, yes," I said. "We had tea at the Kentworthy house just the other day. Mr. Charles Kentworthy mentioned that his brother-in-law was engaged to Mr. Laurence Ayles. Congratulations, sir," I added. "I understand that happened fairly recently."

"This past October," Mr. Ayles said with a broad smile.

"What is the young Mr. Hartford like?" Sophia said.

Mr. Ayles considered for a moment. "He has a sweet

disposition, although he is a little unsure of himself in the way young people often are," he said with a chuckle. "I am glad they agreed upon a long engagement. They're both young yet. Well, Laury is one of those people who seems older than he really is, so I wouldn't have worried about him. But Sebastian is only recently turned one and twenty. I suppose that is around the age young people start entering into Society. I think they suit each other very nicely, but it will be good for them to be married after longer acquaintanceship."

I found myself very pensive after this information. When I was one and twenty, I would have certainly felt too young for marriage. Sophia is seventeen, which means she would be expected to marry in the next five or so years, and then Levinia will come right afterwards. To me, they both still seem very much to be children. But I suppose, to the rest of the world, they are practically adults.

"Will your son come home after his visit with his fiancé?" I said. "Or will he return to London?"

"He will be coming home," Mr. Ayles said. "Thank goodness. Algy and I are unaccustomed to being left to ourselves. I daresay we've been quite bereft the past few months. You shall have to come and dine with us when he returns."

"I would be delighted," I said, returning the gentleman's smile.

It seems as though there has been a constant stream of visitors trickling in. I met Mr. and Mrs. Canterbury. Mr. Canterbury is a good ten years his wife's senior and of the opposite temperament. She was all cheerful smiles and pleasant chatter; he was practically gruff in his bearing. I suspect they are a prime example of opposites attracting.

Like the Hearsts, Mrs. Canterbury was keen to know if I had met Miss Hartford and if I found her attractive. When I assured her I had and that I did find her beautiful, she clapped her hands together and assured me the news was delightful. I'm beginning to wonder if Miss Hartford is the only unmarried young person in town. Though I'm fairly sure Mr. Standish is also unmarried. Did they not care if I considered him attractive?

I suspect Miss Hartford has several friends in the neighborhood who are all on the hunt for a husband for her. I cannot say I mind being considered for the position. I am certainly keen to know the lady better and I daresay I will have ample opportunity to do that if we are often thrown together.

One visitor who did surprise me was Viscount Finlington. He came expressly to meet me because he is good friends with Mr. Charles Kentworthy. He was not well acquainted with my family, though he had met my father a few times. I think the viscount was something of a novelty among the children, for almost all of them gathered in the sitting room when he was announced.

"I hope you will not think me presumptuous," Lord Finlington said, "when I say that I have been looking forward to meeting you, Mr. Thorne. Charlie says you seem to be a man of excellent character and I usually trust his judgment."

Elias elbowed Arabella at those words. She rolled her

eyes in response. Sometimes I think the twins have a secret language of their own.

"How are you liking the neighborhood?" Lord Finlington asked.

I told him I found everyone very welcoming and was pleased to get to know my family better.

"You sweet thing," Lord Finlington said warmly. "I daresay Charlie was quite correct about you. I confess I have been remiss in getting to know your family." He smiled at the gathered children. "I am a social creature, but I do tend to get a bit wrapped in my own work and let the the world pass by. If it weren't for my closest friends, I'd probably become a recluse inadvertently."

I had a hard time imagining that the friendly gentleman could be in the least bit reclusive. "What sort of work do you, my lord?"

"I dabble in magic," the viscount said in a casual tone. "Nothing notable, really, but I do get distracted. A dreadful habit." He then pivoted the conversation back to me and learned about each of the children, and even managed to hear about my life in Bath, which is shocking really as there is precious little to tell. By the time he left, I realized the gentleman hadn't said another thing about himself the entire rest of the visit.

I am glad to hear that the concert was to your liking. And I was delighted by your report on the soiree last week. Mr. Brummerton most decidedly deserves such a set down. I don't care what your cousin says. If Brummerton insists upon pursuing you despite your constant rejection of his suit, then he had your honesty coming to him.

Oh, I saw this lovely fabric at the village shop. I know you are always on the lookout for a good shade of green. I am enclosing a small scrap of it for your perusal. If you like it, I will order you more. Simply tell me how much you need.

Do give our friends my regards.

Affectionately,

Basil

Chapter 19
Basil

As Basil settled into his new life, he was at a loss for what to do with himself. He was now the caretaker of a large family though he never had occasion to take care of anyone other than himself. He considered asking Mary for her advice on the subject, but decided against it. For one thing, it was a trifle awkward talking to Mary about how he could do the very thing he had somewhat offered to do. For another, they did not have that kind of a relationship. It occurred to him that he had never really had a relationship with anyone he could go to for advice. He had Modesty, but she had no siblings and would not have much to offer in this situation. He considered inviting her to stay and help him through this new role, but he thought he ought to do it alone.

One reason he didn't know what to do was because he couldn't really think. He had moved to the library to mull things over, but then Levinia had curled up on a settee to read, the twins were discussing routes over their atlas, and Sophia was browsing the shelves. None of them were particularly noisy, but there were occasional bouts of conversation such as, "Basil, you must hear this thrilling line" or "Basil, do you know the fastest route to Japan?" When Sophia calmly commented what a lovely day it was for a trip to the village, he took it as an excellent notion, excused himself from the room, had his horse saddled, and went out for a ride alone.

He arrived at the village and stopped first at the bookshop, bought himself a notebook and pencil, and then moved on to the teashop. He ordered some tea and sat, mulling over his situation. He did his best to examine it critically. After opening his notebook, he wrote:

New Responsibilities:

Property

Children

Dowries

Coming out?

This was as far as he got before he felt worse than when he started. He didn't even know when his siblings might be expected to come out and what his role would be in that situation. Dowries were a relatively easy problem as they revolved simply around figures. He had little idea of property management and felt almost as lost in that problem as he was with the children.

Then there were the children themselves. How long was he staying in Tutting-on-Cress? He had been there almost two months and he didn't know if he'd ever feel as if he truly belonged there. Was his presence needed indefinitely? Was he expected to become a father figure to them? He could hardly countenance such a thing with such short notice or preparation. He felt as though he was letting them down before he'd even begun.

It occurred to him that his problems were not the type that would be solved in a simple teatime, which made him feel even worse. Perhaps he didn't want to be alone with his thoughts after all. He glanced around him at the sunny day and the people milling around the shops. It was unsettling to be a stranger in a strange town and to go through such a crisis alone.

He looked down the street at the spell shop. He felt a bubbly sensation in the pit of his stomach, which always seemed to start when he thought about Miss Hartford. He hesitated for a moment. He was no closer to solving his problems, but he was now in a rather bad mood and the mere prospect of seeing Miss Hartford made his heart feel lighter. So he finished his tea and strode to the spell shop before he could second-guess himself.

The shop was busy when he entered, and he immediately began to have some misgivings about his plan. He had no business distracting the spellmaster when she was trying to work. But then the lady herself saw him and gave him a smile as sunny as the day and Basil felt his worries dissipate.

"How nice to see you again, Mr. Thorne," she said. "I hope you've come to tell me about your marvelous success with the new spell."

"Sadly no, Miss Hartford."

"Have you come to buy something else? I can try to find you something simpler."

He shook his head. "Forgive me. I really came here because I was..." He hesitated, but at her questioning glance he continued. "Well, I found myself in a rather bad temper and I thought visiting your shop would cheer me up."

Miss Hartford's twinkling smile made his breath catch. "What a lovely thing to say. Although I'm sorry to hear you're in a bad temper. I hope you won't think me impertinent if I say you hide it very well."

Basil chuckled. "More a maudlin mood than anything. I came to the village to think and as soon as I started thinking, I realized my troubles were greater than I thought." He was once again shocked by his remarkable honesty around the woman. Embarrassed, he shrugged. "Perhaps it does not do for me to think so hard after all."

Her brow creased in concern. She glanced around the shop and then said, "Excuse me just a moment." Then she stepped away and spoke to Mr. Standish in a low voice. Basil watched her, bemused. When she approached him again, she said, "Why don't we step into the work room, Mr. Thorne?"

Without waiting for a reply, she led the way through the curtain and into the room beyond. Basil followed her, looking around the room with interest. It was just as tidy as the front of the shop, with shelves full of jars and cases of ingredients.

"I have some spells I need to replenish," Miss Hartford explained. "And I've always found that troubles tend to decrease when one is able to talk about them." She paused. "I don't mean to be presumptuous, of course. But if you would like a willing ear, I am happy to listen while I work."

"Thank you," Basil said, wishing he could more adequately express his appreciation for the kindness.

She smiled at him and began measuring ingredients carefully.

Basil watched for a moment and realized that her calm presence had done much to soothe his nerves, and her cheerful disposition had already helped wrench him out of his maudlin mood. He was grateful to her for applying her focus elsewhere and realized she was doing it on purpose so that he might speak without embarrassment.

So he found himself being honest once more and launched into speech: "I am not at all sure where to start. I suppose the gist is that I never intended to stay here, really. But when Mary assumed I would, it seemed the only logical course of action. Now I find myself unexpectedly settled, but I have no idea what is expected of me. I have never taken care of children before, let alone an entire family of them. I don't know what they need from me, but I feel sure they need something. All I do is sit around feeling restless. And that can't be doing anyone any good." He felt winded from his confession.

Miss Hartford listened without interruption. She was silent for a few moments more, as if waiting to see if he would continue. When he didn't, she said, "That is a great deal of responsibility to shoulder all at once. I'm not at all surprised that you're overwhelmed by it."

Basil let out a long breath. "Thank you."

She hesitated for a moment and then said, "If I might suggest..."

"Please," he said hurriedly. "I will gladly take any advice you have to offer."

She smiled at him and then turned back to her work. "I think you probably have better instincts than you realize. I expect the children have been telling you all along what they need and you've been providing it, without thinking twice."

"What do you mean?"

She shrugged. "Sometimes all that's really wanted is someone to listen. Company. Attention." She glanced up at him. "I have a younger brother, Seb, and for some time we were all frightfully worried about him because he had the most dreadful friends and kept getting into trouble. He came to stay with us here, and while it was a bit rocky at first, we eventually learned to give him what he needed: people who would listen, keep him company when he was lonely, and offer advice when it was called for."

He pondered this for a long moment. "Thank you," he said at last.

"Not at all," she said. "I'm happy to help. And you needn't take my word for it alone, you know. My brother Gavin could probably give you advice from the perspective of someone with two younger siblings. And Charles..." She hesitated and then continued, "Charles is the world's nosiest meddler, but he does take care of the people he loves. I know he'd be delighted as anything to advise you." She looked up at him and met his gaze. "I'm sure it feels as though you are alone, considering you are living in a new town with so many new acquaintances. But..." She broke off, blushing, and turned back to her work. "Well, you need not go it alone. You have acquaintances ready to be your friends, if you were to ask."

Basil was distracted by the fact that a curl had gotten loose from her updo and was now dangling in front of her face. He had a sudden and irresistible urge to brush it away. Before he could think better of it, he reached up and gently tucked the curl behind her ear.

Miss Hartford's blush deepened and she looked up at him. "Thank you," she said quietly.

Basil was struck again by how incredibly beautiful she was. She was not only intelligent, savvy, and talented enough to run her own spell shop, but was also wise and understanding on top of it all. He pulled his hand away, as if doing so might squash the new feelings that were beginning.

Then, because he felt he ought to say something, he said, "I greatly appreciate your advice, Miss Hartford. I confess I had not expected any when I came in." He turned awkwardly and headed toward the curtain. Then he stopped. If he were to walk back into the shop alone, leaving Miss Hartford in the back of the shop, it would very likely cause some tongues to wag. He turned back to her. "Is there anything I can carry for you, back into the shop?"

"Oh, no, thank you," she said. "I can manage."

"If you'll forgive me for saying, Miss Hartford, I think I ought to have something to carry so it can be known I had good reason for being back here."

Her eyes widened. Basil was struck by the innocence of the expression, realizing that she had not recognized the situation she had put herself in, and on his account. He felt a surge of protective instincts take over, which added to the possible beginnings of love, unfortunately, and he looked around the room with intention.

He pointed at a large wooden crate. "Could you use that out front? It seems a bit heavy for you."

She exhaled in evident relief. "No," she said. "But this one could be helpful." She indicated a large glass jar filled with fine shimmery powder.

He picked it up and turned to her. "Thank you again."

"Feel free to visit anytime," she said, smiling at him. "And thank you...for the jar...and everything."

"Glad to help."

Before he could do something stupid (like kiss her), he carried the large jar out of the workroom, asked a bewildered Mr. Standish where he could put it, and left.

Basil had a lot to think about on the way home. Of course, he kept thinking about Miss Hartford and her twinkling smile, her pretty blush, the curl in front of her face, and her look of focus as she worked. Then he thought about her advice and how she encouraged him to pay attention to what his siblings seemed to want from him. The moment he stepped into the house, Lucy wanted to be held, Martin wanted to show him a rock he had found, Arabella wanted to report on the travel routes she and Elias agreed upon, Elias wanted to know if Basil was a good rider and if he could go riding with Basil sometime, Levinia wanted to recite a poem she had discovered, and Grace started playing a new song she recently mastered.

As he scooped Lucy into his arms, admired the rock

Martin held out to him, and led everyone else into the sitting room for better conversation, it occurred to him that this was exactly what Miss Hartford had advised. Thus encouraged, he decided to focus fully on the family around him. He rang for tea, even though he had already had some not too long ago, and sat on the sofa.

He pulled Lucy onto his lap and said, "Right. In order, if you please. Martin, this rock is quite remarkable. Have you thought of starting a collection?"

"How do you start one? Will you help me?"

"Yes, I'll help you."

"Basil, I need you to—"

"Just a moment, Arabella, I want to attend to your plans more thoroughly, so we'll talk about the route in a moment, all right?"

She grudgingly agreed.

"Very good. Levinia, how long is your poem?"

"Only four stanzas."

"How long are the stanzas?"

She held the book out to him.

He nodded. "All right then. Please continue."

She gave a dramatic reading of the poem, and Basil gave proper encouragement and told her that he heartily echoed her sentiments.

"Grace, would you be so kind as to play that piece again? It sounded quite lovely."

Grace beamed and played the song again while Basil had his tea.

He turned back to the twins. "All right, you two. Tell me about this route."

"Well," Arabella said. "I think we would do well to go

east, but Elias thinks we should go west. He's wrong, of course, but I need you to back me up."

Basil took a deep breath. "Well, there is no wrong answer to the problem. Not really. However, I think you ought to take into consideration several factors. How many days will each direction take? What supplies might you need? Are there any ports along the route for restocking purposes? And, if there are, are they friendly ports?"

Arabella sent Elias running to the library to fetch a bundle of books for her. "Does it really matter if the ports are friendly? After all, we could be armed."

"Yes," Basil said. "You could be. But you would do better to think in terms of peace first."

Arabella looked dubious and Basil wondered if it was possible to acquire a position for her in the navy. He was fairly sure his younger sister would enjoy it more than was healthy. Well, if she learned to take orders.

Elias came back with a stack of books. The twins sat down and began going through them as Basil provided advice and direction. By the time dinner was served, none of the twins' questions had been answered, but Basil had provided them with enough questions of his own to keep them too busy to notice.

As the children filed into the dining room for dinner, Mary pulled Basil aside and asked him where he had spent his afternoon. "Not that you need to ask permission to come and go as you please," she added. "Only you left rather precipitously, and I was worried one of the children did something to upset you."

"Not at all," he said. "I needed some time and space

to think. I do not mind their company in the least. But I find I have much to think about and it has been difficult to focus of late."

She smiled sadly. "I can understand that. You know you may use your father's study, don't you? He often tucked himself away in there when he needed quiet. I could tell the children not to bother you when you were occupying it."

"Thank you," Basil said warmly. "I'm sure that will do nicely."

He followed her into the dining room and took his seat at the head of the table. It struck him suddenly that he had slowly begun to take his father's place: taking his seat at the table and now making use of his study. He took a sip of wine to disguise the feeling of anxiety that welled up inside him at the thought. Would the rest of the family think him an imposter? After all their kindness, he would hate for them to resent his coming to stay.

Chapter 20
Sophia

"Right," Sophia said when the family meeting had begun. "I think today's attempt was a definite success."

"Agreed," Eli said. "He took his horse out again today."

"And he came back in a much better mood," Sophia said. "So it's reasonable to assume he went and saw Miss Hartford."

"How can you be sure?" Bel said. "He didn't buy a spell bag this time."

"His spirit was much lighter," Levinia said. "Much like it was when he saw her the other two times."

"You're studying spirits now too, are you?" Bel muttered.

Levinia looked prim. "I am an expert on—"

"I think Levinia's right," Grace said. "Basil looked much more...relaxed."

"Clearly we need to stick to that method," Sophia said.

"Won't he catch on?" Bel said. "He must realize at

some point that we keep suggesting he go to town. He's going to think we're trying to get rid of him."

"Nonsense," Levinia said. "He knows we adore him."

"But Bel does make a good point," Sophia said, trying to be fair. "We can try spacing out the suggestions so he doesn't catch on."

"Any word from his fiancée?" Eli said.

"They send letters back and forth," Grace said. "He seems to be a consistent correspondent."

"Why didn't you read the letters?" Bel said. "What kind of spy are you, anyway?"

Grace's eyebrows rose. "I never agreed to being a spy."

"We are conspirators," Sophia said. "It's an entirely different thing. And we will not stoop to reading Basil's letters," she added with a meaningful look at Bel.

Bel sighed and slumped back in her seat. "You're no fun."

"What did you think of Lord Finlington?" Eli said suddenly.

"He was very elegant," Levinia said. "Did you see his waistcoat?"

"I didn't think he was so very special," Bel said.

"I thought he was interesting," Eli said. "Did you notice that he hardly said a word about himself? He kept twisting the topic around to other people."

Bel straightened. "He did? Perhaps he's hiding something."

"A secret love affair!" Levinia said.

Bel glared. "Or nefarious plots."

Eli shook his head. "I didn't get *nefarious* from him.

But I did think it was fascinating. And he did it so well it was difficult to notice." He paused, considering. "He was charming too, rather like Mr. Charles Kentworthy."

Bel scoffed. "That just means you think he was attractive."

"Well, he was that too," Eli admitted.

"He had the most lovely grey eyes," Levinia said.

"And attractive does not mean he wasn't also intelligent," Sophia said. "I didn't notice that he did that, but it would be worthwhile to keep our eyes open next time we meet him."

"Do you think he'll invite us to tea?" Grace said. "We've never been to tea at his house before."

"Hopefully," Sophia said. "Now that Basil is here, we seem to be invited to tea more often." She noticed Luce nodding off in Levinia's lap and said, "I think that's enough for tonight. We will reconvene later."

Then they all hurried off to bed.

Chapter 21
Charles

Charles did feel a little bad for Gerry as he joined her in the sitting room for tea. Pip and Gavin were present as well, so Gerry seemed a bit more encouraged by everyone's presence. Nevertheless, he could tell she was anxious to get the social call over with.

When the first visitors started trickling in, Charles saw Gerry put forth a forced sort of cheeriness, a sham version of her usual temperament. He felt a little heartbroken at the sight and came very close to making everyone go home. But he knew that would cause more of a mess, so instead he sat on the arm of the sofa Gerry was occupying, leaned down, and said, "Who is our next contestant?"

To his relief, she smiled at his joke. "I think Lizzy is bringing a cousin of hers?"

"He lives locally?"

She shook her head. "Visiting."

Charles wondered at the ladies' change in strategy. Surely they knew Gerry would never pick a suitor who didn't live in Tutting-on-Cress. But it was made clear later. When Lizzy Canterbury entered with her cousin, a handsome fellow in regimentals who gave Gerry a very flirtatious grin, Julia caught Charles's eye and motioned him over.

He took a seat beside her and she said, "Have you had the opportunity to meet Mr. Thorne yet?"

"Ah," Charles said in understanding. "Yes, I have had that honor."

Julia smiled knowingly. "His arrival is very timely."

"Indeed," Charles said. "And I daresay it explains this impractical, although I will admit comely, option today."

Julia nodded. "I thought you'd understand."

"Thank you for explaining. Gerry's met him too, you know."

"I know. He was quite impressed with her."

"Of course he was. And she blushes very charmingly when he's mentioned, so take care you don't talk about him until the lieutenant has left."

Julia hummed thoughtfully. "That will certainly help. Are you on a campaign too?"

"Certainly. But our strategies are somewhat different."

"You disapprove?"

"On the contrary, darling. I'm grateful. I'm not of a military mind, you know—that's more for our friend there—but I do believe there's something to be said about approaching a target from multiple sides."

Julia laughed. "Excellent. I felt sure we'd have an ally in you."

"Always, dear."

A footman entered the room, looking troubled. Gavin waved him over and Charles watched as his husband stiffened, paled, and gave a very curt nod. Charles immediately went to his husband's side. "Everything all right?"

"They're here. Early. Blast it."

"John and Veronica?"

Gavin nodded.

Charles leaned down and kissed his cheek. "It's rather good timing, actually. Our guests will help to cushion the blow."

"If you say so."

The John Hartfords descended upon the room. A nurse trailed behind them, holding a child about two years old.

"Oh, good," Mrs. Hartford said. "They have tea for us. Are our rooms ready, Gavin? You know it is very rude not to welcome your guests in the foyer, don't you?"

Gavin and Charles stood. Charles placed a hand at Gavin's lower back. "Yes, your rooms are ready, Veronica," Charles said. "Perhaps you would like to rest or freshen up a bit? I'm afraid you caught us in the middle of a visit. We're entertaining some guests for tea at the moment and did not realize you were here."

Veronica tsked, but John looked around the room. "I think tea would be very refreshing," he said. "But perhaps the infant should go upstairs."

"Yes, do put him to bed," Veronica said, waving her hand dismissively at the nurse.

Gavin sighed and beckoned a footman to escort the nurse to the nursery. Then he proceeded to make introductions. "John, Veronica, may I present Mr.

Standish, Lady Caro Windham, Lady Maria Windham, Mrs. Canterbury, and Lieutenant Sheldon Melbin. I expect you know Rose and Julia Hearst. This is my brother, John Hartford, and his wife, Veronica Hartford."

"I shall have to explain order of precedence to you some time," Veronica said as she took a seat. "The Ladies Windham ought to have been introduced first."

"Oh, we don't mind," Maria said pleasantly.

"Mr. Standish is somewhat part of the household here. It stands to reason that he would be introduced first," Julia put in. "After all, you will likely be seeing him more than you will see us."

Charles glanced at Pip, who looked uncomfortable. Charles couldn't tell if it was because he was the center of attention or if he was realizing for the first time that he'd see a lot more of John and Veronica.

Gavin poured out for the new guests. Veronica commented that Gavin's pouring technique left much to be desired.

Lt. Melbin turned back to flirt with Gerry. "I am sure you pour most divinely, Miss Hartford. You are so very graceful."

"Ah, is this your beau, Geraldine?" Veronica said. "I must say, it's about time. Two Seasons in London with nothing to show for it. I confess we'd all quite despaired of you." She tittered. "But it's good to see you're not quite on the shelf yet."

Lt. Melbin looked at Gerry uncertainly. "I suppose you left your heart behind in Tutting-on-Cress, Miss Hartford?"

"No," Gerry said wearily. "I simply wasn't interested in marriage when I went to London."

"Ah, but now is a different matter, isn't it?" the young man said, with a rakish smile.

"Not so very different, really. I'm sorry," she said, standing up. "But I'm afraid I have a headache. Do excuse me." She stood and left without another word.

"Does she get the headache often?" Lt. Melbin asked.

"She's just being difficult," Veronica said. "I don't know why she doesn't try harder."

Rose looked indignant. "It was all going perfectly well before you came in. Gerry was being quite pleasant. Wasn't she, Lt. Melbin?"

"Of course, she's a charming—"

"And I think it is most inappropriate for you to come in here and start making remarks like you own the place," Rose went on.

Charles hid a smile. He had always liked Rose's forthrightness of nature. He was especially appreciative of it now.

"Exactly," Caro said. "Very well said, Rose. In fact, perhaps I ought to invite Gerry to stay with us if she is to suffer such company here."

"Perhaps," Charles said, "we can consider that generous offer at a later time, Caro. But thank you. I will pass on your invitation to Gerry."

"I think we'd better take our leave," Julia said. "After all, the Hartfords are surely tired after their journey."

Lizzy nodded hurriedly and all of the guests filed out. Charles caught Pip's eye and gave him nod and was relieved when Pip fell in line behind Lt. Melbin and snuck away too.

"Fine company you keep, I must say," John said irritably. "You should not have let them talk to Veronica that way."

"I've never heard an unkind word from any of them," Gavin retorted. "If Veronica had not said such things about Gerry, none of that would have happened."

Charles laid a hand on Gavin's knee. "How was your trip?"

"Exhausting, of course," Veronica said. "It always is to travel. And I declare that driver was purposely going over every rut and bump in the road. He seemed determined to make us uncomfortable. I could hear the infant crying from the other carriage the entire way here."

"That must have been terrible," Charles said in a sympathetic tone.

"Well," she said, taking a bite of cake. "As long as our room is not next to the nursery, I'm sure we'll be all right. I almost left the infant at home, but the elder Mrs. Hartford insisted you'd all want to see him, which is preposterous, as he shouldn't be out of the nursery. Is Mr. Standish your secretary, Kentworthy?"

"No, he works at the spell shop with Gerry."

"I remember Father saying that," John said.

"And he lives here with you?" Veronica said. "I call that very unnecessary."

"We invited him to live with us and we are very happy to have him here."

"If you say so," she said.

"How did you leave your parents?" Charles said.

"They are in excellent health, thank you," John replied tersely.

"Your son is growing up very quickly. It seems as though only yesterday that he was born."

Veronica rolled her eyes. "He's certainly very noisy. I hope he gets over that habit soon enough."

Charles glanced at John and noticed, with interest, that he looked very uncomfortable with the conversation. He also hadn't had a bite of his cake or a sip of his tea. "How is your tea, John?" Charles said.

John looked startled. "It is very good, thank you," he said. "I'm sorry. I'm afraid I haven't much of an appetite after traveling for days."

"That's because you always get so sullen when you travel," Veronica said.

"Perhaps you would like to lie down for a bit," Charles offered.

"No need," Veronica said. "We have better manners than the rest of the Hartford family, I assure you."

"Well, dinner won't be until seven, so you would have plenty of time to rest. Besides, we don't stand on ceremony here."

"Seven?" Veronica said. "Good heavens, I call that very poor taste. We aren't in London, Kentworthy. I think seven is hardly a respectable time for dinner."

"Seven is a perfectly fine time for dinner," Gavin said. "If you don't like it, you don't have to stay."

"Now, Gav," John said. "That was uncalled for."

"I will be happy to have some dinner sent up to your rooms," Charles said, moving his hand from Gavin's knee to around his waist. "I wouldn't want you to be hungry. But I'm afraid we will not be changing our schedule to suit you. Gerry and Pip work every day and seven works well with their shop hours. So dinner will be served promptly at that time every night."

Gavin leaned against him a little and Charles squeezed his waist.

John's lips pressed tightly together and said, "I'm sure the tea will last us until then."

Veronica looked as though she were about to argue, but she turned to see John taking a small bite of cake and let the matter drop.

Charles prided himself on being a very good conversationalist, but talking with John and Veronica was exhausting. Veronica had something negative to say about everything. John had very little to say and when he did, he usually came to his wife's defense or offered some critique about Gavin. After the longest hour of Charles's life, the two finally went upstairs to their room to freshen up for dinner.

Gavin turned and buried his face in Charles's chest. "I'm glad you've already married me," he said, "so I don't have to convince you not to change your mind after meeting them."

Charles chuckled and rubbed a hand down Gavin's back. "You are not responsible for their behavior."

"But they're so dreadful."

"Yes," Charles agreed.

"And Pip and Gerry will be gone nearly every day, so it'll be just us entertaining them."

"Yes," Charles said.

Gavin groaned.

Charles lifted Gavin's chin. "If it ever gets to be too much, just say the word and they're gone."

Gavin shook his head. "We'd never hear the end of it."

"I don't care."

Gavin sighed. "It is much easier with you around. You are far better at taking over the conversation than I am."

"I give you express permission to hide away in your study as often as you need. I can handle them."

Gavin raised an eyebrow. "Careful, Charles. I might never come out of the study."

"They did come by my invitation, so I daresay I deserve it."

"Don't say that. He's my brother, after all. Although I still don't know why you did invite them."

Charles took Gavin's hand and led him up to the bedroom. Once inside, he pressed Gavin to the bedroom door and gave him a long and lingering kiss. "I invited them because I think John has much to atone for and I think that he is attempting to make up for past wrongs."

Gavin frowned. "If that's the case, he's doing a very poor job of it."

"He is. But there's time yet. And I intend to talk to him before too long and see if I can help the matter along."

"You know," Gavin said, leaning his head back against the door with a soft thud. "When you brought me up here, I really thought you intended to change the topic of conversation and distract me. I don't think you're doing a very good job of it."

Charles grinned. "Duly noted, darling. Shall I try again?"

"Good God, yes."

Chapter 22
Gerry

Gerry did not have a headache. But she had no interest in being insulted by John and Veronica on top of having her friends foist assorted men upon her. Lt. Melbin had been far too forward and flirtatious for Gerry's tastes. He had put his hand on her leg and murmured comments about her appearance when everyone was distracted. Gerry had been almost relieved that Veronica had taken it into her head to discourage the man. Gerry hoped he was a distant cousin of Lizzy's for she never wanted to see him again.

When she shut herself in her room, the comparison between Lt. Melbin to Mr. Thorne came unbidden to her mind. She thought of how Mr. Thorne had been respectful of her when they were alone and how he would never have made comments about her figure. She even briefly gave way to the musings of what Mr. Thorne would say to Veronica's insults. The gentleman seemed to regard her with genuine admiration, and the more she thought of it, the more Gerry realized she very much liked being admired. And he didn't merely admire her beauty, for she had experienced some level of that in London; Mr. Thorne admired her intelligence and her insight. She continued to indulge her fancies and compared Mr. Thorne to the first teatime suitor, Mr. Weatherbee. She smiled at the thought that Mr. Thorne was unlikely to ever cringe at the sight of her.

She had been delighted when he confided in her and she felt great sympathy for how lost he seemed to feel. There had been other things too, like the way he had brushed the hair away from her face and the way he looked at her like she was something marvelous. She had been so set on being a good friend that she had very nearly put herself in a compromising position with him, letting him into the backroom without a chaperone. The realization that he was not only a gentleman, but thoughtful of her reputation, made her feel all kinds of inconvenient things.

Finally, she shook herself to be rid of the thoughts and set about trying to decide what to do next. She would have liked to write Rose and insist the teatime visits stop immediately, at least until John and Veronica left. But she could practically hear her friends argue that the visits would be welcome distractions from her unpleasant relations. And she had to agree with the imagined argument. She even admitted to herself that her friends' attempts to find her a husband would likely pacify John, particularly since the attempts were being made by married people and titled people to boot. Nothing ever pacified Veronica.

So she reasoned herself away from writing to Rose

and instead paced her room until she heard John and Veronica being led to their bedrooms. She waited a little while longer to be sure they were in their rooms and then stepped out to apologize to Gavin and Charles. But they were not downstairs either. She returned to her own room and spent the rest of the time before dinner responding to a letter from her friend, Nell, who lived in London, and writing her weekly letter to her mother. She took care not to mention anything about Mr. Thorne. If her mother caught even a whiff of Gerry's interest in a gentleman, she would be in Tutting-on-Cress in a trice, and that was the last thing Gerry needed.

Predictably, John and Veronica both lectured her for her behavior earlier. But afterwards, the talk at dinner focused on Charles and Gavin: whether or not they would have children, whether or not they planned to stay in Tutting-on-Cress, whether or not Tutting-on-Cress was a desirable place to settle. John and Veronica had many opinions about all of these topics. They both seemed personally affronted that Gavin had made up his mind not to have children.

"You will change your mind, you know," Veronica assured him. "Having children is so life changing."

"I'm aware of that," Gavin said. "Which is why I know I don't want them. I quite like my life as it is now."

Charles attempted to hide his grin and covered Gavin's hand with his own. "We have discussed the matter," he said. "We are both in agreement."

"Come now, Gav," John said. "You have a responsibility, you know."

"I hope you will understand, John," Charles said.

"That this is not a topic either of us are compelled to move on. I would never force Gavin to play at parenting when he is disinclined to do so."

"Yes, but what about inheritance?" Veronica said.

"I have a very clever solicitor with whom I have been talking for months," Charles said. "I'm not concerned."

John sighed but subsided. Veronica glanced at her husband, seemed to note that he had given up, and decided to switch topics. "Have you looked at other places you might settle in?"

Gavin glanced at Charles. "We are very content here," he said.

"I can't deny I'm glad," Gerry put in. "I like having you two around."

"You should be focusing on finding a husband," John said.

She rolled her eyes.

"Truly," Veronica said. "Two London Seasons and nothing to show for it."

Gerry felt her face get hot. "As it happens, I'm rather glad nothing did come of it. I love my life here and I wouldn't change anything about it for the world."

"The Marriage Mart in London is very competitive," Charles said. "And there is not a very even distribution of firstborns to nextborns. Before I met Gavin, I was always surrounded by parents of nextborns who were hoping I'd fall in love with their children. It is very overwhelming for everyone concerned. I had the pleasure of escorting Gerry around for her second Season and I can assure you there was nothing wanting in her character or appearance."

"Well, now that we are here, we ought to focus on Geraldine's marriage prospects," Veronica said. "And Mr. Standish's too, for that matter."

"That is very kind of you," Pip said. "But I'm afraid—"

"Oh, don't be modest, Mr. Standish," Veronica said. "I know you only work in a spell shop as an assistant, but you are a very attractive person. I'm sure some people would overlook your social standing."

Pip's expression tightened. "Well, as it happens, much as I appreciate your intentions, I have already given my heart to someone."

Gerry was surprised at this news, but she didn't pry. She also couldn't tell if Pip meant it or if he was being cleverly evasive. If the latter, she was impressed. In any case, it *mostly* worked as an evasion tactic. Veronica was no longer bent on finding him a match; now she was bent on determining who the match was.

"Who is it? Tell us all about them."

"Well," Pip said. "Nothing has been settled, exactly."

"But you have an understanding?" Veronica pressed.

Pip shrugged. "Of a sort."

"Well, now that Mr. Standish is all squared away," Veronica said. "We can focus on you, Geraldine. I'm not at all sure what your prospects are in a small neighborhood like this, but you really cannot afford to be picky. You're getting too old for that."

"Oh, really, Veronica," Gavin said.

"She's right," John said. "It's not entirely your fault," he added, looking at Gerry. "Our parents should have brought you out when you were twenty. Not bringing you to London until you were three and twenty was positively absurd and set you up for failure."

Gerry rolled her eyes. "Thank you for that, John."

"Perhaps we could hold a ball," Veronica said. "Then again," she added, frowning. "Provincial places like this cannot possibly have much to offer in terms of venue."

"You live in a provincial place now," Gerry muttered.

"I think a ball is a wonderful notion," Charles said.

"Really, Charles?" Gavin said. "I'm surprised at you. As if a ball was all that was wanting in Gerry's search for a husband."

"Well, I would like to see what sort of eligible men there are in town," Veronica said. "Perhaps that is her problem."

"Oh, I highly doubt a ball will end in a marriage proposal," Charles said, grinning at Gerry. "I just love to dance. And I think a ball would be a very agreeable way for John and Veronica to meet all of our friends. I shall talk to Bertie about it. He has the most magnificent ballroom."

Gerry frowned at her brother-in-law. Why on earth was Charles encouraging them? Although, as much as she hated to admit it, John and Veronica were in far more agreeable moods for the rest of the evening.

From Geraldine Hartford
  Hollyton House, Tutting-on-Cress

To Nell Birks
  Covent Garden Theater, London

11 March 1818

Dear Nell,

I am so glad to hear about your promotion at the theater! It is very well deserved. I think training new spellcasters will suit you admirably. You are so very practical. I am sending along a book on theory that has been very helpful to me in the past year or so, in terms of understanding how to explain things in a simpler way. Quite frankly, I wish I'd had this when I was teaching Pip magic, for I'm sure it would have made everything a great deal easier for both of us. But I did use it when I was briefly in charge of Seb's magic lessons and I've been applying some of the author's techniques when teaching customers in the shop, so I know how useful it can be.

My oldest brother has come to visit. I am already weary of his company, and he's only been here a couple days. He and his wife are positively dreadful. I'm sure their son isn't too bad as he's barely two at this point and cannot have yet inherited his parents' horrid temperaments. But my sister-in-law has very decided opinions about children and where they belong. I believe they dragged their poor son all the way from his nursery in Sherton merely to take up residence in the nursery here. I have seen neither hide nor hair of him. Charles has assured me that he goes into the nursery daily to see that my nephew is doing well, so at least someone in the house is looking after the child's wellbeing.

You asked about my spell-building and I regret to report that I have done very little in recent months. I've been trying to come up with something to design, but nothing is coming to mind. If you have any ideas, do send them on.

Someone new moved into the neighborhood, which is rather unusual for a small village. I've only met him a couple of times, but he seems very pleasant. I'm convinced that Charles has taken it into his head to play matchmaker, which is highly irritating. I've already detailed to you the manner in which my friends have started their own matchmaking attempts. The last thing I need is more bachelors thrown in my direction. Sometimes I wish I didn't want marriage, for they would all leave me alone. But since I *do* want marriage and they all know it, they seem ready to stop at nothing in finding me a husband. It is perfectly vexing.

Do give my regards to Betsy, Harriet, Patience, and Lino. Someday I shall have to go to London and visit you so I can meet your friends instead of only hearing about them. Unfortunately, I'm always too busy to teach Pip how to manage the shop without me. I suppose I could close it for a few days, but that seems somewhat irresponsible behavior as proprietress.

Affectionately,

Gerry

Chapter 23
Basil

Ever since Mary had suggested Basil use the study, he had struggled to bring himself to step inside. He had yet to examine why this was so difficult for him and he was not particularly keen to probe too deeply.

Instead, he busied himself with a different task that took him several days: thinking of a good reason to go see Miss Hartford again. He finally remembered that he had a perfectly good reason if he were to practice the spell he'd bought.

He spent two more days practicing the spell. He felt ridiculous, if he were honest—splashing water on himself then using a spell to dry it. At one point—thankfully after he had mostly mastered it—Martin saw him practicing in the library.

"What are you doing?"

"I'm learning a spell," Basil explained. "It dries people quickly."

"Can I see?" Martin asked eagerly.

Basil guided Martin to put his hands in the circle and

then he carefully poured some water over them. Even more carefully, he cast the drying spell. Martin laughed and clapped his hands. "Again!"

After the third try, Martin ran into the circle completely. "Again!"

Basil chuckled and accommodated the request, relieved that he could successfully do it, and pleased to have found a way to clean Martin quickly. Martin's laughter brought Lucy in and before she could ask what was going on, Martin had pulled her beside him and begged Basil to do it again.

Basil did. Lucy shrieked with excitement (almost more from the water than the drying, Basil thought). And after nearly an hour, they were still in the circle, hopping about and clapping with every casting.

Just as Basil was attempting to find a way to end the game, Sophia and Grace walked in.

"Splash Sophia and Grace!" Martin crowed.

"I'm not sure they'd enjoy it," Basil said, giving the two girls an apologetic smile. "We've been playing with the Quick-Dry Spell," he murmured.

Sophia beamed. "How clever! I wonder what other spells they might like."

With that, he gathered his courage and rode to the village. He practiced the conversation a bit on the way, trying to think of how he could broach the topic without sounding like he was bragging, particularly when he was pretty sure the spell was supposed to be fairly easy.

He approached the spell shop and found it busy as usual but also found that Miss Hartford greeted him as cheerfully as ever.

"How are we doing today?" she asked.

"Very well," he said, smiling at her. "I wished to tell you that I successfully cast the spell you sold me." It was not the exact wording he had practiced and it did, unfortunately, come out like bragging.

Thankfully, Miss Hartford did not seem to mind. She grinned and said, "Capital! Well done! Would you like to try another?"

Since this suggestion meant he'd have a perfectly good reason to come back, he agreed to it. "And," he added, "perhaps you might be able to suggest something that could have entertainment potential? Martin and Lucy helped me a bit with my practice and they seemed to enjoy getting soaked and then dried."

Miss Hartford laughed, which made Basil feel warm all the way down to his toes (he had made her laugh!). "I think I have a good idea for what you can try next." She led him to the wall and plucked a bag off a hook. "This is a levitation spell, particularly designed for heavy objects. Would you like me to show you how it's done?"

He said he would like that very much, so she led him to the counter and pulled out each ingredient. As before, she showed him everything without rushing and without getting impatient when he needed her to repeat things, despite how busy the shop was.

"You'll do very well," she said, as she put the ingredients back. "This one is a good spell for learning and mastering magic."

"You mean it should be very easy," he said.

"I never said 'should,'" she replied, with her twinkling smile. "And if you do have any issues, please don't hesitate to ask. It is far better to double-check, especially with magic."

"Thank you, I will keep that in mind." Basil could feel the conversation coming to an end and he found himself selfishly wanting it to continue so he said, "Have you designed any new spells lately?"

To his surprise, the lady looked crestfallen. "No," she said. "It's been some time since I designed something new."

"Is everything all right?"

She smiled. "Oh, yes. I'm just...I don't know...not feeling particularly creative lately, I suppose. It's a shame, really, because spell design is the reason I wanted this position in the first place."

"I wish I could help," he said. "But I fear I am far from creative myself."

"Well, if you think of anything that could help make your life simpler, do let me know. I'm sure that would help me immensely."

He considered for a moment. "Perhaps a spell designed to assist with property management?"

She laughed again, and Basil tried not to feel too smug about the accomplishment. "That might be beyond the power of magic, I fear."

"Pity. I shall bend my mind to the matter."

"Thank you. I greatly appreciate it."

"Don't thank me yet," he said. "My mind has not been in prime working order for a long time, so I daresay I'm not offering very much. If you could make a spell to help me think more clearly, perhaps I can have the right mental capacity to give you ideas."

To his surprise (and delight), she looked thoughtful. "I don't know of any spells to help focus the mind. But that is certainly worth considering. Thank you, Mr. Thorne."

"Not at all," he said. And even though he would have enjoyed talking to her for hours more, he said, "I will let you get back to your customers. Thank you for a pleasant chat, Miss Hartford."

He spent the entire ride home picturing Miss Hartford when she laughed and trying to think of what else he could say to get that reaction from her. He was not a particularly funny person by nature, so he would need to treasure each time she laughed as if it was a rare gift. When he got home, he immediately began to practice the spell.

Chapter 24
Gerry

After they closed the shop for the day, Pip left to dine with Bertie, so Gerry walked home alone. She wished she could join him, but she was also grateful for the time to think. Mr. Thorne had come into the shop again and she couldn't put her finger on why she enjoyed his visits so much. He never stayed overlong, but she always found herself feeling happier after talking to him. When she had explained her disappointment in not designing spells, he tried to help.

Most of her friends in Tutting-on-Cress knew her before her step down in society, and she wondered if they would still be as close if she hadn't formed her acquaintances when she was still part of the gentry. But Mr. Thorne had no misunderstandings of who she was and what her station was; in fact, he'd only ever seen her in her shop. Yet he still treated her with respect and friendliness. She almost wished Mr. Thorne would stop being so perfect. If he were to show some flaws, Charles could possibly be convinced to stop meddling quite so much.

As she stepped inside the house, she saw a young man standing in the foyer. "Laurence!" she shouted. Even though it was not technically appropriate, she pulled him into a tight hug.

The young man laughed and wrapped his arms around her waist, untroubled by the lack of decorum. After Gerry let him go, Charles came down the stairs and pulled Laurence into an embrace as well. Then he stepped back and gave Laurence a look over. "You look marvelous, darling."

"Thank you," Laurence said with a grin. "New clothes."

Gerry wrapped her arm around his. "Why didn't you tell us you were coming? We didn't expect you. Is Seb here?"

He chuckled, kissed her cheek without shyness, and said, "In order: I left earlier than planned and there wasn't time to alert anyone. I surprised my parents last night when I showed up on their doorstep. Seb is still with your parents, but he will likely arrive within the next week."

"Is everything all right?" Gerry asked.

"Oh, yes," he said. "Perfectly fine. Seb and I had planned to travel home together, but..." He shrugged and grinned. "Well, your father was not convinced that would be appropriate. I thought it best to waylay any arguments by offering to come home early. I left right away because Seb would have tried to persuade your father otherwise. They've been getting along very nicely.

I didn't wish to tempt fate. I think your father must have recognized and appreciated my tactic because he paid for the carriage himself."

Gerry laughed. "Yes, that sounds like...well...both of them. It looks as though you're already learning."

He winked. "I'm a quick study."

Charles wrapped an arm over Laurence's shoulders. "Stay for dinner. I will not accept a refusal."

"I wouldn't dream of refusing you. I know better."

"Why did you wait for us in here? You know Gavin would love to see you."

Laurence looked a trifle uncomfortable. "Well, I remembered that you had guests. I thought it might be best to be greeted privately, in case it wasn't a good time."

"Oh, good heavens," Gerry said. "You haven't met them, have you?"

He shook his head. "They were staying with Veronica's parents during my whole visit."

"Prepare yourself," she said ominously. "They're quite dreadful."

"Oh, Seb has been telling me a great deal about them. I confess I'm frightfully curious."

"You'll regret that sentiment," Gerry said.

Charles chuckled and guided them all into the sitting room. "I rather think Laury can handle them."

Gerry had forgotten that Gavin was hosting Veronica and John alone. He looked relieved to see Gerry and Charles, and was clearly delighted by Laurence's arrival. Which is to say, his forehead relaxed and the corners of his lip twitched.

"Why didn't anyone tell me you were here?" he said, coming forward to shake Laurence's hand.

"I only just arrived," Laurence said, taking Gavin's hand in both of his own.

"Good to have you back," Gavin said solemnly.

"Who is this then?" John said.

Charles made introductions. "Allow me to present Mr. Laurence Ayles. Laurence is one of our neighbors, the newly appointed Royal Spellcaster to the Crown, and engaged to Seb. Laurence, this is John and Veronica Hartford."

Gerry relinquished her arm around Laurence's so he could bow appropriately.

"It is a pleasure," he said.

"You are Sebastian's young man?" John said. "My father speaks very highly of you."

Laurence gave him a wide smile. "Thank you, Mr. Hartford. That is very kind of you to say. I'm sure you will be pleased to know that I left your parents in good health."

"Where is Seb, by the way?" Gavin said as if he'd just noticed he wasn't there.

"Still at home. Your father thought it best if we travel separately, so I came back ahead."

"Most appropriate," Veronica said. "I'm glad someone in this family has an idea of propriety."

Laurence laughed. "I hate to disappoint, Mrs. Hartford, but I should confess it was more a matter of keeping in their father's good graces. If he hadn't voiced a concern, I would have happily traveled back with Seb."

Veronica tsked.

"As it is," he continued. "He will likely arrive at our originally planned time next week. He will not have the benefit of a speed spell, so I don't know how long the journey will take."

"Have you mastered the speed spell?" Gerry asked as Charles directed them all to sit down. She sat next to Laurence on one sofa, John and Veronica took the other sofa, and Gavin sat in the remaining chair with Charles perched on the arm. Veronica curled her lip slightly at the casual arrangement, but said nothing.

"I'm not sure I'd go so far as to say I've mastered it," he said. "But his lordship showed us the way of it en route to London and I've practiced it on every trip since. I shall be pleased when he shows me how to feel magic, for I'm sure that will make it easier."

"That is something I wish to know too," Gerry said. "We're both so busy all the time, it's well-nigh impossible to work out a training schedule."

"As if you need to focus on anything other than finding a husband," Veronica muttered.

"How is business, by the way?" Laurence said, not acknowledging Veronica's commentary.

Gerry grinned at him. "Capital, thank you."

"Any new spells?"

"No," she said sadly. "Lately I've felt a bit blocked, creatively speaking."

"I've had that," he said sympathetically. "I'll be home for a month or so. If you'd like to talk out some ideas, I'm at your disposal."

"I'd love that!"

"You're going back so soon?" Gavin said.

Laurence nodded. "I shall likely be back and forth quite often for the first year or so of my appointment. Bit of a wrench, but nothing for it, I'm afraid."

"Does Seb know?" Charles said.

"He does. And he was not best pleased, poor lamb."

John scoffed. "Sebastian has never possessed a talent for maturity. It will be good for him to learn patience and responsibility."

"He's young yet," Charles said. "He grew up quite a lot in a short time when he came to stay with us. I'm not worried about him."

"I confess I was surprised," Veronica said, "when I'd heard he was engaged. I know he's a horrid little flirt, of course. But I never expected him to actually become serious about anyone. He was such a brat when he was sent down. But then I don't suppose you knew him then, for you surely wouldn't have proposed if you had."

Gerry was horrified by this speech. "Well, I like that," she said.

"Don't pretend Sebastian isn't a horrid little flirt," John said in his wife's defense. "He would never listen to a word I said the entire time he was at Oxford, no matter—"

"Oh, do shut up, John," Gavin said.

Everyone began talking at once, except Laurence. Then suddenly Gerry realized she was staring at Laurence, and then she realized that everyone else was staring at him too. Like her, they had all stopped talking. He hadn't spoken and he was still looking as calm and pleasant as usual. But she noticed a small sprig of holly tucked under his thumb. Holly was the sort of plant that was good for volume spells, charisma spells, and glamour spells. It attracted focus and attention.

Gerry felt a small tingle down her spine at the reminder that Laurence was a tremendously powerful spellcaster, for all his calm demeanor and cheeriness. He was, after all, the Royal Spellcaster to the Crown. It was a prestigious position that he fought for amongst a half dozen talented spellcasters. If she had not known him so well, she might have been frightened at the casual and subtle display of power.

Laurence smiled with his usual calm. "You wish to talk about Seb? I'm sure I don't mind. He's quite my favorite topic of conversation, with the exception of gardening. I am mad for gardening, you know. When I first started to fall in love with him, I often wondered how such a sweet man came to be so thoroughly uncomfortable with himself. I've come to learn that he had the most abominable friends at school. Wretched creatures who told him they supported him, only to tear him down at every opportunity. I wondered for months why he was so unforgiving of his past mistakes, why he was so carelessly cutting about his own character, why he was so afraid to trust himself." Laurence let out a deep breath. "I met one of his school friends in London, as it happens. I thought then that I understood why Seb was constantly abusing his own character." He tilted his head thoughtfully, smiling at Veronica. "But perhaps I was giving his friends more credit than they deserved."

Gerry noticed out of the corner of her eye that Laurence rubbed the holly between his fingertips gently, and she felt her focus pull back to him, even though it had never left.

"You are surprised that anyone could love Seb enough to want to marry him. Shall I tell you then, why I love him? I love him because he is kind to others, even though he is still learning to be kind to himself. I love him because he has one of the most open minds of anyone I know—open to all kinds of people and all kinds of knowledge. I love him because he is brilliant, but doesn't seem to realize it. I love him because he is so very curious and is constantly learning. I love that he is forever working to improve himself and to change and grow and I cannot wait to find out what sort of man he grows into. I love him because I can practically read his mind sometimes and yet I am always eager to hear him speak it. I love him because he is beautifully flawed and yet, almost by magic, he is quite perfect for me."

Laurence tucked the holly into his palm and Gerry immediately felt vaguely distracted in the usual way of conversation.

"Does that answer your question, ma'am?" Laurence said mildly and with a gentle smile.

"My soul," Charles said softly. He was grinning hugely. "It is prodigiously good to have you back, darling."

Laurence laughed. "Even if I get too eloquent about my betrothed?"

"Especially then," Charles said.

John and Veronica looked stunned and confused. Gerry wondered if they had any idea they had been inclined to listen to Laurence's speech through magical means. She glanced at Gavin to see if he had noticed. He gave her a small smirk and she winked back. Gavin had definitely noticed.

Dinner was announced and the tension in the room dissolved as they stood to go into the dining room. Laurence told them all about his job and his time in London, as well as his time with Gerry's parents and Seb at the family estate in Sherton. He spoke with his usual cheery, open nature, as if he hadn't just given Veronica and John the friendliest set down they'd likely ever had. He answered their questions with the same tone he answered everyone else's.

Gerry had been worried about Seb's return with John and Veronica still in the house as he had never gotten along with them. She felt comforted by the knowledge that Seb was likely to be perfectly safe from any of their bullying when Laurence was around. Laurence, clearly, was as stalwart a protector of his beloved as Charles was of Gavin.

Gerry sighed happily to herself. She was glad her brothers were so well looked after.

Chapter 25
Charles

Charles led Laury outside to the carriage. As soon as they were outside, he said, "I'm so glad you're here, darling."

Laury grinned up at him. "I expect you must be, with visitors like that."

Charles chuckled. "She is a character, isn't she?"

Laury tilted his head and looked at him thoughtfully. "Not him?"

"He's...a little lost, I think."

Laury smiled. "That's what I like about you, Charles. You're always trying to help people. In fact..." He paused.

"Yes?"

"I might ask you to help me with something."

"Anything, darling."

"I would like to talk to you all, well, you, Gavin, and Gerry before Seb comes back."

"Is everything all right?"

"Oh, yes. But I'd like your advice and it would be

simpler to explain it all at once. I was hoping I might induce you all to come to Copperage Farm soon. My parents can help entertain your guests while we talk."

Charles nodded. "It would have to be on a Sunday so Gerry can come."

"Sunday will be perfect. Thank you. And if you need anything from me, please don't hesitate to ask. I can see you have your hands full."

"I'm so glad you brought that up," Charles said. "Because I'm going to enlist your help." Laury looked at him expectantly. "I think I've found the perfect husband for Gerry."

Laury burst into laughter. "Of course you have. Good heavens. I'm gone for a few months and you've already matched up the last single Hartford."

"Well, the timing did work in my favor," Charles admitted.

"Who is the lucky man?"

"Are you familiar with Mr. Thorne?"

Laury gave him a sharp look. "Mr. Basil Thorne?"

"Yes."

"I knew his father rather well. I've never met the son," Laury said.

"I barely met the father, but the son is charming."

Laury raised an eyebrow. "Attractive?"

"Devastatingly handsome, dear. And kind and generous."

"Hmm," Laury said. "His father spoke very highly of him, but they had a very...distant relationship, from what I gather."

Charles laid a hand on Laury's shoulder. "You were close?"

Laury nodded.

"I'm sorry, darling."

Laury gave him a small smile. "Thank you. My parents invited the family to visit tomorrow. I'm not sure if Mr. Thorne will be there."

"I wouldn't be surprised. He invited the family to stay at the house and I think they've taken to accompanying him practically everywhere."

Laury chuckled. "That sounds like them. Frankly, that's as good an endorsement as any. Some of those Thornes are frightfully prickly. If they've taken a liking to him, he must be a good sort."

"Gavin liked him."

Laury's eyebrows raised. "Ah. Well, that's a good endorsement too. Father did write to me about how Mr. Thorne invited his family to stay. Father seems to like him as well. I confess, I'm pleased by the prospect of our families joining together in a more permanent manner."

"So you'll help?"

"Do you even need to ask? What is it you want me to do?"

"Be on the lookout for opportunities to encourage Gerry in that direction. And if you do meet Mr. Thorne..."

"It wouldn't go amiss to talk about how wonderful Gerry is?"

"Exactly."

"Is there a grand plan in action?"

"Well, as it happens, there are several. Gerry's cousin

Rose and some of her friends in town have started inviting eligible gentlemen to tea. I learned recently that the younger Thorne siblings are hoping to match Gerry and Mr. Thorne as well."

"Are they really?" Laury looked amused. "That will be something. I'm not sure if it will help or hinder your cause, but they are clever children. I expect their attempts will be effective in causing *something* to happen."

"Bertie is going to throw a ball, only we're waiting for the right opportunity."

"Ah, good," Laury said. "So everyone is in on the scheme. Mr. Standish?"

"I think he likes Mr. Thorne. In fact, he's the one who brought the gentleman to my attention. But he's not the scheming type."

"Very honorable too. Well," Laury said as he turned toward the carriage, "I will gladly lend you my aid. I'll send you a note tomorrow about their visit. If Mr. Thorne is there, I'll learn what I can from him. If he isn't, I'll talk to the children."

"Perfect. I knew I could depend on you, darling." He laid a hand on Laury's shoulder. "By the way, I intend to talk to John before Seb arrives. If he's unkind to him, he's leaving."

Chapter 26
Basil

Basil stood on the threshold to his father's study, surprised by how nervous he felt.

He had finally set aside the new spell in order to tackle the problem of the study. He told himself the previous night that he would go into the study first thing in the morning. But then, of course, there had been breakfast. And then there were conversations to be had and questions to be answered and poems and piano songs to be attended to. Before he knew it, he was sitting down to lunch.

The study had not been used since December. Basil could see that everything was where his father must have left it. He had a sudden and powerful fear of upsetting that tableau.

Mary approached him and said she was taking her children to Copperage Farm to have tea with the Ayles family. "I'm still in mourning," she added. "But they're old family friends. I think it will do me some good to see them."

"Of course," Basil said. "Well, I'd love to come along, thank you."

She looked surprised by this and Basil realized, belatedly, that she was telling him more along the lines of information rather than invitation. It occurred to him that Mary might have been intentionally getting the children out of the house because he had mentioned needing some space to think. He felt absurd, but his anxiety about entering the study was too strong as yet, so he quelled his feeling of foolishness and prepared to leave.

Copperage Farm turned out to be a cottage on a small plot of land. There was a long drive leading up to the house where pigs and geese milled about. Basil could see a garden plot toward the back and into the treeline. There was a small stable for the horses and a dogcart, but no conveyances larger than that.

The carriage pulled to a stop in front of the house and three men strolled out to greet them. Basil recognized the oldest man, Mr. Robert Ayles, who had called on him for tea. The bald man with dark skin and broad smile was clearly the gentleman's husband—Basil thought he remembered the name Algy. The young man who was currently greeting Mary could only be their son, Mr. Laurence Ayles. The youngest Mr. Ayles was short and trim but muscular, with medium brown skin, large brown eyes, dark brown hair that curled tight to his scalp, and a ready smile.

The children dashed about the gentlemen for greetings. Basil noticed that the youngest Mr. Ayles was as animated as the children as he scooped them into embraces and planted kisses on their cheeks. For the little ones, he swung them around with a whoop first.

Mr. Robert Ayles stepped forward and made introductions. After he had formally introduced everyone, he said, "Mr. Thorne, would you like to come inside for tea or would you like to explore the gardens? Laury always takes charge of the children on these visits, so I don't wish you to think you need to do one or the other."

Basil glanced at Mr. Laurence Ayles, who was lifting Martin onto his back.

"Basil, you simply must come look at the treehouse," Arabella said in a tone that brooked no argument. It was her normal way of speaking, but Basil fancied she had a particularly sharp note when she was giving orders.

"Oh," Basil said. "Well, I'm sure I would love to see it and the gardens. I'll come in for tea shortly."

Mr. Laurence Ayles hoisted Martin farther up his back and grinned. "Lovely." He took Grace's hand and said in a loud voice, "All right, you lot. Fall in line."

Lucy pulled on Basil's leg and Basil obediently picked her up. Mr. Laurence Ayles's grin widened, then he turned and marched toward the back of the house. The twins marched behind him. Levinia took Basil's free arm.

Basil noticed that Sophia followed sedately after them and it made him ponderous that Sophia still considered herself one of the children. He was sure she would have been welcome to join the others for tea. He wondered if she still believed herself to be responsible for her siblings.

"Levinia, did I tell you I brought in a new plant?" Mr. Ayles said.

Levinia gasped. "Is it portrait-ready?"

"Just about. I want you to look at it and see if you can sketch it for me. I'll need to study it, you know. I only trust you to do it justice."

She nodded gravely.

He tilted his head to the side in a gesture meant to point. "I've got it next to all of the herbs. You'll know it for the mound of fresh soil about it. Mind you don't pluck it, though. I've only got the one. If you need the sketchbook, you can go get it. It's in the usual place." Levinia went back toward the house.

As soon as they reached the gardens, Lucy scooted out of Basil's arms and ran around the plot. "Oh dear," Basil said. "She'll step on something or—"

"Not to worry," Mr. Laurence Ayles said as Martin slid off his back. "The garden is used to them. They know which parts to avoid stepping on anyway."

"Oh," Basil said, breathing out a sigh of relief. "That's good."

"Did you get the music I sent you?"

Basil turned in confusion and saw that the young man was still holding Grace's hand and was looking down at her expectantly.

She nodded. "Yes, it will be a beautiful piece. But it is far too difficult for me."

"Nonsense," he said. "You're a musical genius, my girl. I'll wager with a bit of practice, you'll have that piece down by summer."

Grace giggled.

"How's Eli coming along?"

Grace skipped a bit as she walked. "He's good. It's hard to get him to practice, though. Bel doesn't like it when he leaves her to her own devices."

The young man scoffed.

"Elias can play?" Basil said.

They both looked up at him. "Oh, yes," Mr. Ayles said. "Gracie and I have been teaching him."

"You can play?"

Mr. Ayles chuckled. "I learned when I was younger. When did you start playing—seven, wasn't it?"

Grace nodded.

"I learned at about that age, too," Mr. Ayles continued. "Eli has a good ear for music, but he compares his efforts to mine and Gracie's, which is not particularly fair. To him, I mean. I've been trying to talk him out of it."

"Me too," Grace said primly. "But Bel says it's a waste of time because he won't need to know how to play when he is older since they'll be onboard ships most of the time. So he always has to sneak off to do it."

"And you know Bel," Mr. Ayles said to Basil. "It's hard to sneak anything by that one."

Grace gave a solemn nod.

"Well, I'll talk to them," Mr. Ayles went on.

"Good," Grace said. "They listen to you."

Mr. Ayles flashed another wide smile and gave her hand a squeeze.

Basil looked ahead and gave a start. "Good heavens," he said. "There really is a treehouse."

"Care to go inside?" Mr. Ayles said.

"Well, I—"

Mr. Ayles didn't wait for an answer. He dropped Grace's hand and framed his mouth to shout, "Bel! Eli! Report!" The twins ran up to stand at attention. Mr. Ayles gave a salute and said, "In the shed, I want you to fetch the box of tools. It is big, so you'll both need to carry it."

They saluted and ran off.

Mr. Ayles looked around and said, "Ah, good. Sophia, be a darling and fetch my spellcaster kit, will you? It's in my room. Papa or Father will show you where."

She turned and walked back to the house.

"Can you make sure Martin gets up the ladder all right?" he said, turning back to Grace. "And make sure he doesn't fall out of any windows."

Grace nodded and followed her younger brother up to the treehouse.

"Right," he said. "That's everyone accounted for, I think. I'll get Luce and we'll show you up, shall we?"

He didn't wait for Basil to answer but strode forward and caught Lucy as she was running around a flowerbed. He scooped her into his arms and then pulled her into a close hug. "How are you, my little ladybird?"

Lucy giggled.

"Ready to go up?"

She nodded and wrapped her arms tightly around his neck.

Mr. Ayles laughed and turned in place to look around. "Excellent," he said, as if to himself. "Come along then," he said to Basil.

Basil realized why the young man had Lucy gripping

him tightly. Mr. Ayles climbed swiftly up the ladder into the treehouse with Lucy clinging to him like a small monkey. Once he reached the top, he gently let Lucy down and leaned out to look at Basil.

"All right?"

Basil followed tentatively.

Mr. Ayles grinned when he reached the top and offered a hand to help him into the house.

Basil was unsure about taking the offered hand—the fellow was shorter and smaller than he was. He decided it would be impolite to reject it, so he accepted Mr. Ayles's assistance as he hauled himself inside.

"Do you have any feathers on you?" Mr. Ayles said.

Basil shook his head, mystified.

"Pity. Me either. Fresh out in my kit too." Mr. Ayles continued to lean out of the doorway and yelled down, "Twins! Use the rope to bring it up."

Basil looked down to see Elias and Arabella carrying a crate between them. They set it down on the ground and propped it open. Arabella pulled out a long bit of rope. She cast it over her shoulder like a sailor and climbed nimbly up the ladder.

Once she had reached the treehouse, Mr. Ayles helped her secure the ends to a hook outside one of the windows. Mr. Ayles complimented Arabella on her clever knotwork. Then Arabella tossed the rest of the rope out the window. As Elias set the crate into it, Basil realized it was a rig of some kind. The crate nestled into the center of the rig and Elias hopped about, getting it balanced. Then he stepped back and Arabella hauled the crate up with Mr. Ayles subtly helping from behind. Once the crate was safely inside, Elias clambered up the ladder. Sophia came up after him, a leather satchel over her shoulder.

Mr. Laurence took the satchel out of her hands and said, "I hear you've been practicing more."

She nodded even though the gentleman had already turned to kneel on the floor.

He unbuckled the straps on the satchel, which fell open to reveal a great many pockets and compartments. He looked over the ingredients in the pockets, wiggling his fingers as if indecisive. "Can you handle a lateral movement spell?"

"I think so," she said hesitantly.

He plucked a bit of reed out, tucked the satchel against the wall of the treehouse, and then turned back to her. "I'll show you in a minute, but hold on to the reed for me." She took it as he stood up and framed his mouth again to be heard above the din. "All right, everyone. Listen up. I have a task for each of you, but I need you not to squabble over it. My mind's made up on who is doing what. There will be no arguments." He gave a steely look to Arabella. "All right?"

The children nodded.

"Very good. Bel, you're on nails. There's a hammer in there. I want you to go through and make sure all of the planks are secure from the inside. Understand?"

"But I can—"

The young man raised his eyebrows.

Arabella huffed. "All right."

"Martin? Luce? You see that sack of straw in the corner? That's for the roof, you see. Eli is going to

187

clamber up top and fit the straw into the grooves. He can use this," he said, plucking a tool out of the crate and passing it to the boy, "to facilitate easier work. Gracie is going to hand you a bit of straw at a time so you can bring it across the treehouse and hand it to him. Mind you don't rush and mind you don't give him too much. He can only take one handful at a time because he'll be using the other hand to balance." This was said with a look at Elias as if it was an instruction for him, too.

Elias nodded. Arabella looked irritated. But Martin and Lucy excitedly ran over to the pile of straw and began pulling it out quickly, despite the recent instructions otherwise. Grace ran up behind them, scolded them a bit, and then began pulling the straw out with more care and putting it into the little ones' hands.

Mr. Ayles chuckled next to him. "We're going to have straw everywhere soon enough," he said quietly. Then he turned to Sophia. "Let me show you how to do the lateral movement spell. How are you with going up top?"

He taught her the spell as Basil watched with interest, then he led Sophia out the side window.

Basil looked around the treehouse, noting Arabella irritably hammering nails into the wall and the three youngest chattering around the straw. He could see Elias sitting carefully wedged onto a tree branch so that he was secure enough to collect the straw and then lean forward to stuff it into the roof. Basil looked out the window to see Mr. Ayles showing Sophia how to use the spell she'd just learned to help move the straw to the opposite side of the treehouse, where it was too far for

Elias to reach safely. He backed away from the window when the young man climbed back in.

Mr. Ayles leaned down to talk to Arabella. Basil couldn't hear what was said because of all the noise and chatter but she nodded frequently, looking progressively more mollified, until he patted her on the shoulder and walked back to the center of the treehouse.

"Right," Mr. Ayles said. "That takes care of everyone. The twins will keep an eye on the little ones and Sophia will keep an eye on the twins. Care to see the gardens?"

"They'll be safe up here?"

"Oh, yes," he said as he began to climb back down. "They're here quite often, whether I'm here or not. I actually have a spell set up near the bottom of the tree to catch any fallers."

Basil hurried to climb down after him. "It is a marvelous treehouse," he said when he was back on the ground.

Mr. Ayles smiled at him. "Thank you. My papa has been helping me. It's nearly done, actually. If I'm honest, most of what they're all doing is...well...somewhat unnecessary, but it keeps them busy and they quite like doing it."

A bit of straw floated down as if to emphasize this point.

Basil followed the gentleman as he strode away. "You're very good with them."

"Thank you. I've known them all their lives, so we all sort of grew up around each other. Well, I was eleven when Sophia was born, so there is quite an age difference. But I adore all of them, so I love when they come visit."

Basil felt uncomfortable that this young man knew his family so much better than he did. "I'm afraid I don't know what I'm doing," he muttered, half to himself. "You talk to them all with such ease."

"You'll learn," Mr. Ayles said in a gentle voice. "They obviously adore you and I find that to be half the battle."

Basil nodded, not really believing the words. He felt so horribly inept—trying desperately to fill his father's shoes, when he didn't even know his father. How could he fill the shoes of the man when he couldn't even enter the man's study? A tiny part of him wanted to say all of this to Mr. Ayles, for he had an inkling the gentleman would understand. But he didn't quite dare. He had spent so much of his life without guidance, he didn't know how to ask for it when he needed it.

"I wanted to talk to you alone," Mr. Ayles said after a moment.

Basil looked up in surprise. "You did?"

"I'd like to offer my condolences. Your father was a great man. One of the best men I knew. His was a deep loss."

Basil cleared his throat, feeling even more uncomfortable. "Thank you." He could feel Mr. Ayles looking at him, so he said, "That seems to be the general consensus. I'm glad to know he was well loved. Only it makes me wish I knew him better."

"Yes," Mr. Ayles said. "I can imagine. You're very like him, you know."

"I am?" Basil said, shocked.

Mr. Ayles smiled. "You take after him by looks and, I think, by temperament."

Basil felt warmed by the words. "Thank you," he said, with more feeling than the first time.

"My father wrote to me about his passing and how you moved into the house. I don't know how much was arranged in advance, but I'm sure your father would have been very pleased to see his family all together, even if he wasn't there to enjoy it."

Basil did not know what to say to that. "Thank you," he said again, but softly. "He knew I didn't intend to send them away. We spoke of it before...you understand. I hadn't actually planned to move in. Not really. I had intended to make sure everything was in order and then leave them to carry on with their lives. But everything happened all at once and suddenly it was taken for granted that I'd be staying."

Mr. Ayles gave a small smile. "And now?"

"Now?"

He nodded.

"Now I can't quite fathom leaving them again."

Mr. Ayles's small smile broadened again. Basil thought privately that the young man seemed inclined toward smiling and doing so openly. "I can certainly understand that. They are all wonderful, aren't they?"

Basil nodded. "They are." He glanced at Mr. Ayles and decided to be bold with a bit of truth, even though he barely knew the gentleman. Mr. Ayles put him surprisingly at ease. "I grew up apart from my family, you know. So I'm unaccustomed to it. But I have to say, the way they've accepted me into their lives so readily and so easily, it...well, it has meant more than I ever thought it could. I don't know if they realize it."

"I imagine they do, in their way. The Thorne children are clever. It feels as if they've adopted you in much the same way you've adopted them."

Basil smiled. "That's a nice thought."

Mr. Ayles led them in a loop and began strolling back toward the treehouse. "I believe my father told you that I'm engaged to Mr. Hartford."

"Yes," Basil said, surprised by the change of subject. "Congratulations."

"Thank you," Mr. Ayles said, flashing him a smile. "I mention it because Seb, my fiancé, grew up much like you. That is, he grew up in a somewhat isolated fashion. He knew his father so little that he was quite afraid of him until recently. I'm not at all sure he would have begun to know his father if he hadn't strengthened his friendships with his siblings first. I rather think the poor fellow was a bit lost before he came to live here; he had no one he felt comfortable turning to for advice or guidance."

The young man stopped and turned to face Basil fully. "Your father was a friend of mine and my family. In fact, my family and yours have always been very close. What I'm trying to say, very clumsily, is that I suspect you might have suffered from a similar form of isolation. And while you are certainly not isolated now," he said with a small smile, "you gained family, but not a great deal of support to go with it. I know we've only just met, but if you ever need someone to talk to, whether it be advice on the children or anything really, I hope you know that you can count me your friend. I should be happy to assist you in any way that I can."

Basil felt floored by this speech. "Thank you," he said, yet again. "Your assessment was quite spot on, I'm afraid. I feel thoroughly out of my depth. Miss Hartford... well, Miss Hartford said something similar. It is nice to be surrounded by such good people. Although..." He paused and glanced at Mr. Ayles. "It is nice to know someone who knew my father well and understands the children better than I do. I'm sure I shall need your advice."

Mr. Ayles grinned. "Gerry is one of the best people I know. I'm glad you went to her for advice; she's very good at it. In fact, I'm planning to ask for her advice on something myself. And Charles and Gavin, of course. I'm glad you've met them all. And I'll be happy to be of service. Even if it's just tea and telling you stories of your father."

"I should like that," Basil said earnestly. He gave a self-deprecating laugh and ran his hand through his hair. "Mary told me recently that I could use his study if I needed the privacy; I'm quite ashamed to admit that I've completely avoided stepping into the place."

Mr. Ayles looked thoughtful. "I can see how that would be hard."

"Can you really?"

"Entering into another man's space, one who was closely connected to you and yet you barely knew? Yes, that would be very difficult."

"Thank goodness. I thought it was so foolish of me. I

confess, I came on this visit because it kept me from having to go in."

Mr. Ayles chuckled. "I'd offer to go in with you, but I rather think you need to do it alone."

"Yes, I suppose so." And because Mr. Ayles had been so kind and understanding, Basil said, "It...it will feel too much like I'm taking his place, I think. I already feel that enough as it is. As if I'm filling his shoes and yet I'm poorly equipped to do so. A shadow version of the man that was."

"You aren't taking his place, Mr. Thorne," Mr. Ayles said gently. "You're taking yours. It is enough for you to be their brother. If you were strolling through the house and stripping away all reminders of him, then I could see that as being a shoddy replacement. But you care about your family; it shows in the way you check to make sure they're safe and it shows in the way you try to make them happy. I don't think leaving that study vacant is doing anyone any favors."

"I suppose you're right. Thank you."

Mr. Ayles smiled and clapped him on the back. "Let's see what havoc they've wrought in our absence, shall we?"

Basil laughed and followed the young man back into the treehouse.

Mr. Ayles climbed inside and looked about with his hands akimbo. "Bel, I want a status report."

Arabella stepped forward with her back straight. "We lost a great deal of straw because Martin and Lucy keep throwing it out the window. But we're about a quarter way through filling the roof and I'm about halfway down this wall."

Mr. Ayles nodded. "Very good. Can you lot carry on without us? We're going in for tea."

Arabella saluted.

"Excellent work. As you were."

Basil was a trifle exhausted by the time he climbed back down.

Levinia was on the ground to greet them. She held out a sketchbook. "Will this do, Laury?"

Mr. Ayles took the sketchbook and looked over it appraisingly. "Mighty fine, Levinia. You're even better than the last time you sketched for me. Been practicing, have you?"

She nodded, pleased. "I was going to start the identification, but I wasn't quite sure."

"Oh, do go ahead if you want to. I'll be happy to check your work or answer your questions. We're going in to tea just now, but you can come along inside anytime you like. What do you think, Mr. Thorne? Isn't she marvelous?"

Mr. Ayles held out a sketch of a flower. The lines and the shading were intricate and precise.

"It's beautiful," Basil said. "Don't tell me you did that? In this short a time?"

Levinia beamed at him.

Mr. Ayles passed the sketchbook back to Levinia and they walked into the house. Inside, the house was homey, filled with old knick-knacks and gently worn-down furniture. Basil followed his host down a narrow corridor but paused at a collection of family portraits. Family members of both parents were clearly represented, but what caught Basil's eye was a cluster of portraits of the same child in various stages of life: one as an infant, one at Grace's age and at the piano, and another at the twins' age, dressed in a floral frock and posed with a doll. The final one was slightly larger than the others, and showed the child around Levinia or Sophia's age, with close-cropped hair, wearing a dark blue suit, a crisp cravat, and a smile that was, if possible, even more joyous than the previous portraits.

Mr. Ayles came to his side, apparently having noticed Basil's distraction. "I was fifteen," he said.

"I...was thinking you looked to be about Levinia or Sophia's ages," Basil said.

"You have a good understanding of ages."

Basil chuckled. "Far from it, I assure you." He looked over the different portraits. "Your smile hasn't changed."

Mr. Ayles smiled in response. "My parents like to say the same. I still have the doll too." Then he gave Basil a wink and led him into the sitting room.

Chapter 27

Gerry

Gerry spent all day at the shop thinking hard. She couldn't get the spellcasting Laurence had done out of her mind. She didn't know what spell he had used and she was sure it was one she had never heard of. And what made her think even more furiously was what Mr. Thorne had said when they talked at her shop. He mentioned needing to think more clearly. It occurred to her that even though there were spells for manipulating the emotions and thoughts of others—Love spells which made a person fall in love; Glamour spells, which made the spellcaster irresistible to others; Charm spells, which made other people inclined to like the spellcaster —there were no spells to manipulate the emotions and thoughts of oneself. How convenient it would be if there were a spell for clarity, a way to focus the mind and solve a problem, or a spell for calm, or a spell for good humor. Then again, such spells could run the risk of becoming addictive if misapplied. But it didn't seem any more dangerous than manipulating someone else. Did it?

So as Gerry chatted with customers and replenished the stock and put together spells, she turned the matter over and over in her head. Pip commented on it on their walk back home. "Are you all right?"

She looked at him in surprise. "Why shouldn't I be?"

"You've been very quiet today."

"Oh. Yes, I suppose I have. I've been thinking about a spell."

"A new one?"

"Yes."

"Oh, good," he said, breathing out.

She gave him a quizzical look. "You're relieved?"

"Very. You haven't experimented in months. I've been worried about it."

"It hasn't been all that long," she protested.

"I think the last time you designed a spell was the letter copying one Seb requested."

She considered. "Yes, I suppose you're right. I told Laurence yesterday that I've been having a bit of a creative block. It's never happened before."

"I don't mean to criticize," Pip said hastily. "I've just always known you to be inventing some spell or other. I was worried you might be unhappy or something."

"Oh. No, I don't think I am. I've just been busy and, I don't know, sort of dried out with ideas."

"What's this new spell?"

"It isn't anything yet. Just an idea. Or an idea of an idea."

He smiled. "Sounds exciting."

"I'm not even sure if it would work. I'd like to talk to Bertie or Laurence about it before I get too excited."

"Why don't you come with me for dinner? You know he'd love to see you."

"Well..." she hedged. "I'm not sure I should."

"I'm sure Gavin and Charles would understand."

She hesitated. It would be nice to have an evening out of the house. "Would you mind if we stopped by home first? I'd like to tell them myself that I won't be there. And then we could go on with the carriage?"

"Of course I don't mind."

"Or if you like the walk, you could go on ahead and I'll catch up."

He shook his head. "I'd be afraid you'd get too dutiful and stay behind after all."

She laughed. "Oh, all right." She considered for a moment. "Can I ask you something personal?"

"Surely," he said.

She gave him a steady look. "It's a very personal question. Quite impertinent, actually."

He chuckled. "I don't mind."

"Is Bertie the person you spoke of the other day? The one with whom you have an understanding?"

Pip blushed but didn't appear bothered by the question. "It isn't generally known. Although I'm sure Charles knows. Those two tell each other everything."

"And if Charles knows, there's a good chance Gavin knows too."

Pip smiled. "Probably. Gavin is good at keeping secrets so it's hard to tell." He paused. "Seb knows."

"He does?"

He nodded. "He walked in when we were having tea together once. We weren't doing anything," he added.

"But I think he understood there was...affection between us. And I sort of brought it up later. When he was asking for advice about Laurence."

"He came to you for relationship advice?"

Pip chuckled. "Strange, isn't it?"

"Not really. You're very observant. I'm just surprised Seb picked up on it."

"It was when Laurence first proposed. Seb was anxious because he wanted to say yes but he didn't think he was ready."

"What did you say?"

"I told him that I was in a similar situation. That I was in love with a gentleman as well but wasn't ready for marriage. I told him to wait."

"You're waiting too?"

"We're not engaged. We're not even courting, really. And I expect I shall have to be the one to propose in the end, as he won't want to rush me." Pip puffed out his cheeks. "I hate to admit it, but I'm awfully worried I'll go on forever being too frightened to ask him."

"I don't think you will. It hasn't been that long since you moved here."

"I know. But it feels as though it should be long enough by now."

"There's no 'should' about it, Pip. And you know Bertie would agree."

He smiled. "You're right. I'm sorry I haven't told you yet. You might be the last Hartford sibling to know."

"John knows?" she said in mock horror.

He laughed, dimpling. "Goodness, no. Is it horrible that I forget he is your sibling? He's so unlike you all."

"I forget he is too. Well, I try to. He was always a bit of a prat, but he got so much worse when he got older. And Veronica brings out all of his bad parts."

"I've wondered about that. Could it be like Seb, do you think? Bad influences?"

"It could be," she said. "I suppose I never thought about it. John and I never got on, so when he got worse, it seemed perfectly natural. But Seb and I were always friendly, so it was noticeable when he started to pull away and grow distant."

Pip looked thoughtful. Which made Gerry thoughtful too. She felt a little guilty that she had never thought of John in anything other than unkind tones. Had he been as lonely as Seb or as withdrawn as Gavin in his own way? But when she told Charles that she would be accompanying Pip to dinner with Bertie, and John had come in and scolded her for inviting herself over to other people's houses, her guilt evaporated immediately.

Bertie, however, had no such scoldings. "Darling!" he said when she walked into the house. "What a delightful surprise! It has been far too long!"

She gave him a hug and kissed his cheek. "I hope it's all right that I came. I know I wasn't invited."

"Good heavens, my sweet. I should hope we're past the point of invitations now." He led them both to the sitting room. "How's business, darlings?"

"Business is going very well," Gerry said. "I'm getting ready to increase production on the Personal Quick-Dry spells, as we're getting close to the rainy season."

"Very wise," Bertie said approvingly.

"Gerry has an idea for a new spell," Pip said. "Or

201

maybe it was more of a...what did you call it? An idea of an idea?"

Gerry laughed. "I was just thinking. It's not really anything yet."

Bertie raised his eyebrows inquiringly.

Gerry took a deep breath. "Well, I should probably explain what made me think of it. I talked to Mr. Thorne at the shop and—have you met Mr. Thorne, Bertie?"

"I called on him for tea. He seemed a very good sort of person, very kind eyes."

"Yes, he does. And...yes, he has. Well, anyway, he came by the shop the other day and we got to talking about my spells and I explained that I haven't been coming up with any new ideas. And he made a sort of suggestion about making a spell to think clearly. Later, Laurence came to the house to visit and John and Veronica were being dreadful, as usual—good heavens, you haven't met them yet, have you?"

Bertie smiled. "Not yet. Charlie wanted to get a good gauge on them first. We're plotting to have our households collide fairly soon, though."

Gerry gave a snort. "Plotting. That sounds like you two. Anyway, Laurence came to visit last night and John and Veronica were being cutting about Seb, because of course they were, and we all jumped in to defend him—"

"Because of course you would," Bertie put in with a grin.

"Yes," she said, grinning back. "And then Laurence did some sort of spell to pull our focus to him. It wasn't a quieting spell, but none of us were compelled to speak and it drew our attention. I've never seen anything like it."

Bertie looked thoughtful. "Do you know what he used?"

"I saw holly in his hand, but I don't know if he had anything else."

"Interesting," he said. "I shall have to ask him about it."

"We're having tea with them tomorrow, so I might ask him about it too."

"Your spell idea has something to do with it?"

"Well, I got to thinking: there are plenty of spells for manipulating other people's thoughts and emotions, but nothing for manipulating one's own. And I thought if there was a spell for, say, clarity..."

Bertie hummed thoughtfully. "Very clever notion, darling."

"There's something to it then, you think?" she said, feeling hopeful.

"Oh, undoubtedly. Mind you, there are drawbacks."

"Yes, I know. People might get dependent on them, and of course it could be dangerous to cast a spell on oneself."

Bertie nodded. "But you're already thinking of those, so I'm not worried about it. However..."

"Yes?"

"I wonder if you might consider finding another spellcaster to work on it with you."

"Would you like to?"

He chuckled. "Well, I'd certainly love to help, but I

mean to say...your shop is very popular. I'm not sure if you're aware of that."

"I thought it was a normal sort of popular."

"As a matter of fact, it's a good deal more than that. Do you realize you have customers who travel from other counties to buy from you? You have about as much business as a London shop, if my accountant is to be believed."

Gerry gaped. "Not really?"

"And London shops, typically speaking, have several employees. Well, the nice ones do. There's always Smelting's on the seedier end of town. He only employs one person at a time, but that's more out of stinginess than budget. But if you were to hire one, or even two more people, I don't think it would go amiss. Proficient spellcasters who could help Pip with the customers and the cleaning, or help you with the spell-building or the ingredient preparation."

Gerry considered this. "We have been very busy the last few months." She looked at Pip. "What do you think?"

"I think it could help," he said. "One person at the till, one person on the floor, one person doing inventory and building spells?"

"Goodness," she said.

"And when we have slow periods, you could teach me, or the others, some of the things we haven't had time for yet. I'd be happy to learn more about ingredient preparation or spell-building, but I can't countenance doing it alone; someone has to be out on the floor at all times as it is."

She nodded. "You're right."

"And then," Bertie said. "You could have someone to assist you with these new spells you have in mind. That person could be Pip, if he were interested, or someone else."

A liveried footman came in to announce that dinner was ready. Bertie stood and offered them each an arm. "Think on it, at any rate, my sweet. There's no hurry in the matter as I know you two are handling everything splendidly as it is. But that shop of ours is quite the success and we'd do well to think in the long term. Since I'm suggesting it, you can know that I'm prepared to work out the finances for your employees' salaries, although the shop itself can afford a good portion of that."

"I suppose I ought to learn the business part of it, shouldn't I?" she said.

He laughed. "If you like. The most successful shop owners in London hire accountants for just such a purpose. I've never owned a shop before, so I had my own accountant keep track of things."

They went into dinner and conversation moved on from business to local gossip, Bertie's own magical projects, and life in general. When she and Pip finally got back into the carriage to ride home, Gerry breathed out a long sigh. "Bertie's so very lovely to be around, isn't he?"

"He is," Pip said. "He's very restful."

"I hope you don't mind, but I'm prodigiously happy now that I know about you two."

He chuckled. "Why would I mind you being happy?"

"Well, I'm liable to say things like 'you two are so perfect together' or 'you two make a lovely pair.' I say these things when someone I like falls in love with another person I like."

"I don't mind it," he said. "I'm not particularly comfortable with outward shows of affection. That is, I can be, but it has to be on my own terms...which sounds terribly selfish—"

"No, it doesn't."

"The man I was with before," Pip said slowly. Gerry held her breath. Pip rarely talked of his life before he came to Tutting-on-Cress. "He made a point of showing affection in front of others. He liked the evidence that I belonged to him. As a result, I was somewhat constantly..." He cleared his throat. "At any rate, it is nice to be with a man who doesn't need to prove our love to others. I am trying to...well, you know Bertie. He's so naturally affectionate. Rather like you, I think. And it doesn't seem fair to deprive him of that... comfort. So I'm trying to give him that, when I can."

"I'm sure he understands."

"We've discussed it, so I know he does. But I....well, I'd like to be more for him."

"More?"

"More...deserving, I suppose?"

"Pip—"

"Anyway, let's change the subject. Don't think it escaped my notice that you had a chat with Mr. Thorne the other day. How was it?"

Gerry smiled. "It was nice. He's lovely, you know."

"Oh, I know."

She laughed. "Well, I don't expect it to result in anything other than friendship."

Pip raised his eyebrows.

"I don't," she said.

He gave a small smile.

"Oh, all right. What did you notice this time?"

"That every time you laughed, he practically glowed with pleasure."

"He did not!"

Pip's expression was sympathetic.

She sighed. "I suppose I ought to take your word for it. You are a good judge of character."

"Thank you."

"But please don't tell Charles."

He chuckled. "I would never." He was silent for a long moment. "But I hope you'll forgive me for saying so...I may not have to."

"What do you mean?"

"I mean that every time Mr. Thorne comes up in conversation, you blush. And he came up in conversation tonight. And you know very well that Bertie is apt to mention it to Charles sooner or later."

"Oh dear. And now I'm going and making a spell specifically for him too, aren't I?"

"Are you?" he said in a curious tone.

She sighed. "Yes. And I would appreciate it if you told no one of this, but I would very much like to see Mr. Thorne's reaction when I tell him I've made a spell at his request."

Pip gave her a dimpled smile.

Chapter 28
Basil

Basil stood, once again, on the threshold to the study. He wished briefly that Mr. Ayles was there to go in with him, and then he felt foolish for such a desire. Then he thought about what Mr. Ayles had said, that Basil wouldn't be replacing anyone, and that he was not invading his father's space. He wondered if this meant his father would have wanted him to be in his study. Or perhaps that was wishful thinking?

Basil sighed and stepped over the threshold. He closed the door behind him and stood in the quiet. He thought his hands might be shaking so he tucked them into his pockets. The trouble was, he considered, as he stood still and stared about him, he hadn't told Mr. Ayles all of what was worrying him.

He hadn't known his father, so Basil had barely felt any grief when the man died; it was hard to mourn someone he didn't know. But he had a feeling that if he occupied the study, he would come to know his father to an extent. Basil was not at all sure he was prepared to grieve. But then, had the lack of grief been so very satisfying?

He closed his eyes and leaned back against the door. There was the slight scent of tobacco in the air. He remembered vaguely that his father had smoked a pipe. There was a brief flash of memory of climbing into his lap as a child and watching the pipe smoke curl around him.

It was this, oddly, that caused him to open his eyes and step forward into the room. He kept his hands in his pockets and looked about him as if he were in an art gallery. The study had a large bay window on one wall, art hung on the wall opposite, and the wall behind the desk was lined fully with bookshelves. At first, Basil noticed that among the art were portraits of the family, including one with him and his mother, and a painting of the house, but then he noticed rougher pieces. He realized after looking at several of these pieces that they must have been art created by the children. He wondered suddenly if anything done by him as a child was hung on the wall. His own childhood felt too distant for him to remember much detail. He wondered if Mary would know the artists of each piece.

Most of the books on the shelves were what he might have expected: books on finance and estate management that his father might have favored, but the farthest case, the one closest to the window, was different. It was a barrister's bookcase with eight shelves. On each of these eight shelves was a tiny framed portrait of one of the children. Basil stepped back to note that all of them were represented and realized that the bottom shelf was newer and had likely been added when Lucy was born.

Looking more carefully at the topmost shelf, he saw that it had a portrait of him. Next to the portrait were books, papers, files, and a dark mahogany box. Basil opened the glass door at the front of the shelf, pulled the box down, and set it carefully on the desk. His hands were definitely shaking now.

He opened the box to discover letters. A quick shuffle revealed that they were all the letters he had ever written his father, from when he was a boy at Eton to when he was a man living in Bath. His father had kept them all.

He returned the box back to its place and glanced through some of the papers. They contained drawings and notes, certificates and messages from his schools. He recognized one of the books from his childhood. The spine was worn from frequent readings. Basil was afraid to open it for fear of damaging it, but he was sure if he did, he'd experience a rush of memories. The other books were ones he did not recognize but were, oddly, uniquely to his taste.

A glance through the other shelves showed similar mementos, drawings, notes, essays. The other children's shelves were no more or less full than his own. There were books to each of the children's tastes—although this was more evident in the older ones.

His father, it would seem, had been equally fond of all his children. This discovery answered a question Basil had held in his heart for years. It was a question that had kept him from coming home after his father's second marriage, had kept him from writing as often, had kept him from crying at his father's funeral. It was a question he had held close to guard his heart from sorrow. He sat on the window seat with a thump, folded forward with his head in his hands, and started to cry.

Once the tears began, it was shockingly difficult to stop. He was filled with regret and longing and loneliness. The pressure of his responsibilities weighed on him anew. He had a sudden wish that he had a shoulder to cry on and shuddered at the realization that he had so carefully kept himself independent for most of his life, that he had no one he knew well enough to offer that kind of support. Modesty probably would, but he had never developed the talent of asking for help. He had no idea how to start learning now. He focused on taking deep, calming breaths and used his handkerchief to dry his face. He considered ringing for tea but did not want any of the servants to see him in such a state.

He looked at the desk, but knew he was not ready to face that, so he strode back to the shelf, plucked out one of the books next to his own portrait, and sat back down to read. It was, he concluded, a way of getting to know his father—to read something his father had picked out for him. After some deliberation, he rang for tea after all, and spent the whole of the afternoon reading on the window seat.

Chapter 29
Gerry

Gerry was not entirely convinced that a trip to Copperage Farm would be enjoyable with John and Veronica along. If they were a different sort of parents, her nephew might have enjoyed the visit. But she hadn't seen the baby since the family's arrival; Veronica was of the opinion that children belonged in the nursery.

However, she needn't have worried. Laurence and his parents had the situation well in hand. As soon as they arrived and introductions were made, Mr. Algernon Ayles directed Veronica and John to sit on one sofa, the two gentlemen sat on the other sofa, rang for tea, and recommended that Laurence show the others his progress on the treehouse. This suggestion sounded so abhorrent to John and Veronica that neither was the least bit interested. So Gerry took Laurence's proffered arm and allowed herself to be led outside with Charles and Gavin following them.

"Don't fret," Laurence said, as soon as they were out

in the yard. "Father and Papa are consummate conversationalists."

Gerry breathed a sigh of relief.

"I noticed Pip did not come, nor was he at dinner the other night," Laurence said.

Charles laughed. "Astute observation, darling. He's taking refuge at Bertie's."

"Good," Laurence said.

"You handled yourself very well with them the other night," Gerry said. "I rather wish you could be at our house all the time."

"I'm glad you brought that up, actually. I fear I owe you all an apology."

"Whatever for?" she said.

"I used a spell on you that night. It was not very polite of me. I hope you know that ordinarily I would never dream of spellcasting on my friends, but—"

"Don't be stupid, Laurence," Gavin said. "It was remarkably efficient."

Laurence laughed. "Thank you. It's become a bit of a bad habit, I'm afraid."

"What do you mean?" Gerry said.

"Well, for the first month in London, no one really cared about anything I said. They took for granted that I was from the country and a nobody, and there was a general assumption that I would be easy to push around. I could barely get a word in edgewise."

"Oh, dear," Gerry said.

He shrugged. "I let it pass for the first month because I was trying to get the lay of things. But if I didn't do something about it, it would get progressively more difficult to fix." He took a deep breath. "So I started using that spell. It draws focus to the spellcaster. It's very good for speeches and that sort of thing. But it isn't long-lasting."

"I noticed you recast halfway through," Gerry said, half to herself.

"When I used it at your house...well, after I'd started, I wished I hadn't."

"I'm on Gavin's side on this one," Gerry said. "John and Veronica are dreadful and you did what you had to in the circumstances."

"Besides," Charles said, "your speech was charming, darling. I didn't mind a jot being made to hear it."

Laurence laughed. "Thank you. You're all too kind. I'm glad you're not angry."

"Never," Gerry said. "In fact, I might have to ask you more about it later."

Laurence grinned. "That would be delightful."

"Is that what you wanted to discuss with us?" Gavin said.

"No," Laurence said slowly.

They had reached the back of the house by now and were in the garden proper. Gerry had never explored the gardens at Copperage Farm. She knew Laurence had a whole magical section planned. She was curious to know if he'd already started it, but she focused on her friend.

"It's about Seb," he said.

"Is everything all right?" Charles said.

"Oh, yes," Laurence said. "We're fine. It's just... when I came from London to your parents' place, well, I was exhausted from my time away. I told Seb that

I'd have to be in London more than we had anticipated and..." He stopped walking and turned fully to them. "I know we said we'd make it a long engagement, but I think Seb had it in his head that this meant a few months, a year at most, since my proposal. Rather like yours," he added, with a nod to Charles and Gavin.

"But?" Charles said.

"I think we should wait a while longer. I have no desire to make Seb sit around at home, waiting for me. He'd have Papa and Father for company, of course. But that's no proper way to start a marriage. Not to my mind. And as I told him when I first proposed, I'm in no hurry. The trouble is...I think Seb is getting anxious about that prospect. I fear he thinks that if we wait longer, I'll 'come to my senses' or something and take it all back."

He smiled ruefully. "Of course he never said this out loud or I could have corrected him. But you know how he is; he's so adorably easy to read sometimes. Anyway, I don't think either of us is quite ready for marriage yet. But it's no good me telling him that. He'll think I've changed my mind or that I'm putting it off for some negative reason. I was rather hoping you all might help plant the seed, as it were...perhaps congratulate him on making plans so far in advance or something? It will mean a different thing entirely if you were to tell him to wait than if I did."

Charles nodded. "We'll be delighted to help, darling."

"Seb is dashed stubborn. So it might take some doing," Gavin said, glancing between them all. "If you

215

ask me, the best method might be a combination of encouragement and...distraction."

"How do you mean?" Gerry said.

"Seb gets restless," Gavin said. "If he's rattling about by himself at home, he'll spend all his time thinking about how he ought to be here and married."

"Very observant, dearest," Charles said fondly, kissing Gavin's temple.

Gavin blushed, but didn't object to the show of affection.

"I've been thinking that too," Laurence said thoughtfully. "That's something else I've been meaning to talk to you all about. You see, Seb is...well, he's frightfully clever, you know. The way he goes about spells—it's brilliant. I think he could really make a career for himself, if he had a mind to it. The trouble is, I worry he thinks there's only room for one person to be ambitious in our relationship."

"You might be right," Charles said. "I think he anticipates running the house as his career."

"And there's nothing wrong with that," Laurence said. "But will that make him happy? I don't think it would. He needs more of a challenge."

"He's still working with Bertie, isn't he?" Gerry said, looking at Charles.

"Yes," Charles said. "I could talk to Bertie. He really only needs him a few hours a day. But he might be able to come up with projects to keep him busy. And I did tell Seb I would make him learn a whole curriculum on running a house," Charles added with a wicked grin. "I could make good on that promise."

Laurence laughed. "I'd certainly appreciate it. If any of you think of a good career for him, I hope you'll tell him, or me. I don't expect us to be married until the end of the year at the earliest. There's more than enough time for him to sort himself out and try his hand at something spectacular."

"We certainly shall," Charles said. "I'm of the same mind, actually. I think if he settles down too quickly, he'll get restless."

"Exactly," Laurence said. He let out a long breath. "Thank you. I knew you all would understand."

"Was that everything, darling?"

Laurence nodded. "That was everything."

"Before we go in," Gerry said. "Can you show me where you're planning your plot of magical plants?"

Laurence brightened and went into a long explanation of his plans for expansion. Charles and Gavin wandered off to explore on their own while Gerry listened, riveted, and asked a great many questions. Finally, Laurence suggested they return to the house and they all trooped back inside.

After they entered the building, a maid handed Laurence a letter with a curtsy. Laurence looked at the direction and smiled to himself.

"Is it from Seb?" Gerry said.

"No," he said. "It's from a friend of mine. Actually, I think he said he's met you. Mr. Thorne?"

"Oh, you've met him?" Charles said. "He's a delightful fellow."

"He is," Laurence said. He glanced at the envelope. "Do you mind if I read it now?"

"Not at all, darling. We'll go in and join your parents," Charles said. He took Gavin's hand and strode inside. Gerry lingered; she was curious and a little nosy.

Laurence didn't seem to mind. He opened the letter and read it, smiled, and murmured, "Oh, good."

"Everything's all right?" Gerry said.

He looked up at her and grinned. "Yes. Everything's lovely. He did something difficult. And he invited me to tea tomorrow."

"You know his family then?" Gerry said.

He opened the door into the sitting room. "Where do you think I got the idea for having a lot of children?" he said with a wink.

Gerry followed him in and stopped on the threshold when she realized everyone in the room was talking about her.

"Well, I rather think the young lady knows her own mind," Mr. Robert Ayles was saying.

"It's disgraceful," Veronica rebutted. "She should have been married an age ago. I'm sure I don't—"

"Ah, Miss Hartford," Mr. Algernon Ayles said, standing. "Do come sit down."

Mr. Robert Ayles gave her an apologetic look as she sat down on the sofa between Laurence's fathers. Charles and Gavin were sharing a chair, with Gavin in the seat, and Charles propped on the arm. Laurence sat on the arm of the sofa, blithely ignoring Veronica's annoyed expression.

Mr. Algernon Ayles poured out for Gerry and Laurence, having already given Charles and Gavin their tea. "We were just discussing your prospects, my dear."

"Oh," she said. "That seems to be a popular topic these days."

Veronica tsked.

"I'm surprised Lady Windham hasn't put forth more of an effort," Mr. Robert Ayles said. "Considering she's a friend of yours. That woman sticks her nose into everyone's business."

Gerry laughed. "She's doing her level best."

"Much as I disliked the way your friends spoke to Veronica," John said. "I confess I would like to be better acquainted with them. I am impressed that you keep such august company. You should invite them to tea."

"That's a marvelous idea," Charles said. "We'll have all of the ladies to tea. Won't we, darling?"

Gerry stared at him. "We will?"

"Yes," he said. "I'm sure they'll adore meeting Veronica and John again."

"It is difficult to plan around your schedule," Veronica said with a sniff. "I don't see why you must work in that shop every day."

"I take one day off a week," Gerry said. "It is good for business to be open most days."

"Perhaps a dinner party, then?" Charles said.

Gerry stared at him. What was he up to?

Gavin was staring at his husband in much the same way. "Have you gone quite mad?" he said, his voice carrying despite the fact that he had spoken quietly.

"John is right," Charles said, sliding his hand down Gavin's arm in what was probably a signal that he knew what he was doing. "We have been shockingly lax in introducing our guests to our friends in town. This is the

219

first time they've been to Copperage Farm and they've been staying with us for an entire month. And they haven't even met Bertie yet. We shall have a dinner party as soon as I can throw one together. It will be delightfully good fun. Won't it?"

Silence met that.

"Seb might be back in time as well," Laurence said, offering support. "I'm sure he'd like a dinner party."

"That would be marvelous, wouldn't it?" Charles said. "I shall write to Mr. Hartford to see when he intends to send him."

"Good," John said. "I'm glad that's settled."

"I'll start making plans immediately. It might take me a month or so to get a date that works for everyone," Charles said, standing. "Perhaps we ought to return home so I can start today."

John and Veronica hastily agreed, clearly eager to be out of the small sitting room. Charles thanked the Ayles family enthusiastically before slinging an arm over Gavin's shoulder and walking him out of the house. Laurence offered Gerry his arm.

"What on earth can he be up to?" Gerry said as she took it.

"I'm not sure," Mr. Robert Ayles said. "But I wouldn't worry, my dear. Mr. Kentworthy is usually up to something."

"He doesn't like people to be single," Mr. Algernon Ayles said with a laugh. "Unless they have an express desire to be so."

She looked at Laurence. He shrugged. "At the very least, it will be entertaining. Can you imagine your sister-in-law verbally sparring with Caro Windham? Or trying to out-talk Lizzy Canterbury?"

Gerry laughed aloud. "You're right. That will be entertaining."

He walked her out the door. "And," he said in a low voice, "there's Bertie to consider. He and Charles are a force to be reckoned with, you know."

"Too true," she said.

He helped her into the carriage and closed the door. "Well, goodbye, you lot. Do come again soon."

The carriage rattled down the long drive.

"Their house is very small," Veronica said, as if she had been fit to burst with the criticism.

"Oh, do hush," Gavin said.

John's lips pinched together, but he merely turned his face to the window and said nothing. Veronica seemed more irritated with her husband's silence than Gavin's admonition. She hissed her disapproval at him all the way home.

Much to her annoyance, Gerry was unable to talk to Charles alone in order to get an explanation. As soon as they returned from tea at Copperage Farm, Charles excused himself to his study and Gerry needed to help Gavin entertain John and Veronica. She was surprised by how excited their guests were about the upcoming party. She supposed it could be dull to have the same four people as company. Then again, she thought irritably, they were the ones choosing to stay.

She was finally able to talk to Charles before dinner the following evening. Pip had gone to Bertie's again and Gerry entered the house alone. No one came out to greet her, so she made good of her unnoticed arrival and headed straight for Charles's study. To her relief, he was inside and alone.

"Oh, good," she said by way of greeting as she shut the door behind her.

"Good evening, darling," he said, smiling at her placidly. "How was your day?"

"Charles," she said, sitting across from him. "Please tell me what is going on in that scheming mind of yours."

He grinned but said, "Could you possibly be more specific, my dear?"

"This dinner party. What are you on about? I'm sure you're not seriously planning to find me a suitor in this fashion. You know perfectly well that I know everyone in the vicinity."

"Oh, dearest, if introductions and social events were the only things standing in your way of matrimony, I would have assuredly done something about it a long time ago."

"Then what are you up to? Why are you humoring Veronica and John like this? And...and why won't you leave my marriage prospects to me?"

He set aside the papers he was looking over and folded his hands on his desk. "All you Hartfords are so adorably stubborn," he said fondly. "It is one of the many things I love about you. And I do relish the challenge it provides. But it does mean that I am not disposed to tell you of my schemes because you will surely resist my involvement. Rather than proving I am right, it is vastly easier to go about my plans without confiding them to you."

Gerry rolled her eyes. "I'm not my brothers, you know."

"Yes. I do know. Which is why I have left you alone. You are not as prone to making yourself miserable. But I'm very worried that you're on the verge of doing so. Thus, I mean to interject before family habits get in the way of your happiness."

She sighed and walked around the desk. "You're impossible. But I'm so glad you're part of the family now, I can't be irritated at you for long." She leaned over and kissed his cheek.

He took her hand in both of his. "Trust me, darling. I have managed to get half your family straightened out —or mostly straightened out; dear Seb is still a work in progress, poor thing—but I will not rest until you are all happily situated."

She frowned at him. "Half? Are you worried about John?"

"Exceedingly," he said, with far more seriousness than was usual.

"I rather think John's unhappiness is of his own making."

"Perhaps," Charles said with a small smile. "But that could arguably be said about all of us, couldn't it? Or at the very least, most of us?"

She nodded and strode back to the door. "I suppose Bertie would be an unhelpful source, wouldn't he?" Bertie and Charles told each other everything so she was fairly confident Bertie would be aware of all of Charles's schemes. It was a source of curiosity to Gerry how the two men had become such good friends and yet never lovers.

Charles laughed. "Undoubtedly. Compared to Bertie, I'm a frightful amateur in the art of being mysterious. But I give you leave to try. I'm sure he would find the attempts entertaining and I could never begrudge him that."

Chapter 30
Basil

Basil felt very silly writing the letter to Mr. Ayles, but he had swallowed his pride and done it anyway. He had a feeling the gentleman would not think him foolish for taking pride in entering his father's study. Nor did he think Mr. Ayles would find the invitation to tea an exceptional one. However, despite his gut feelings on the matter, he was prodigiously relieved when he received a response congratulating him and heartily accepting the invitation.

He was pacing his father's study when Mr. Ayles arrived. He knew the moment the gentleman entered the house because there was a great cacophony of greetings, as all Basil's siblings rushed to welcome the visitor. Basil walked out and found Mr. Ayles holding Lucy with one arm with Martin tugging on the other, and the twins and Levinia chattering excitedly in front of him. Sophia and Grace stood to one side, clearly wanting to be a part of the conversation, albeit a quiet part. Mr. Ayles took it all with good humor, and Basil took the opportunity to observe the man's interactions to see if he might learn from it.

"Well, of course, I would love to see it, Bel," he was saying. "But as it happens, I am not here to look at your atlas."

Mary walked in at that juncture and scolded her children gently for hounding Mr. Ayles in such a manner. Mr. Ayles laughed and kissed Lucy on the cheek before passing her to her mother.

Mary turned and said, "Oh, good. Here's Basil. Basil, Laurence has arrived for tea. Would you like to have the sitting room to yourselves? I'm sure I can keep the children out," she said with a look at the twins.

"No, thank you, Mary," Basil said. "We can take tea in the study. I know Levinia has set up her art supplies in the sitting room and I don't wish to disrupt it."

Mr. Ayles grinned and eased himself out of the crowd to follow Basil to the study. When Basil offered to let Mr. Ayles enter the room first, he smiled knowingly and said, "After you, Mr. Thorne."

Basil was a trifle nervous about bringing someone into the room, and he had a feeling the other man had guessed this. Not wishing to keep his guest waiting, Basil squared his shoulders and strode in.

Mr. Ayles closed the door gently behind him as he followed. "It will get easier, I expect," he said.

Basil let out a huff. "It is ridiculous."

"By whose standards?" Mr. Ayles said mildly.

Basil tilted his head in acknowledgement.

Mr. Ayles gave a small smile and tucked his hands into his pockets. "It is a nice room."

"Did you ever come in here with..." Basil cleared his throat. "Did my father ever see you in his study? I remember you said you were friends."

"He did. And we were. It was your father, in fact, who encouraged my pursuit of magic. Both of my parents are proficient, of course, but neither possesses a particularly strong talent for it. Your father saw the inclination in me quite early on and gave me a great deal of books to study on the subject."

Basil felt a little hollowed out knowing another young man had been fostered by his father in a manner he had never enjoyed.

"Your father spoke of you often," Mr. Ayles went on, his voice softer. "It troubled him greatly that he had sent you away at such a young age. But he was so certain you were living a better life without his interference that he did not know how to send for you."

Basil looked down. "I suppose we were alike in that way," he said at last. "That was the exact reason I never came home. They all seemed to be living a perfectly fine life without me. It seemed silly to..." He waved his hand expressively, "remind my father of his previous marriage by returning. My mother's death brought him so much grief."

"You are very like him," Mr. Ayles said. "He used to say the same thing about you."

Basil ran a hand over his face. He realized that he invited Mr. Ayles to tea and had not yet rung for it, so he pulled the bell rope. Then he realized that both of them were standing in the middle of the room, as he had not yet invited his guest to sit.

"Good heavens. Where are my manners? Please take a seat, Mr. Ayles."

"Call me Laurence. Everybody does. Or Laury, if you prefer, like your siblings. I'm not particularly formal by nature. Do you have a preference in where we should sit?"

Basil was grateful for the question. He had been worried Laurence would sit on one side of the desk with the expectation of him taking his father's seat, and he hadn't quite managed that yet. So he waved a hand toward the window. "Will the window seat suit?"

"Admirably."

Though Laurence had not asked, Basil said, "I haven't managed to go through the desk yet, you see. I made it as far as the paintings and bookcases."

Laurence nodded as he sat. "Grief is an exhausting thing. There is no rush for you to go through it all. Although I expect it may help you."

Basil sat on the other side of the seat. "I did not feel grief when he died. I did not know him well enough."

Laurence did not say anything. Basil chanced a glance to see if the silence was one of judgment. He was unsurprised to find that it wasn't.

"It would be hard to grieve a man you barely knew," Laurence supplied.

"Yes," Basil said. "And I'm sure it is cowardly of me, but I have a feeling that the more I explore this study of his, the better I shall know him. And what—" He broke off, unsure if what he meant to say was wrong. Laurence did not push him to continue, which made him feel as if he should. "What good does it do to know him now?"

Laurence did not say anything. The maid brought in the tea trolley, so Basil was saved from having to say anything further. Neither of them spoke until the maid was gone and Basil had poured for them both.

Laurence took a sip of tea and said, "I cannot claim to be an expert, of course, but I expect that not knowing your father was not from lack of wanting to."

Basil closed his eyes and let out a long breath. He was relieved by how comforting Laurence's quiet presence was, so he allowed himself to be brave enough to say the thing he'd been wanting to say all along, the whole reason he had invited Laurence to tea, the suspicion that he needed confirmed. "I always thought that he didn't love me very much. That my mother's death had made our relationship too...unappealing for him. When he remarried and had all those children and was so busy taking care of his new family, it seemed to prove my suspicions." He sighed. "You know of that barrister bookcase, I presume. The one with a shelf dedicated to each of us."

"I do," Laurence said softly.

"I did not know of it until I came in yesterday. And—" His voice broke, so he took a sip of tea to steady his nerves and then set the tea on the tea caddy. "And it would appear that I was wrong. It took him dying for me to realize that. I can never forgive myself for such—such foolishness."

He was very pointedly not looking at Laurence when he said this, so he heard rather than saw Laurence put his own teacup aside. He felt a hand on his shoulder and then a handkerchief came into view.

229

"You must not blame yourself," he said. "Your father really should have sent for you a long time ago. Casting blame on either party is useless. You were both grieving and both afraid to cause the other more pain. You were both acting out of love and consideration, misguided though those decisions may have been." The hand on his shoulder squeezed slightly. "It is too late to form a relationship with your father, but it is not too late to know what sort of man he was. Nor is it too late for you to form relationships with the rest of your family, which is what your father surely would have wanted above all things. You cannot change the past, but you can use it to guide your way to the future."

Basil wiped his face, grateful that Laurence had been unembarrassed by his show of emotion. "It is a wrench. I am in desperate need of guidance right now, and I could very much do with my father's advice. But it is my father's death that puts me in such a need for advice."

Laurence gave his shoulder a final squeeze before withdrawing his hand. "I cannot give you the advice of a father, but I can give you the advice of a friend, should you desire it." Laurence did not prompt him further, simply picked his tea up and sipped it.

As before, it was Laurence's lack of pushing that led Basil to expound on the subject. "Well, it's a great many things. I have never been responsible for other people, and now I find myself responsible for not only my seven siblings, but my stepmother as well. I haven't the faintest notion what to do. I did talk to Miss Hartford about that briefly, and she said the children were likely already telling me what they need and all I have to do is listen. Which has helped. But the trouble is..." He took a breath. "The trouble is that I still feel as though I'm taking my father's place. Even if that is not the case, I'm still taking on a new role and I haven't the slightest notion how to fill it. Moreover, I don't know the first thing about property and estate management. And then there's the children's dowries and futures to think about."

Laurence listened without interruption. Finally he said, "I think Gerry has the right of it. And, of course, if you're ever at a loss with something specific, you can always ask Mary, or me. You're not alone."

"Thank you."

"As for estate management, I'm afraid my skills are rather lacking there. But Charles could certainly provide some advice and I know he'd be only too glad to help."

"Charles?"

"Kentworthy."

"I hardly know him."

"You hardly know me," Laurence pointed out.

"And I hardly know Miss Hartford. Strange, really, that I've taken to confiding in people so quickly."

"Perhaps you're making up for lost time," Laurence said with a smile. Then, after a moment, he added, "What did you think of Gerry?"

Basil raised his eyebrows. "Is that even a question?"

Laurence looked amused.

Basil rolled his eyes. "Miss Hartford is incredibly beautiful and shockingly easy to talk to. I most certainly should not be telling you this, but I think I'm falling in love with her and it is most unfortunate as the timing really isn't the best."

Laurence grinned. "Excellent. I think you two will suit admirably."

Basil was somewhat cheered by this, but said, "Did you not hear the part about the bad timing?"

Laurence chuckled. "Oh, I don't know. Might be helpful to have someone to muddle through with you. I know I've found problems significantly less daunting now that I have Seb to talk to."

"I feel as though I ought to have things sorted out before I start looking for a spouse."

"Well," Laurence said. "There are always long engagements, you know. Seb had similar concerns and we've decided to wait because of that." He paused for a moment and then said, "In fact, I've recently asked Gerry, Charles, and Gavin to encourage Seb to make the engagement even longer. I don't think either of us are quite ready for marriage yet, but I also want to be sure he knows it isn't out of uncertainty on my part."

Basil sighed. "We are very far away from talk about engagements. I only recently discovered my feelings for the woman. I'm not about to propose. Besides, what do I have to offer her: a house full of siblings, a stepmother who has a firm handle on the household, and a husband who has no idea what he's doing? I cannot imagine any nextborn wanting such a marriage."

Laurence tilted his head, looking thoughtful. "You never know." Then, he changed the subject, and they chatted amiably about their families until Laurence took his leave.

"I cannot thank you enough," Basil said, seeing him to the door. "You should know I don't usually take people into such confidence after so short an acquaintance."

Laurence laughed. "It was my pleasure, Basil. And I must say that with how close our families are, how often your father spoke of you, how our gatherings were filled with reports of your life, I feel as though we have been friends all my life." He grinned as he tilted his head. "I own that I have a certain advantage in this friendship, having heard more of you than you have of me, but I think I can safely promise to make up for lost time as well."

Basil grinned in reply. "Please do. I particularly want to hear all about this fiancé of yours. He's due back soon, isn't he?"

"Yes," Laurence said, looking fond. "And thank you for the open invitation to tell you everything. I promise to abuse it entirely."

Chapter 31
Charles

Charles sat at his desk, reading a note from Laury. Laury was unusually vague in his missive, but he had high hopes for their schemes pertaining to Gerry. Charles was in the process of putting Laury's letter away when he heard a knock at the door.

John stepped in and said, "You wish to talk to me?"

"Yes," Charles said. "Do take a seat, dear. I'll only be a moment."

John did as he asked and Charles took the opportunity to organize his desk and his thoughts, and get a read on the other man's mood. Like Gavin, John kept his emotions guarded. Charles had a great many theories on why John was the way that he was. He had made assumptions based on his own relationship with Gavin and Seb, and had a strong suspicion that Mr. Reginald Hartford was at the heart of many of his children's emotional issues. Charles liked Mr. Hartford, but he felt the gentleman had done his sons a great disservice in being so austere and distant. It was one of the many reasons Charles had encouraged the John Hartfords to visit, despite Gavin's reticence. He not only wanted to mend the relationships between siblings, but he felt sure that John could do with a good friend.

John shifted impatiently in his chair, waiting for Charles to speak. Charles fought back a smile. He had wanted John to be a bit unsettled before they started speaking. It seemed he was getting his wish.

He finished shuffling papers around, folded his hands on the desk, and met John's gaze. "Thank you for your patience," he said. "I want to talk to you because Seb is expected to return tonight or tomorrow."

John nodded. "Yes, I am aware."

Charles took a deep breath. "You are my guest, John, and I'm pleased to say, a member of my family, so I hope you will understand that what I'm about to say is out of affection."

John frowned.

Charles continued, "I know that you do not always get on with your siblings. I do not pretend to know the whole history of your relationships with them. But I do know Gavin is still healing from some of the things that have been said to him over the years. And Seb is still trying to shake off the feeling that he is a disappointment."

John's lips pressed together. Charles wondered if Gavin had picked up the trait from his brother. He waited a moment for John to speak. Finally John said, "That is part of my reason for coming here."

Charles nodded. "I suspected as much. I do appreciate you making an effort. However, you will forgive me for observing that you have not stopped criticizing your siblings since you arrived. If you are seeking to improve your relationships with them, you are not going about it the right way."

John's frown deepened.

Charles took pity on him. "John, darling, I understand you are worried about them. But you are not conveying your concern appropriately. It is only coming out as criticism."

He was relieved when John pinched the bridge of his nose. It was a small sign of emotion, enough to indicate that John had registered the rebuke. "I have never had a talent for communication," John said at last.

"I know," Charles said gently.

"Veronica is much better at this sort of thing than I am."

Charles smiled. "I think you might be surprised. I'm sure Veronica has many talents, but expressing your wish for your siblings to be happy does not appear to be one of them."

John gave him a long look and then turned his gaze to the floor.

"I would like to help you, if I may. I flatter myself that I do have a talent for communication. And I know your siblings very well."

John winced.

Charles stood and moved to the chair beside John's. He laid a hand on the man's arm. "I'm going to tell you something harsh first, my dear, but I promise to say something kindly afterwards."

John glared at him. "You do not need to coddle me, Kentworthy."

"Very well. As pleased as I am to have you as guests and as much as I wish to help you improve your relationships with your siblings, Seb is my priority. If you say anything unkind to him, if you make him feel like a disappointment, or that he's foolish, or in any way unworthy, I will ask you to leave."

John looked up at him in surprise and, Charles thought, with a little fear. Good. John nodded. "Understood."

"Now, that is what you are *not* to say. If you would like advice or help in what you *should* say, I am happy to be of help."

John swallowed. "I daresay you think me a very great fool."

"No," Charles said. "I think you are a man who has had very little instruction in how to talk to the people he loves."

John heaved a sigh. "Oh, very well. What would you have me say to Sebastian when he comes?"

Charles smiled. "You might ask him how his trip went. Ask him about Laury. If you want to win Seb's favor, you might point out anything you found impressive or good about Laury when you met him."

"Veronica was not overly fond of their cottage, I'm afraid."

"Well, to be perfectly frank, darling, I don't much care about Veronica's opinion in this instance. I care about yours."

John glanced up at him and then away. Charles had a

sinking feeling that John had been so desperate for connection that he had attached himself too deeply with the horrible woman he'd married. Now he barely knew her opinion from his own. After a long moment of silence, John nodded again. "I understand."

"I felt sure you would. Thank you, John. Please know that my door is always open, should you wish for advice or conversation."

John's lips pressed together. "Thank you." He hesitated. "Is that all?"

"Well, since I have you, I might add that it wouldn't go amiss if you were to be a bit kinder to Gavin and Gerry. But they're less vulnerable than Seb is right now, so I haven't said anything about that."

"I'm sorry," John said quietly.

"I'm not the one who needs to hear it, darling."

John's expression was bleak. Charles wanted very much to wrap the silly man in a tight hug and make him talk about his feelings. But John was not ready for that yet. Charles was a patient person, generally speaking. He knew when it was appropriate to wait. Besides, he suspected John needed to think through everything they'd discussed. He told John that was all and watched him exit the room.

Chapter 32
Gerry

Charles remained tight-lipped about the dinner party for days, which annoyed Gerry exceedingly. She didn't even know who was invited. When she attempted to pry information out of Gavin, he was irritated at being brought into it.

"God's teeth," he said. "You honestly think he's telling me anything?"

"Well, he *is* your husband."

"And you're my sister. He knows perfectly well that I'd tell you all I know."

She sighed. "Isn't it technically your responsibility to send out invitations?"

He gave her a dour look. "I have been married long enough to know I am passing good at everything expected of me. But I have also been married long enough to be perfectly happy when my husband does some of my work for me. You truly expect me to complain about it?"

Gerry started to grumble about lazy older brothers.

"I daresay this is not the time to say you will understand when you get married."

"Decidedly not. And please be so kind as to never say such a horrid thing."

Gavin gave a snort and walked away.

Pip was no help for information either. "Bertie said he'd be there," he offered.

"Did he say who else might be there?"

Pip shook his head. "I did ask. Not because I was curious about what the two of them are scheming, but because I wanted to find out if I'd know everyone. But he just said I wasn't to fret and it was sure to be a good time."

"Oh, those two!"

Pip smiled and continued sweeping the store.

Since her dinner with Bertie, Gerry had paid more attention to how busy her shop was. She had so little experience of other shops to draw comparison. It never occurred to her the shop was particularly busy. But now that she noticed, she could see how having an extra pair of hands would be useful. She had even begun to categorize how she would designate the work and was trying to determine the best way to find more help. She supposed she might ask Bertie, but decided she'd probably have to wait until after the dinner party, since she was too annoyed at her friends' scheming.

"I suppose I shouldn't be surprised," she said, as she finished hanging spell bags. "Not after the way they both maneuvered Seb into his relationship."

"My primary introduction to both of them was planning things out on my behalf," Pip put in. "Granted, it was more saving my life rather than finding me a husband. But I've come to know that's just how they...I don't know...show their love."

She sighed. "Yes, I know it's all well-intentioned. It's just a nuisance. I have a strong suspicion Charles plans to have me fall in love with Mr. Thorne, but I can do such a thing perfectly well without his help. You're lucky they haven't started in on you."

"Well," Pip said, dimpling. "Bertie is not likely to scheme anything in regards to me when he's the other party involved. With Charles, however, I expect it's only a matter of time."

"That doesn't bother you?"

"Not particularly. If Charles starts teasing me about Bertie, then I'll know I've taken too long and really ought to get a move on. So I confess I'm somewhat relying on him for that. Especially since I have no idea how I'll..." He glanced at her. "How did we start discussing my problems?"

"Oh, very well," she said laughing. "I'm due for it, I know. Before we moved to Tutting-on-Cress, Charles was tasked with finding me a husband. He took the job very seriously until I was offered this shop. Silly of me to think he had put it out of his mind entirely."

"At the very least, this dinner party is working to distract your guests," Pip said. "They've been talking about it ever since they went to Copperage Farm."

"I daresay you're right," she said, reflecting on it. "Will you be eating dinner at home tonight then?"

"I actually intend to eat dinner at home every night until Seb gets back. I am looking forward to seeing him and I should hate to miss his arrival. I was very regretful at missing Laurence's visit the other night."

They walked to the back room to hang up their aprons and put on their coats.

"I've missed him too," she said. "I can't deny I'm worried about how he'll be with John and Veronica here. John has always been very hard on Seb, and Veronica makes it even worse, of course. In the past, Seb always retaliated by playing pranks on them, but he doesn't do that anymore, thank goodness, so I don't know how he shall cope."

"I expect having you, Gavin, and Charles there will help. I wouldn't be surprised if he went to dine at Copperage Farm more often than not, or if Laurence came to dine with us while he is still here."

"You're probably right. That is good at least."

They walked home, keeping a leisurely pace. When they reached the house, a carriage was parked outside the door with luggage being hauled down by servants.

"Good heavens!" Gerry said. "What perfect timing he has!"

They hurried inside to see Seb being embraced by Charles with Gavin looking on fondly. Gerry didn't hesitate to jump in and give her younger brother a tight hug.

"Thank goodness you're back," she said. "We've all missed you."

"I've missed you lot too," he said, grinning wearily back at her. "But if the journey hadn't been so awful, I would have gone to see Laury first. So I daresay you're all very lucky."

"Well, I like that!" Gerry said in mock offense.

Gavin cuffed his brother's shoulder. "You just saw him a fortnight ago, you goose."

"Yes, but he kisses so well."

Charles laughed and ruffled Seb's hair. "All right, you rascal. Go upstairs, change your clothes, and get refreshed. We'll wait dinner for you."

Seb hurried to do as he was told. Gerry worried he might run into Veronica or John on his way to his room, but Gavin quietly followed Seb upstairs. She guessed he was thinking the same.

Fortunately, Seb did not encounter John or Veronica until everyone was waiting in the sitting room for dinner to be called. Seb was the last to arrive—not surprising as he had just finished a long journey. But Gerry was relieved everyone was present when he finally entered the room.

He looked around at everyone's expectant faces and blushed. "I'm sorry I kept you all waiting."

"Don't think a thing of it, darling," Charles said. "We're more than happy to wait for you."

Veronica raised an eyebrow, but did not comment.

Gavin led Seb to the sofa where Charles was still sitting and pulled him down to sit between them.

"How was your trip, Sebastian?" John asked.

Seb's eyebrows shot up at the polite inquiry. "Er...long and rather dull, to be honest. I'm glad it's over."

John nodded. "Yes, it is always dull traveling alone."

"I had hoped to travel with Laury, but Father said it was out of the question."

"Yes, we met your betrothed the other night," John

said. He paused. "He seemed very kind and respectable. Congratulations."

Seb blinked. "Thank you?"

"And we had tea with his family the other day," John said. "They were all very pleasant."

"Yes," Veronica said. "Quite respectable, I'm sure. Although, their drawing room is very small. I'm sure when you get married and move in, you will consider getting rid of the piano in the corner. It takes up far too much space. And with no one in the house to play it, it is a dreadful waste."

"Laury plays it," Seb said.

"He plays very well too," Gerry said. "He's almost better than I am."

"In fact," Seb went on. "I think he's hoping to purchase a newer piano in the future. It will likely be a bigger one too."

Veronica tutted. "But where will you entertain your guests? We were all piled on top of each other as it was."

Seb's face reddened at this criticism.

"I'm sure when you move in, you will make it a very comfortable home," Gavin said.

"I quite agree, darling," Charles said.

"And perhaps we will be able to hear your gentleman play at the dinner party," John added.

"Dinner party?" Seb said.

"Oh, that's a capital idea," Charles said. "I daresay we shall. And Gerry as well."

"Charles is hosting a dinner party on an as yet undisclosed date," Gerry explained, as Seb still looked bewildered.

"For me?" Seb ventured.

"I rather think it's for us," Veronica said. "After all, we have been here over a month and have barely met any of their friends."

"Who will be there?" Seb said. Gerry turned eagerly to Charles.

He grinned. "I've settled on a date about a month from now. I've invited a nice collection of people, I think. I'm sure we shall all have a marvelous time."

"But Laury is coming?"

"Of course."

"Oh, good," Seb said on a sigh.

"I'm not sure it is at all proper for you to refer to the young man with such a familiar name," Veronica said.

"Laury is very affectionate by nature," Charles said. "You'll understand when you get to know him better."

Dinner was called before Veronica could argue the point. To Gerry's surprise, John continued to attempt to make the conversation somewhat civil. "How did you leave our parents, Sebastian?"

"They're well." Seb considered. "And...how have you been enjoying your time here, John?"

John seemed pleased even though he didn't smile. "It has been very nice getting to know Charles at last." He paused a moment and then said, "And I'm relieved that Gavin is so well settled now."

Gavin looked surprised by this comment.

"Although Geraldine will keep leaving every day," Veronica said. "We've barely seen her at all."

"You mean because she's working?" Seb said.

"Not to mention the fact that she goes off to have dinner elsewhere."

"It was one time," Gerry said.

"Well, not at all a proper way to treat a guest."

"You aren't her guest," Gavin said. "You're Charles's and my guests. Gerry is, quite frankly, a guest as well. She has no hostessing responsibilities, so she is free to go about however she chooses. Including, might I add, to her place of business."

"I've noticed she still pours tea," Veronica said.

Gavin sighed. "Only when I'm not there to do it. Which I'm sure you know as you seem to love pointing out every mistake I make when pouring."

"I say, Gav, that's hardly fair," John said. "Veronica is only wishing to help you."

"Is this how dinner has been every night?" Seb whispered to Pip, but his voice carried.

Veronica looked on the point of scolding him for the question.

"Quite right," Charles said. "Thank you, Seb. This is hardly appropriate conversation for the dinner table. Perhaps we can turn our attention back to more pleasant topics."

There was a small lull while everyone tried to come up with a change of subject.

"Sebastian," John said. "Perhaps you could tell us how you met Mr. Ayles? I don't think he ever described your meeting."

Seb lit up wonderfully at the question and then launched into a very detailed description about working for Bertie when he was auditioning spellcasters for the

246

position of Royal Spellcaster and how he had fallen in love with Laurence. He even talked about how Laurence had proposed and how anxious he had been about giving a response before settling on the decision to ask for a long engagement.

"Thankfully," he concluded. "He agreed that a long engagement was a good idea. Although I really would like to have a date worked out."

"Oh, I don't know," Charles said. "We didn't set the date for our wedding until just over a month before."

"Personally," Gavin said, "I think the way you two are going about it is quite perfect: stay engaged until you're both ready, then decide on a date and use that time to get everything prepared."

"You know we're happy to have you live with us for as long as you like," Charles said.

Gerry was worried they were both laying it on a bit thick.

"I've never seen the appeal of long engagements," Veronica said. "To my mind, it shows an indecisive nature."

"Well," John said slowly. "I must say our father was pleased with Sebastian's decision. He worried you might be young yet for marriage."

Veronica gave her husband a very dirty look and Gerry realized tonight was the first time she had ever heard John disagree with her. She looked around the table to gauge everyone else's reactions. Gavin and Seb looked equally mystified, Pip looked uncomfortable with the slight tremor of conflict, but Charles looked remarkably pleased—not just pleased, Gerry realized—

he looked proud. Had he said something to John before Seb's arrival?

After a brief quiet moment, Seb said, "Yes. He did mention that. Thank you, John."

John nodded awkwardly.

After dinner, Seb pulled Gerry aside. "What the blazes is wrong with John?" he asked in a frantic whisper. "I'm not complaining exactly but...I don't know how to handle a civil John. I can't say I know how to handle John in his usual temper, but he's thrown me off-balance."

"Your guess is as good as mine," she said. "He certainly hasn't been like that the entire time he's been here."

"So, he's doing it on my account?" Seb said, his forehead wrinkled in confusion.

She shrugged, although she had a pretty good idea who was behind John's sudden change of mood.

Chapter 33
Basil

Basil was buoyed by Laurence's visit. For the next several days, he spent the morning with the children and Mary, gradually getting to know them all better. He persuaded Elias to show off his piano skills and he checked in regularly on Levinia's art projects, Grace's progress on the songs she was practicing, the routes the twins were planning, and Martin's running speeds.

Every day after lunch, Basil would retire to the study and begin the arduous and sometimes painful process of going through his father's desk. He had to decipher a great deal of documents, ledgers, and notes to determine their meanings. Every time he found something he thought he ought to review again to fully understand, he'd set it aside. Soon he had a pile of things he didn't understand. It was all very trying. On top of that were the small hints and indications of his father's character: reminders scrawled in the margins of papers, notes detailing upcoming social engagements, the small stool under the desk that was perfect for hitching a heel onto when working. These were the things that were the most challenging; they made his heart feel tight, particularly when he discovered things that reminded him of himself. He recognized the tightness of his father's handwriting in his own penmanship, noticed the precision of blots on the ink blotter, and even the way his father organized his pens. He was coming to learn that Laurence was correct: they had been very alike.

Fortunately, these discoveries did help Basil understand his father's organization process. While he still had no idea how to manage an estate, he gradually came to recognize patterns in the documents and ledgers. Soon the large pile became smaller, more manageable piles. Basil supposed he'd have to take the piles to another expert once he had sorted through everything, although he wasn't entirely sure who that expert might be.

After he had gone through every drawer and cabinet in the imposing piece of furniture, Basil put off all responsibilities, and spent his afternoons reading on the window seat.

His evenings were spent with less guilt than the afternoons, as he started to devote his evenings to spell practice. He found the levitation spell surprisingly easy to master. Martin and Lucy gave him their rapt attention as he practiced first with handkerchiefs, then throw pillows, and leatherbound books.

"Try it with us, please!" Martin begged.

Basil weighed one of the largest books in his hand, deciding it was probably about as heavy as Lucy. "All right," he said with a hesitant smile.

They stood impressively still as he prepared the spell for different focuses. Basil was cautious at first, only allowing them to hover a few inches into the air. But it hardly mattered, the children shrieked with delight and wiggled their feet. Predictably, they both shouted "Again!" as soon as their feet returned to the ground. Basil increased the power to move them a foot off the ground. He worried when their shrieks grew louder, but as they also continued giggling and grinning, he decided they were safe enough.

The twins poked their heads in. "What are you doing?" Arabella asked.

"Basil is making us float!" Martin said.

"Float, Basil, float!" Lucy shouted.

The twins approached, looking intrigued. "We could use something like this in our adventures," Arabella said. "It could make going into the crow's nest safer and easier."

"And faster," Elias put in.

"Not to mention climbing trees or buildings when we're at port."

"Why would you need to climb buildings?" Basil asked.

"Can we try?" Elias asked.

"It's for research," Arabella added.

Basil chuckled and started over, making the circle large enough to accommodate four children. At one point, Elias even lifted Lucy into the air while being levitated himself. It made Basil's heart leap in his throat, but seeing both children unharmed and their cheeks pink with delight gave him an enormous sense of satisfaction.

After nearly a week of practice, he finally decided he was ready to go buy a new spell. The spell shop was busy, as usual. Mr. Standish noticed him first and gave him a friendly nod and smile. Basil noticed that the other man did not approach to assist. A few minutes later, Miss Hartford greeted him and asked him how the practice was going.

"If my siblings tell me true," he said, "I have, in fact, mastered levitation."

She grinned. "Smashing. I knew you could do it. Are you ready to try another?"

"I certainly hope so."

"Do you want something more advanced or—"

"Good heavens, no!"

She laughed. "Very well then. We can do the lateral movement spell. It's very similar, actually, to the one you just mastered."

The term stirred in his memory. He thought back to what Laurence had taught Sophia in the treehouse. "Does it use a reed?"

She beamed at him. "It does! Excellent memory, sir!"

He shook his head, embarrassed by her praise. "A... friend instructed Sophia on how to do it recently." He paused a moment and then said, "I think you know him: Mr. Laurence Ayles?"

"Oh, yes," she said. "Laurence is engaged to my brother, Seb."

"Yes," he said. "He has promised to tell me more about your brother than I could possibly want to hear. I am looking forward to it."

Her smile turned fond. "Well, Seb returned home very recently, so you may well get to meet him yourself."

"I'd like that." He wanted to add that he'd like to meet everyone related to her, but didn't. He found himself incredibly curious to learn if the rest of the Hartford family was cheerful and friendly like Miss Hartford or shy and serious like Mr. Gavin Kentworthy. From what Laurence and Mr. Robert Ayles had described, the youngest Hartford sibling was a little unsure of himself and had a history of being very lonely. He realized that all of the Hartford siblings he knew of were definitely nextborns, so he said, "Do you have an older sibling? Older than Mr. Kentworthy, I mean?"

Her smile vanished and was replaced by a tight expression that Basil did not like to see on her normally cheerful face. "Yes," she said. "My brother, John. He's staying with Charles and Gavin too, actually. So you might meet him as well."

"You say that like it's a bad thing," he said hesitantly.

She sighed. "None of us have gotten on well with John. He's very disagreeable." Her expression turned thoughtful. "Although he's recently shown some signs of improvement...but I'm not putting much stock in it, not yet." She turned to the wall of spells and plucked a spell bag off a hook. "Are you ready to talk lateral movement?"

"Of course." He would have loved to spend all day

talking about her and her family. He wanted to know why she didn't get on with her oldest brother and what she had been thinking of that made her look so fond when thinking of her youngest brother. He wanted to know how she seemed closest to a brother who was so dissimilar in temperament. He wanted, in short, to know everything. But instead, he applied himself to knowing a new spell.

Miss Hartford did her usual style of teaching him, and Basil realized he was no longer shy about learning in such a public space. As she was packing all of the ingredients away, she asked him how his siblings were doing.

"They are well," he said. "I've taken your advice. I still don't know what I'm doing, of course. But I'm learning to notice when it doesn't matter. At least, I think I am."

She smiled. "I'm so glad."

"Of course, I should have probably brought some of them with me. I'm sure they would love to come to the village."

Her smile turned into a smirk. "Well, I imagine you wind up having to buy a great many more presents when you do that."

He chuckled. "Yes, you're probably right. I confess I —" He broke off.

She raised an eyebrow. "Yes?"

He'd been about to say that he wanted to keep her to himself, at least for a bit. But that would have been far too forward and far too honest. He grappled for something else to confess. "I...I confess I'd love...to bring you around to see them."

Her eyes widened. "You would?"

"Yes," he said, latching onto the idea. "How would you like to join us for lunch? And Mr. Standish, of course."

She blinked in surprise. And then, to his delight, she said, "I would love to."

Chapter 34
Gerry

Gerry knew it was the height of folly to accept the invitation. She was fairly sure he hadn't initially planned to make it, but to say something else entirely. But she was also sure she wanted very much to continue talking to Mr. Thorne and, for once, to see him outside of the shop.

After she agreed to his invitation, he looked stunned. "Really?"

She smiled and nodded.

"Lovely," he said. "Well, then, perhaps I'd...perhaps I'd better return home and tell Mary so we can prepare places for you both. Would that suit? I can send round our carriage for you."

Her smile widened. "That would suit admirably, Mr. Thorne. But please don't worry about the carriage. Pip and I can walk."

He glanced over her shoulder at where Pip was talking to other customers and nodded. "Yes, of course. Whatever you'd like. Well then, I shan't keep you from your customers. Would you like a note sent to your house letting them know of your plans?"

"No, no," she said hastily. Then she smiled. "Please don't bother. I can send it."

He returned her smile. "Very good. We'll expect you then." He bowed and left, taking his spell bag with him.

Then Gerry came back down to earth. "Right," she said to herself. She turned to find Pip, but he was already approaching her, looking amused.

"That seemed like a pleasant conversation."

She knew she had to be blushing and was grateful that Pip was the only one seeing it. "It was. He...er... invited us to join his family for lunch."

Pip raised an eyebrow. "That sounds delightful. I assume we're going?"

"Oh, yes."

Pip gave a small smile. "And what are we telling Charles?"

"That we are dining with friends," she said firmly. "I shall write the note, so you don't have to worry about it. And we're not lying," she added. "But...I will have to figure out what I'm going to tell him and I'd like more time to do that."

"Of course."

He walked away because he was tactful like that. Gerry wrote a note to Charles and found an errand boy in the village to take it for her. Then she spent the rest of her morning trying to not think about lunch with Mr. Thorne and his family. She was not in the least bit successful.

Finally, it was time to close the shop for lunch. Pip

offered his arm and they walked to the Thornes' house. Gerry had never been before. It turned out to be a house about the size of Charles's or a little smaller. There was no garden, which made her curious. Pip had told her how much the Thorne children had loved Charles's garden. She wondered if Mr. Thorne would have one designed for his siblings now that he was in charge of the house. She gave in to a brief flight of fancy, imagining what she would put in a garden if she were mistress of the house, and then quickly realized what she was thinking and directed her thoughts elsewhere.

As soon as they entered the house, they were greeted with chatter, questions, and enthusiasm. Apparently, the children were delighted to have them both as visitors. Gerry noticed that Levinia and Elias were particularly keen to talk to Pip, and that the latter was remarkably shy around him. Mrs. Thorne came forward and welcomed Gerry and Pip inside, looking just as pleased as her children.

"When Basil told us that he'd invited you to lunch," she said, "I could hardly believe it! I'm so pleased. It is nice to see him making friends, you know." She gave Gerry a knowing smile.

Gerry heartily wished that her complexion was not quite so inclined to blushing.

Mr. Thorne walked into the room and smiled at the sight of her, as if he couldn't believe she'd really come.

Mrs. Thorne said, "Ah, there you are, Basil. Would you like us to leave the sitting room for you and your guests? Or you could go into the study if you'd like more privacy, like you did with Laury. Lunch won't be for another half hour or so."

To her surprise, Mr. Thorne looked alarmed at this suggestion. But he said, "Of course, Mary. We can go into the study. Thank you."

Then Pip said, "Actually, I would be delighted to join you in the sitting room now, if that would be all right."

"That will be lovely," Mrs. Thorne said, and turned to lead the way.

Pip gave her a winning smile. As he passed Gerry, he leaned over and, in a barely audible whisper, said, "Positively glowing."

The rest of the family followed Pip out of the room. Mr. Thorne looked a bit bewildered for a moment. Then he cleared his throat and said, "So, the study?"

"By all means."

He offered her his arm and they walked down the hall to a pair of doors. He seemed to hesitate and then opened the doors and stood back, gesturing for her to go first. She walked into the room and he followed. She noticed that he did not close the door and she was, once again, grateful for his consideration.

Gerry stood for a moment and glanced around. There was a strange sort of stillness in the air. The room appeared lived in, but she noticed the piles of documents on the desk were stacked with meticulous neatness. And then she noticed that Mr. Thorne was still standing behind her. He seemed tense. Not only tense, but as if he was holding his breath.

"Is everything all right?" she said gently.

He gave a stiff nod. "Of course." Then he gave her a

small smile. "I'm still...getting used to this room, you see. It was my father's."

"Oh," she said. It explained some of the conflicting emotions crossing his face. Although she realized she couldn't identify all of them and, what was more, she very much wanted to. "We don't have to sit in here if it makes you uncomfortable."

He looked pained. "Not at all. Please." He gestured weakly at the room, though not at any particular furniture for her to sit in.

Gerry studied the room, verifying her options. There was only one chair in front of the desk, with the worn leather seat behind it, and a lovely wide window seat by the window. Gerry moved forward, intending to take the seat in front of the desk. But then she realized he would have to take the seat behind the desk and it occurred to her that this might have been what made Mr. Thorne so uncomfortable. She glanced at the window seat and immediately dismissed it as an option as they'd have to sit too close to each for propriety. So she didn't sit down at all and instead looked at the artwork with interest.

"Is this you?" she said, pointing to a portrait of a boy and a woman.

"Yes. And my mother."

"She was beautiful."

"She was," he said, his voice soft.

She smiled at the sight of the pictures done by children, wondering idly if any of them had been done by Mr. Thorne in his youth. She almost asked, but didn't quite dare. She started to inspect the bookshelves behind the desk and then turned back to him. "Do you mind if I look?"

"Not at all."

She glanced over the spines, noting with interest the books on magical theory. There were a few she wanted to pick up and read, but she had a feeling Mr. Thorne was still working through his feelings on the room, so she didn't touch the books for fear of disrupting him. She couldn't quite resist the urge to run her hand along the edge of the shelf, however.

She had just reached the final bookcase, which was made up of a stack of barrister bookcases, when Mr. Thorne said, "How is your design work coming along? Any developments?"

She turned and smiled at him. "A few. I talked to my friend, Bertie, Lord Finlington—I think you've met?"

He nodded. "I like him. He is very nice."

"Yes," she said, pleased to hear him say so. "We were talking about some ideas I've been contemplating. I have nothing concrete as yet. As I told Pip, it's more an idea of an idea."

He smiled. "Sounds exciting."

She laughed. "That's exactly what Pip said. I hope it turns out."

She paused. She wanted to tell him all about it, even though there wasn't much to tell, but she felt nervous admitting that he had inspired the idea, especially when there was nothing substantial to show him. She much preferred the idea of having a real spell to present, rather than promising something that might never work out.

But when she turned back to continue her perusing of the bookcase, she thought she saw him tense slightly and a brief glance told her that there were portraits of the children on every shelf. She realized that whatever was on the shelves was something Mr. Thorne was not entirely ready to share. Considering the fact that he'd spent most of his life away from his family, it occurred to her he was still sorting through his own thoughts on how he fit into the family dynamic.

With this realization came the understanding that Mr. Thorne had been very vulnerable in bringing her into his study. She was so touched by the gentle show of vulnerability that she immediately turned away from the shelf and said, "As a matter of fact, you inspired the idea."

His eyes widened. "I did?"

She nodded. "You said something the other day about how you'd like something to help you think better, or well, something along those lines."

He smiled. "Remarkable that you remembered that."

She couldn't very well tell him that she remembered everything he said, so instead she said, "Well, it got me thinking. There are a number of spells that manipulate emotions and thoughts, but they're usually used to manipulate other people: Charm Spells, Glamour Spells, Love Spells. So I thought it might be worth exploring doing something on one's own self. Something to improve one's mood, or perspective, or to focus the mind." She shrugged. "I'm not at all sure if it will become anything other than an idea. But I'd like to explore it a bit and find out."

His smile widened. "That's truly incredible."

She laughed. "Please don't get too excited yet. Spell experimentation has a lot of failures. I may not find what I'm looking for."

"Even if you don't, I'm still impressed that my comment spurred such a thought process." He shook his head. "You're very creative. I don't know how you do it." When she opened her mouth to reiterate that it might not succeed, he stepped forward and said, "I know it's still only a theory. Barely even that. But all the same, the way your mind works is...well, it's astonishing."

People had praised her for her spell designs, for her spell casting, for her abilities on the pianoforte, and for a great many other things that took time, energy, practice and study. But she didn't think anyone had ever praised her just for thinking of something, for the way her mind worked. Gerry felt herself on extremely dangerous ground with the compliment.

She was so muddled by the line of thought that she gave Mr. Thorne her cheeriest smile and said, "Thank you! How kind of you to say! Should we go join the rest of your family now?"

She was relieved when he didn't comment on the change in topic and he didn't seem to mind returning to the noise and bustle of his family.

Chapter 35
Sophia

Sophia was surprised when Basil came home from the village and announced that Miss Hartford and Mr. Standish were joining them for lunch—surprised and thrilled. Her mother assured him it was perfectly all right to have a couple guests over for lunch.

"You are the one hosting, technically speaking," she said. "I could stay upstairs, but with only two guests, it will not be objectionable. It has been nearly four months now," she added softly. "Once we reach six months, it will get less strict."

Basil nodded and put a hand on her arm in a comforting way.

She smiled, patted his hand, called him "a dear boy," and hurried off to prepare the house for visitors, despite her explanation that she was not hosting.

There hadn't been time for a family meeting, but Sophia gathered Levinia, Grace, and the twins and discussed what was to be done.

"We need a plan," Bel agreed.

"But if he invited her of his own volition," Eli said, "there may not be much we need to do."

"Nonsense," Levinia said. "We must throw them together as much as possible."

"But they're actively throwing themselves together," Grace said.

"We don't even know what he plans to do when she arrives," Eli said.

"I doubt he knows," Sophia said.

"Swept up in the moment," Levinia said, clasping her hands. "His heart spoke what his mind could not."

Bel snorted.

"Right," Sophia said, trying to get them back on track. "Let's make a few plans just in case. If we are all pulled together in the sitting room, let's see if we can get them to sit together."

"Hushed conversations in a corner," Levinia whispered.

"But Miss Hartford might try to join in our conversation," Grace said. "She's so friendly."

"If she does, we can direct the conversation to point out Basil's good qualities."

Bel looked quizzical.

"But be subtle," Sophia added.

"Do you think Mr. Standish will act as a chaperone? And keep them from being alone together?" Eli said.

Sophia considered. "He might. But even if he does, I can't imagine he will hinder things too much. He's so quiet."

They dispersed, as prepared as they could be with such short notice. In the end, the planning was hardly necessary as Basil and Miss Hartford went to the study, and Mr. Standish joined the rest of the family in the sitting room. Bel snuck off to check on the couple and reported to Sophia and Eli that the door had been left open.

"He's so honorable," Eli said, half disappointed and half proud.

Mr. Standish was quietly charming, as usual, looking at Bel's atlas with interest and listening to Grace play. He even talked about painting with Levinia and admired her latest pieces. Basil and Miss Hartford returned shortly before lunch was called.

The family had assigned seating at the table to ensure the little ones were closest to their mother or an older sibling who could help them. But Sophia and Levinia managed to maneuver things so Miss Hartford sat closest to the head of the table, where Basil sat, with Mr. Standish sitting across. They were a bit worried that Mr. Standish would distract the couple from talking together, but he proved to be incredibly helpful in the situation, turning to his left to continue his conversation with Levinia and ask for recommendations on poetry.

Sophia kept an ear to the conversation between Miss Hartford and Basil, while also trying hard to not look like she was listening, and by making sure Martin didn't make a mess of things. From what she could tell, Basil was inquiring into a spell Miss Hartford was building and asking her how she would go about designing it. She seemed pleased by his inquiries and talked about potential ingredients or what books and resources she would need to employ. She explained the amount of research that went into spell design well before the actual experimentation took place. And how she usually worked off of another spell to start and then modified it to reach her desired results.

"And what spell do you think you will start with?" he asked.

"I'm not entirely sure," Miss Hartford admitted. "I recently learned about a spell used to pull focus in a room, so that might be worth looking into. Although it was a Motion spell, which are harder to use as starting points; they're so minimal to begin with. I think I need some sort of manipulation spell and then find a way to redirect the focus."

"It sounds rather dangerous," he said. "How will you experiment without inadvertently manipulating yourself too much?"

"That's a good question," she said. "And one I'm not at all sure of yet. I will likely figure out the theoretical points first and then ask someone—maybe Bertie—to help me when I cast it."

"Does it have to be cast on oneself?" he asked. "Would it be just as effective to create a spell that one casts on another person to give them better mental focus?"

She considered. "Perhaps. That might be easier to start with. Thank you."

He gave her a self-effacing smile. "Sorry, I'm merely curious. Please don't take any of my questions too seriously. I haven't the faintest idea what I'm talking about."

"No, no," she said, reaching out and putting her hand

over his. "You aren't offending me. They're good questions."

Sophia dared a glance at Basil's face. He looked as if he was trying not to breathe.

"Thank you," he said. "I'm glad to hear it."

Miss Hartford glanced down at her hand over his, blushed, and pulled it back. "I'm sorry."

"Please don't be," he said, so softly that Sophia could barely hear it.

Miss Hartford took a sip of her drink. "Anyway, you've helped me to see the problem from some different angles." She smiled at him. "Perhaps I should come to you for these ideas more often."

"I'd like that," he said.

Her blush deepened. Then she looked at the rest of the table and Sophia hurriedly turned to Eli to ask him to pass the salt, hoping she looked like she'd been trying to find it.

Shortly after lunch, Miss Hartford and Mr. Standish left to go back to the village. To the family's delight, Basil insisted on escorting them. After the door closed behind them, their mother said, "What a lovely couple they make."

Sophia wanted to cheer. Everything was going beautifully.

Chapter 36
Basil

Basil held out his arm for Miss Hartford and Mr. Standish quietly stepped to the back.

They started to turn down the lane, but Miss Hartford stopped in her tracks, looking mildly horrified. "Rose!" she said.

Basil looked up to see the Hearsts approaching the house.

"Gerry, dear," Mrs. Julia Hearst said warmly. "We were just coming to call on the Thornes for tea."

"We didn't expect to see you here," Mrs. Rose Hearst said.

"It is a lovely surprise," Mrs. Julia Hearst added.

"Mr. Thorne was kind enough to invite Pip and me over for lunch," Miss Hartford said. She gave a cheery smile. "We're going to the village now, you see."

"Indeed?" Mrs. Julia Hearst said, grinning.

"Well, we won't keep you," Mrs. Rose Hearst said.

"We'll just go inside and call on Mary. I know she's technically in mourning, but we've been meaning to see how she's doing. I'm sure old family friends will be all right by now." Mrs. Julia Hearst added, "It was lovely to see you again, Mr. Thorne."

"Yes," Mrs. Rose Hearst added. "Do call on us soon."

"I would be delighted," Basil said. He glanced between them and Miss Hartford, who still looked discomfited. "Are you unwell, Miss Hartford? Should I send for the carriage?"

"Oh, no, I'm quite well, thank you," Miss Hartford said crisply. "Just surprised to see my cousins here, that is all. But I don't wish to keep you from your guests. Thank you all the same." Then she extricated herself from Basil, took Mr. Standish's arm, and hurried away, practically hauling the other man along with her.

Basil looked after them, trying to figure out how the lovely afternoon had dissipated so quickly. "I hope I did not offend her."

"I'm sure you didn't," Mrs. Julia Hearst said. "Gerry likes to get to her shop at a particular time, you see. So I'm sure our arriving for tea made her realize what time it was."

He was both relieved and guilty at this assessment. "Ah, that must be it. Well, I am sorry to have delayed her."

Mrs. Rose Hearst waved her hand airily. "Nonsense. Everyone thinks Gerry works far too much as it is. I'm sure we'd all be very grateful if you invited her to lunch much more often."

Her wife looked like she was trying not to laugh. "Indeed. It would probably do her good."

He gave them a small smile. "Well, then. I suppose I'd

better. Thank you." Then he stepped aside to let them enter ahead of him.

Mrs. Julia Hearst returned the smile. "I'm so glad to see you've already made friends in town. Gerry is such a delight, is she not?"

"Indeed, she is," he said, amused. "Have you known her long?"

"I met her a few years ago when she came to stay with Rosie for the summer. We had a marvelous time."

"Yes," Mrs. Rose Hearst said. "That was when Gerry decided she wanted to design spells."

"Is it?" Basil said.

"Yes," Mrs. Rose Hearst said. "The old spellmaster— what was his name?"

"Mr. Fenshaw," Mrs. Julia Hearst supplied.

"Fenshaw, that's right. Well, he was the one who taught Gerry how to design spells, how to build them, and so on. She spent hours learning from him and then experimenting at home with me." She paused and then added hastily, "Mr. Fenshaw is rather old, you know."

"Ah," Basil said. "I see...er...thank you."

Mary approached at that point and there were a few moments spent in explaining why Basil was not accompanying Miss Hartford to the village like he'd said. "I'm so glad you invited her to lunch, Basil," she said, leading them all to the sitting room. "She's such a sweet young woman."

"Yes, she is," Mrs. Rose Hearst said, sounding pleased by Mary's approval.

"Mr. Standish too," Mary added. "I hope you intend to invite them again."

271

Basil glanced at the Hearsts and then said to Mary, "I certainly intend to. The question is whether Miss Hartford will ever accept again."

"Oh, don't be silly," Mary said. "She clearly likes you. I could see her blushing all the way from my end of the table."

"Gerry does blush very becomingly," Mrs. Julia Hearst said.

"Don't you agree, Mr. Thorne?" Mrs. Rose Hearst said, without any subtlety.

Basil laughed. "To be sure, I do, Mrs. Hearst. And if you came here to tell me how wonderful Miss Hartford is, you won't find a difficult audience. I'm much inclined to agree with you."

"How marvelous," Mrs. Julia Hearst said.

"Do tell us everything you like about her," Mrs. Rose Hearst said, leaning forward.

Basil shook his head. "That would be ill-advised of me. But please rest assured that I like the lady very well."

"That's enough to be going on with, I think," Mrs. Julia Hearst said, smiling at him.

Thankfully, Mary pivoted the conversation to other topics, asking after the health of their cook, the activities of Mrs. Rose Hearst's family, and general gossip in town.

"I do miss everyone so," she said before they left. "Mourning is so very isolating."

"It is," Mrs. Julia Hearst said feelingly. "I read through my entire collection of books twice over when my husband died."

"At least I have the children to occupy my time, and dear Basil," Mary said, smiling at him.

Basil was startled. Did he occupy her time? And it helped?

"And I am glad we are still at Verdimere Hall," she went on. "I would have been very sad to quit it."

"It was very kind of you to let them stay," Mrs. Julia Hearst said.

"It wasn't a difficult decision to make," he assured her.

"He even lets me run everything my own way," Mary put in. "He is the kindest young man. I love running the house, you know. I shall step aside when he marries, of course, but it won't be easy."

"I suppose the best option is for Mr. Thorne to marry someone who is not opposed to letting you run the house." Mrs. Rose Hearst said, with a mischievous glint in her eye.

"That would certainly make all parties most comfortable," he said cautiously.

After the couple left, Mary turned to Basil and gave him a long look. "Basil, dear, I hope you won't mind my saying so, but I'm worried about you."

He was alarmed by the statement. "Are you? Whatever for?"

She flattened her skirt over her lap as she seemed to try to find the right words. "I know we don't know each other as well as I'd like, but...I have noticed a worrying propensity of yours to...well, to be overly cautious."

He blinked in surprise. "That is likely true," he said slowly.

"I had spent years thinking you weren't visiting us because you didn't care for me or your father's second marriage," she said, speaking the end of the sentence in a rush. "But I've come to realize that such a decision is wholly outside your personality and you were likely staying away out of caution." She reached forward and took his hand in hers. "If I may give you the advice of a mother, dear, don't be overly cautious when it comes to matters of the heart. As we both know from recent experience, life doesn't always wait for us to do what we truly want to do."

Basil swallowed and gently turned his hand so he could clasp Mary's hand in return. "Thank you," he said quietly.

Chapter 37
Gerry

Gerry spent the afternoon in a confusion of thoughts. Mr. Thorne had been sweet, vulnerable, attentive, and respectful. He had asked her questions about her work with genuine interest and curiosity. And while he seemed concerned about the dangers of her experiment, he never suggested she not attempt it, but had merely asked what measures she planned to take to make it safer, as if he truly trusted her to think it all through. Gerry had been so swept up in the conversation that she'd barely noticed there were other people at the table. When she laid her hand over his, in an unguarded moment, he had neither pulled away nor pressed his advantage. It was, frankly, almost infuriating how perfect the man was.

And then Rose and Julia had to come and ruin everything. Gerry knew her friends well enough to recognize the gleam in their eyes. Now that they had seen her with Mr. Thorne, they were bound to try pairing them up. It was bad enough to have Charles pushing them together; her friends would be even worse. She would be horrified to walk into tea and find Mr. Thorne sitting there, waiting to be offered up. Why couldn't they trust her to fall in love without their interference?

After all, the more time she spent with the gentleman, the more she could see how easy it would be to fall in love with him. She gave herself a few moments to imagine how she might fit into the Thorne household: Mary running the house, the children growing up and playing with any children she might have, Gerry going home to a bustling house every night. She always liked to be surrounded by people. And she'd have Mr. Thorne to keep her company at night—she shook herself mentally and thought fiercely of something else.

It didn't help, of course, that Pip kept giving her a mixture of amused and sympathetic glances throughout the afternoon. As they were walking home, he said, "I know we are probably not to talk about it, and I promise not to bring it up at home, but please allow me to point out that Mr. Thorne didn't seem to notice anyone else was in the room while you were there."

Gerry sighed. "I hardly noticed anyone else either."

He squeezed her hand that was wrapped around his arm. "I will not bring up the subject, but you do know I could never lie to Charles or your brother."

"No, neither could I."

"You know they're going to ask where we were."

"If Rose didn't already tell them."

"You think she will?"

"I don't know," Gerry said. "Probably not. I'm not sure they're working together exactly."

"Although their aims seem to be the same."

"Yes," she agreed. "It is very inconvenient."

He kindly didn't say anything else, like the fact that Gerry was helping her friends' and Charles's cause perfectly well on her own. He didn't need to say it because she already knew. Gerry debated how to handle Charles's inevitable inquisitiveness. Finally, by the time she reached home, she had come to a decision.

"I'm going to tell him myself," she said.

"Do you want me to come with you?" Pip said.

"No," she said, smiling at him. "I can handle the dragon on my own. But thank you."

"Good luck."

She squared her shoulders and went to Charles's study. She was relieved to find him alone.

"Good evening, darling," he said. "Did you have a pleasant day?"

"Yes," she said.

"How was lunch?"

"It was delightful."

He grinned. "Are you going to tell me who invited you? You were very vague in the details—very out of character, dear."

She sighed and flopped into a seat. "Yes, because I'd rather tell you now than have you find out later."

He raised his eyebrows.

"Mr. Thorne invited me to lunch."

Charles's grin was wide. "Why, darling, how wonderful. How was it?"

"It was very pleasant, of course."

"Of course."

277

She glared at him. "And I hate to disappoint you, but he did not offer up any declarations of love over the course of the meal."

"Plenty of time for that."

"Well, I should like to be sure of my own feelings, let alone his, before anyone lets their imaginations run away with them. Including mine," she added. "And Mr. Thorne, despite how wonderful he is, how much he asks me about my work, seems to want to know everything about me, and thinks everything I do is interesting, is still barely more than an acquaintance. So kindly refrain from sending out any wedding announcements."

"Of course, darling. You will be the one to send those out anyway. I'd never dream of taking that task away from you. And did he really ask you about your work and want to know everything about you and think everything you do is interesting?"

"Yes."

"He really is perfect, darling."

"I know," she moaned. "It is appalling, really."

He laughed. "Well, chin up. I'm sure he'll have some faults. Practically everyone does, you know."

She sighed and stood. "Yes, but there are very few I can imagine him having that would really make him unappealing."

He raised an eyebrow.

She flapped her hand at him. "Don't look at me like that. I know perfectly well what I sound like."

"Hmm," he said. "Then you know that you sound like a person in—"

"Don't," she said, holding a hand up. "Do not say it, Charles."

He cocked his head.

Gavin stepped into the room. "Oh, am I interrupting?"

"Not a bit," Gerry said.

Gavin looked between them. "Is he meddling again?"

"Of course," she said. "That's what he does."

Charles shrugged. "Gerry and I were merely talking about what it looks like for her to be in love."

"Oh, really, Charles!" Gerry said, realizing she sounded just like Gavin.

Gavin, for his part, looked equal parts amused and alarmed. He glanced at Gerry. "Now you know what I have to put up with." And then to Charles, "Is she really?"

Chapter 38
Charles

Charles grinned as Gerry stomped out of the room. He turned back to Gavin. "Yes," he said. "And she knows it."

"Huh," Gavin said, turning and looking at the door his sister had just exited. "And here I was thinking she was irritable or ill."

Charles chuckled and stood, pulling Gavin into his arms. "Well, it looks different on everyone, you know."

"Are you continuing with your schemes then?"

"Oh, yes. In fact, I think we can begin on the next step."

"Dare I ask what it is?"

"Well, things are already in motion, of course. But I should like to throw the two of them together at every possible opportunity."

"Won't that be a trifle difficult with her working and everything?"

"Oh, I don't know," Charles said. "We have the dinner

party to think of. Bertie is going to invite us all to tea—"

"He is?"

"Yes, dear, and then of course there's the ball."

"Are you really doing that?"

"Yes, dear. That will be the near final step in the plan."

Gavin glanced over his shoulder. "I don't know," he said. "If Gerry takes love in this manner, I don't think a ball will have the usual effect. Especially if John and Veronica are present."

Charles smiled. "Don't worry. Mr. Thorne thinks everything she does is interesting. I expect it will all work out in the end."

"Thank God."

From Basil Thorne
Verdimere Hall, Tutting-on-Cress

To Modesty Munro
23 Royal Crescent, Bath

27 March 1818

Dear Modesty,

I have much to say in regards to your conversation with Miss St. John, but I am quite sure you would flay me alive if I did not first report what happened today.

You see, I rather impulsively invited Miss Hartford and Mr. Standish for lunch. I cannot properly explain what caused me to do such a thing, but I also cannot say I regret it. The only downside to the event was that as she was leaving, the Hearsts came to call, and Miss Hartford seemed embarrassed at seeing them. She left most precipitously. I rather wish I could tell her that she has done nothing wrong and that she has nothing to be ashamed of.

Mary encouraged me to show Miss Hartford into the study, probably because I took Laurence in there the last time he visited. She showed very kind restraint in not touching the books and only lightly brushed her fingertips over the shelves. She even turned away from the family shelf as soon as she noticed it. It seemed as though she had recognized how private and difficult the room was for me. I find that the more I know of her, the better I like her. And isn't that something?

The Spellmaster Of Tutting-On-Cress

Over lunch, she talked about a spell she was building and grew wonderfully animated at the topic. I could have listened to her talk on the subject for hours, learning from her, learning about her. It hardly mattered that I barely remembered anything about Constitutional Properties and theorems and principles. She spoke plainly enough for me to follow the thread of her thought process. She wasn't offended or annoyed by my questions. If anything, she seemed pleased by my curiosity. I quite liked that, too. If she enjoys having a curious audience, I'm sure I could offer years of genuine curiosity. As a friend, of course. And I love that she thinks of her work from every angle; she is cognizant of the dangers, and takes steps to be safe. I confess I dislike the idea of her being in danger, but she is sensible in her approach and is unashamed of being supported by other spellcasters when it was called for. She has been doing this for longer than I've known her, so she clearly knows what she's doing.

Everyone here is doing well. Sophia has asked for another spell the next time I go to the spell shop. I suppose having the spellmaster here put her in mind of it, for I would have purchased it for her while I was in the village today if I'd known. The twins are bending their focus to the Far East, which is unfortunate as I know precious little about the ports there. Not that I know much about the ports of northern Africa, which was their previous interest. I rather wish they would spend more time on European ports, for those are far easier to discuss.

Grace has been practicing a piece that Laurence gave

her. She told him it was too difficult for her, but he was clearly right in thinking she could do it. She always scrunches her nose when she makes a mistake and I've noticed her nose scrunches a good deal less these days when playing. Martin has started practicing leaps, which I fear I do not care for quite as much as the running. His mother, the servants, and I are forever having to discourage him from using assorted pieces of furniture for jumping points. And of course Lucy likes to imitate him a great deal, which makes it all the more difficult.

I have forestalled Levinia on doing a portrait of me. She argues that she has done a portrait of everyone else by now and that I am next. I suppose it is silly of me to resist her attempts. But frankly there's only so much I can take of comments about the curious shape of my eyebrows and the aristocratic tip of my nose.

I should end this letter soon as it is almost twilight. I wonder if we should have a garden. The children would love it. Clearly they love gardens, if the way they ran through Laurence's and Mr. Kentworthy's is anything to go by.

I wonder what time Miss Hartford closes her shop. I do not like to think of her walking home in the dark. She walked to our house for lunch, you see. I imagine she is the sort of person who enjoys a good walk. I enjoy a good walk myself.

Now, regarding your Miss St. John, I do not remember the lady in question very well. I seem to recall she was invited to a number of dinner parties, but I cannot recall what she looks like. Kindly provide a description. In any case, regardless of what she looked like, I think the compliments she paid you speak very highly to her character, not to mention her good taste. If you are interested in courting her, she sounds like a promising prospect. If you are not interested in courtship, well, she sounds like she might do for a friend. I do feel as though I abandoned you somewhat. Not that you don't make friends wherever you go. I don't mean to suggest that. And I daresay our friendship is more along the lines of you adopting me more than anything else. But in any case, I will be happy to know that you have more friends in Bath since I quit it.

It is kind of you to offer to buy Levinia that painting, but I do not know what we could get for the others that would match it in price and quality. So perhaps we had better save that gift idea for another time.

Affectionately,

Basil

Chapter 39

Gerry

Gerry was relieved that Charles did not pursue the topic of her visit with the Thornes. In fact, her absence at lunch had only been remarked upon by Veronica, who quieted somewhat after Charles explained that Gerry had a great many friends in the village and it was wholly unexceptional for her to be away for occasional mealtimes.

After dinner, she decided a distraction was in order. She went into the library and began pulling down books to help with her new spell experiment. When the door to the library opened, she was alarmed, but blew out a breath of relief when Seb walked in.

"Oh, good," he said. "It's only you."

"How have you been surviving?" she said.

"It isn't as bad as I feared. Veronica is beastly, of course. John is still acting dashed strange, though. He isn't mean, so I can't say I mind it. But I have no idea how to talk to him. Not that we ever talked much before. But now he seems to want to talk?" He shook his head. "I don't understand it."

"What do you talk about?"

"Well, it's always very awkward, but he asks me about Laury and what my plans are for the house and what I think of Laury's parents. He keeps complimenting me on having everything planned out so young and saying it's good to see that I'll be well settled." He shrugged. "It isn't bad, but it is very stilted. I'll be glad when Bertie has me back to work again."

"Oh, good," she said. "I've been wondering about that."

"He told me to take the week off and get settled first. And Charles has threatened to put me on a new lesson plan with his staff so I can learn to run a house." He grimaced. "Dreadful man." He looked around as if only just realizing where he was. "What are you doing then?"

"Research for a spell."

He brightened. "Really? What sort of spell?"

"Well, I want to create something to improve focus."

"You want the spellcaster to cast better focus on themself?"

"Yes."

"I don't know of any spells like that," he said, his voice pensive.

"I know. Everything else that's remotely similar is made to impact other people."

He walked slowly to the bookshelf and pulled out a thick spell book. "Have you thought about trying—" He broke off, his face turning red. "I'm sorry. Am I intruding? I don't mean to."

"Don't be silly. I'd love to have your help. The research part is always the least interesting to me, to be honest."

He grinned. "Really? I love this part. With Bertie's lessons, he has me pulling all sorts of spells to work through. It's like solving a mystery."

"Wonderful! I'll gladly take your help."

He opened the book in his hands and started flipping through pages. "Hmm. Not exactly what I was looking for. I'll keep trying."

They fell into a companionable silence, occasionally broken by one or the other suggesting a spell or an ingredient. After several hours, Gavin came in.

"There you are." He looked at the piles of books on the desk. "What are you two doing?"

"I'm helping Gerry work out a new spell," Seb said. Gerry was pleased, and surprised, at how proud her younger brother sounded.

Gavin's mouth quirked. "That sounds nice. I imagine you two will work well together. But it's quite late now. I think you'd both better go to bed."

Gerry rolled her eyes. Seb groaned. "You sound like Father."

Gavin raised an eyebrow. "You'll thank me in the morning when you aren't overly grumpy from being up late."

Seb stomped out of the room. Gavin watched him go and then turned back to Gerry. "That was clever of you."

"What do you mean?"

"Having him help you with spell work. He's dashed canny about it. It would solve both of our problems perfectly."

"What problems?"

"Well, Laurence asked us to find something for Seb to do, a distraction or a hobby or a career. And Charles told me you might be hiring someone else for the shop."

"Oh, my heavens," she said. "That's a marvelous idea!"

"You thought of it."

"No, I didn't! It's brilliant. Thank you, Gavin!" She paused and considered for a moment. "How did Charles know? I only talked to Bertie about it."

"That's all you needed to do. They tell each other everything."

"You're right." She turned her mind back to Seb. "We'll have to suggest it to him gradually, I think. Not spring it on him too suddenly. I might not suggest it at all until we've finished designing the spell, make sure he likes the process from beginning to end, you know."

Gavin looked amused. "Sounds like a good plan. Do you mind if I tell Charles?"

"Please do," she said, beaming.

Gavin ushered her out of the library, making sure she went to her room. Gerry considered the matter as she got ready for bed. It seemed like a perfect distraction not only for Seb, but also for her. Perhaps designing a spell and training Seb at the same time would make her too busy to be the target of everyone's schemes.

Chapter 40
Gerry

Gerry hoped her friends would quit their scheme after catching her visiting the Thornes. Unfortunately, that did not appear to be the case; the following Sunday, Mr. Applebough joined them for tea. Thankfully, she already knew him, so she was more at ease than she had been during any of their other tea times.

Then again, when John and Veronica joined, Gerry was no longer quite at ease, but conversation did flow more pleasantly than the first time they had met her friends. Caro pointedly did not talk to Veronica, and Mr. Applebough and John seemed to get along very well. In fact, Gerry hardly talked to the vicar at all after John entered the room. In the end, Mr. Applebough chatted amiably with John and Veronica, and Gerry turned in her seat to talk to the other guests. By the time the gentleman left, everyone was in surprisingly high spirits.

"A very pleasant fellow," John said. "I am pleased to see he is in your social circle, Geraldine."

"Indeed," Veronica said. "Very proper. Of course, the

rectory is probably very small, but that shouldn't bother you. After all, you cannot afford to be picky."

"So you keep telling me," Gerry said.

"But I daresay being a vicar's wife will improve your social status and somewhat rectify your reputation."

"I have no intention of being a vicar's wife, Veronica."

Veronica pursed her lips. "Well, I find that very foolish of you. He is a nice young man, very amiable, very respectable."

"That he is. But he has not proposed to me, and even if he did, I would not accept his offer, for I do not love him."

Veronica scoffed. "Love has nothing whatsoever to do with marriage."

Gerry gestured about herself indicating Gavin and Charles, Rose and Julia, Caro and Maria, and Lizzy. "Well, considering that practically everyone in my social circle, not to mention Seb, have formed attachments before marrying, I do not think it impossible to say that I would like to do the same."

"Hear, hear," Caro said.

"Besides," Julia put in. "There is no real urgency. Believe me when I say that we all have hopes for Gerry to be well situated. But none of us would wish for her to settle for a marriage that would make her unhappy."

"Love does not guarantee happiness," John said. "Passion fades over time."

"And compatibility shifts," Gerry countered. "Nothing is ever guaranteed. I do not need to be married, so I certainly would not be tempted with a gentleman of whom I hold nothing more than warm regard."

"No need for marriage?" Veronica said shrilly. "What an outrageous thing to say! A person of your situation? You do not have the luxury of such silly talk. You are in no position to decide—"

"I am, in fact, in precisely the position to decide that," Gerry replied coolly. "I have a career. I know it is not the career you would have chosen for me. But I am happy, I do it well, and I am well respected within my community. I am living with Charles and Gavin because I choose to."

"In fact," Charles said, "she could very well afford to live on her own if she wished. But we haven't mentioned it because we like having her here. The shop is doing marvelously well, you know. Bertie says it's the most popular spell shop in the county."

John looked thoughtful. "You are right that it is not the career I would have chosen for you, Geraldine," he said at last. "But I suppose I cannot object if you are doing as well as you say."

Gerry felt her eyes widen at the statement. It was the first time John had ever said anything remotely supportive of her career. "Thank you, John," she said at last. "I'm glad to hear it."

He nodded curtly.

Charles beamed. "Agreed. Personally, I think the career suits her very well. It is good to see her succeeding in a position that makes her so happy."

John nodded again. "Yes, it is."

Gerry blinked. "Er...thank you," she said. She gave a questioning look to Gavin, who shrugged.

Veronica appeared to be at a loss. "I still say it is not a respectable position."

John gave his sister a long look before turning to his wife. "If she is respected by the community, then perhaps we were mistaken in that assumption."

His wife glared at him.

John stood and said, "I think I'll go take a walk in the garden now. It was pleasant to see you ladies again." He gave a stiff bow and strode out.

Veronica turned back to the assembled party and said, "I hope you have found more eligible gentlemen for Geraldine to consider. I don't care what my husband says: it is absurd for her to still be single."

Rose straightened and said, "Nonsense. Gerry can remain unmarried for as long as she wants. She is surrounded by friends and family, and none of us would abandon her simply for remaining single. We are making sure she has options, that's all."

Gerry grinned at her.

"Exactly so," Caro said.

Then, she did a singularly Caro thing and turned her back on Veronica and proceeded to chat with Gavin, who happened to be in her new line of vision, to prove a point. Gavin looked thoroughly bewildered to be the focus of Lady Windham's attention. Gerry was fairly sure he had hardly exchanged two words with the woman before. Lizzy seemed to catch on to Caro's intention and drew Charles and Maria into a conversation. Julia smiled and began chatting to Pip.

Rose glanced at Gerry, who smiled and leaned toward

her to begin a quiet conversation. "That was a very pretty speech, dear."

Rose sniffed. "And I meant it."

"Thank you." Gerry hesitated. "Does that mean the parade will stop?"

"If you really want it to," Rose said, looking disappointed.

Gerry chuckled. "I would prefer it, but I would so hate to derail your plans. How many more am I expected to endure?"

"Three, I think."

"I suppose I can handle that."

Veronica, having no one else to talk to, left the room in a huff.

"Good riddance," Caro muttered.

Chapter 41
Basil

Basil thought about his conversation with Mary for days. He was struck by her honesty and the motherly way she'd spoken to him. He barely remembered his own mother; it was an unfamiliar concept to imagine having another one. As he had entered the house as an adult, he tended to think of her as a co-conspirator rather than a parental figure. But he realized she had spent more time with his father than he had, had likely heard his father talk about him, and had come to think of him as a child and a son rather than a grown man.

Thus, he gave her advice due thought. Though it took him several days to work up the nerve, he finally convinced himself to talk to Miss Hartford again. In the meantime, he practiced the lateral movement spell. He did not have it mastered as well as the previous two, but it was enough to consider himself proficient. Once again, he saddled his horse and rode into town.

He was nervous as he entered the busy spell shop. He wondered idly if Miss Hartford could afford to hire a third person. He did not like the idea of her being run off her feet with fatigue after handling so many customers every day. As his thoughts often did these days, he began to imagine what he might suggest if she were his wife. He would probably find a way to pay for another person to work there. He filed that thought away as the lady approached him.

She gave him a slightly less cheery smile than her usual one. "How nice to see you again, Mr. Thorne."

He bowed. "A pleasure, as always, Miss Hartford."

"You wish to buy another spell?"

"Gladly, and I would also like to talk to you."

Her expression turned wary and Basil was saddened at the sight. "Of course," she said.

"I hope I did not offend or unnecessarily distract you when you came to visit the other day."

She relaxed a little. "No, not at all. I'm sorry I left so quickly."

"You were surprised to see your cousin, I think."

"Yes."

He paused for a moment and said, "I hope seeing her will not discourage you from visiting us again. I'm sure I can speak for my entire family when I say we all very much enjoyed having you there."

Her blush deepened.

"I mean," he added hastily. "We all enjoyed having you to visit. And I would be very saddened to learn that coming to call had lost its appeal."

"No, not at all," she said, looking apologetic. "I...I had a very good time, actually. I'm sure I would love to come again."

He smiled in relief. "I'm so glad to hear it. How is your spell project coming along?"

"It's coming along rather well, actually. Thank you. My brother, Seb, has started helping me with the research. He's in the back right now, as it happens."

"Is he really? This is the brother engaged to Laurence?"

"Yes, the youngest of us."

Basil was very curious to meet the young man, but he didn't wish to be presumptuous. "Well, I'm glad to hear you have someone to help you."

"Thank you. Now how can I help you? You said you wanted a new spell?"

"Yes. The lateral one was not as easy as the previous two, but I think I have it down well enough. And Sophia requested I buy her a spell as well. She wrote the name for me."

Miss Hartford took the note. "Ah yes. I have these in stock. Are you still looking for spells with entertainment possibilities?"

He chuckled. "If you have any more."

She plucked two spell bags off their hooks, walked him back to the counter. and started laying out the ingredients for one of the bags. "This one is a wind spell. No doubt the children have seen one like it, but I expect you can—"

"Gerry!" a new voice said from behind Basil. "I think I've found something promising. What do you think of this?"

Miss Hartford gave the newcomer a disapproving look.

"Seb, you really shouldn't interrupt when I'm with a customer."

Basil looked down to see a young man around Miss Hartford's height with orange-red hair, the same pale skin, dark eyes, narrow nose, and small mouth. The young man turned to look up at Basil and blushed—Basil was amused to note that the young man blushed similarly, and just as adorably, as Miss Hartford. He knew immediately that this had to be the youngest Hartford sibling, and Laurence's fiancé.

"I beg your pardon," the young man said to Basil.

"Please don't worry, Mr. Hartford," Basil said, without thinking. "I don't mind."

Mr. Hartford started and gave Basil a quick up-and-down look. "Do we know each other?"

Miss Hartford laughed. "No, but I just told him you were in the back. We look too much alike for him to mistake you for anything other than my sibling. Seb, this is Mr. Thorne. Mr. Thorne, my brother, Sebastian Hartford."

Basil and Mr. Hartford bowed to each other.

"Pleasure," Mr. Hartford said, smiling up at him. "Laury's told me a lot about you. Said you were a good sort."

Basil smiled in return. "Thank you, Mr. Hartford. I've heard about you as well, and I've been looking forward to making your acquaintance."

Mr. Hartford glanced at his sister. "I should probably leave you alone, shouldn't I?"

Miss Hartford sighed. "Not at all. If you don't tell me now, you'll be hopping about in the work room until I get back there. Mr. Thorne said he doesn't mind. Go ahead and show me what you found."

Mr. Hartford dropped a large book on the counter and pointed to a passage. "I think this one might do. At least for a start. It has most of the ingredients we thought we'd need anyway. And we can substitute nutmeg for turmeric, see? That should provide the Constitutional Properties we're looking for." He scrunched up his forehead and leaned closer. "My only concern is that they're using this symbol in the sigil and I think that might make it a bit...temperamental."

Miss Hartford tilted the book so she could see it better. "I see what you mean. But I do agree with you on the substitution. This would make an excellent starting point. Mark this one and see if you can find any sigils that will suit our needs better."

Mr. Hartford nodded. "Right. Will do. Thanks." He gave Basil a bow. "Pleasure." Then he hurried back to the workroom.

Basil chuckled. "I believe I can see how he and Laurence are so well suited for each other."

Miss Hartford grinned. "Yes, they complement each other perfectly."

Basil made a mental note to call on Laurence soon. He wanted to learn more about his friend's fiancé. After all, if his friendship with Laurence continued to improve, he would likely see a lot more of Mr. Hartford. He suspected that learning about Mr. Hartford from Laurence would also give him a chance to learn more about Laurence too.

He returned his full attention to Miss Hartford. "I hope that's a promising step in your project."

She nodded. "I will have to give it another look, of course. But it contained most of the ingredients I expected I'd need to use."

"It is good that you have some help on the matter."

"Seb and I come at this sort of problem from different angles, but I think that will be a good thing."

"What do you mean?"

"Generally speaking, I look at a spell I wish to modify and see how I can expand or tweak it. Seb likes to come at spell work from his anticipated result. He works backwards, in a way. And this project is really more along the lines of his approach: I'm trying to achieve a specific end result. I did have some other spells in mind I thought to work from." She gestured vaguely in the direction her brother had left. "But I think he found a better one."

Basil smiled. "That's excellent. I'm so pleased to hear it. Does your brother work with you then?"

She laughed. "It's funny you should say that. He doesn't, but I'm hoping to use this project as a sort of trial period to see how we work together."

"Oh, good."

She raised her eyebrows.

He quickly added, "I mean to say that it's always busy here. Not in a bad way, of course. I'm delighted that you always have plenty of customers. But I've worried about you and Mr. Standish having to do so much by yourselves."

She gave him a warm smile. "Thank you. It is sweet of you to worry."

He would have liked to tell her that he seemed to be filled with worries for her—worries, hopes, plans, dreams—but instead he shrugged and said, "I always worry for my friends. I like to see them succeed." Then he realized what he'd said and added shyly, "I hope we can be friends, Miss Hartford."

Her smile widened and she held out her hand. "I think we already are, Mr. Thorne."

"Excellent."

He shook her hand and very nearly bent down to kiss it. But that gesture would have suggested courtship, flirtation, and romantic interest. While these were all very much on his mind and among his eventual hopes, it felt too soon. So instead, he framed her hand with both of his and gave it a light squeeze.

Miss Hartford beamed and blushed becomingly. Basil was pretty sure she did everything becomingly. He dropped her hand and she proceeded to teach him the spell. He was almost disappointed with how much he was learning of magic as the lessons were getting progressively shorter.

Chapter 42
Gerry

After Mr. Thorne left, Gerry let out a long breath, squared her shoulders, and returned her attention to the shop full of customers. She was grateful that Pip always took over when she was teaching customers how to work spells—and he seemed to take particular care to never interrupt when Mr. Thorne came in—but she hated the idea of burdening him with extra work while she flirted with a handsome gentleman.

She sighed. He had offered her friendship. It felt like a beginning, like a gentle start to something bigger. It didn't feel anything like one of her first fancies, or Arnold Hornsby, who had clapped her on the back when she was eighteen and said he was so glad she was so easy to talk to and it felt like talking to a sister. Perhaps even if this fascination with Mr. Thorne went no further, at least she might be able to preserve his friendship. That gave her a small bit of hope.

Once the shop was quiet enough for Pip to manage

alone, she went back to check on Seb in the workroom. "Any luck?" she said as she walked in.

Seb was perched on a stool by her work bench, several piles of books in front of him, and poring over two books at once. "Hm?"

"Have you had any luck finding a good sigil?"

"No," he said, glancing back down at the books. "Not yet." He looked up at her. "I say, that Thorne fellow is prodigiously handsome. I take some exception to the fact that no one told me that."

"Who's been telling you about Mr. Thorne?"

Seb blushed. "Laury. Didn't I say that?" He looked decidedly guilty. Seb was particularly bad at lying as his emotions usually played on his face very easily.

She sighed. "And Charles, I suppose?"

Seb shrugged and hunched back over his books. "He might have mentioned there was someone new in the neighborhood."

Gerry rolled her eyes. "Hm."

"Don't you think he's handsome?"

"Of course he is."

"He seemed nice too. And he was listening to our conversation as if he was interested in our project. I liked that."

"You seem to have formed quite a strong opinion of him."

Seb attempted to appear uninterested. "Just observing that it's nice to see other people who are as interested in magic as we are. That's all."

"Mr. Thorne is not interested in magic. Not really."

"No? He looked very intrigued for someone who wasn't interested."

"That's because he—" She broke off and felt her face flush.

Seb cocked his head. "That's because he...?"

"That's because he's polite."

Seb smirked. "Hm. For a moment there I thought you were going to say he was intrigued because he was interested in you."

"And I thought you weren't nosy."

Seb put a hand to his chest in mock offense. "I? A Hartford? Nosy?" He dropped his hand and said, "I seem to recall a certain sister asking me probing questions about Laury not too long ago."

"That was different."

Seb hitched his foot on a stool rung and leaned his elbow on his knee and his chin on his fist. "Different? Really? Please do elaborate. I would simply adore to hear how you coming over all bashful in front of the impossibly attractive Mr. Thorne is vastly different from when I was confused about Laury."

Gerry was saved from having to respond by Pip poking his head around the curtain. "Sorry to interrupt," he said. "Do you think you could whip up some more wind spells?"

"Yes, of course," Gerry said, relieved.

Seb narrowed his eyes. "Wind spells? I rather thought Mr. Thorne was learning a wind spell today. At least that's what I gathered from all of the ingredients you had laid out. I'm so grateful you made me learn the Constitutional Properties so completely, Gerry. Are you going to drill Mr. Thorne on the same lessons? I'm sure he'd enjoy it. I recall it took simply hours of studying. It seems to me he'd appreciate that."

Gerry glanced at Pip, who gave Seb a little smile and said, "You really do liven things up around here, Seb. I think I like it."

Seb looked smug.

"I'm not sure I do," Gerry said. Then she made Seb help her assemble wind spells. He kept teasing her, but she noted with interest that he learned how to assemble very quickly. Despite her irritation with her younger brother, she had to admit he was turning out to be a very good asset to the shop.

Chapter 43
Charles

Charles strode into dinner, pleased that he had an announcement to make. "Bertie has invited us all for tea on Sunday," he said. He smiled at John and Veronica. "He is very much looking forward to meeting both of you."

"John's met him," Gavin said. "In London. You remember Viscount Finlington, don't you?"

John's eyebrows raised. "Ah, yes. I met him briefly. I did not realize you were so well acquainted, Kentworthy."

"We're old friends, dear," Charles said.

"A viscount, did you say?" Veronica said, looking pleased. "Well! That will be nice. Although I have heard Finlington is something of an eccentric."

"The best ones usually are," Charles said with a grin. "I'm sure you will love him. Gerry, I hope you will not take it amiss if I advise your friends to postpone their social call until the week after?"

Gerry beamed. "I should be delighted to do that."

Veronica sniffed. "Dreadful manners, Geraldine. To

cancel on your friends simply because you've been invited by someone else. Suggests contempt, you know."

Gerry glared at her.

Gavin frowned. "Why the devil would Gerry's friends mind? They know she only has one day off a week."

"Besides," Charles said, "their teatime visits are rather more casual in nature. They happen regularly."

"I shall write to Rose immediately after dinner," Gerry said. "I am sure she will understand."

"Do you think it would be all right if I invited Laury to come with us?" Seb asked.

Veronica clicked her tongue. "Really, Sebastian. You cannot invite people to others' houses."

"I cannot imagine Bertie would object, my dear," Charles said. "But I will ask him for you. I expect he'll invite Laury's entire family."

Seb grinned.

"How was your afternoon at the shop, Sebastian?" John asked as they all sat down to dinner.

"It was very enjoyable, thank you," Seb answered. Charles was pleased to see that Seb was getting progressively more at ease with John's attempts at conversation. "I think I found a spell that will suit what Gerry is looking for. And she put me on another assignment to fine-tune. It's a lark."

John said, "I'm glad to hear it."

"And I taught Seb how to assemble some spells with me," Gerry said. "He was very helpful."

"Oh, dear," Veronica said. "Must you drag your younger brother down in status with you, Geraldine? Such a terrible example. John, you must make her stop."

John blinked at her, looked between Seb and Gerry, darted a quick glance at Charles. Then he took a sip of wine and said, "If my parents could allow Geraldine to work as a spellmaster, I'm sure they would permit Sebastian to work alongside her. Besides, he's already engaged. So there is no need to worry about his prospects."

Veronica looked angry and then thoughtful. "I suppose you are marrying a farmer, Sebastian. So you are practically lowering yourself to his level. I daresay that is all right then."

Seb's face flushed. "'Lowering myself to his level?' Are you mad? You did meet him, didn't you, Veronica? I think you'd be hard put to find anyone as good as Laury. If anything, I'm still endeavoring to deserve him."

"Not to mention," Gavin said, "Laurence is the Royal Spellcaster to the Crown. That's no small thing. He will be a powerful political figure in his own right."

"And for one so young," John said, "he really does appear to have a good career ahead of him."

"Indeed he does," Charles said.

"Besides," Seb went on. "I'm not even working in the shop. I was just helping."

"Did you enjoy helping?" Charles said.

"Oh, yes," Seb said with a grin. "That was fun too." He hesitated a moment and then said, "And it was nice to meet some of the other villagers today."

Gerry gave Seb a frightened look.

"I met one of Laury's friends—Mr. Thorne, I think his name was. He seemed like a very nice chap. So I was quite glad to meet him."

313

Charles bit back a laugh and tilted his wine glass in a slight salute before drinking from it. "I'm delighted that you had the opportunity to meet him. We had him over for tea not too long ago. Gavin and I both liked him tremendously. Didn't we, dearest?"

"Yes, we did. He was very understanding. And very patient with all those children."

"Children?" Veronica said. "Who is this man? Another farmer, I take it?"

"No," Charles said. "A young man of some property. He recently inherited everything from his father and graciously took responsibility for his half-siblings. How many of them are there, Gavin, do you recall?"

"Seven," Gavin said.

"Very active little brood," Pip said. "And very intelligent."

"Indeed," Charles said. "I have not met their mother, yet, but the Ayleses say she is charming."

"Is he unmarried then?" John said. "Might he be a good choice for Geraldine?"

"He is unmarried. And he and Gerry might suit. Although I confess I haven't yet considered it. He's so new to the neighborhood, you know." He glanced at Gerry and saw her arch an eyebrow at this remark.

"It seems to me as if the young man is hardly a good match for anybody if he is truly housing a whole swarm of half-siblings along with his stepmother," Veronica said.

John looked pensive. "Perhaps..."

"Well, at any rate," Charles said. "I think you'll get to

meet him soon. Unless I'm much mistaken, Bertie has invited them to call for tea on the same day."

Gerry choked a bit on her wine at this.

"So, I'm very glad Gerry will be able to put off her tea with her friends in order to join us. It will be good to all go together as a family," Charles said, giving her a cheery smile.

After dinner, Seb hustled Charles into his office. "Good Lord, Charles," he said as soon as the door was closed. "That man was outrageously handsome. I wish someone had warned me."

"You liked him then?" Charles said.

"Hard not to like him. He's so agreeable. He didn't mind a jot that I'd completely interrupted his conversation with Gerry and then he seemed very interested in the spell we're designing. Gerry said he isn't interested in magic at all and that he's just being polite. But he watched her a great deal, so I rather think he wants to know as much about her as he can."

Charles grinned and clapped Seb on the back. "Marvelous work, darling."

Seb blushed. "I'm not very subtle, you know. I didn't really mean to get John and Veronica on the hunt too."

"Oh, don't worry about that. I actually think it might work in our favor. I know from personal experience how difficult John can make a situation if he doesn't approve of a person. If he's predisposed to like our Mr. Thorne, then so much the better."

Seb looked dubious. "But will Gerry still want to marry him if John approves of him?"

Charles chuckled. "She probably wouldn't if he had been the one to introduce them. But since they've already met several times now, I doubt it will matter too greatly."

"Oh, good," Seb said. "I was worried I'd bungled the whole thing."

Charles framed Seb's face and kissed his forehead. "Not a bit of it, darling. You did marvelously well. Thank you."

Gavin knocked on the door and walked in. He glanced between the two of them and shut the door. "Congratulating Seb on being such a successful accomplice?"

"You should see the way she blushed when I mentioned him in the shop," Seb said, grinning.

"Are they really coming to tea? Or did you just say that to irritate her?" Gavin said.

Charles dropped his hold on Seb's face and reeled Gavin in. "Why do you think the tea is happening, my darling?"

"John and Veronica," Gavin said. "You, Seb, Laury, Bertie. Not to mention all of the Thornes. You really are putting a great deal of pressure on her, you know. On both of them."

"Pressure?" Charles said in an innocent tone. "I'm sure I don't know what you mean, dearest."

Gavin sighed. "Impossible man."

Chapter 44
Sophia

Sophia was passing a very pleasant afternoon in the library with her siblings. She and Basil were each reading their own book, the twins were poring over their atlas and plotting naval battles, and Levinia was sighing over a gothic romance.

"Basil," Levinia said. "You must hear this passage."

"All right," Basil said, looking up from his book. He glanced at the book in her hands. "Is it not poetry?"

She shook her head. "It's a romance and it is too, too beautiful. Just listen: 'He held her hand in his and could hear their hearts beating as one, the sounds of the world drifting to silence around them.'" She sighed. "Is that not enthralling?"

He gave her a small smile. "Very. It ends well, then, I take it?"

She shook her head again. "It cannot possibly. For she is engaged to be married to a horrid duke who owns half the country."

"I can't say I'm one for tragedies."

"Well, they *might* end up together."

He reached over and tilted the book in her hands so he could see the title on the spine. "Hm. Well, let me know how it ends. If it ends happily, I daresay I'll read it after you."

Sophia was relieved that there was finally someone in the house who appreciated Levinia's taste. Clearly Levinia was too, for she sprang out of her chair and wrapped her arms around Basil's neck. "How thrilling! I cannot wait to discuss it with you."

Basil chuckled. "Yes, that will be fun. We can form a club if you'd like."

Levinia gasped. "Wouldn't that be wonderful? Who else would join, do you think?"

Sophia put down her own book, eager to use the opportunity to her advantage. "I think Miss Hartford would like romances."

"Oh, yes," Levinia breathed. "She must be a romantic. One can sense it."

"Can I join?" Eli said from his spot on the floor. "I think I'd like to read a gothic romance."

"You're too busy," Bel said. "We can't fill our ship with a bunch of silly romances."

Eli slumped a little.

"I actually think that it is good for officers to be well-rounded," Basil said. "You'll want your crew to be sensitive and educated, Arabella. It will make them better at command and reasoning."

Bel looked conflicted. Finally, she said, "Oh, all right. But don't tell me I have to read any of that nonsense."

"Of course not," Basil said soothingly.

"You'd be ruining our fun anyway," Levinia said with a toss of her hair.

Basil gave her a stern look. "But if you change your mind," he added to Bel, "just say the word. Who else would like our club, Sophia?"

Sophia considered. She had actually only wanted an opportunity to throw Basil and Miss Hartford together. But perhaps it wouldn't do to be too obvious. "Perhaps the Hearsts?"

"And Mrs. Canterbury," Eli said.

"And Mr. Kentworthy," Levinia said.

"Which one?" Basil said.

"Mr. Charles Kentworthy," Sophia said decisively. "I know his husband reads poetry. I'm not sure if he likes other books."

"He said I could borrow some books from their library," Levinia said.

"That was very generous," Basil said.

Their mother walked in at that juncture. "Basil, dear, we've been invited to tea at Lord Finlington's house this Sunday. I'm sure it's due to you, dear boy. The viscount invited your father a few times, but he's never invited the whole family." She held out a letter.

Basil took it and read over it. "We are of a similar age," he said. "I expect it's more due to that."

She nodded. "Quite right. I'm so glad you're making friends."

He looked thoughtful as she bustled out.

"Is everything all right?" Eli said.

"Yes, of course," Basil said, smiling at Eli. "I was just thinking that when I came here in December, I had no idea I was going to stay indefinitely. And now that I am making friends, as your mother pointed out, it seems as if I really am settling here after all."

Sophia felt herself tense at her brother's words. "Do you not want to?"

He turned his smile to her and reached over to cover her hand with his. "I cannot imagine myself leaving Tutting-on-Cress now that I've gotten to know all of you. I was only thinking about how unexpected it all is."

Sophia felt some of the tension leave. "Does that mean you'll be sending for Miss Munro?"

He frowned, confused. "Well, I would like her to meet everyone, of course. And some of the other people I've met in town."

"So you'll be getting married to her then after all?" Eli said quietly.

Basil's eyebrows shot up. "What?" He laughed. "No, of course not. Good heavens, I do keep forgetting you all think that." He patted Sophia's hand. "Modesty and I aren't engaged. I don't know how you got that impression."

Sophia was shocked. After the initial surprise passed, she felt immensely relieved. "Levinia said you'd proposed."

"I did. She rejected my suit."

"And you're still friends?" Bel said quizzically.

"Yes, she's still dear to me," Basil said.

"Why did she reject you?" Levinia said, leaning forward in her seat.

Basil shrugged. "She said I'm too easygoing. She wants to marry someone who challenges her. Besides, we have a great fondness for each other, but it's not what I'd call passion. And Modesty said she needs passion in her life."

"She sounds wonderful," Levinia said.

Basil chuckled. "Yes, I think you'll all like her very much. I'll write to her soon and ask her to come visit."

From Basil Thorne
Verdimere Hall, Tutting-on-Cress

To Modesty Munro
23 Royal Crescent, Bath

9 April 1818

Dear Modesty,

Do you recall in one of my earlier letters that some
of my siblings had gotten the notion that we are
engaged? Well, I finally managed to correct that rumor.
On the bright side, they are very eager to meet you and
have encouraged me to invite you to visit. So do
consider this your official invitation. On the other hand,
allaying the rumor has seemed to give everyone
permission to discuss my marriage prospects.

Mary asked me the other day if I will be considering
any of the young people of the neighborhood. I was
surprised by the question, but relieved she brought it up
after breakfast and the children had left the room to go
about their various activities.

I told her I wasn't sure about the immediate prospect
of marriage, as everything is rather uncertain
right now.

"Is it? I thought you intended to settle here."

"Well, yes?" I said. "I mean to say that I am still
figuring out my place in this family. I do not wish to be
too distracted."

Mary smiled. "Of course you may do as you wish,

Basil dear, but I think having a spouse might help rather than hinder that particular puzzle."

"Perhaps," I said, unsure.

"Will you be inviting Miss Hartford to join us for lunch again? I do hope so. Such a sweet girl."

"She is. Although her last visit ended so abruptly, it might be best to give her some time before repeating it."

Mary laughed. "Oh, yes, the Hearsts' arrival. Well, I'm sure she's quite over it by now. I would love to see her again, and dear Mr. Standish too."

I assured her I would ask Miss Hartford to lunch soon.

"Do you know," Mary said, thoughtfully. "It really is a pity that we cannot host events here. It would be so nice to throw a dinner party. We would invite all the lovely people you've been meeting and those you'd like to know better."

"I should like that very much," I said. "Though I confess I've never hosted anything before."

"Well, until you get married, I can keep hosting responsibilities. I do love hostessing. But it wouldn't be proper when I'm in mourning. It is a shame, really, for I would like to help you make new friends."

"Thank you. I'm sure the friends will keep until the year is out."

"I suppose," she said doubtfully. "Who would you invite if you could?"

I considered for a moment and then listed off everyone I had met from the Kentworthy household, the Ayles family, the Hearsts, and Lord Finlington. "Although it may be presumptuous of me to suggest the viscount,"

I added, uncertain. "I don't know him all that well. But I'd like to."

"Well, you're going to his house for tea on Sunday," she said. "So I can only assume he wishes to continue the acquaintanceship."

"Oh, that's right. That will be nice."

"Yes, the children are ecstatic. It is the largest house in the district and they have always wanted to see what it is like inside."

I chuckled. "I hope the viscount is prepared for the havoc we will wreak." Mary beamed at the word "we" but didn't say anything. I confess I felt my face flush when I realized I'd said it. I didn't mean to sound presumptuous or overbearing. I grappled for something else to say. "It is all hypothetical, of course, but who else would you recommend for a future dinner party?"

"I think who you mentioned would do nicely to start with. I might invite Lily and Gregory Talbot, Rose Hearst's parents, you know. Lovely people. And perhaps the Canterburys and the Ladies Windham? Oh, and the vicar, of course."

I agreed to all of her additions. "That would be a lovely group. Well, Levinia and I are thinking of starting a book club, so perhaps I can make more friends that way in the meantime."

"Really?" Mary said.

"It is only in the planning stages," I admitted. "But she so loved the idea, I think it would be nice. It's only a matter of where to have it. It wouldn't be fair to make you stay upstairs while I entertained here."

"I wouldn't mind."

"I would," I said. "I'll see if someone else will host. It may take some doing, but it will likely happen sooner than a dinner party."

She chuckled and left the room to check on Lucy and Martin.

I should add that if you are present during this book club, you are most heartily welcome to join. I know you enjoy a good lively discussion and I'm quite sure you will love all of my new acquaintances.

This anecdote should clear up your previous question as to why I haven't invited more of my new acquaintances to visit. Since having Miss Hartford and Mr. Standish for lunch, however, I haven't invited anybody. It hardly seems fair to Mary. Once this mourning period is over, I will be sure to take your advice.

Do write and tell me when you can visit.

Affectionately,

Basil

Chapter 45
Charles

Going to tea at Bertie's turned out to be something of an event, mostly because Charles had to corral his group more than he'd anticipated. Gavin, Gerry, Pip, Seb, John, and Veronica didn't all fit in one carriage. Gerry was evidently anxious about the visit and Charles was not at all surprised when she announced that she was going to walk to Bertie's rather than take the carriage. Seb jumped at the chance to join her and Charles encouraged Pip to walk with them as well.

Gavin took his hand as they walked to the carriage and said, "I almost wish I could go with them."

"Why don't you?" Charles murmured back.

Gavin gave him a small smile. "And leave you to handle my horrid older brother and his horrid wife alone? I'm not heartless."

The remaining invited guests got into the carriage and were the first to arrive at Bertie's. Veronica and John were suitably impressed by Bertie's large and stately home, although they both declined the offer of a tour.

Just as Veronica was complaining about how long it was taking Gerry, Seb, and Pip to arrive, the Ayles family walked in.

"Seb didn't come?" Laury said as he greeted them.

"He chose to walk," Veronica said with a sniff. "Completely preposterous, of course, as Kentworthy has multiple carriages."

Laury gave Charles a knowing smile. "Ah. Well, he does love a good walk. Besides, I expect he'll be making the journey every day again before too long. Isn't that right, my lord?"

"Too true," Bertie said. "Although I do wish you'd call me Bertie, m'dear. I certainly consider you a good friend."

"I'm surprised, my lord," Veronica said. "I think society has gotten far too lax. It isn't at all a bad thing for Mr. Ayles to have some sense of decorum. Young people these days so very often lack it."

"Very kind of you to say, Mrs. Hartford," Laury said, but he gave Bertie a wink when Veronica's back was turned.

"One hopes," she continued, "that you influence Sebastian's manners. That boy is horribly behaved, you know, always was."

"Really?" Mr. Algernon Ayles said. "Sweet Sebastian? Poorly behaved? I'd never have believed it."

"Then you clearly didn't hear about his escapades at school," Veronica said smugly.

"Ah," Mr. Algernon Ayles replied. "I do recall hearing that. But he has matured a great deal since he left school, I think. Besides, I never think it good manners to remark on a young person's past behavior. It is something they cannot fix, after all."

"I will say," John said slowly, "that Sebastian does seem to have grown up a great deal since last spring when he was sent down." He glanced at Charles and blushed. "I daresay you had something to do with that."

Charles smiled at him. "I had some help. Gavin, Gerry, Pip, Bertie, and I did our best to ensure Seb had what he needed to become who he was to be." He paused. "And he would never have gotten there if he did not work hard himself. No one can change involuntarily."

John looked thoughtful at this.

Laury ginned. "And I must say that one of my favorite things about Seb is his capacity for growth, even now. He does so dearly want to be the best version of himself. It is impossible not to want to encourage him."

"Too true, my sweet, too true," Bertie said. "I am looking forward to spending more time with him again. I've certainly missed his good company. I've been waiting until you return to London before resuming Seb's work with me."

"I appreciate that," Laury said with a warm smile.

"Sebastian is working with you?" John said.

"I thought he was working at Geraldine's shop," Veronica said. "So very flighty."

"Seb worked as my assistant last year," Bertie said. "I like to dabble a bit in magic, you see. He has been an immense help to that end, so I am eager to have him back. But I didn't know he was helping Gerry as well. That is a delightful prospect."

Charles had written to Bertie about it, so this was a complete lie, but Gavin jumped in to say, "Yes, I think it happened rather fortuitously. Gerry has been working on a new spell and Seb has been helping her with the research component."

"How marvelous," Bertie said, beaming. "I think that will suit both of them very nicely. He is excellent at research. I've long thought so. And he learns very quickly, so I imagine if his work at the shop expanded, he'd do well there."

"You don't mind that he would be working less with you?" John said.

"Not in the least, m'dear," Bertie said. "I like his company, of course. But so much of my work is done with pen and paper, and there is little he can do for that. So if he were to work with me two days a week and at the shop two days, I think that would be quite perfect."

"But of course," Veronica said. "He would have to give it all up once he was married. You couldn't possibly have a husband who only keeps house three days a week," she said to Laury.

Laury smiled. "Well, as my parents are still at home, I doubt it would matter. And all I really care about is Seb's happiness. If he is happy working, that would suit me just fine. Besides, my work takes me away from home so often, I think Seb keeping himself occupied is rather perfect. I would certainly worry about him less."

Seb walked in at that moment. "Why are you worried about me?" he said, going straight to Laury.

Laury wrapped his arm around Seb's waist and kissed

him briefly. "Just trying to make sure you're happily occupied after our marriage."

Seb glanced around the room, looking embarrassed. "Oh."

"It's about time you arrived," Veronica said.

"Oh really, Veronica," Gerry said as she stood next to Seb. "We kept a very good pace."

Bertie stood and ushered everyone to sit. Charles noted with interest that Pip took the same sofa as Bertie, though on the opposite side. Both men seemed more at ease with the arrangement. He dearly wanted to see an official declaration between the two of them, but had been keeping his distance due to Pip's troubled past. Theirs was a situation that required finesse, which was not something Charles was always very good at.

"Is this everyone then?" Mr. Robert Ayles said. "A lovely little group, I think. I'm so grateful that you invited us to join."

Bertie smiled at him. "Thank you, m'dear. But we are actually waiting for a few more, so it will not be quite so little a group soon enough."

"Anyone we know?" Mr. Robert Ayles said.

"The Thornes."

Mr. Algernon Ayles looked delighted. "Ah, how wonderful. Our families are very close. Have they ever been here to tea?"

"No," Bertie said. "A negligence on my part, to be sure."

"And have you met the new head of house, Mr. Basil Thorne?" Mr. Robert Ayles.

"Briefly," Bertie said. "But I am hoping to continue that friendship. He seems like a delightful sort."

"He is," Laury said. "Have you met him, my love?" he said to Seb.

Seb nodded. "He came into the shop earlier. He seemed very nice."

Laury smiled and kissed Seb's cheek. Veronica tutted. "I quite dislike how informal you all are in your affection. I think it is very bad taste."

Before anyone could respond, the Thorne family arrived.

Charles couldn't resist complimenting them on their excellent timing.

Chapter 46
Gerry

Gerry had never been so relieved to see a crowd of children enter a room. The awkwardness of the conversation evaporated instantly as hasty introductions were exchanged and the children took over. The twins were talking excitedly about how large the house was and Arabella was asking Bertie if they could explore it. Levinia was eloquent on the beauty of everything in the room. Martin was dashing to each window and exclaiming at the sight of the garden and the grounds. Lucy tugged on Mr. Thorne's coat until he obligingly picked her up. Gerry tried very hard not to be charmed at the sight. Grace sat quietly and shyly between Pip and Bertie. Neither of them seemed bothered by her presence. In fact, Pip was talking to her in his own quiet manner. Sophia had taken a seat on a chair. Gerry felt herself relax as she saw to it that everyone was accounted for.

Bertie was in the process of telling the twins what rooms might be best for exploring.

Laurence laughed when not only the twins but Levinia gasped at learning the library had two stories. "Why don't Seb and I take the children on a tour, my lord?" he said. "We can keep them out of trouble."

"Oh, how kind of you, my sweet," Bertie said. "That would be marvelous."

Seb looked startled to be volunteered for such a mission, but he gamely followed Laurence's lead, even offering Grace his hand as she stepped up to follow them.

"Should I go with you?" Mr. Thorne said.

"Not at all," Laurence said, cheerfully. "Stay and have tea, Basil. Seb and I can handle them." He took Lucy out of Mr. Thorne's arms, gave him a wink, and corralled the twins out of the room. Sophia and Levinia followed behind.

"Well," Veronica said into the ensuing silence. "And I thought my child was loud." She gave an unconvincing titter.

"I am so glad you were able to come and bring your family," Bertie said, smiling at Mr. Thorne.

"It was very kind of you to invite us," Mr. Thorne replied.

"Are you planning to settle here?" Charles said.

Mr. Thorne nodded. "I wasn't sure at first, but I can't imagine myself leaving now."

Gerry tried to ignore the instant feeling of relief that welled up inside her.

"How lovely," Charles said. "I must admit we all felt the same. At least, I don't think Gavin and I necessarily planned to stay here forever. Now with Seb and Gerry all settled here, it feels right to stay close."

Gavin nodded.

"Geraldine is hardly settled," Veronica said. "She's still living with you. Quite frankly, I think it is ridiculous for so many adults to live under one roof."

"It's the same number of adults who live under your roof," Gavin retorted.

"Yes, but we are all married," Veronica said.

"And what difference does that make?" Gerry said, wishing she wasn't arguing with Veronica in front of Mr. Thorne.

"It makes all the difference," Veronica said.

Gerry opened her mouth to respond, but Bertie said, "My goodness, how absurd of me. I invited you all to tea and yet I haven't offered anything to you. Do forgive me, m'dears. I was so engrossed in your conversation."

"Please don't think a thing of it, my lord," Mr. Robert Ayles said, accepting a cup from Bertie. "We are honored that you invited us."

Bertie smiled at him. "Glad to do it, m'dear. Glad to do it. I confess I have been remiss in socializing more. I'm delighted to make up for lost time."

"I fear I am similar," Mr. Thorne said. "I've barely called on anyone without express invitations."

"Please consider our house completely open to you any time you wish to visit," Charles said, grinning at him.

"Ours as well," Mr. Algernon Ayles said.

"Perhaps we should combine forces," Bertie said in a musing tone. "We could venture forth together to call on various people of the neighborhood."

Mr. Thorne smiled. "I would be delighted, my lord."

"Excellent! I shall draw up a calendar and send it to you."

"I'm at your disposal, sir."

Gerry was torn between pleasure at Bertie's evident approval of Mr. Thorne and suspicion that her friend was privately scheming.

"As one of the few married persons in the room," Veronica said, "I feel bound to point out that if you gentlemen are both of the masculine persuasion, people will assume courtship between you, particularly as you are both unmarried."

Mr. Thorne shook his head. "I hope you will forgive me for disagreeing with you, ma'am. It is kind of you, I'm sure, to hint at such a thing. But I am quite openly of all persuasions. I enjoyed a very close friendship with a lady in Bath, yet no one there ever mistook our friendship for more than what it was." He shrugged. "It is a privilege to be born a firstborn, but part of that privilege is more freedom. Yes, the viscount and I may both be single gentlemen of masculine persuasion, but we are also both firstborns. I think people may be more inclined to think we are on the hunt for spouses together, rather than courting."

Bertie laughed. "Indeed, m'dear. I quite like the notion of that gossip."

John gave Mr. Thorne a considering look. "Are you on the hunt for a spouse, Mr. Thorne?"

"I don't think I'd say I'm quite that active in the search."

"But you are searching?"

Mr. Thorne chuckled. "I fear I have a great deal on my plate right now. It hardly seems an appropriate time to get married when I'm taking care of so many things at once. I am still open to the idea, or trying to be, at least. But I think I'd prefer to offer a spouse more stability than what I have currently."

Gerry privately thought that the right sort of person would help with all of the things on Mr. Thorne's plate. She certainly had a great many ideas of ways to make things easier for him. She very carefully kept silent.

"Oh, I don't know," Charles said. "You have property and income. That's certainly enough to be going on with."

"The property is one of my current difficulties," Mr. Thorne said. "I can hardly make heads or tails of it all."

"I'd be delighted to help you with that, young man," Mr. Robert Ayles said.

"As would I," Charles said.

"You see," Mr. Algernon Ayles said. "You are not without friends, Mr. Thorne."

Mr. Thorne gave a wide smile. "It seems I am not. Thank you," he said, with a nod at both Mr. Robert Ayles and Charles. "I may take you up on your offers."

"Please do," Charles said.

"My cousin helped my mother manage our property when my father died," Bertie said. "If you would like, I could write to them and see if they have any advice for such situations."

"I would be grateful for that," Mr. Thorne said.

"I can understand your concern about property management," John said. "I myself have struggled to understand it." He glanced at Veronica. "But I don't think marriage has impeded that at all."

Mr. Thorne gave John a small smile. "That is good to know. Thank you, Mr. Hartford."

"You said you're of all persuasions?" John said.

Mr. Thorne nodded. "I don't generally have a preference." He shrugged. "Frankly, I find most people attractive."

Charles raised his teacup. "Hear, hear."

"I must say," Veronica said. "There are more single people here than I would have expected of such a small vicinity. Perhaps Geraldine's case is not quite so hopeless after all."

Mr. Thorne frowned at Veronica. "Hopeless?"

Gerry noticed that John was looking at her very thoughtfully and she didn't like it at all. She set aside her own teacup and stood just as Veronica opened her mouth to elaborate on her meaning. Before Veronica had a chance to utter a word, Gerry said, "Perhaps I ought to check on the children."

"Oh, don't worry, dear," Mr. Algernon Ayles said. "Laury is with them. He is very good at wrangling them."

Mr. Robert Ayles laughed. "And he's likely teaching young Sebastian some of his tricks."

"The children can be rather active, though," Mr. Thorne said. "They aren't poorly behaved or anything, but I do worry about what they're getting up to in your house."

Bertie looked amused. "You sweet thing. I'm not at all concerned. But if you are worried, you are welcome to go in search of them. Perhaps Gerry can go with you and give you a small tour of the house."

Veronica straightened. "That would not be appropriate, my lord. I think I'd better join—"

At that moment, Gerry's friends arrived, and she could not decide whether or not she was pleased to see them. After all, she had canceled her tea with them and had been relieved to avoid more pointed conversations about her single status. But apparently Bertie had invited Rose, Julia, Caro, Maria, and Lizzy, and they had clearly traveled together. They bustled into the room, greeting everyone fondly. The ensuing commotion made it impossible for Veronica to put a word in edgewise for nearly a quarter of an hour. Gerry was beginning to think she was pleased by their arrival, seeing her friends greet her family so warmly.

But then Julia turned and gave her a wry smile and said, "It seems as though we were interrupting something."

"I was just encouraging Gerry to give a tour of my home to dear Mr. Thorne here."

"Gavin and I can help in the search," Charles said, taking Gavin's hand. "I think combined forces are the best solution."

"How marvelous," Rose said.

"Why don't you stay with the others, dear?" Julia said, kissing her wife on the cheek. "I'll join Charles and Gavin. I've seen precious little of his lordship's house."

Gerry decided maybe she wasn't so pleased by her friends' arrival.

Charles turned to Gerry. "Now, darling, if you and Mr.

Thorne will join us, I'm sure we'll have plenty of adults to corral the children." Then he led Gavin and Julia out of the room.

Mr. Thorne stood as well, looking baffled. He offered his arm to Gerry. Gerry had no idea how her plan to exit the room and the conversation had gone so wrong, but she took his arm all the same.

Chapter 47
Basil

Basil was relieved to have an excuse to escort Miss Hartford away from what was sure to be an unpleasant conversation, but he also regretted the inability to contradict whatever Mrs. Hartford had been about to say. He was grateful to both of the Kentworthys and Mrs. Hearst for offering their chaperonage. The three chaperones were a good ways ahead of them down the hall and it was evident that the situation had been arranged so he and Miss Hartford could talk comfortably without damaging her reputation.

"It would appear I have now met all of the Hartford siblings," he said as tactfully as he could.

She huffed in amusement. "Yes, I saved the best for last."

"I take it Mr. Hartford is your older brother? The one who is not as supportive?"

She nodded.

"How long has he been married?"

"Three years."

He hummed thoughtfully. He couldn't get a good gauge on Mr. John Hartford's age, but he had a quality about him—what was it Mr. Robert Ayles had said of Sebastian Hartford? A lack of self-assurance that young people often have? He couldn't determine if Mr. John Hartford was simply prone to it, or if it really was a matter of his age. He noticed that the oldest brother had not contradicted his wife, but he had also not agreed with her either.

Miss Hartford looked up at him. "What are you thinking?"

He gave her an apologetic smile. "I was wondering how old your oldest brother is." He hesitated and then said, "And I was wondering how much his wife influences his judgment."

Miss Hartford sighed. "He's thirty. As to your second thought...up until this visit, she influenced his judgment very strongly. In fact, I'd say she likely...directed his judgment."

"And now?"

"Now I'm not sure. John has been acting differently since he arrived. I'm not sure what happened. Although I can only assume Charles had words with him. John used to criticize everyone just as much as Veronica did. Only now he...well, he's curbing his words more often. I can't tell what he's thinking anymore. It's unsettling."

Basil nodded. "I can imagine it would be. I'm impressed that Mr. Charles Kentworthy has such influence."

She laughed. "Charles is highly influential in our family."

"Even to you?"

"Yes, even to me. He's taken us all under his wing, really. His courtship with Gavin was a friendship months in the making as he coaxed Gavin out of his shell."

"Must have taken some doing," Basil said with a smile.

"Yes," she said, returning the smile, "it certainly did. And then when Seb came to stay with us, Charles was, I think, the biggest influence in helping Seb to—"

"Get out of my own way," Mr. Sebastian Hartford said, leaning out of a doorway. Martin was on Sebastian's back, with his arms wrapped around the young man's neck. Mr. Sebastian grinned at his sister. "That's what you were going to say, I think. Although, to be fair, you all did your part." He frowned at them and said, "What are you doing out here anyway?"

"Looking for the children," Miss Hartford said. "The ones you're supposed to be keeping an eye on."

Mr. Sebastian raised his eyebrows and then looked over his shoulder into the room. "Laury! Gerry is accusing me of shirking my duty. Come defend my honor."

Laurence appeared, laughing, at his fiancé's side, with Lucy on his shoulders. "Not to worry, Gerry. We have the two youngest in here."

"But what about the others?" she said.

He glanced at Basil, looking mischievous. "Try the conservatory."

"That's not at all alarming," she said. "Did you really let five children run rampant in Bertie's house?"

Mr. Sebastian rolled his eyes. "The two oldest are hardly likely to run rampant."

"Neither is Grace," Laurence said.

"Is that the quiet one?" Mr. Sebastian said.

Laurence smiled and kissed Mr. Sebastian's cheek. "That's right. I told her Bertie had a very fine piano in the ballroom. You don't need to worry about her."

Miss Hartford sighed. "Oh, all right. Mr. Thorne and I will go look in the conservatory." She continued to lead him down the hall.

Basil noticed that the chaperones were no longer in sight. He hoped that simply walking through the house alone was safe, but supposed that the Kentworthys wouldn't do anything to hurt Miss Hartford's reputation.

"I'm sorry my brother lost your siblings."

He smiled. "I'm not worried. They were correct, you know. The only two I'd worry about are the twins. They can be rather very easy to lose, so I can't exactly blame your brother and Laurence."

She laughed. "I'm glad you're not worried then. What were we talking about when Seb interrupted us?"

"You were telling me about Mr. Charles Kentworthy taking you all under his wing."

"Oh, that's right. I'm sorry. I didn't mean to talk about myself and my family so much."

"Please don't apologize. I believe I brought it up." He hesitated and said, "Besides, I never tire of learning more about you."

She glanced up at him, blushing. "Oh."

"I apologize if that was presumptuous of me. I did not mean to upset you."

"You didn't upset me. I...um...I suppose it is normal to learn as much about new friends as possible."

"Yes," he said, relieved. "I'm sure it is."

She breathed out. "Good."

"You were saying that Mr. Charles Kentworthy had helped your youngest brother."

"Yes," she said. "And he was probably the biggest proponent of his relationship with Laurence."

"And for you? How does he help you?"

"Well, he is housing me and has essentially assumed the care of me, in terms of finances and chaperonage and everything..." She tapered off, frowning.

"But you wish he hadn't?"

Her frown cleared. "No, no. It isn't that. I was just thinking. Charles has begun to interfere with my...well... my marriage prospects. I rather wish he wouldn't. But I was thinking that from his point of view, he has every reason to believe it's the right thing to do, considering how much he's helped my family already."

"I can see how that would be unsettling. Although if he is acting as an unofficial sort of guardian, I suppose he has society's support in his intervention."

"Yes," she said with a sigh. "That too. But I suppose, as much as I'm annoyed by it, I'd rather have his interference than Veronica's, or even my mother's."

"I can well imagine. Your sister-in-law has...very decided opinions about that topic, I think."

"She has decided opinions on everything. And everyone seems to have an opinion on my marriage prospects." She said it like it was a bad thing. Basil very much wanted to ask why. Did she already have her heart set on someone in particular? His chest tightened at the thought. Or was it simply fatigue from having to deal with suitors? He had met enough nextborns in his time in Bath to know that the Marriage Mart was serious business. Perhaps she did not wish to be married? This was a worrying thought too.

Before Basil had time to put his thoughts into words, she said, "This is the conservatory." She opened a pair of French doors at the end of the hallway.

"It's lovely," Basil said.

"Basil!" Elias said, jumping out from behind a plotted plant. "Have you ever seen such a wonderful room?"

Basil smiled, relieved he had found one of the twins and pleased to see Elias so happy. "This is a marvelous conservatory."

Elias looked disappointed. "Oh, you've seen one already?"

Arabella's voice came from the other side of the room. "Of course he has, you goosewit. He's worldly."

"Oh," Elias said.

Basil wondered if he ought to scold Arabella for her harsh words. Was such a thing his responsibility? He had no idea. He decided instead to try and cheer Elias up. "I would never call myself worldly. Besides, I've never seen one as grand as this. It is magnificent."

Elias beamed.

"What are you two doing?" Miss Hartford said.

"Using this room to plan out surprise attacks in the jungle."

"Yes," Arabella said from a different corner of the room, still hidden. "And you can consider yourself either killed or captured at this point because you are terrible at hiding."

345

Elias looked embarrassed.

"Oh, I don't know," Miss Hartford said. "I rather think he played his part very well. After all, if we were an enemy force, then you would have had plenty of opportunities to surround us and launch a surprise attack."

"Exactly," Basil said. "In fact, I think you ought to reconsider your strategies. A good captain plays to her crew's strengths. Elias is good at conversing with others. Perhaps he could be used for diplomacy."

"Diplomacy?" A fern bristled in evident agitation.

"Or distraction," Miss Hartford offered. She gave Elias a wink. Elias grinned again.

The fern gave an expressive sigh. "I'll think about it."

"Mind if we continue looking around?" Basil said. "Elias can hone his skills and you can anticipate our next moves."

"I suppose that would be acceptable," Arabella said in a decidedly happier tone.

"Now," Basil said. "Why don't you show us the finer points of the room?"

Elias began conducting a very informal tour, pointing out the prettiest plants, the best places to sit, Arabella's hiding spot, and the door leading out to the garden.

"Thank you," Basil said, when it was concluded. "Carry on. But be so kind as to stay in here all right? Find Laurence or myself when you leave?"

Elias nodded. "We will."

"Utterly guileless," Arabella muttered disgustedly.

Chapter 48
Charles

Charles got Gavin situated in the library and strode through the house with Julia on his arm, easily outstripping Mr. Thorne and Gerry.

Thankfully, Julia didn't seem to mind his tactic. "How are things going on your end?"

Charles grinned. "Quite well, I think. Thank you."

"I was afraid we'd bungled something when we arrived so late."

"Actually, dear, your timing was quite fortuitous. Veronica was just about to talk about how hopeless Gerry's marriage prospects were."

Julia rolled her eyes. "Dreadful woman." She glanced over her shoulder to check on the couple they were chaperoning.

"They're a good ways back, I think."

She chuckled. "Indeed. They really do make a lovely couple."

"I quite agree. I think we're all hoping for a match at this point. Even John is amenable to the idea."

"It's only a matter of time," she said, patting his arm. "They can barely take their eyes off each other. And Mr. Thorne has all but admitted that he's in love with her."

"Has he?" Charles said, unable to keep the excitement out of his voice.

"Yes, but he seems very unsure of himself, poor thing. I'm afraid we may be in for a bit of a wait."

"Well, that might be better for Gerry. I think easing her into love may work out well."

She grinned. They passed the ballroom, where Miss Grace was playing on the piano. Satisfied, they headed into the conservatory. A couple bushes moved, but Charles and Julie tactfully crossed through and into the garden without a word.

"I'm glad the twins are accounted for," Julia said once they were outside. "They are the trickiest to keep track of."

They found the two oldest girls exploring the garden. Charles asked if they'd managed to find the library. When they admitted they hadn't, he gave them both directions on how to locate it. He led Julia to a bench and sat down next to her.

"Gavin and Miss Levinia will get along splendidly," he said.

She raised an eyebrow. "I'm afraid Levinia might be a touch too dramatic for your husband."

Charles laughed. "He needs more friends who like poetry."

"Well, she can certainly provide that."

"And I think her energetic nature will be beneficial for him. He does well around me, of course," he added. "And those in our close social circle. But the darling man still gets disconcerted around other people. Miss Levinia is a good young person for him to get to know. They have many similar tastes."

They heard the conservatory door open and looked to see Gerry and Mr. Thorne exit the building, her hand still on his arm.

"Marvelous," Charles said.

The couple appeared to be having a cheerful conversation and when Mr. Thorne spotted Julia and Charles, he waved and led the way over to them.

"How are you enjoying your tour?" Charles said.

Mr. Thorne smiled. "Well, we narrowly escaped an attack, I think. But otherwise, we are doing quite well. Most of the children are accounted for."

"I take it you found the twins then?" Charles said.

Mr. Thorne laughed. "More like they found us. Elias was very excited to show off the conservatory."

"He didn't show us the conservatory," Charles said in mock disappointment.

Julia patted his arm. "There, there, Charles. We can't all be exciting older brothers."

"Is that what I am?" Mr. Thorne said.

Gerry smiled at the gentleman's surprise. "It does explain his eagerness to show us around. He definitely wanted your approval."

Mr. Thorne looked back at the conservatory. "I wish I'd known that. He doesn't need to try for my approval. He certainly has it."

Gerry's smile turned unmistakably fond and Charles's heart turned unmistakably hopeful at the sight. "I think he'll understand that in time," she said. "You're very good with him."

"I am?"

"Yes," she said, laughing. "The way you talked to both of them speaks well of your understanding of their character."

Mr. Thorne looked both pleased and embarrassed by the praise. "It is kind of you to say so, but I cannot take all of the credit. You handled that difficulty with Arabella beautifully."

Gerry blushed.

Charles couldn't resist saying, "What an excellent team you make, darlings."

Gerry's blush deepened and she glared at him.

"You said you found most of the children. Which ones are you missing?" Julia said.

"Well, we haven't stumbled upon Sophia or Levinia, but I'm not too concerned about them," Mr. Thorne said.

"They're in the library," Charles said. "With Gavin."

Gerry raised an eyebrow. "You think he'll still be in there?"

"I expect so," he said, grinning.

"Oh dear," Mr. Thorne said. "She's liable to talk about poetry."

"Yes," Charles said. "I'm hoping that is the case."

"But your husband is so shy," Mr. Thorne said. "I'm not sure he'll know how to handle Levinia's enthusiasm. Perhaps I should check on them and make sure he's all right."

Gerry huffed. "It seems to me as though Charles

should check on them since he did orchestrate the situation."

Mr. Thorne was still looking anxiously back at the house.

Considering Charles had just been telling Julia about how wise it was to ease Gerry into the notion of love, he decided it was time to give the couple some distance. "Why don't I show you the library, my dear? Then we can both go and take a look."

Mr. Thorne looked relieved. "Thank you. I would appreciate it."

Julia, thankfully, seemed to understand Charles's strategy and said, "Gerry, would you like to join me? The shade is quite comfortable."

Chapter 49
Sophia

Sophia had dutifully followed her siblings out of the sitting room. However, once they were all out in the hall, Laury took Martin's hand, gave Grace directions to the ballroom and gave the twins directions to the conservatory. When he said, "Where would you two like to go?" to Sophia and Levinia, she realized she was rather tired of always being considered a child. She wished she could go back to the sitting room.

Instead, she looped her arm around Levinia's and said, "We'll go out to the garden. Do you know where it is?"

Laury had smiled knowingly and told her which door was closest. "Don't worry about the two littlest. Seb and I will keep an eye on them. Go enjoy yourself."

She was mollified by the news that she was not responsible for Lucy or Martin. She gave him a nod and led Levinia out to the garden.

Levinia, thankfully, had been delighted to have a companion who didn't mind her being overly poetic all the time. She gamely walked through the garden, her arm still linked around Sophia's, and exclaimed with delight every time she found a flower she thought was beautiful (which was often). Sophia was content to listen to her sister chatter, allow the sunshine to wash over them, and enjoy the peace of not having to worry about her younger siblings. Perhaps, she thought, it was time she considered staying inside sitting rooms instead of following the others out to play.

Some time later, Mrs. Julia Hearst and Mr. Charles Kentworthy came outside. Mr. Kentworthy informed them where the library was, and Levinia took Sophia's hand and dragged her back inside. Sophia didn't mind this either. The library was huge, with two levels.

Levinia stood in the doorway and gasped dramatically. "Is it not the most beautiful sight you have ever seen?"

Sophia agreed that it was. Levinia walked past the shelves, skimming her fingertips across the spines as she went. Sophia followed in her wake. Neither of them even noticed Mr. Gavin Hartford until they were practically upon him.

"I'm sorry if we're disturbing you," she said when she saw him look up from his book.

"Not at all," he said. "It is an impressive library," he added with a small smile. "I can...er...leave you to it."

"What is it you're reading?" Levinia said.

He glanced down as if he'd forgotten. "Shakespeare's sonnets."

Levinia gasped. "My favorite." Then she sat down beside him as if he'd invited her. She exclaimed when she bent over the book. "There are illustrations!"

"Yes," he said, his mouth quirking at the corner. "This

is one of my favorite editions. I often revisit it when we come here."

Levinia gazed up at him with adoring eyes. "The words are indeed like old friends, are they not?"

"Indeed. Would you care to—"

"Yes! We must read it together. I have always longed for a friend who loves poetry as much as I do."

"Oh," he said as she tilted the book and leaned over the pages.

"Which one were you reading?"

Sophia left them to it. She walked up the staircase, relishing how the distance made the voices grow softer. She was so rarely alone. Even at home, she was forever being interrupted by someone. Granted, sometimes she pursued company, but people like Basil and Grace were restful companions. Sophia wandered past the tall shelves. After a brief moment of hesitation, she allowed herself to skim her fingertips across the spines like Levinia had. She admitted that it did feel romantic. She found a section of essays and pulled out a few titles that looked interesting. After flipping through a few volumes and deciding on one that seemed promising, she made her way to an alcove and leaned against the side, looking out into the sunny garden.

She watched as Mr. Charles Kentworthy and Mrs. Julia Hearst talked in the garden and then watched as Basil and Miss Hartford joined them. Standing alone and simply observing made her feel strange. She looked down at the book of essays in her hand. Why had she chosen that book? Was it simply to make her feel more grown up? If that was all she wanted, why hadn't she stayed in the sitting room with the others, or outside in the garden, instead of following her sister around? Would she forever be defined by her siblings? This was a troubling thought. She stewed over it as she watched the two gentlemen leave the garden and the two ladies sit together on the bench.

Chapter 50
Basil

Basil followed Mr. Charles Kentworthy into the house. They went through a different door than the one they'd taken to the garden and Basil was relieved they wouldn't be disturbing the twins so soon. He made a mental note to talk to each of them later and make sure they weren't still bickering. It worried him that Arabella was so dismissive of Elias's strengths. He didn't think she was a cruel person and he suspected there was more going on than what he was seeing.

He was suitably impressed by the library. They found Mr. Gavin and Levinia discussing something in heated tones. Basil was immediately alarmed, but Mr. Charles Kentworthy looked amused and walked slowly toward them.

"But it isn't nearly as romantic as 116," Levinia was saying. "How can you say so?"

"Sonnet 130 is the most sincere and genuine declaration of love," Mr. Gavin Kentworthy replied. "To love someone despite their flaws? That is true adoration."

"But the lover should not even notice their beloved's flaws," Levinia said. "Love should be steadfast, unbroken."

"But it is not realistic," Mr. Gavin Kentworthy said. "It —oh, Charles." He blushed. "We were just discussing poetry."

His husband smiled. "Yes, darling. So I gathered. I never knew Shakespeare to be so divisive," he added, glancing at the open book on the table.

"I'm afraid I got a bit carried away," the young man said. "I do apologize, Miss Levinia."

Levinia reached forward and clasped Mr. Gavin Kentworthy's hands, startling him. "Not at all," she said. "It was a most invigorating discussion. I hope we can talk again."

Mr. Gavin Kenworthy's mouth twitched slightly. "Gladly," he said. He looked up at his husband. "Were you looking for me?"

"Just making sure you were both doing all right," Mr. Charles Kentworthy said, running a hand through his husband's hair. "Would you two like to join us in the garden?"

Levinia sighed. "So romantic."

Mr. Charles Kentworthy grinned. "It comes easily sometimes."

Levinia smiled. "That is exactly the sort of relationship I would like."

"I'm not as romantic as Charles," Mr. Gavin

Kentworthy said. "The way he speaks sometimes, it's—well, I'm not nearly so good with words."

"You have the soul of a poet, Mr. Kentworthy," Levinia said to the young man feelingly.

Mr. Charles Kentworthy took the seat on the other side of his husband. "I quite agree, darling."

"It is kind of you to say so," Mr. Gavin Kentworthy said. "But really—"

"But what you said earlier," Levinia said. "About loving someone despite their flaws. Were you thinking of your husband?"

"Rather more thinking about how he saw me," the young man replied, glancing at his husband.

"That is too, too beautiful," Levinia breathed.

Basil glanced around the library. "Where did Sophia go?"

"She went upstairs, I think," Levinia said, before turning back to the two gentlemen to ask them more about romance.

Basil walked up the stairs in search of his eldest sister. He found her sitting on a window seat looking out wistfully. "Are you all right?" he asked quietly as he approached.

She started and turned to him. "Yes. I'm sorry, I didn't see you."

"That's all right," he said. He sat on the opposite side of the seat. "You looked very pensive."

She shook her head, glanced out the window, and then turned back to him with a conflicted expression. She opened her mouth, closed it, and then said, "Do you think of me as a child?"

He blinked at the direct question. "I suppose in a way I do."

She looked sad but unsurprised by the answer.

"But that's more a matter of me not having much experience with children. How do you see yourself?"

"I don't know. I was just wondering about it. I'm so used to being one of the children. And today it occurred to me...maybe...I need to grow up?"

She looked so apprehensive in admitting this that he reached for her hand and clasped it gently. "I think that you've long taken responsibility for your younger siblings; you probably grew up a long time ago."

She gave a small smile, but still looked worried.

"Do you know that Mr. Sebastian Hartford was twenty when he met Laurence?"

She shook her head, mystified.

"And," Basil continued, "Mr. Ayles was worried that Mr. Hartford might be too young for marriage?" He squeezed her hand.

She sighed. "I just feel as though I'm in between too much. I'm not young enough to want to go and play, but I don't like sitting around at tea and discussing..." she gestured vaguely.

He laughed. "Why do you think I leave sitting rooms so much? Sometimes those conversations are a dead bore."

She smiled.

"I think you're at a rather perfect age. You have time to figure out what you like and who you are. You're welcome in sitting rooms anytime you want to test the waters of conversation. But you also have an easy excuse to check on your siblings whenever you need to escape."

He tapped the book on her lap. "What are you reading?" She held it out to him. He read the spine and then flipped it open. "Essays?"

She shrugged. "It looked interesting."

"You know," he said slowly. "There are a couple of volumes in...in the study at home you might enjoy."

"Father's study?" she said, her eyes wide.

He nodded. "Remind me to give them to you."

She gave him a broad smile. "Thank you, Basil."

He handed the book back to her. "And we can ask our host if you can borrow this one."

"Really?"

"Really." He glanced out the window. "Should we go check on the others?"

She slid off the window seat, looking in a much better mood.

Basil felt a vague feeling of accomplishment, unlike any he'd experienced before.

Chapter 51
Sophia

"Mr. Gavin Kentworthy is exactly what a gentleman ought to be," Levinia said as Sophia followed her into the carriage at the end of the visit. "He understands the soul of a poem, the depth of meaning."

"You do realize he's married, don't you?" Eli said in an irritable tone.

"I know," Levinia said. "But I always knew I was destined for sorrow. It seems fitting that my soulmate should be in love with another."

Bel rolled her eyes. "You only talked to him for one afternoon."

"We connected on a deep emotional level," Levinia said archly.

Basil interjected at this point. "I do hope you're not falling in love with the gentleman. He really is quite a bit older than you, not to mention married."

Levinia sighed. "I suppose I shall have to reconcile myself to simple friendship."

Basil looked thoughtful. "Friendship isn't something one settles for. It has a great deal of value on its own."

Levinia did not look convinced. Sophia suspected her sister wanted to feel maudlin.

Sophia looked out the window, thinking about her conversation with Basil. She couldn't put a finger on why the conversation made her feel better about things, but it had. He hadn't even offered advice, really; he had more or less told her she needn't worry about where she fit. The way he had asked Lord Finlington if they could borrow the book (the viscount had generously agreed and invited her to come and borrow another when she was done) and the way he had offered her a book from his own study—it reminded her a great deal of her father. And that had created a whole mess of feelings.

She still missed her father terribly. Offering a book from the study was exactly the sort of thing Papa would have done. He had never made a poor recommendation. Sophia hugged the book to her chest, feeling both saddened by the memory of her father and relief that Basil had unwittingly done what their father always did: he saw her as unique and important.

It gave her a rush of warmth and gratitude for her brother. She started thinking of ideas to show her appreciation, landing inevitably on her schemes for his marriage with Miss Hartford. She waited for a lull in the conversation and said, "Did you have a nice conversation with Miss Hartford?"

Basil seemed surprised by the question but nodded. "Yes, I did. Thank you." He smiled and added, "It would probably be hard to not have a nice conversation with her."

Sophia smiled in response. It seemed as though marriage was quite definitely in the future.

From Geraldine Hartford
Hollyton House, Tutting-on-Cress

To Nell Birks
Covent Garden Theater, London

17 April 1818

Dear Nell,

I have enclosed a packet of a spell for your friend Harriet. I believe it will help them with the pain in their feet. If you need any more, do tell me! I know you said that you are accustomed to spending long hours on your feet, but it seems they are working you frightfully hard. Please take care of yourself, dear.

We visited Bertie's for tea the other day and had a marvelous time despite John and Veronica's presence. In fact, I spent most of my time with Mr. Thorne, which was pleasant for all that it was orchestrated by Charles and Bertie.

I have begun working on a new spell. I am relieved to finally have an idea. I shall tell you more when it is ready. It is rather different than anything else I've worked on, which makes the whole endeavor both exciting and intimidating.

I am sorry I have not been writing more. The shop has been keeping me very busy lately. And when I am home, I am either listening to John and Veronica's nonsense— well, really it is more Veronica's nonsense these days— or working on spell-building.

I hope you are well and missing you terribly,
Gerry

Chapter 52
Gerry

Gerry allowed her pleasant memories of tea at Bertie's to buoy her through the week. She thought about the way Mr. Thorne had spoken to his siblings, playfully encouraging their imaginations while also tenderly taking care of them. She thought of the way he had been concerned on Gavin's behalf when he'd learned that Charles had instigated conversation between Levinia and Gavin. She thought about how he'd asked if his sister could borrow one of Bertie's books. These happy thoughts distracted her from Veronica's cutting remarks and John's hints that Mr. Thorne seemed to be very respectable.

She was so distracted, in fact, that it was several days before she realized that Seb was in a progressively worse temper. When Seb nearly burst into tears over a measurement gone wrong, though, she did take notice. "Good heavens! Whatever is the matter?"

"This won't add up like it's supposed to," he said. "I did everything you said."

She looked over his work. She had started Seb on assembling cooling spells for her. "This Merlin's ivy isn't treated. The measurements I gave you are for the treated kind."

Seb squinted at the leaves. "How the devil can you tell?"

She pointed at them, trying to sound soothing and patient. "Do you see how the tips are white? They turn a purplish hue when they've been treated."

He sighed and slumped in his seat. "Oh."

Gerry carefully cleared a space on the workbench. "Seb. What's the matter?"

"I just told you."

"No. What's really the matter?"

He glanced up at her and looked away. "You're going to say I'm foolish."

"I doubt it."

"Laury has to go back to London. He's leaving the morning after the dinner party."

She'd completely forgotten about the dinner party. "When is that?"

"Day after tomorrow."

Gerry gave herself a moment to be infuriated at Charles for not giving her better warning. Then she smoothed down her emotions and said, "Why don't you go and spend the day with him then?"

Seb looked up, hopeful. "But don't you need me?"

She smiled. "I like having you around and you're an immense help but—"

"But not when I'm messing up spells?"

She laughed, framed her brother's face, and kissed

his forehead. "But I won't keep you from your love when you clearly want to be with him. You don't work here anyway. You're free to come and go as you choose."

This statement was met with a surprising reaction. Seb blushed and said, "Oh, that's true," in a small voice.

She ruffled his hair. "We'll discuss it when Laurence has left. Go and be saccharine."

He rolled his eyes and slid off his stool. "Thanks." He put on his coat and hat, then turned back when he reached the curtain. "Speaking of saccharine, are we going to ignore the fact that you've been in an utter daze since Bertie's tea?"

Now it was her time to flush. "Whatever do you mean?"

Seb was clearly in a much better mood now that he was on his way to visit Laurence. He grinned at her. "I mean that you looked very sweet with your hand around Mr. Thorne's arm. Has anyone told you what a lovely couple you make?"

She threw a rag at him and he ducked out of the room.

When she got home, she wasted no time in approaching Charles, who was with Gavin in the sitting room waiting for dinner. "Charles, why didn't you tell me the dinner party was going to be tomorrow night?"

"Good evening, darling, how nice to see you. And I'm so glad you brought that up," Charles said cheerfully. "The dinner party is going to be tomorrow night."

She sighed.

John and Veronica walked into the room. "Geraldine,

that is no way to speak to Kentworthy when he's
practically your guardian."

Gerry ignored Veronica and glared at Charles. He gave
her an unconvincingly innocent look. "I hope you have
not made other plans, my dear."

"Of course I haven't," she said. "I'm sure you've
invited everyone I would have made plans with. Besides,
you haven't divulged the guest list to anybody."

He looked smug.

"Are you displeased with the idea of a dinner party?"
John said, clearly confused.

"No," Gerry said. "I quite like dinner parties. I dislike
scheming."

John looked even more confused. But he changed the
subject, asking where Seb was.

"He's probably at Copperage Farm," Gerry said.
"Laurence leaves soon and I advised him to spend time
with him until then."

"He went unchaperoned?" Veronica said.

"Laurence's parents will be there," Gerry said.

"I still say it is impolite for people not to be at dinner
when they have guests."

Gavin sighed. "You're not Gerry's guests and you're
not Seb's guests. You're Charles and my guests. Gerry
and Seb are free to spend their time however they wish.
As is Pip," he added.

"I see that he is absent yet again," Veronica said. "He
hardly ever seems to be at home."

"Weren't you just complaining that there were too
many adults in the house?" Gerry said. "And now when
those adults go off to various activities, you disapprove.

Seb is out with his fiancé, which is perfect considering they will be married soon. The more time they spend together now, the sooner they will probably be able to get married. Pip is out...and it's his own business what he's doing, but he did confide that he has an understanding of a sort with someone. It is reasonable to suppose he is spending time with them."

"And what about you?" Veronica said. "Are you out with prospective gentlemen?"

Gerry laughed. "Well, sometimes I'm spending time with friends who are intent on matching me up, like the Hearsts, the Ladies Windham, Lizzy, or Bertie. And sometimes, yes, I am meeting eligible gentlemen. So perhaps you ought to stop criticizing everything and let them take their course."

Veronica opened her mouth, but John laid a hand on her arm. "Geraldine," he said. "I would ask you to not speak to my wife in that tone." He glanced at Veronica, who looked triumphant. "However," he went on. "I am pleased to hear you are meeting with eligible gentlemen. Are there any prospects to that end?"

Gerry had been prepared to argue with John about her tone, but his question had been a reasonable one, considering her recent speech. She debated for a moment and then said, "I'm not sure yet," surprising herself with her honesty.

John gave a small smile. "That sounds promising."

Chapter 53
Basil

Basil turned over the conversation with Sophia in his mind for days. He realized that he had grown accustomed to thinking of challenges with the children as a unit, when really, the biggest challenges were likely on an individual level.

He felt as though he had handled the interaction reasonably well, so he tried to feel encouraged about what that said of his abilities. However, he kept thinking about the twins and how dismissive Arabella had been and how much Elias had glowed at the little praise Basil had given him. And what was it Mrs. Hearst and Miss Hartford had said in the garden? That Elias wanted Basil's approval? What did he need to do to show his brother that he had already had it? That, in fact, Elias had to do nothing to earn Basil's favor?

He turned the matter over and over in his mind until he came to the conclusion that he didn't need to solve the problem alone. He had been informed multiple times that he had friends now who were happy to help him.

The next question was, who best to ask? He liked the idea of going to Miss Hartford, if only for her good company. But he reluctantly rejected the idea as he suspected Miss Hartford didn't know the children much better than he did.

This led him to decide on Laurence. Laurence had stated in their very first meeting that he would be happy to help with any questions about the children. Moreover, one of Laurence's fathers had mentioned he was welcome without official invitation. Thus decided, Basil had his horse saddled and rode to Copperage Farm.

He found Laurence in the garden. The young man was wearing a pair of trousers that were covered in dirt and grass stains. He was kneeling on the ground, so it was easy to determine how the well-worn trousers had come to that state. He wore a shirt rolled up at the sleeves with no waistcoat, looking very handsome—well, Laurence was handsome in general—and Sebastian Hartford was clearly approving of the overall look, considering how he was gazing at his fiance with unabashed adoration.

Laurence turned as Basil approached and gave him a broad smile. "How nice of you to come visit."

"I probably ought to have warned you," Basil said.

Laurence shook his head. "You never need to ask to come and see us." He stood and gave Basil a hug. Basil was only recently becoming accustomed to hugs, but he had to admit he did like it.

Laurence called for a servant to come and take care of Basil's horse. "I should tell you," he said, "that you are welcome anytime, but you may catch us in less than glamorous appearance when you do." He opened his arms wide and grinned. "As you see."

Basil chuckled. "You look marvelous, actually."

"See?" Mr. Sebastian said.

Laurence laughed. "All right. Why don't you put down a blanket and join us? I'm weeding and I do like the company." He gestured at a pile of blankets by the door of the house.

Basil fetched a blanket and sat down on the other side of Laurence, who resumed his work. "Can I help?"

Laurence shook his head. "I quite like doing it, actually. I'm trying to get as much done as I can before I leave."

"When do you leave?"

"The day after tomorrow. I'm staying long enough to go to Charles's dinner party tomorrow night, but I can't stay any later than that, I'm afraid."

"Oh," Basil said, saddened by the news. He'd forgotten that Laurence's job took him to London. He also realized belatedly that he was taking up his friend's time while Mr. Sebastian was evidently soaking up as much time with Laurence as possible.

"Did you come by for an informal visit or did you have something on your mind?"

"I do have something I wanted to ask you," Basil admitted. "But I don't wish to take away from your time with Mr. Sebastian."

Mr. Sebastian shook his head. "It's quite all right. I'm sure Laury could stand a break from my chatter anyway."

Laurence reached up and smudged a bit of dirt on his fiancé's nose. "I adore your chatter. Don't be silly."

Mr. Sebastian blushed.

"Was I interrupting anything?" Basil said. "My question can wait."

Mr. Sebastian shrugged. "I was just complaining about Veronica. I don't know how we'll survive the dinner party. She's sure to be horrid."

"I'm still surprised your brother married her," Laurence replied.

"I'm not," Mr. Sebastian said. "He's horrid too."

"Your sister said he's been acting differently recently," Basil said.

Mr. Sebastian flashed him a smile at the mention of his sister. "Yes, he has. We think Charles said something to him. Of course, Charles won't admit it but..." He shrugged. "It's the sort of thing he'd do."

Laurence grinned as he continued to weed. "It is. He likes to take care of his family."

Mr. Sebastian sighed. "I'm not saying I mind it. John is much easier to be around these days. But I must admit... well, I can't decide if it's bothersome that John is so horrid that Charles had to intervene or if it's good that John actually listened."

"It could be both," Basil said.

Laurence sat back on his heels to give the conversation his full attention. "I hardly know John. But I will say that I wouldn't be at all surprised if he experienced some of the same things you did."

Mr. Sebastian cocked his head. "What do you mean?"

"Well, you've told me how Gavin and Gerry played

together all the time as children. Perhaps John was just as lonely as you were."

"Oh."

"And when he went away to school, perhaps he was similarly influenced by unkind people."

"I never thought of that."

"I'm not saying it's so," Laurence said, leaning forward to continue weeding. "But it would explain a great deal. It doesn't excuse the unkind things he's said in the past, so I'm not suggesting you forget they happened. But I do think it is very telling that he is currently listening to Charles over his wife." He shrugged. "To me, that suggests he wants direction. Perhaps he's always wanted direction. Veronica is certainly a person who offers that, as dreadful as her influence is. I can easily imagine a young man who is lonely and wanting guidance latching onto a strong-minded woman. I confess it's strange that he latched onto that particular woman because I don't think I've heard her say a single nice thing, but all the same..."

"She's very pretty," Basil said. "Depending on when they met, that probably helped. And she may have been less...acerbic prior to their marriage."

Laurence smiled at him. "Very true."

Mr. Sebastian was frowning pensively. "I'd never have believed that I might relate to John of all people. I know it's all conjecture, but it does make sense." He sighed. "Why are people so complicated?" He flopped back onto his blanket and draped his wrist over his eyes to block out the sun.

Laurence gave his fiancé a fond look.

Mr. Sebastian squinted at Basil. "Did I take over the conversation? I do chatter too much."

"Not at all," Basil said, chuckling. "It was an interesting topic, and one that has been on my mind lately."

"Has it?"

"I'm curious about...well, everyone I've met since I came here."

Mr. Sebastian smirked. "Some more than others?"

"Naturally."

Laurence gave him a knowing grin. "Now what was it you wanted to discuss?"

"I wanted your advice on the twins." Laurence nodded encouragingly. Basil went on to describe the conversation in the conservatory. "I feel as though I ought to talk to them about it or...I don't know...provide some...well, as we were just discussing, direction. Only I have no idea how to go about it."

"That is an excellent question. Do you mind if we scoot over to the next plot while I answer it? I've run out of weeds." They obligingly shuffled to where Laurence had indicated. "Now," he said, as he got back to work. "Before I give you advice, I think I ought to tell you what I've observed of the twins. Do you mind?"

"Not at all," Basil said hurriedly.

"Let's start with Bel. Because she's bossier and has all the ideas, people tend to think that Eli can't do without her. But I've long suspected it's the other way around. Bel needs Eli. She depends on him. He's her...I don't know...her support, if that makes sense. What's a captain without a crew? What's the sense of having good ideas if no one will believe in them? I'm quite sure that if you were to split the two up for any length of time, Bel would lose a great deal of her sense of purpose. And furthermore, I think she knows this. In any case, she can be quite prickly as a general rule, so most people don't realize all of that.

"Now, Elias," he went on, "is different. He's a bit quieter, gentler. He has...he has a very soft heart, that one. It's probably why he understands Bel as well as he does. But Eli has plans and dreams that go beyond whatever Bel has cooked up. He plays the piano, he likes to read, he loves meeting new people. He is keenly observant. If you ever want information on the rest of the siblings, go to him. He notices everything. He's very intelligent too—just as smart as his sister, but everyone overlooks that because he's not as loud about his cleverness. Does that all make sense?"

Basil nodded. "Perfect sense."

"Good. Now the trouble is that Eli needs some time by himself, or at least away from Bel, if he's going to truly come into his own. My advice is to offer that to him: either by taking him on outings by himself or finding tasks that only he can do."

Basil thought back to the treehouse and how Laurence had divided the twins up, positioning Elias not only away from Arabella, but also away from the rest of the siblings. He nodded his understanding.

"However," Laurence continued with a small smile, "that leaves with you the problem of what to do with Bel. I think that Eli needs space, but Bel needs purpose. So if you are going to give Eli time apart, your best bet is to give Bel a task of some kind. There's no doubt that she has a gift for command, but she also does well at following directions herself. You just have to give it confidently and it has to have value. She's smart enough to know when she's being sent to do something inane. But if she's in charge of watching Martin or if she's delivering a message to the kitchens or if she's going in search of a book you've been looking for, if it's something she can see the value and purpose of, she'll do it."

Basil recalled the way Laurence had made sure Bel kept an eye on the three youngest during the treehouse afternoon. "That makes sense. Thank you."

Laurence smiled. "Good. Was there anything else?"

Basil considered. "Someone said that Elias wanted my approval. Do you think that's true? And if it is, how do I...I don't know...convey to him that he already has it?"

Laurence's smile broadened. "Yes, I expect he does, poor thing. He's often overlooked, I'm afraid. Overshadowed by his twin sister. Overshadowed by his two older sisters. But I think if you keep on doing as you've done and tell him when you're proud of him and let him know he isn't forgotten, you'll do just fine."

Basil breathed out in relief. "I can do that."

Laurence glanced over at his fiancé, who had returned to lying on his back on the blanket. He cupped Mr. Sebastian's cheek. "Angel," he said softly.

Mr. Sebastian beamed up at him. "Hm?"

"Can you do something for me?"

"Anything—what?" he said, sitting up.

"Will you go inside and ask my parents where my

378

orange tincture is? And then will you have one of them apply it to your face?"

"Oh," he said with a slump. "I thought I was going to do something useful."

Laurence leaned forward and kissed him. "It *is* useful. You're helping me look after you, which you know makes me happy."

Mr. Sebastian rolled his eyes. "Oh, all right." He huffed and walked into the cottage.

Laurence turned back to Basil. "He gets frightfully burned when he's outside with me."

"And freckled too, probably."

Laurence laughed. "Yes, well, the freckles are pretty adorable. I don't entirely mind that. But his sister-in-law would say something. I don't want Seb to feel ashamed for spending time in the garden with me. So I've been careful since we got back."

"I won't be sorry when they leave," Basil said. "I wouldn't mind getting to know the older brother better, but she really does bring down the conversation."

Laurence nodded. "That she does. But while Seb's gone, I did want to ask you about something."

"Oh, what is it?"

Laurence looked mischievous. "Any developments with Gerry? You two seemed to be enjoying yourselves at Bertie's the other day."

Basil chuckled. "No developments, I'm afraid. I'm simply trying to get to know her better. Getting to know her family is helpful too, though."

"Good. The dinner party will be a good opportunity for that."

"What dinner party?"

"Charles is throwing a dinner party tomorrow. Didn't you know?"

Basil shook his head. "Mary's been handling all of my social obligations."

Laurence laughed. "Yes, that sounds like her."

"Fortunately, there haven't been all that many social obligations to handle. And I imagine I'm not the easiest person to plan for as I tend to ride out to the village at a moment's notice or impulsively invite people to lunch or come see you with no warning."

"Who did you invite over for lunch?"

Basil gave him a small smile. "Miss Hartford and Mr. Standish."

Laurence threw back his head and laughed. "Marvelous! And how was it?"

"Do you even have to ask?"

Laurence playfully flicked a bit of dirt at him.

"Mary suggested I talk to her in my father's study. And without my even saying anything, she was respectful of the space. She looked at the bookshelves and then told me about a spell she's designing." He hesitated. "And...er...she's designing a spell inspired by something I said, which is...well, it's remarkably kind."

"To say the least," Laurence said. "What else?"

"Well, I asked her all sorts of questions about it. Probably sounded like a complete idiot because I know very little about magic, let alone anything that advanced. But she answered all of my questions, and when she left I was already trying to think of a reason to invite her again." Basil sighed. "The more I see her, the more I like her. But sometimes I get the sense that there's something...I don't know...holding her back somehow. I wish I knew what."

Laurence looked thoughtful. "Well, as a man engaged to a Hartford, I can tell you the entire family is remarkably stubborn. I'm not sure if something is holding Gerry back but if there is, it may take some doing to persuade her out of it."

"I have no desire to woo the lady against her will."

Laurence smiled. "Well, I didn't say you were doing that. From what I could see, she very much enjoys your company."

"You think so?"

"Oh, yes. And besides..." Laurence hesitated for a moment. "I imagine you're not the only one who likes the idea of you two as a pair."

"Yes, I've gathered that. Mary seems wholly approving of it and I think Miss Hartford's cousins and friends are playing matchmaker."

Laurence nodded. "Yes, I believe you're right. I'm glad Mary approves of it. That will make things more comfortable for everyone. Although I can't say I'm surprised."

"You talk as if it is a foregone conclusion. I haven't proposed and I'm not sure I will until my suit would be met favorably."

"Well, I think if you keep on as you've been doing, it may very well work out in the end."

Basil did not understand his friend's confidence, but Mr. Sebastian came back, his face shiny with whatever tincture had been applied, and the subject was dropped.

"Well," Basil said. "I think I'd better take my leave and let you two have some time together."

Laurence stood along with him. "Thank you for coming by. I'll send you my address in London so you can write to me if you have any more questions."

"Thank you," Basil said. "You've been an immense help." He shook Mr. Sebastian's hand. "It was a pleasure to see you again, Mr. Sebastian."

"Oh, do call me Seb," he said. "You call Laury by his given name."

Basil chuckled. "Gladly. And you can call me Basil."

Seb grinned in what was a decidedly mischievous expression. "Capital. Thank you."

As Basil rode home, he tried to focus on Laurence's advice, and not on the fact that Seb's grin reminded him of Miss Hartford and that he already found himself missing her company.

Chapter 54
Sophia

Sophia and her mother were listening to Grace practice piano when Basil came home.

"How was your ride, dear?" her mother said to him.

"Excellent, thank you. I called on Laurence and had a very nice talk with him and his fiancé." He paused a moment. "Was I invited to a dinner party tomorrow night?"

"Yes, dear. Didn't I tell you?"

"I don't believe you did. Did you accept?"

"Yes, I did—" She broke off and covered her mouth with her hand. "Was that all right?"

He smiled. "Yes, quite all right. It must have slipped my mind. The Kentworthys', isn't it?"

"Yes, dear. I think you ought to wear your dark blue suit. It looks very becoming."

"Thank you," he said in a slightly bemused tone. "I will."

"She won't be able to take her eyes off you."

He raised his eyebrows and laughed, before taking a seat. "It would seem the entire county is conspiring now."

"You two look so well together."

"Yes," Sophia said. "You'll be the handsomest couple in Tutting-on-Cress."

He gave her a warm smile. "Thank you." He leaned back in the seat. "Shall I bring the children with me?"

"I don't think so," her mother said. "I want you to have the opportunity to just talk with your friends without worrying about the children."

"Sophia might enjoy it."

Sophia felt a thrill at being included. Basil remembered their conversation! She considered the invitation and imagined herself in the dining room with so many people. Strangely, the idea made her feel sick rather than giddy. She shook her head. "I'd better not. Thank you anyway."

His smile was full of understanding. "Maybe next time."

That night, Sophia called for a family meeting.

"Basil has been invited to a dinner party," she began.

"We're going to a dinner party?" Levinia said, clasping her hands together.

"No," she said. "Mama suggested he go alone."

Levinia wilted.

"That will be good for him," Eli said. "He won't have to keep looking for us the entire time. He can just enjoy himself."

Sophia nodded. "That's essentially what Mama said."

"How can we be sure he'll fall in love with Miss Hartford without us there to help?" Grace said.

"They were pretty friendly the other day at tea," Bel said. "We might have been able to observe them if Eli hadn't gone and given himself away."

Eli looked chastened. "They didn't seem to mind."

"Your orders had been to keep quiet and you couldn't do it."

"Yes, but it got them to agree on something together. I thought that was nice."

"What do you mean?" Sophia said.

"Bel was scolding me and Basil said it was actually a good strategy for Bel to hide and me not to. Miss Hartford agreed with him and said Bel might have attacked us while we were talking because I would have helped her to draw out their weak points—"

"That is not what she said," Bel huffed.

"It was close."

"That's wonderful!" Sophia said. "If they get married, it will help if they agree on things like this."

"Particularly when they have children of their own," Grace agreed.

"Won't their children be beautiful?" Levinia said.

"So what's the plan?" Martin said, confused.

"There is no plan," Bel said. "We aren't invited."

Sophia considered. "We will have to give him lots of confidence when he leaves and then the next day, we will ask him what Miss Hartford wore and try to get him to talk about her as much as possible."

Eli nodded. "I like it."

With that, Sophia adjourned the meeting, privately relieved that she had not confessed to her siblings that she had been invited to the dinner party and had turned the offer down. She was quite sure Bel would not be pleased.

Chapter 55
Charles

Charles was very busy on the day of the dinner party. He had assured Gavin he would take care of everything, so he had sent out the invitations more than a month before and approved the menus a fortnight ago. On the day of the party, on top of his usual daily routine like his morning ride, checking in on his nephew in the nursery, and responding to the letters he'd received, he had to make sure everything was set up properly for their guests. While he was talking through the seating arrangements with the butler, John strode into the dining room.

"Looking for me, darling?" Charles said.

"Yes," John said. "But I suppose this is a bad time."

"Not at all," Charles said. He verified that the butler needed nothing more and dismissed him . "How can I be of service?"

"I was wondering if there is a particular reason my sister is so agitated about this dinner party?"

Charles smiled. "Oh, she's just concerned that it's an attempt at matchmaking."

"Is it?"

"Not exactly. The initial plan had been to introduce you to our friends here in town. Although I think you've met most of them at this point."

John nodded. "Are the Thornes coming?"

"I believe they are," Charles said.

John looked thoughtful. "Mr. Thorne struck me as a rather good match for Geraldine."

"Indeed?"

"You disagree?" John said, frowning.

"Not at all. But I'm curious about your thoughts on the matter."

John blushed. "I have few thoughts on the matter. Veronica said no one would want to marry a man with that many children running around, but..."

"But?"

"Well...it seems to me he is a thoughtful gentleman of significant property. Geraldine is—well, she's many things of course, but no one would deny she's intelligent. I think a man of good sense would suit her. And...and he seemed respectful of her, which I liked. I am unfamiliar with the family name, so I don't know very much about him, but he certainly...he certainly seems very respectable." John looked at him doubtfully.

Charles smiled and put a hand on John's shoulder. "I'm inclined to agree with you."

John let out a breath.

Charles gave John's shoulder a squeeze. "How are you enjoying your visit?"

"You and Gavin have been very good hosts."

"Thank you, dear. That isn't what I asked."

John blinked and pressed his lips together for a long moment. "It has been an...interesting visit."

Charles figured that was the best he would get. "I'm glad to hear it. And by the way, you've been doing very well."

John gave a humorless laugh. "Very kind, I'm sure."

"No, darling, I mean that sincerely. You've done exactly as I asked. I want you to know I appreciate it."

John's lips pressed together again.

"What are you trying not to say?" Charles said.

John rolled his eyes. "Don't worry. It wasn't anything cutting about you. Or any of my siblings."

"Ah," Charles said. "Something cutting about yourself then?"

John glared at him.

Charles sighed and said, "John, has it not yet occurred to you that words can inflict damage?"

John winced.

"I am not speaking of what you've said to your siblings. I am speaking of what you are thinking about yourself."

John gave him a startled look, which was a pretty good indication that Charles had guessed correctly.

"You've been choosing your words with care ever since Seb got home. Don't think I haven't noticed. Do try and show yourself the same kindness."

John pinched the bridge of his nose. "Kentworthy, you know better than anyone how little I deserve that sort of kindness."

"Everyone deserves that sort of kindness, John. And I suspect you have been inflicting a great deal of damage on yourself for years now."

John slipped out from under Charles's hand. "Be so good as to stop trying to fix me, Kentworthy. I'm doing as you asked in regards to my siblings. It's not enough, but it's the best I seem to be able to manage."

Chapter 56
Gerry

After weeks of fretting about the dinner party, Gerry
was relieved to see that the guests were almost
predictable. She wasn't entirely sure what she'd been
worried about—her parents, perhaps? The Dukex of
Molbury? Some sort of authority figure who would add to
the petition that she marry Mr. Thorne? In the end, it
was Bertie, Rose, Julia, Caro, Maria, Lizzy, Mr. Canterbury,
the Ayles family, Aunt Lily, Uncle Gregory, Rose's older
brother Clarence, the vicar, and, of course, Mr. Thorne.
Gerry was almost surprised to see him without the
children accompanying him. She was not surprised,
however, that they were seated next to each other.

She glanced around the table and saw that Charles
had arranged the guests with a complete disregard for
formality: spouses sat beside each other, Seb and
Laurence were paired together, as well as Bertie and Pip.
At one point, Veronica complained that Gavin ought to
know better than to seat a married couple together at a
dinner party, and Charles promptly had her moved to sit

between Mr. Algernon Ayles and the vicar. He did it so seamlessly that Gerry had a feeling he intended to do it all along. John wound up seated between Mr. Robert Ayles and Pip, who both seemed perfectly content to chat with him. She noted that Laurence had been seated next to Mr. Thorne and that Julia had been seated on Gerry's other side—two people who would most certainly leave her and Mr. Thorne alone so they could talk. She had to give Charles credit: he definitely knew what he was doing. He practically guaranteed that she would be able to chat with Mr. Thorne for the entirety of the meal. She tried not to be too excited about it.

Mr. Thorne leaned close and said quietly, "I see what you meant about Mr. Kentworthy looking after his family. Your oldest brother looks more at ease than I've ever seen him."

She was surprised to see that he was right. "Yes, he is. How have you been? I...er...haven't seen you in some time."

He looked chagrined. "My apologies. I've been remiss in going to your shop."

"I didn't mean for you to apologize," she said hastily.

He smiled. "Well, all the same. As your friend, I have been remiss in visiting you."

She returned the smile. She liked hearing him say that. "I haven't seen you since the tea at Bertie's. Have you two gone to make social calls together yet?"

"Not yet. I was hoping to ask him about it tonight, but I'm not sure I will have the opportunity. There are quite a lot of people here, more than I'd expected, to be honest."

"Does it make you uncomfortable?"

He smiled again. "No, not exactly. I daresay the dinner parties in Bath were larger than this one. But it's been so long since I've socialized on that scale. I guess I'm a bit out of practice."

"I've been wondering..." She tapered off, realizing she didn't know how to ask the question without sounding nosy.

"Yes?"

"How did you end up in Bath?"

He chuckled. "That's a good question. Let me see if I can explain it in a way that makes sense. I think I'll have to go back a bit to my school days—is that all right?"

She nodded. She didn't want to admit it, but she was curious to know everything about him.

"I spent most of my childhood in school. After my mother died, I was sent away and...it became too difficult to come back."

"Why?" she whispered.

"My father's grief was...very great. It seemed kinder to leave him in peace. Keep in mind," he added after seeing her quizzical expression, "I was about eight years old, so my reasoning was not all that sharp."

"Of course," she said. "Go on."

"Anyway, from then until I was about Seb's age, I spent in school."

She tried to ignore how nice it sounded to hear him refer to her brother by his first name, as if he were part of the family.

He continued, "I hardly ever came home. My father remarried when I was about fourteen. I suppose I ought to have tried visiting more often then, but I felt too much like an outsider." He cleared his throat. "This is all to say that I was rather lonely by the time I was about twenty. I still didn't feel comfortable coming home, so I sort of flitted about, visiting my schoolmates. I wouldn't call them friends exactly, as I was never particularly close with any of them. But I was well-mannered and wealthy enough to be considered a good addition to dinner parties and balls. Anyway, that's where I met my friend, Modesty. She is a cousin of one of my schoolmates and was eighteen when I met her. I was six and twenty. This will sound strange, I know, but she sort of adopted me as soon as we met." He gave a fond smile at the memory. "We became very close. I moved to Bath because that's where she lived. Until I came here, Modesty was the closest thing to family I...well, experienced. Which is ridiculous to say now, considering I'm completely surrounded by family."

"How dreadful that you were alone for so long."

He gave a self-deprecating shrug. "I was somewhat accustomed to it, I'm afraid. Although I don't think I shall have to worry about that ever again," he added with a grin.

"No, I think not. If you intend to stay here until Lucy is married, you have quite a long time ahead of you."

He smiled. "Yes. It is quite wonderful to think of, isn't it?"

She returned his smile. "Indeed it is."

"And what of your childhood?"

"Oh," she said. "Well, it was very different from yours."

"I'm glad to hear it. Do tell me about it."

So she told him about growing up with three brothers, about going to school, about her parents. She felt embarrassed to regale him with stories of a childhood so different from his own, but he seemed to hang on every word, asking questions about her family, learning the name of the dog she had growing up, her favorite tree to climb in Sherton, the lake she and Gavin used to swim in. He was so invested in what she had to say that it was easy to forget they were in the middle of a dinner party.

Chapter 57
Basil

Basil felt as though the dinner party was some sort of dream. He had been able to ask Miss Hartford about her family and her childhood. But it wasn't enough. He wanted to know more. He wanted to know everything. He wished his own story had been less pathetic. As satisfying as it had been to see her look at him with such sympathy, he would have preferred to give her amusing anecdotes or tidbits about an idyllic childhood, much as she had with him. He would have preferred to see her laugh. Nevertheless, it felt good to have told her so much, to admit that there was so little to his past. He was accustomed to thinking of himself as rather boring, so he was glad to have the boring part over and done with. Perhaps that was why he enjoyed talking about his siblings so much; they were anything but boring.

As they moved into the drawing room, Basil noticed a similar level of attention was made to the seating arrangements as there had been at dinner. He and Miss

Hartford were seated together on a sofa toward the back of the room with Mr. Gavin Kentworthy on one side of them and his husband sitting on the arm of the sofa. The Ladies Windham were in chairs closest to Basil and he found himself, once again, left to talk to Miss Hartford without any distractions.

"I'm afraid I talked too much about myself," she admitted.

"Not at all," he assured her. "I'm sure you didn't talk enough for there is still much I want to know."

She smiled. "That's very kind of you. But I really shouldn't. Can't you tell me about your time in Bath?"

He shrugged. "There isn't much to tell." Feeling bold, he leaned closer to her and said, "The horrid truth is that I'm dreadfully boring. My siblings are a hundred times more interesting than I am."

She laughed. "I disagree with you on the first point. But do tell me more about your siblings."

He was delighted and launched into descriptions about what Levinia had been painting, a song Grace was learning to play, the twins' latest nautical plans, and even some of his concerns about Sophia. "She's practically an adult. I find myself completely unprepared for how to give her what she needs at this stage."

"It is a difficult age," she agreed.

He was about to go on when there were calls from other guests for Miss Hartford to play the piano.

"Oh dear," she murmured. "There's an end to our conversation."

"It's a pity," he agreed. "But I would love to hear you play."

She gave him one of her twinkling smiles. "Well, in that case..." She stood up and strode to the piano and played three songs at her friends' encouragement.

Basil was transfixed watching her. He felt that he could watch her play for hours. How on earth was she so talented at so many things? He allowed himself to imagine what it would be like to have her in the house, playing the piano in the evenings, perhaps helping Grace or Elias with their practice.

After she was done, Mr. Hartford, of all people, suggested that Laurence play.

Laurence did and Basil felt the absurd pride one feels when a friend does something well. Laurence played a few songs, as Miss Hartford did. Then Lady Maria Windham sang while Miss Hartford accompanied her, and Mr. Algernon Ayles sang while his son accompanied him.

It was late into the evening when Basil finally returned home. As tired as he was, he couldn't help but wish the evening had gone on longer, if only so he could have stolen a few more words with Miss Hartford or watched her play a few more songs.

Chapter 58
Charles

Charles spent nearly a week riding the pleasure of a job well done. The dinner party had been an immense success. Gerry and Mr. Thorne had spent the entire evening talking only to each other, and had seemed even closer by the evening's end. John had spent nearly the whole event away from his wife and had been markedly more at ease because of it.

So Charles was inclined to think everything was going remarkably well. One afternoon, he strode into his study and then stopped short, quickly reassessing his previous satisfaction: Julian, the Dukex of Molbury, was sitting in a chair in front of Charles's desk, looking regal and imperious as ever. They turned to Charles, arched an eyebrow, and then held out their hand.

"Do pick up your jaw from the floor, child."

Charles closed the door, stepped swiftly across the room and kissed Julian's knuckles. "Forgive me, Your Grace. I did not expect you."

"So I gathered," Julian said with a smirk. "However, I have much to discuss. Kindly ring for tea."

Charles did as he was told, refraining from the urge to roll his eyes at being bossed about in his own home. He was pleased to see Julian, though.

He sat down behind his desk. "I hope you'll forgive me for observing that my last letter did not ask you to come just yet."

"No, it did not. I am not here at your request, as it happens. I am here at Bertram's."

Charles's eyebrows rose in surprise. "Indeed?"

"Yes," Julian said, picking invisible dust from their coat sleeve. "He was concerned about your visitors. I understand he met them recently. He seemed to think reinforcements might be appreciated."

Charles did roll his eyes at that. "Very considerate of him, but I think I have it well in hand."

"I'm surprised you are allowing such unpleasant people to stay under your roof."

Charles took a deep breath. "She is, unfortunately, a required addition. He is...learning."

A maid came in and Charles instructed her to bring in a tea trolley.

"And do see if Mrs. Barlow has any of her delicious lemon cake," Julian said with a smile. "I have very much missed it."

The maid glanced at Charles and he nodded his approval. After she left, he turned back to his guest. "So you came to keep us all safe from Mrs. Hartford's vitriol?"

"I thought I might lend my aid," Julian said primly.

"But that was not the only reason. I have been eager to come stay since your letter in February."

"We have the matter well in hand," Charles said. "I had not planned to send for you until the ball, or possibly after," he admitted.

Julian folded their hands in their lap and waited.

Charles sighed. "Everything seems to be going very well. Gerry and Mr. Thorne have met several times—and most of their meetings have not even been arranged by others. I gather Mr. Thorne goes to see Gerry in her shop often."

"That sounds promising."

"Yes, and Gerry's friends have been orchestrating teatime visits to introduce her to various suitors. They're all quite unsuitable, of course, but I think they're leading up to Mr. Thorne eventually."

"Very painful plan from Geraldine's point of view, I should think."

Charles tilted his head in acknowledgement.

"What else?"

"Laury—that is, Mr. Laurence Ayles—you remember, Seb's fiancé?"

Julian nodded.

"He has befriended Mr. Thorne and has been working to encourage him in the right direction. Bertie invited us all to tea just this month. The Thorne children are, I think, working to unite the couple. So I rather think things are going quite well." Charles was annoyed by how defensive he sounded.

Julian gave a small smile. "It seems as though you've all been very busy."

"He's perfect for her, Julian. I wouldn't push nearly so hard for this except I'm quite sure Gerry likes him a great deal; she blushes every time his name is mentioned. She joined his family for lunch once—Pip was there too, and Mrs. Thorne was able to act as chaperone —and one has only to talk to her to know she is in love. Not to mention, we hosted a dinner party last week and you'd think they were the only two in the room with how much they talked to each other."

"But?"

Charles sighed again and leaned back in his seat. "But Gerry is being stubborn and I don't know why. She keeps saying she wants to find romance naturally and doesn't want it forced upon her. She cites Gavin meeting me or Seb meeting Laury, despite the fact that both of those instances were very orchestrated. I feel sure that the only thing for it is to keep trying as we have been."

The maid reentered the room with the tea trolley. Charles stood and took the seat next to Julian. Charles poured for both of them and cut Julian a generous slice of lemon cake.

Julian didn't speak until after the maid had left, and even then they sat silently for a long moment, stirring their tea and looking thoughtful. "I take it the young man is equally interested in Geraldine, if shop visits and luncheon invitations, not to mention dinner parties, are anything to go by?"

"From what Laury says, Mr. Thorne is quite smitten."

Julian carefully set their spoon on the saucer and took a sip of tea. "So, your primary difficulty is in getting Geraldine to fall in love despite her insistence that she couldn't possibly fall in love under contrived circumstances?"

Charles was irritated at how absurd it sounded when phrased like that. He took a sip of tea.

Julian smiled knowingly and gave Charles's leg a pat. "Don't take on so, poppet. You've done marvelously well by her, by all of them. I give you a great deal of credit for creating such a safe and pleasant environment for Geraldine that she feels comfortable in eschewing marriage until she is absolutely ready. That is no small thing."

Charles took another sip of tea, mollified. "Thank you. I just don't understand why she doesn't trust me. I would never push her to marry someone who wasn't suitable for her."

"She's strong-minded."

"As am I."

They gave him a long look. "Why are you in such a rush?"

"She's lonely. Practically everyone around her is happily matched up."

"Not officially."

"All the same. If she were of a less romantic temperament, then I wouldn't worry so much. She deserves someone who will take care of her and who will sweep her off her feet."

"By the sounds of it, she's waiting for that to happen. You can't orchestrate foot sweepage."

"I think they would make each other happy. I'm impatient for them to start doing so."

They took another sip of tea. "How often do I need to

remind you, child, that it is not your responsibility to see personally to everyone's happiness?"

Charles was silent for a long moment. The urge to fix things had always felt instinctual; it was as much a part of him as the color of his eyes. He was pretty sure he was sitting next to the reason this urge burned so strongly. Julian had helped Charles more times than he could count. Was it so wrong that he wanted to do the same for those he loved? Was it so wrong to do everything in his power to build and repair the family he'd found? He shared such happiness with Gavin, he merely wanted everyone he cared for to have the same.

Charles thought of how it physically pained him to see John so miserable, how Seb's restlessness made him itch to give him peace. He thought of Gavin and how every frown, every bit of tension his husband experienced felt like a wrinkle he needed to carefully smooth out. He thought of Bertie and Pip and worried their mutual inaction was keeping them both from healing past pain. These things weighed on him.

Finally, he said, "I don't know how to change that part of who I am."

Julian set aside their cup and cupped his cheek. "Sweet child. Not everyone's burden is yours to bear."

"What if I want it to be?"

Julian sighed and rubbed his cheek with their thumb. "Sometimes I fear I did you a disservice in raising you the way I did."

Charles shook his head. "You don't really mean that. Look at you: you came all the way from London because you were worried I had unpleasant guests."

"But when will you rest, Charles, and simply enjoy life?"

Charles gave them a wry look. "You tell me."

Julian rolled their eyes, leaned back in their seat, and picked up their teacup. "I suppose I should take some comfort that your social circle is so reduced these days. You're rapidly running out of people to fix."

"Oh, I don't know," Charles said. "After Gerry, I need to see to Bertie and Pip. And once you meet John, I'm sure you'll understand why he's on my list."

"I've met him. There's precious little you can do for him at this juncture, I'm afraid."

"I disagree. He needs a friend."

Julian took a sip of tea. "He needs a great many things, actually. But you're not wrong. You said he's learning?"

"Yes. I told him if he was unkind to Seb I would ask him to leave. And offered some advice on how to talk to Seb. The conversations are very stilted, but he is trying."

"I see." They gave him an assessing look. "You've always had a knack for absorbing the lessons that suited you and disregarding the ones you didn't care for. Can you possibly imagine which one I might be alluding to?"

Charles had a very good idea what Julian was hinting at, but he said, "Oh, I don't know. Never whistle around others? Limit yourself to one waltz at any given assembly? Avoid public displays of affection?"

"Impertinent child. You just told me you had no idea how to convince Geraldine to your way of thinking."

Charles heaved a sigh. "Oh, very well. I suppose I do

need your help after all. Will you help me sort Gerry out?"

Julian gave him a wide grin. "I thought you'd never ask. Has she left for the shop yet?"

"Yes. I don't expect her to be back until dinnertime."

Julian nodded. "Good. That will give me time to call on Mr. Thorne. Be so good as to accompany me. I shall need introduction."

Charles stood. "I would have thought you needed no introduction."

Julian arched an eyebrow. "Sit down and finish your tea. I haven't had time to eat my cake. Now that we've talked through the matter at hand, I wish to know everything else. How are you? How is Gavin? How are Sebastian and his sweet beau? And tell me more about the couple visiting you."

Chapter 59
Basil

Basil had gone out for a ride. He was not yet confident enough in his latest spell to revisit Miss Hartford's shop, and he did not feel comfortable calling on anyone for tea, besides Laurence. So he had simply ridden around the estate and the surrounding area, wishing he had a destination. He had never enjoyed aimless wandering, so when he returned home, he was feeling more unsettled than when he'd left. When Mary approached him in the hall looking flustered and announcing quietly that the Dukex of Molbury had come to call on him, it only added to his unease.

He thanked her, handed his outerwear to a servant, and went into the sitting room. He was relieved to see Mr. Charles Kentworthy sitting with the dukex, who turned out to be an older person in their sixties, short and round, with a handsome and pleasant face.

"Ah, Mr. Thorne," Mr. Kentworthy said. "Please allow me to present the Dukex of Molbury. Your Grace, this is Mr. Thorne."

Basil knew little of the aristocrat, other than their connection to the royal family, but that knowledge was a good start. He bowed. The dukex held out a hand and Basil kissed their knuckles.

"It is a pleasure to meet you," the dukex said.

"I am honored by your visit, Your Grace," Basil replied.

The dukex seemed pleased by this response. They gave him a small nod. Then they turned to Mr. Kentworthy and said, "Thank you, Charles. Be so good as to absent yourself for a while."

Mr. Kentworthy sighed, but bowed and said, "Of course, Your Grace." He gave Basil a bow as well and left the room.

"Shall I ring for tea, Your Grace?" Basil said.

"Thank you, Mr. Thorne. Very kind of you."

Basil was relieved to have something to do, although ringing the bell pull did not take very long, and then standing around waiting for the maid to come in made him feel awkward. The dukex did not say anything as they waited. After the maid came in and was sent to bring in some tea, Basil cautiously took a seat.

The dukex gave him a small smile. "I have been wanting to meet you for some time, Mr. Thorne."

Basil wasn't sure if this was a compliment or not. "Did you know my father, Your Grace?"

"We met a few times. I lived in Tutting-on-Cress for about six months and we became somewhat acquainted. Your father did speak of you, but I was not really referring to his description of you."

"Oh," Basil said.

"Charles and Bertram write to me quite frequently,"

they explained. "They had both described meeting you, and Charles, in particular, was eloquent in explaining how you came to stay here."

"Oh," Basil said again. He tried to think of something to say in response. Finally, he decided on, "And how long are you staying in Tutting-on-Cress, Your Grace?"

"About a month or two, most likely. I believe Bertram intends to hold a ball soon, and I should like to be here for that."

Basil nodded. "You are staying with Lord Finlington then?"

"Yes. He is my cousin."

"And you came for the ball?"

The dukex smiled. "Not precisely. I came to see to some matters that are of great importance to me. The ball is a convenient entertainment."

"The viscount recently offered to go with me to call on some of my neighbors. Perhaps you would like to join us as well?"

Their smile widened. "Thank you, young man. I would be delighted."

"I'll be honored by your company," Basil said. It felt like a silly, but necessary thing to say. He was relieved the maid returned at that juncture so he didn't spend too much time worrying that it had been more silly than necessary.

The dukex accepted their cup of tea, sat back in their seat, and said, "Now, please tell me about yourself, Mr. Thorne."

Basil was taken aback. Was it normal to walk into a stranger's house and request an account of themself? He considered for a moment, wondering what on earth had put him in the dukex's purview. As he wondered about this, it occurred to him that it hardly mattered why he garnered the attention of such an illustrious personage. The fact was he had, so he might as well make the most of it.

"I am two and thirty, Your Grace. I moved to Tutting-on-Cress at the end of December to take over the estate and help take responsibility for my siblings after our father's death."

"As I understand it, you are more than helping to take responsibility for them."

"Well, I suppose I'm their legal guardian now. I am in charge of their dowries and so forth."

"Was it part of your father's will that they be under your protection?"

Basil frowned in confusion. "No. I mean, he did ask me to take care of them. We spoke before he died and he asked that I see to their comfort and safety and so forth."

"An understandable concern on your father's part," the dukex said. "Many firstborns would not be so generous to half-siblings."

Now Basil's frown was one of irritation. "I hope you will forgive me for saying so, Your Grace, but I do not understand why so many people are surprised by my choice. I will confess that I never planned to play such an active part in their daily lives, but I would never have sent them away, even without my father's request."

"But surely you will agree that it was an unusual choice to make."

"No, I will not agree," Basil said. "I apologize for my curtness, Your Grace, but if it is unusual to take care of those related to you, even through only one parent, and when they are vulnerable and powerless, then I would argue that society should alter what it considers usual behavior. It should not be exceptional that I took it upon myself to see that a widow and her seven young children were not left to fend for themselves with a meager living. If the law cannot be better designed to protect nextborns, then it is our duty as firstborns to make up for the law's deficit."

Far from being offended by his argumentative tone, the dukex grinned in response. "Well, I can see my expectations of you were well-founded. I am very glad to know you, Mr. Thorne."

"Thank you," Basil said. Now that his irritation had abated, he was a little embarrassed. He was thankful the dukex considered what he'd said a good response rather than a poor one. "Was there anything else you wished to know?"

"Oh, I wish to know a great deal," they said. "I would like to know if you plan to settle here, whether you like the area, who you have met here in town, and whether you intend to marry."

Basil was surprised enough by the list of questions to laugh. "Very well," he said. "In order: I plan to stay. I hadn't when I arrived, but I'm finding I like the company of my family and wish to stay close. As the youngest is only two, it will be some time before they're all grown and ready to settle into their own homes, so I expect I'm here somewhat permanently. I like the area, although I'm still learning it. I have met several people: Miss Hartford, Mr. Standish, the Kentworthys, the Ayleses, Lord Finlington, Mr. Sebastian Hartford, the Hearsts, the Ladies Windham, the Canterburys, and Mr. Applebough. Oh, and I suppose I should count Mr. and Mrs. Hartford, although I understand they are only guests of the Kentworthys." He paused, trying to remember if he'd left anyone out. "As for marriage, yes, I do intend to marry. But I'm not at all sure if it is the right time."

"Why not?"

Basil shrugged. "I only recently moved here. I'm still getting to know my family. I'm trying to understand property management—it's rather difficult, you see, as I never had the opportunity to learn it from my father. Now that he's gone I've had to learn it all very quickly."

"Well, that is easily remedied. I will be happy to teach you while I am here. And both Charles and Bertram are very knowledgeable." They considered for a moment. "I think I would recommend Charles for you, however. Your estate seems to be of an equitable size to his."

"Thank you," Basil said, a little floored by the offer. "Laurence—that is, Mr. Laurence Ayles said something similar about Mr. Charles Kentworthy being a good resource. I confess I haven't taken his suggestion as I don't know the gentleman well enough to solicit his advice."

"Believe me, Charles would be delighted if you asked for his help. And my offer to assist is genuine. I've handled my own property and helped Bertram's mother to manage hers when her husband died. So I know what it is like to step into someone else's organizational system and try to sort it out."

"Thank you," Basil said again. "I may take you up on that offer. I should tell you that I am unaccustomed to being surrounded by so many friends and family, so I am out of practice when it comes to asking for help."

"It is a skill that can be honed, child. I would hazard a guess that you've had a lot of practice in the recent months. If you are nervous to write out the actual words, simply send a note to me at Bertram's house and invite me to tea. That will suffice."

Basil let out a long breath. "I am deeply grateful, Your Grace."

"It is my pleasure. Now, about marriage. Once we have your property concerns sorted out, do you have any other concerns keeping you single?"

"No," Basil said, chuckling. "Other than the ones I've already mentioned."

"Ah yes, you think you should wait until you are better settled."

"Yes."

"I've always been a firm believer in marriage being an expedient to that particular problem."

"My stepmother seems to be of the same mind."

"Good. So do you have any prospects in town?"

Basil wanted to laugh again at their directness. "I have met a few single people, yes."

"That was not exactly what I asked."

"You wish to know if there is anyone I have met who I would consider marrying?"

"Yes."

Basil hesitated. If the dukex was so well acquainted with Mr. Charles Kentworthy, it stood to reason they were well acquainted with Miss Hartford too. He wasn't at all sure he wanted his interest in the lady known.

The dukex smiled at his hesitation. "Ah, good. So there *is* a person in mind."

Basil huffed out a laugh. "Yes, but I hesitate to confide the name."

"Why?"

"I hardly know you."

"I am a matchmaker, child, not a gossip."

Basil grinned. "Very well. In that case, I suppose I can tell you I very much enjoy the company of Miss Hartford."

The dukex smiled again, more broadly. "Delightful. Yes, I think you two would suit very well."

"My stepmother said something similar."

"I assume you would not object to her continuing in her work."

"That, Your Grace, might be assuming the lady returns my interest. But, for the sake of discussion, no, of course I would not object."

"Excellent. I'm glad to hear it. Now, since you are clearly uncomfortable with that topic, I shall take pity on you. Tell me about your siblings."

Basil settled into his seat, coming to the conclusion that he liked the dukex exceedingly despite how intimidating they were. He proceeded to describe each of his siblings in exhaustive detail and was absurdly grateful that the dukex asked questions and seemed genuinely curious about them. He found himself saddened that they did not live locally and were only staying for a short visit.

Finally, the dukex stood. "Well, I have enjoyed myself very much. Thank you, Mr. Thorne, for indulging my curious spirit. I shall see what can be done about your marriage prospects and I shall be on the lookout for invitations for tea. When do you and Bertram plan to make social calls?"

"I don't think we've made any concrete plans."

"Well, I shall remedy that. I look forward to the outing," they said, giving Basil's cheek a pat as if he were a child. "Let's see what Charles is up to, shall we?"

Mr. Kentworthy, as it turned out, was deeply engrossed in a discussion with the twins over the best way to defend against a pirate attack.

The dukex stood in the doorway, looking fond.

Chapter 60
Gerry

Gerry put up her apron in the backroom. As soon as Laurence had gone back to London, Bertie started Seb's work as his assistant again, so Gerry only saw Seb in the shop a few days a week. She intended to write Bertie about splitting up her brother's week, but hadn't gotten around to it yet.

A knock came at the shop door and Pip touched Gerry's shoulder. "I'll get it."

Assuming it was a customer who had missed business hours, Gerry proceeded to put on her coat, hat, and gloves. She was surprised when she heard several voices in the shop—Pip knew better than to let in customers after the shop was closed. She poked her head out the curtain and was shocked to see the Dukex of Molbury and Charles.

"You're looking very well," they said, cupping Pip's cheek. "I quite like this suit on you."

"Your Grace!" she said.

They looked up and smiled at her. "How are you, poppet?" they said.

She ran up and gave them a hug. "When did you arrive? And how long are you staying?"

They kissed her cheek. "I just arrived last night and I'm not yet sure how long I will be staying. At least until Bertram's ball, that's certain."

She gave them a wary look. "Are you part of the scheme as well?"

"What scheme is that, child?"

She narrowed her eyes and glared at Charles. "Are they?"

Charles attempted to look innocent. "Now, darling, you know perfectly well that I have no sway over Julian—"

"That's not an answer."

"Well, don't argue about it, child. Charles and Pip will take the carriage to pick up Bertram and you shall accompany me to your home. I would like to talk to you."

She knew better than to protest. They filed out of the shop, she locked the door, and took the dukex's offered arm.

"You're looking very well," they said. "Charles and Bertram both tell me the shop is doing very good business."

"Thank you," she said. "I am doing well. Is there...a particular reason for your visit, Your Grace?"

They chuckled. "There are several reasons for my visit, and you are correct about one of them."

She groaned. "Why is everyone so bent on seeing me married all of a sudden?"

"Probably because a rather perfect man practically dropped from the sky."

"Just because he's perfect doesn't mean he's perfect for me."

"Very true."

She gave them a suspicious look. "You agree?"

"I agree with that statement in general, although I am inclined to approve of Charles's assessment of the young man's suitability."

"You met him?"

"We had a very pleasant chat this afternoon. Do you really dislike him?"

"No, not at all. I like him very well, actually."

"Then why, may I ask, are you so resistant to these matchmaking efforts?"

"Because it isn't very romantic!"

They walked in silence for a moment before saying, "Kindly explain to me what you think romance looks like, Geraldine."

"Romance should be...it should feel powerful, overwhelming. It should feel certain."

"And you don't feel these things with Mr. Thorne?"

"No."

"Then what do you feel?"

She sighed. "I like him. I like his company. I think he's very kind and intelligent and he's enjoyable to be around. I miss him when I haven't seen him and look forward to spending more time with him. I'm sure you're aware that he's very attractive."

"But?"

"But...I don't know. I don't feel the urge to be with him every day. I don't need him to write me sonnets or give me flowers or...or anything like that. I always thought that's how it would feel. I thought it would be overpowering, so I'm sure it isn't love."

"Do you remember Bertram's protégée, Miss Nell Birks?"

"Yes, of course," Gerry said, surprised by the change in topic.

"I seem to recall her mentioning that she didn't want romance, that she never felt the sentimental pull that others did."

"Yes, I remember that," Gerry said, frowning. "But I'm not like Nell. I want that. I just don't feel it in this instance."

"People are rarely made up of extremes," they said. "They tend to be a blend of complexities and contradictions."

She looked up at them questioningly.

They patted her hand. "In other words, is it possible that you don't feel romantic toward the gentleman because that isn't a feeling that comes frequently to you? You are six and twenty and have met a wide variety of people. Have you ever felt yourself to be in love with anyone?"

"Well...no. But that doesn't mean I'm not interested in love and romance, like Nell."

"No, it doesn't. But it is possible that you're similar to her, in a way. Perhaps somewhere in the middle between Miss Birks and, say, Charles or Bertram?"

She considered the question. "Charles says that he fell in love with Gavin as soon as he saw him."

"Precisely. Now, he does tend to be a bit dramatic, of course, but even if he fell in love within his first conversation with your brother, that doesn't mean everyone experiences that. Your brother certainly didn't."

"No, he didn't," she murmured.

"Just think about it," they said. "And consider the possibility that you are waiting for a feeling that might not actually come to you."

"Oh," she said. "Where do you fall...in the range between Nell and Charles? If you don't mind my asking?"

They chuckled. "Oh, somewhere around the area that you're in, I suspect. I think Gavin is as well, actually."

"You were married once," she said. "How did you know that your spouse was right for you?"

They paused mid-step for a moment. "Well, in point of fact, I was mistaken in my late husband's character. But that's a danger that can befall anyone, regardless of whether or not they fall in love. Actually, I rather think those who tend to fall in love more frequently might be in more danger of that sort of thing. And I don't think that will be a problem for you, at any rate. At least not with Mr. Thorne."

"No, I think you're right," she said. "His siblings very clearly adore him and I don't think they would if he was a bad sort." She sighed. "I've waited my entire life to fall in love. Do you really mean to say I won't?"

"That isn't quite what I said," they replied. "But I think you might be expecting the sensation of falling in love to feel a certain way and to come immediately, and I'm not sure that will be the case for you. But don't fret about it, poppet. Just examine your thoughts and your feelings the next time you're around the gentleman. I would urge you not to wait for it, but to look at the matter more practically: does being in the gentleman's company make you happy? Does he make you feel safe? Does he make you feel valued? You see what I mean?"

She nodded. "Did you say there are several reasons for your visit?"

They smiled. "Well, I always like to see all of you, of course. I've been meaning to talk to Bertram. I was concerned about Charles playing host to your sister-in-law. Although I'm pleased to learn that Charles seems to be handling your oldest brother quite well. I'm attending Bertram's ball."

"And you wanted to see me get engaged to Mr. Thorne?"

They laughed. "It would be the highlight of my trip, my dear."

Chapter 61
Basil

Basil was unsurprised to receive a message from Lord Finlington the day after the dukex's visit, suggesting a day and time for them to start making calls. He immediately responded with a confirmation to the plan.

They arrived in a carriage to collect him and he dutifully climbed in, feeling strangely nervous.

"How are you, m'dear?" Lord Finlington said. "You look very well, if you don't mind my saying so."

"Thank you, my lord," Basil said. "It is good to see you, and you, Your Grace."

The dukex nodded in acknowledgement. "That color suits you, child."

"Who are we visiting first?" Basil said.

"Well," Lord Finlington said, "my cousin wishes to call on the Ladies Windham and Lord Antony Caldwell."

"Order of precedence," they explained.

"I can't imagine our visit to the Windhams will take very long," Lord Finlington said with a smile. "And I hardly know Lord Antony."

The dukex sighed. "You've been here for two years, child," they muttered.

Lord Finlington chuckled. "I know. In my defense, I did not anticipate settling here."

Basil was surprised. "What changed your mind, if you don't mind my asking?"

"Of course I don't mind you asking, my sweet. To put it simply: I decided to stay because those I love most were living nearby."

"The Kentworthys?"

"Yes, and others. Quite similar to your situation, I think," he said in a light tone. "Which is why it seemed such a perfect opportunity to join forces in such a way."

Basil had a feeling the viscount had intentionally deviated from the subject, so he smiled and said, "I'm sure Mrs. Hartford will be pleased that we now have a chaperone for our adventure."

Lord Finlington threw back his head and laughed.

"I'm surprised she expressed concern," the dukex said.

"Oh, she was most insistent that it would give the wrong impression," Lord Finlington said. "Quite frankly, I think if the gossip does abound, it would be no bad thing. I rather like being speculated about."

"Particularly if it's wrong, I assume," Basil said.

The viscount's smile was wide. "Precisely, darling."

As Lord Finlington predicted, the Ladies Windham did not visit with them for long, although both of the ladies were strangely curious about whether or not Basil wanted to have children of his own. He wondered aloud about the topic when they returned to the carriage.

"If I were to guess," Lord Finlington said, his attention focused on adjusting his cuffs, "I'd say they were gleaning the information for matchmaking purposes."

Basil thought back to the visit from the Hearsts. "Ah," he said. "I see."

Lord Antony Caldwell chatted with them for longer. He turned out to be a foppish sort of fellow who spent most of the visit admiring the viscount's cravat and the dukex's waistcoat. He had very little to say to Basil. Basil suspected it was because his own style of dress was rather plain, regardless of how well the color supposedly looked on him.

After visiting Lord Caldwell, the viscount asked if they minded stopping by the village. "I need some supplies from the bookshop and Gerry's shop," he explained.

Basil was eager to see Miss Hartford again, as he hadn't seen her since the dinner party, and he readily agreed.

Lord Finlington stopped at the spell shop first and Basil was gifted with the sight of seeing Miss Hartford's face light up when they entered. "I'm just here to buy some supplies, m'dear," Lord Finlington told her. "I'll avail myself of Pip's assistance."

"How were your social calls?" she asked Basil.

"They were interesting."

She smiled. "Who did you go see?"

"The Ladies Windham and Lord Antony Caldwell."

"I don't know Lord Caldwell very well, but the Ladies Windham are two of my closest friends."

"They seemed very nice," he said. "But our visit with them did not last particularly long."

She looked amused. "I'm afraid that doesn't surprise me, but I hope you didn't take it personally."

"Well, I will now," he said.

She laughed.

He watched her for a moment, delighted by the accomplishment, then said, "Are visits with them always so short?"

"They are if there are no ladies present," she said.

"Ah, I see. Well, then I suppose I shall have to bring you with me next time if I want a longer interview."

She laughed again. "You see? You're already learning the neighborhood."

"I'm practically a local."

She beamed. "And what did you think of Lord Caldwell?"

"He had little interest in me either, I'm afraid. My clothes were not quite fancy enough to suit him, I think." He hesitated and then leaned forward. "Are you sure you want to befriend a man with such boring clothes?"

"Oh, I don't think they're boring," she protested. "The color suits you."

Which was when that coat became Basil's favorite. "You're the second person to tell me that today. Perhaps I ought to change over my entire wardrobe to match."

She smiled at him again and Basil thought he might expire from giddiness. "Who do you intend to call on next?"

"I'm not sure," he admitted. "Lord Finlington said he

needed to buy some supplies in the village. I'm rather at his and the dukex's disposal."

"You're in good hands," she said. "They're two of the best people I know."

"I'm glad to hear it."

She seemed to shake herself mentally. "I should probably get back to my customers. Unless, of course, you wished to buy a spell?"

He fancied she sounded hopeful, so he told her he had been planning to buy a spell and asked for advice on which one to get. They went through their usual routine of her teaching him a spell. He found he had missed it. When he finally let her return to her work, he saw the dukex standing patiently by the door.

"I do apologize if I kept you waiting," he said, hurrying over to them.

"Not at all, poppet," they said. "I would not have broken up that conversation for the world. Bertram already went to the other shop. Shall we join him?"

Basil nodded, embarrassed.

"It might comfort you to know," they said as they walked down the street, "that if you hadn't disclosed your interest to Geraldine before, I would have most certainly determined it for myself."

"Er..." Basil said. "I'm not entirely sure that is a comfort, Your Grace. Am I so very obvious?"

They chuckled. "You looked as if you wanted to bottle up her laughter and keep it for a rainy day."

"That's...remarkably accurate, Your Grace."

They smiled. "I know."

Chapter 62
Gerry

Gerry did not know what her friends had been thinking in suggesting Lord Antony Caldwell as a suitor. She had barely spoken a dozen words to him in the two years she'd lived in Tutting-on-Cress. They had nothing in common. The man was completely obsessed with his own appearance. He kept absently touching his cravat, as if afraid a deep breath would affect the fall of the fabric. He didn't have a word to say to Gerry. In fact, he barely noticed she was sitting next to him.

She was almost glad John and Veronica had decided to join them yet again. Lord Caldwell spoke very precisely and haughtily and Veronica seemed to think he was very fine indeed. Gerry was amused to note that John looked at the gentleman with some distaste.

After Lord Caldwell finally left, Julia turned to Gerry and said, "Well?"

Gerry rolled her eyes. "I'm not sure he realized I was in the room. He was dreadful. Is that really the best you can do?"

"Nonsense," Veronica snapped. "He just has good taste." She patted her hair. "Although I can't say I'm surprised he didn't talk to you, Geraldine. You may be beneath his notice with your career. Perhaps if you offered to give it up, he would consider you as a wife."

"Well, in that case," Gerry said, "I'll do no such thing. I have no intention of being his wife."

"But you would be a lady!"

"I hate to disagree with you, Veronica," John said slowly. "But I'm not sure he is suitable for my sister."

Veronica glared at him.

"There is nothing wrong with taking care of one's appearance," he added hastily. "But I fear the gentleman may be a bit too vain."

"You just don't understand the titled," his wife said.

"I have the same title," Caro said, "and I'm inclined to agree with your husband."

Lizzy giggled.

"Perish the thought," Rose murmured.

Maria elbowed her, stifling a giggle as well.

Gerry slumped back on the sofa. "How many more of these must I put up with, ladies?"

"Just two, dear," Julia said. "Although if you do find a gentleman without our help, you can be sure these visits will cease."

Gerry almost said she had but then thought better of it. "Well," she said, "if you will excuse me, I have a spell I've been working on and I'd like to get back to it."

"Geraldine!" Veronica hissed. "Don't you dare leave your guests alone in this manner!"

Maria laughed. "Don't worry about it, Mrs. Hartford. I rather think we deserve it."

Julia smiled and stood. "Exactly so. Besides, we're all dear friends. There's no need to stand on ceremony with us."

They all stood, said their goodbyes, and left.

Back in her room, Gerry sank onto her bed. The visit definitely ranked as one of her least favorites. After all, Mr. Thorne had little in common with her either, yet they never seemed to run out of conversation.

She lay across the bed, letting her feet kick idly, and tried to think of why conversations with Mr. Thorne were so pleasant. He always seemed willing to talk about magic, despite knowing little about the subject. And he enjoyed talking about his siblings. Quite frankly, she enjoyed listening to him talk about his siblings. He looked so fond and happy when he did. She wondered if that was how she looked when she talked about magic.

She sighed and sat up, deciding she might as well work on the spell since that had been her excuse in leaving. She pulled out the case of supplies she kept under the bed, rolled up the rug, and began laying out ingredients.

Seb had already done a great deal of work in helping her determine the right spells to build from. Next up was her second-favorite part: running tests. She wasn't ready to cast the spell yet and the nature of the spell being what it was, she couldn't even do partial casting of some of the ingredients to see how they'd react with the sigils. But she did need to see how certain ingredients interacted with certain spells to verify if they would do anything dangerous or underwhelming.

She drew a chalk circle on the floor and laid a piece of glass in the center. She had collected broken fragments from a bottle that had fallen for just such an occasion. Then she chalked out a sigil and cast a spell. The glass sparkled. That was a good sign. She took it out of the circle and rubbed away the sigil.

She did it again with some nutmeg, which exploded. Not quite what she wanted. Thankfully, it stayed within the confines of the circle. She cleaned it up, replaced the nutmeg with more, and tried another sigil. This time it turned to mush. Blast. She cleaned it up again and cast a different spell. This time, the nutmeg spun in a circle. Much better. She tried with an adjustment to the sigil. It flew in an arc and landed back in place. Perfect.

She made a note in her notebook about the glass and the nutmeg. Then she moved on to a piece of granite. This one took three sigils to get the reaction she was hoping for. She made another note. She tested some dried petals from the Eye of Robin Goodfellow flower next, then a bit of twine, and then a piece of gauze. She made notes, crossing out ingredients that wouldn't work and testing different ingredients in their place.

She was so engrossed in her project that she didn't realize there was a knock on her door until her maid was in the room. She cleaned up her work while her maid set out a dress for dinner. Gerry didn't usually change for dinner when she was eating at home, despite Veronica's criticisms to how she ought to do it anyway. But after lying on the bed and then experimenting with spells on the floor, it was worth changing clothes.

Veronica gave her another lecture on leaving the room when she had visitors and Gerry blithely ignored her, her head still filled with experimentations and occasional thoughts about what sorts of questions Mr. Thorne might ask if she described her process to him. She daydreamed answers to imaginary questions, basking in imagined compliments.

3 May 1818

Dear Nell,

Thank you very much for passing on Harriet's message. Please assure them I will be happy to send more of the same spell whenever they have need of it.

I find myself in need of some advice. How did you know you didn't want romance? And when? You see, I keep waiting to fall in love and I have met someone who is exactly the sort of person I'd expect to fall in love with. Only it hasn't happened and I'm not sure what to do. I cannot determine if I will never fall in love with him or if I have been misunderstanding what love will feel like. I blame Gavin for all of his poetry readings. I know you are not married to Patience, but you two seem very happy together.

Julian—that is, the dukex—says I might not be the sort of person who falls in love easily. They suggested I might be more along the lines of what you experience, only somewhat more romantic in nature. I don't understand it, quite frankly, and I don't understand why things should be so very complicated. But I also know that I've never fallen in love. When I was in London for both of my Seasons, I met a great many handsome, kind, intelligent, and dashing gentlemen. Some of whom were definitely interested in forming an attachment, but it never felt right. This friendship with Mr. Thorne feels more right than any of those acquaintances did but...I always expected more.

At any rate, I will be very grateful for any advice you have to offer on the matter.

Please give my regards to everyone in London.

Affectionately,

Gerry

Chapter 63
Basil

Basil had worried it would be awkward to have Mr. Charles Kentworthy over, but he quickly learned that Mr. Kentworthy, like so many of Basil's new acquaintances, had a way of taking charge in a conversation. Considering the gentleman had married a shy and reserved person, Basil reasoned this was not altogether surprising. He observed in past conversations that Mr. Kentworthy had a habit of using terms of affection with practically everybody. He rather liked it. It reminded him of Modesty, who had a similar tendency.

Basil handed Mr. Kentworthy the pile of notes and documents he needed help with. Mr. Kentworthy looked through them, and then answered all of Basil's questions without condescension. Miss Hartford had described her brother-in-law's protective character, so it occurred to Basil that he was likely on the receiving end of Mr. Kentworthy's desire to fix problems. Remembering that this desire was one reserved for his family made Basil feel strangely comforted. He was unaccustomed to being taken care of. He decided he liked the notion, as odd as it was, and found himself relaxing under his new friend's tutelage.

They had just stopped their work to have tea when Basil heard a very familiar voice trilling down the hallway, "I'm here, darling! I have come at last!"

Basil scrambled up and ran out the door. A tall woman with dark brown skin, wavy black hair, large dark eyes, high cheekbones, and full lips was striding confidently down the hall toward him. "Modesty!" he said.

Modesty Munro was looking more fresh and beautiful than anyone had a right to look after traveling over a hundred miles. She held her hands up in greeting, as if she were at the forefront of a parade. "Basil, darling! I've come to lend you my aid." Then she grabbed his shoulders and kissed both of his cheeks. She pulled back and gave him an assessing glance. "You look very well. The country air has done you good." She patted his cheek. "Oh, do stop looking so shocked. I told you I'd visit, didn't I?"

Basil quickly gathered his wits about him. "Good heavens, I'm glad to see you. But why didn't you tell me you were coming?"

She gave him a wide smile. "Surprise!"

Basil rolled his eyes. It was just like her, really. He instructed a servant to have Miss Munro's things taken to a spare bedroom.

She glanced over his shoulder. "You have company, darling?"

"Oh," he said, turning. "This is Mr. Charles Kentworthy. Mr. Kentworthy, this is Miss Modesty Munro."

"A pleasure," Mr. Kentworthy said, bowing. "Shall I come back another time, my dear? Leave you two to catch up?"

"Not at all," Modesty said airily. "I am here to meet all of Basil's new friends. He mentioned you in a few of his letters, so we are practically friends already. Although I must admit I was expecting a dozen children to spring out of the woodwork. The house is shockingly empty. Basil, have you been exaggerating about your siblings' liveliness? That would be most unlike you."

"They've gone to visit the Ayleses."

"Ah," she said. "The ones with the farm. That would explain it. I shall have to meet them too. And Miss Hartford, of course. And you mentioned a viscount." She began taking off her gloves. "I shall be quite busy while I am here."

Basil had forgotten how winded he could get from listening to Modesty. It pleased him, though, to hear her accept all of his acquaintances as friends before meeting them.

Mr. Kentworthy stepped forward. "We've heard about you as well, Miss Munro, so I know we shall all be glad to get to know you. You must be exhausted from your trip. Mr. Thorne and I were just sitting down to tea. Would you care to join us?"

She gave him a sunny smile and then peeked into the study. "In here? Is this your study, Basil? It's lovely. But I couldn't possibly step foot on such hallowed ground. Let's go into a sitting room."

Basil was grateful, even though it meant calling for a servant to move the tea. He had written to Modesty about his father's study and he was relieved she remembered his conflicted feelings on the space.

Modesty looped one hand around Mr. Kentworthy's arm and her other hand around Basil's and started to lead the way in a random direction. The three of them were close in height and both men were so bewildered by her taking charge that they followed without even thinking.

"Modesty, you have no idea where the sitting room is," Basil pointed out.

"Of course I don't," she said blithely. "But they're usually in this general vicinity, aren't they?"

He sighed and pointed her in the right direction.

"Oh, this is lovely," she remarked when they entered the sitting room. She gestured to a corner. "This is where Levinia works?"

"Yes, she's been working on some paintings."

Modesty peeked at the canvas. "You were right. She's very talented." She perched onto the sofa and looked Mr. Kentworthy up and down. "You are the first person who invited Basil for tea, correct? The one who's married to the shy gentleman? Your good friend is a viscount and you're entertaining two relations who may or may not be unpleasant? And...you are hosting several people who live with you, including the intriguing Miss Hartford? How did I do, Basil?" she said, turning to him with a grin.

Mr. Kentworthy laughed as he took a seat across from her. "Correct on all counts, Miss Munro. I'm very gratified to hear Mr. Thorne has spoken so much of me and my family."

Modesty patted the sofa cushion next to her. "Do stop hovering, Basil, dear. Yes, he has told me all about everyone. I was very relieved to hear he had made friends. He isn't shy exactly, you know, but he doesn't promote himself very well. He usually needs someone to push him forward. But from what I can tell, his stepmother seems to be doing a good job of that. And that viscount fellow who's been going visiting with him. So it seems I don't have to worry overmuch about him." She turned and gave him a small pat as if he were a well-behaved puppy.

Basil smiled at her fondly. "How on earth are you so bubbly when you just traveled from Bath?"

She lifted her chin. "First impressions are frightfully important. I stayed at an inn last night and used a speed spell this morning."

"You are a proficient spellcaster then?" Mr. Kentworthy said.

"Oh, yes," she replied. "So I shall be eager to see the spell shop in the village. I have heard so much about it."

Mr. Kentworthy's smile was broad. Basil wanted to pull a sofa pillow over his own head in embarrassment. "I do hope you don't intend to talk like this to everybody," he said. "I don't exactly wish for everything I wrote to be announced to my new acquaintances."

She put her hand to her chest in shock. "Whatever can you mean, dear? Besides, you told me that Mr. Kentworthy was a very knowing sort of person. I'm merely testing that observation to see if you are correct. And," she went on, gesturing at the gentleman, "I can happily say that you are correct. He knew exactly what I was talking about. So, well done, you! You always were much better at reading people than you think."

Mr. Kentworthy's shoulders were shaking with barely repressed laughter.

The tea trolley was brought in and Basil was grateful for the small lapse in conversation as he poured. Finally, he said, "You know, I'm very nervous now about you meeting the children. I'm quite certain the house will descend into utter chaos."

She stirred her tea and gave him a bright smile. "Don't be silly, dear. You need a little chaos."

"I already have plenty, actually."

"And see how well it looks on you!" she exclaimed. "Why, you are the peak of health! I've never seen you looking better. A little chaos can do wonders for the constitution, don't you agree, Mr. Kentworthy?"

"I do, indeed, my dear."

Her eyebrow quirked at the endearment. "Oh, I think we shall get along very well."

He smiled. "As you said, we are friends already."

She laughed. "Excellent. Now, Basil, darling, about your siblings, I know I shouldn't choose favorites, but I am simply dying to meet Arabella. Tell me, Mr. Kentworthy, is she as sly and bossy as Basil describes? Oh, and Levinia, of course. She sounds like an absolute delight. I brought them all gifts, so I certainly hope your descriptions were apt. I'll blame you if they don't like them." She paused to take a breath and sip her tea. "You know, I'd imagined a place in the country to be provincial, but you really are a nice distance from London. Barely a day's travel by speed spell. I call that very comfortable. And you inherited a London townhouse too, did you not? That will be nice when the children start coming out."

Modesty had a way of talking where only about half of her questions really needed answers. Basil found himself settling into the familiar sensation of having his friend's conversation wash over him like a rather powerful breeze. It was comforting, even if it was a bit brisk. He put his hand over hers and said, "You're going to turn my quiet life here completely upside-down, but I have missed you."

She gave him a fond smile and kissed his cheek. "I know."

He couldn't tell which of the two parts of his statement she was agreeing to, but it hardly mattered.

"How long do you intend to stay?" Mr. Kentworthy said.

"I'm not sure," she answered. "Long enough to see Basil get married, I suppose. But beyond that, I haven't made any plans."

Basil sputtered into his tea.

Mr. Kentworthy grinned. "Ah, you are a matchmaker then?"

"Well, ever since he proposed to me—did he tell you about that? Yes, good. Not that I don't love him completely, of course, but we really wouldn't suit as a couple—I have made up my mind to see him happily married. I did try introducing him to various people in Bath, but he never seemed to notice."

"You what?" Basil said.

"Exactly. But when he started writing about a lovely spellmaster with copper-colored hair and twinkling smiles who patiently teaches him magic spells and makes him more curious than he usually is, well!" She smiled and sipped her tea. "I waited until the moment felt right."

Basil gave her a wary look. "The moment feels right?"

"It's close. You're not quite at the point where you're going to hover uncertainly for ages, but you're nearly there. I wanted to be in position for when that time comes. Then I can push you out of the nest like the sweet baby bird you are."

Basil glanced at Mr. Kentworthy and then turned to Modesty. "You know, I haven't actually been proclaiming my interest for the lady for all to hear."

"You wear your heart on your sleeve, darling. I'm sure everyone who knows you is aware of your interest by now. Am I correct?"

Mr. Kentworthy nodded and gave Basil an apologetic smile. "Neither of you seem to be aware that anyone is in the room when you're together. Besides, you two look very well together, darling. We are all hoping for a match."

Basil let out a relieved breath. "All the same, some subtlety would be appreciated."

She scoffed. "Subtle heart never won fair lady."

"That's not quite how the saying—"

"Don't be pedantic, darling. Now, once you finish your

tea, we can go see the spell shop. Will you be joining us, Mr. Kentworthy?"

Basil tried not to sound exasperated. When Mr. Kentworthy said he would like nothing better, Basil couldn't decide if he was relieved or agitated. But then the children returned home.

Chapter 64
Sophia

When she followed her mother into the house, Sophia was shocked to see Basil entertaining a stunning woman who sat far too close and seemed far too friendly. She looked how Sophia imagined Amazons to look, with sharp cheekbones, cunning eyes, and thick black hair. She was as tall as Basil with wide shoulders and delicate wrists, and when Basil introduced the lady as Miss Munro and she smiled with her full lips, Sophia felt her breath catch.

Basil introduced everybody and Miss Munro was effervescent in her reaction.

"Why, aren't you all as charming as Basil described? My goodness, but good looks do carry on in the family, don't they? You can call me Aunt Modesty, darlings. Oh, that sounds horribly patronizing, doesn't it? Never mind, call me whatever you like. I'm sure we shall all get along famously."

Lucy tugged on Basil's trouser leg until he picked her up. Miss Munro leaned toward Mr. Kentworthy and said,

"My word, doesn't he look adorable like that? Do tell me Miss Hartford has seen this. She has? Oh, good. No, Basil, don't be so bashful. You look very sweet. Is Miss Hartford fond of children? I suppose I should have asked that sooner. Thank goodness, that is good to know. Well, then, it really is very simple, isn't it?"

Mr. Kentworthy appeared to be amused as he replied to Miss Munro's rapid-fire inquiries. Basil seemed embarrassed but looked at Miss Munro with unmistakable fondness.

Levinia whispered in Sophia's ear, "I think she might be an ally! How marvelous!"

Miss Munro noticed them whispering and beckoned for Sophia to sit beside her on the sofa. "Which one are you? Sophia? Lovely. Do you ever go by Sophy? No? Well, I think it suits you." She touched fingertips under Sophia's chin and tilted her face. "Very beautiful. I am sure you will be a darling of the ton. Basil has no contacts in society, really, but I'll see to it you are all introduced to advantage."

"Actually," Mr. Kentworthy said, "since moving here, Mr. Thorne has met several influential people."

"Really? Who?"

"The Dukex of Molbury, Lord Finlington, and myself."

She gave a bubbly laugh. "Excellent. I cannot abide false modesty. But did you say the Dukex of Molbury? How did you never mention this, Basil? Wait, I think you did."

"I did, yes."

"Well then, there you are. I shall have to meet them as well. Do they really live here? Oh, visiting, I see."

Sophia felt swept up in the lady's nonstop conversation. She wanted to hang on every word.

"Did you say you can't abide modesty?" Bel said. "Isn't that your name?"

Miss Munro gave her a wide smile. "I said I can't abide *false* modesty. However, to be honest, I think modesty is vastly overrated in general. That's partly why I chose the name."

"You chose it?" Sophia said.

Miss Munro nodded. "Yes. I was about your age actually. I was going through the process of being formally recognized as a woman and I thought Modesty was a funny name to choose. It makes me sound simpering and missish, and I quite like the idea of people underestimating me."

"You chose a name because you thought it would be funny for people to make incorrect assumptions about you?" Bel said incredulously.

"I like to catch people off guard" was the reply, accompanied by a dazzling smile.

Sophia began thinking about her own name. Miss Munro said that Sophy suited her. She began to try on the name mentally, determining if it fit.

"So you're like Laury then?" Eli asked.

Miss Munro looked questioningly at Basil, who nodded and said, "Yes, quite like."

"Will you be staying for lunch, Mr. Kentworthy?" her mother asked.

"Actually," Mr. Kentworthy said, with a smile towards Miss Munro. "I thought it might be nice to have you both over for lunch at our house. You can meet everyone there. We can even go by the shop to pick up Gerry and Pip."

Miss Munro threw a hand up in the air and said, "Brilliant! I knew I'd like you. Dear Mrs. Thorne—may I call you Mary? You know Basil always calls you Mary in his letters. I can hardly think of you as anything else. Unless, of course you'd prefer—oh, good. Well, dear Mary, I hope you don't mind us leaving so suddenly. I'm desperate to meet everyone Basil has told me about."

Having received Sophia's mother's assurances that it was a very good plan, Miss Munro kissed all of the children goodbye as if she were indeed a long-lost aunt and not someone they had just met. Sophia felt her face get hot when she received her goodbye kiss. She watched as the three left.

"My word," Eli said. "She's...something else, isn't she?"

Sophia could only nod.

Bel huffed. "I quite detest being kissed on the cheek. Who does she think she is, anyway?"

"I think she's wonderful," Levinia said. "And did you hear her? She must be on our side about the whole Miss Hartford plan."

"How long do you think she'll stay?" Bel said in a wary tone.

"I don't know," Sophia said, but she secretly hoped it would be a long visit.

Chapter 65
Gerry

Gerry had been enjoying a busy morning. She was nicely distracted by thoughts of her spell experiment, trying to think of what else she could do to make it effective. She was not thinking about Mr. Thorne at all, imagining how his eyes might light up if she told him the spell had been successfully designed, or how he might smile and congratulate her. She was definitely not wondering when he might come by the shop again or trying to decide what spell she should give him to learn next. No, it was all spell-related thoughts in her head. When Mr. Thorne did open the shop door, Gerry's heart leaped despite herself. Her heart then sank at the sight of a beautiful woman striding in after him, followed closely by Charles.

Charles's appearance baffled her almost as much as the strange lady's. Charles seemed notably pleased, which made Gerry wonder even more who the lady was. After all, if Charles thought she was a prospective match for Mr. Thorne, he wouldn't have been nearly as cheerful.

Mr. Thorne saw her first and smiled and then, with surprising tentativeness, he brought the lady forward.

Before he could open his mouth, the lady said, "Oh, let me guess. You must be Miss Hartford. I'd recognize you anywhere. Basil does excellent work in describing his friends via letters. I am Miss Munro, but do call me Modesty. My word, but you are lovely, darling. And this shop is perfectly charming." She paused to clasp Gerry's hands and kiss her on both cheeks. "Do tell me we can be friends."

Gerry laughed. She knew she could have a habit of overwhelming people on first acquaintance; it was strange to be on the receiving end. She found herself unable to dislike the woman, even though she was still unsure of what she meant to Mr. Thorne. "I would be delighted to be friends, Miss Munro—I beg your pardon—Modesty. When did you arrive?"

"Oh, about an hour or two ago, I think" was the airy reply.

"Goodness," Gerry said. "I've never been so full of energy after traveling."

"I cast a speed spell from my inn this morning, so I really only traveled about two hours." Speed spells were notoriously difficult spells to cast. Gerry was immediately intrigued by the hint of the lady's talents. "I understand you have an exceptional magical talent," Modesty went on. "And you certainly have a great deal more patience than I in teaching Basil spells. I confess I always just cast them myself. But Basil is profuse in his praise about your genius."

Gerry felt her face get hot. "That's very kind of him. He's learning magic very quickly, actually, and been very pleasant to instruct."

Modesty squeezed her hands and gave her a sly smile. "Basil never exaggerates, except when it comes to his own virtues. Then he's always woefully insufficient in his descriptions. So you can see why I've been eager to meet you. I want to hear all about the cunning spell you're designing. We've come to collect you and Mr....Standish—did I get that right?—for lunch. Mr. Kentworthy said you usually come home at this time. And oh, look, the shop's already clearing out. It seems everyone knows it is time for you to depart."

"Yes," Gerry said. "Lunch sounds lovely. If you'll excuse me, I'll go get my things."

Modesty nodded. released her hands, and turned to exclaim to Mr. Thorne about how delightful the shop was.

Pip followed Gerry into the back room. "Who is that?" he whispered.

"A friend of Mr. Thorne's, I think. Miss Modesty Munro."

"She seems very...erm...friendly."

Gerry chuckled. "Indeed."

He glanced at the curtain. "I must say, I think I shall like her."

"Oh?" Gerry said, surprised.

He nodded. "It can be much easier to talk to people

who like to carry the bulk of the conversation, far less pressure."

Gerry looked at him thoughtfully. She sometimes forgot how shy Pip was. His manner was so easy around her and her family—well, other than John and Veronica. Although when she thought about it, she realized Pip was also fairly easy around John, and mostly seemed to avoid Veronica. She was lost in this train of thought when she followed him back into the shop.

Modesty had, apparently, instructed Mr. Thorne to point out the spells he had learned. She turned when Gerry and Pip came out of the back room. "I shall have to come back when you are not about to go to lunch," she announced. "There are so many spells that I should like to try. I want to buy all of the ones of your own invention."

"That is very kind of you."

Modesty gave Pip an assessing look. "Mr. Standish, is it? Yes, you are just as pretty as Basil said." She laughed. "You know, from the way he writes, I thought this entire village must be impossibly full of attractive people. But so far, I can see he was right. Everyone I've met has been stunning. Even Basil looks better from his time here. The water in Bath apparently has nothing to this country air."

This question did not seem to require a response as Modesty offered her arm out to Pip and followed Charles out the shop and into the carriage.

"What brought you to visit, Miss Munro?" Pip asked once they were all seated.

455

Sarah Wallace

"I came to help Basil. He's always describing himself in his letters as hopelessly lost and without any notion of what to do. I come all the way out here to rescue him to find he's doing perfectly well by himself." She laughed again. "Ah well. I can't say I'm surprised. He really is very capable, you know."

Gerry had a sudden suspicion that Modesty was in the exact same scheme as Charles, Bertie, Seb, Rose, Julia, Caro, Maria, and Lizzy. Although whether the lady had come upon the notion on her own or from meeting Charles was yet to be determined.

"Did you say Mr. Thorne does well in describing people? I wish you'd teach my brother, Gavin," Gerry said, smiling at Mr. Thorne. "When he lived in London, it was nearly impossible to get him to describe people properly. And I always wanted to know simply everything, so it was torturous to be at the tender mercies of his pen."

Mr. Thorne chuckled. "Well, you've met Modesty," he said. "As you can imagine, she is very demanding when it comes to details."

Gerry could well imagine that.

"Don't be silly, darling," Modesty said. "I am an excellent correspondent. You must be too, Miss Hartford, or you wouldn't be dragging out details of your brother. Which brother, did you say? Is it the one married to you?" She pointed at Charles. "Ah, yes, the quiet one, right? He sounds lovely. But I can imagine he would be difficult to pry information from. Basil said he was very shy."

"He is," Gerry said, wondering suddenly how her shy

456

and quiet brother would handle this one-woman storm. "But he writes surprisingly long letters." She glanced at Charles. "I felt as though I knew Charles before I'd even met him, Gavin described their interactions in such vivid detail. All that was lacking was a description of his looks."

Charles chuckled. "And he was adorably embarrassed about it. I tried to find out how much he was discussing me and he was always very evasive."

"Did you have to draw him out, Mr. Kentworthy?" Miss Munro asked.

"It was a months-long process."

"You shall have to tell me all about it. You know, I'm only staying for a short while, so I hope by the time I leave we're good enough friends that you will write to me. Basil is an excellent letter-writer, but a person likes variety. It's good for the soul."

"Like chaos," Mr. Thorne muttered.

"Exactly! Now, Basil did say there was a strong family resemblance with your siblings, Miss Hartford. Can you tell me anything distinct that I should be able to remember so I don't mix your brothers up? From what I understand of their characters, that would not be appreciated."

"Well," Charles said, "Gavin is the one that I will be greeting with a kiss, so that's an easy way."

She threw back her head and laughed. "Marvelous. Is the youngest going to be there?"

"Seb?" Gerry said. "He went back to working with Bertie several days a week, so I think he'll be having lunch there."

"That is a pity," she said, sighing. "Basil, can we visit them this afternoon?"

"Let's take it one visit at a time," he said carefully.

"Oh, very well," she said. "We'll plan on visiting them tomorrow. That will do just fine. I'm in such a rush to meet everyone, you know."

Chapter 66
Charles

Charles adored Miss Munro immediately. He loved her theatrical manner, her obvious affection for Mr. Thorne, her complete lack of subtlety, and the hilarious way she took over the conversation. He was intrigued by the knowledge that Mr. Thorne had spoken of his new acquaintances in such detail but had not missed the fact that Miss Munro clearly paid very close attention to everything Mr. Thorne had written.

When the carriage reached the house, Charles was eager to see how Miss Munro would interact with the other members of the household. Gavin came out of his study as soon as they were all inside. Charles pulled his husband in for a kiss.

"Who's that?" Gavin whispered.

"Oh, you must be Mr. Gavin Kentworthy," Miss Munro said. "Your husband promised I would be able to recognize you by his greeting and he did not disappoint. I'm Basil's friend, Miss Munro. I've heard so much about you."

"You have?" Gavin said.

"Yes, and I can see you're quite as charming as described. And you must be Mr. and Mrs. Hartford. What a pleasure. I hope you don't mind Basil and me disrupting your usual routine. I was quite mad to meet everyone, you see."

Veronica sputtered in disbelief. "Well, I must say—"

Gavin glanced between Miss Munro and Veronica and then timidly stepped forward. "Not at all, Miss Munro. We are very happy to have you. Any friend of Mr. Thorne is welcome here. Shall I show you to the dining room?"

Miss Munro gave him a wide smile and tucked her hand around his arm. "Such a dear! Thank you, Mr. Kentworthy. I was sure I would like you."

Gavin blushed and led her out of the room as promised. John stared after them and then turned to Mr. Thorne. "A pleasure to see you again, Mr. Thorne."

"Thank you, Mr. Hartford," Mr. Thorne said pleasantly.

John nodded and held out his arm for Veronica. Mr. Thorne offered his arm to Gerry, who took it, blushing. Pip and Charles took up the rear.

"What do you think of her?" Charles said quietly to Pip.

Pip chuckled. "I like her. I'm...interested to see how this conversation goes."

Charles grinned in response. "Never a dull moment, eh, darling?"

"Not if you can help it."

Charles laughed.

For part of the meal, the conversation went almost

exactly as it had gone since Miss Munro arrived. She kept up a near steady stream of observations, questions, and comments. She praised the meal as excellent and complimented Gavin on employing such a good cook, told Gerry her dress was lovely and how well the color suited her complexion, asked John and Veronica who their favorite people were in Tutting-on-Cress, talked about how impressed she had been by Gerry's shop, asked Pip what he did in the shop and whether he liked it there, asked Charles if there was anyone she ought to meet who Mr. Thorne hadn't met yet, and finally asked John and Veronica about their son.

"He is about two years old," John explained.

"A lovely age! And what is his name?"

"John."

"Ah. A very steady name. I would love to meet him. Did you bring him with you?"

"He is in the nursery," Veronica explained. "Where he belongs."

"Does he like the garden? You seem to have a lovely garden. Have you met Basil's family? I think their youngest is about little Johnny's age—"

"It's not Johnny," Veronica snapped. "It's John. I can't abide nicknames. They're insufferably common, to my mind. And no, we haven't introduced him to Mr. Thorne's siblings. He does not accompany us on our social calls."

"Whyever not?"

"Because he's too loud and chattery to do well in polite society." Veronica looked smug, as if she had delivered a well-worded insult.

Miss Munro waved a hand airily. "That is how children are. Why, you should see Basil's family. They are the liveliest creatures, and so adorable."

"Yes, I've met them. I found them to be very poorly behaved."

"I beg your pardon," Mr. Thorne said. "I hate to contradict you, Mrs. Hartford. But how were they poorly behaved?"

"They asked too many questions, they wouldn't sit down for the space of two seconds, they insisted on exploring a strange house on their own. It was far too demanding."

Mr. Thorne looked pained. "I...was not aware that was inappropriate."

"Of course it wasn't inappropriate," Gerry said hotly. "They were being children. Bertie didn't mind. If he did mind, he wouldn't have invited them, and he wouldn't have given them leave to explore the house. They didn't do any damage and they even left the room so the adults could converse easily. To my mind, they were perfectly behaved."

Mr. Thorne gave Gerry a small smile. "Thank you, Miss Hartford."

"Very well said, darling," Miss Munro said. "I've always said if you can't handle children being children, then you shouldn't have them. Of course, Basil was somewhat dropped into the situation, but all the same. I don't hear him complaining about them."

Veronica gaped. "How dare you, you vulgar creature! John, did you hear what she said? The idea." She turned back to Miss Munro, not waiting for her husband to agree with her, which was just as well, as John didn't respond. He had gone rigid and pale, his lips pressed close together.

"Mr. Hartford?" Mr. Thorne said softly. "Are you all right?"

John gave a stiff nod. "I'm afraid I'm not feeling altogether the thing. Do carry on, please." He quickly left the table.

Mr. Thorne looked conflicted, then quietly excused himself and followed John.

Veronica rallied despite her husband's departure. "I think it is a pretty low thing that people have forgotten their moral duties and responsibilities in this day and age."

"Moral duty?" Miss Munro said, laughing. "What a strange way to go about that decision. Moral duty won't help you to love a child more."

"But inheritance!"

"That's what entailments are for," Miss Munro replied, shaking her head in disbelief.

Veronica gasped in horror. "How dare you say such a thing."

Miss Munro smiled. "I do adore a lively debate. It has been far too long since I've enjoyed one. Basil is wonderful, but he is not one for this sort of conversation, you know what I mean? I am glad we're getting on so well, Mrs. Hartford. Do go on."

Gerry choked on her tea. Gavin's mouth twitched.

"Lively debate?" Veronica said. "What, is this some sort of game to you?"

"It's such fun! What else shall we discuss? You can pick the next topic."

Veronica sputtered some more.

Charles leaned forward and said to Miss Munro, "I would love to hear your thoughts on the importance of order of precedence."

Miss Munro lit up. "Excellent!"

Chapter 67
Basil

Basil wasn't quite sure why he was following Mr. Hartford. He felt as though the other man's discomfiture was, in a way, his fault. He was relieved when the gentleman went to the garden and not upstairs. Basil stepped outside and Mr. Hartford gave a start at the sound of the door.

"Oh," he said. "Mr. Thorne. I...I didn't know you were there."

"I wanted to apologize," Basil said, approaching carefully. "Modesty can get a bit carried away in the excitement of conversation. I assure you, she didn't mean anything cutting."

Mr. Hartford pressed his lips together. "No," he said finally. "I fear that I am the one who ought...my wife is very outspoken in her opinions. Rather like Miss Munro, I expect."

"Rather, yes," Basil said.

Mr. Hartford nodded, as if that settled it. Basil

couldn't help but think that the man still looked miserable.

"Are you all right?" he said.

"Miss Munro said something that, er...I just...needed a bit of fresh air. That's all. It was...good of you to come and ask."

"It was nothing. You looked as if you might faint before." Mr. Hartford didn't respond, so Basil said, "Well, if you are quite well, I suppose I ought to—"

"I...my sister was right. Your siblings were not poorly behaved. They were...loud, yes, but not..." He cleared his throat. "I suppose that I...I mean, my wife and I are not altogether...that is, we're not accustomed to a great many children all at once."

Basil had a feeling he knew what Mr. Hartford was keeping himself from saying. He wondered if the gentleman knew that his younger brother, Mr. Kentworthy, shared a discomfort around children. "Thank you," he said at last. "I am relieved to hear it."

The other man gave a brisk nod.

Basil hesitated. "You know, Modesty is right. Your son is only a little younger than my youngest sister. You would be more than welcome to bring him over sometime so they could play together."

Mr. Hartford gave a humorless huff. "I rather think you have more than enough on your plate as it is, sir."

"What's one more child in the house?" Basil said with a small smile.

Mr. Hartford gave him a long look. "Thank you," he said quietly. "I'm afraid my wife has very particular...

ideas about the matter. So I'm not sure I shall take you up on the offer. But it is kind of you."

Basil nodded and, deciding to give the gentleman some time alone, returned to the dining room. He was not altogether surprised to find Modesty in an enthusiastic debate about order of precedence with Mrs. Hartford. Well, Modesty was enthusiastically debating; Mrs. Hartford was practically spitting in agitation. He wished he could have warned her. Glancing around the table, it seemed as if the rest of the household was in varying states of amusement and shock.

Finally, Mrs. Hartford turned to Basil. "Where is my husband, Mr. Thorne?"

"He went on a long walk," he lied.

She gave them all a scathing glance before she swept out of the room, righteous indignation echoing in every step.

"Brava, my dear," Mr. Charles Kentworthy said, raising a glass to Modesty.

"I have never seen anyone take on Veronica in such a manner!" Miss Hartford said, grinning. "It was incredible!"

"Would you consider staying with us until they leave?" Mr. Gavin Kentworthy said in a tone that suggested he was not entirely joking.

Modesty laughed. "I haven't had so much fun in ages," she said. She patted Mr. Gavin Kentworthy's hand. "I will gladly come over as often as you want, darling. Is she always like that?"

They all nodded.

"You poor dears," Modesty said feelingly.

"Pip and I have the excuse of going to the shop," Miss

Hartford said. "So it's really Charles and Gavin that have to really put up with her."

"And poor Gavin was left alone today," Mr. Charles Kentworthy said.

"Oh, I was *very* busy in my study," Mr. Gavin Kentworthy said, "with strict orders that I was not to be disturbed."

They all laughed.

Mr. Standish turned to Basil and said, "How was Mr. Hartford?"

Basil was pleased to see that someone else had been concerned for the gentleman. "I'm not sure," Basil replied honestly. "But he wasn't sick or faint, as I'd feared. Not particularly forthcoming, though, I'm afraid."

"No," Mr. Charles Kentworthy said quietly. "He rarely is. Did he really go on a walk? He usually paces the garden."

"I left him in the garden," Basil admitted.

Mr. Charles Kentworthy flashed a smile. "Wonderful. Very kind of you, darling. I'll go and check on him shortly."

Basil nodded, relieved. He glanced at Miss Hartford. "He told me that you were right about my siblings. Thank you for standing up for them. I do appreciate it."

She smiled. "It was nothing. Veronica is dreadful, but it was unthinkable that she would turn her vitriol onto you as well."

"It wasn't nothing," he said softly.

She blushed.

He tried to ignore the fact that both Modesty and Mr. Charles Kentworthy were grinning like fools. "Right," he said briskly. "Thank you very much for your hospitality. I think Modesty and I had better be going."

Modesty obligingly stood and proceeded to tell them all how wonderful it was to meet them, what darlings they all were, how she couldn't wait to see them again, extracted a promise from Mr. Gavin Kentworthy that he was to write if he needed her to intervene with Mrs. Hartford again, and assured Miss Hartford that she would come to the shop as soon as possible in order to buy as many spells as she could pack in her trunk.

Finally, they were in the carriage going home. Modesty sighed and leaned against him. "They are lovely people, darling. You did very well in befriending them."

He chuckled. "Thank you. Although I rather think they took me under their wing."

"That doesn't make you any less charming," she said. "And Miss Hartford is exquisite. I thoroughly approve. Do go on falling in love with her. She's very good for you."

He wrapped his arm around her shoulders. "Thank you," he said. "I rather think I will."

Chapter 68
Gerry

Gerry almost hated to admit that Mr. Haines was actually not too bad of a suitor, all things considered. He wore spectacles and sat perched on the edge of the sofa, looking eager to talk. He asked Gerry what she liked to read and then discussed history, which was apparently his great passion. He shyly admitted that his library did not boast much of a fiction collection but that he would happily take any recommendations she had to offer.

This was another part of her friends' scheme that Gerry did not like. She rather liked Mr. Haines and would have been pleased to get to know him better, but she couldn't imagine being married to him. She hated the idea of disappointing him and hoped he hadn't gotten his hopes up about the encounter. Compared to the other suitors she had met, Mr. Haines was exemplary. However, she couldn't help also comparing him to Mr. Thorne. Mr. Haines had none of the other man's charms, his good looks, his gentleness of temper, or his curiosity.

The Spellmaster Of Tutting-On-Cress

As soon as her guests were finally gone, she wrote to Bertie and asked if he could spare Seb for the next few weeks; she needed a distraction and spell-building was the best distraction she could think of.

Every day for the rest of the week, Gerry, Seb, and Pip stayed late after the shop was closed. Gerry performed more tests, putting all of the ingredients together and casting spells to make sure they didn't cancel each other out. Toward the end of the week, she placed herself in the circle, and performed more tests to see what calculations needed to be changed to accommodate herself as part of the spell.

It was an exhausting business and she felt drained every night when she went home. On the bright side, she felt as though she was making progress, and she had little time to spare for thoughts about Mr. Thorne. At least, that was what she told herself. Thoughts of him snuck into her mind when she was least prepared for them. She would look up when any tall gentlemen entered the shop, hoping it was him, and was disappointed and annoyed with her own disappointment when it wasn't. She kept a clean copy of the spell, redrafting it every time she made adjustments with the vague expectation that she would give Mr. Thorne the copy when the spell was complete. Sometimes when she stepped into the circle, she would think about him and wonder what he might use the spell to think about. Would he use it to think about her? Was he as conflicted over the idea of being in love with her as she was with him?

By the end of the first week of experimentation, she

finally cast it on herself. Pip sensed the magic, offering suggestions for when ingredients weren't straight or centered. Seb took notes. The first time she cast it, she was nervous, and when her mind quieted with the magic, she panicked briefly that she might have done something truly dangerous. But then she had a moment of clarity and found herself reasoning through the panic more calmly than she ever had before.

But before she had time to think anything else, Pip said, "The magic's fading. Oh, it's fading quickly," and the spell dropped completely.

Seb looked at her anxiously. "Did it work?"

"I think so," she said slowly. "But it was hard to say when it lasted as short as it did. Did anyone keep time?"

They both shook their heads regretfully.

"No matter," she said brusquely. "I didn't ask you to. We'll do it next time."

Then, it was another solid week of experimentation. This time, they knew they were on the right track, which helped. Gerry assigned Seb the task of looking up ingredients with the same Constitutional Properties that had longer-lasting effects. Then she stayed up late in the library doing calculations to adjust for the difference in ingredients. By the end of the second week, they were up to five minutes of the spell working.

"I need at least ten," Gerry told them.

Seb nodded wearily. "Five minutes of focused thinking wouldn't do much, would it?" He yawned.

"I'm sorry," she said. "I daresay you aren't used to these long hours. Perhaps you should take tomorrow—"

"Don't you dare suggest I take tomorrow off," he

snapped. "I'm not used to these hours, but it's fascinating and I will never forgive you if you figure this out without me."

"I only meant that you don't officially work here," she said. "So if you need to rest, you can. Pip and I are used to these long days, but you aren't."

His face fell. "Sorry. I didn't mean to—I'd like to come back in tomorrow, if I may." He glanced at her and then looked away. "It is fascinating. And besides, I miss Laury. I miss him less when I'm busy all day."

She gave him a hug and told him not to be silly and of course he could come every day that he wanted to.

After another week of experimentation, Gerry deemed it ready for another casting. She let out a deep breath. She wanted the spell to work this time. She needed it to work. It felt more urgent a need than any of her previous experiments. She wanted the clarity the spell would bring. Seb was perched on a stool, leaning sideways over the workbench so he could jot down notes at Gerry's dictation and keep an eye on the watch. Pip stood beside her, prepared to sense the magic as soon as she cast it and let her know if anything felt off.

Pip smiled encouragingly.

She set about preparing the spell, taking care of the placement.

"A little to the left, I think," Pip murmured and, "And that one's a bit off-center."

She followed his advice, relieved that she'd asked him to help. Then she chalked out the sigil and sat herself carefully in the center of the circle. She glanced at Pip, who gave her a nod. She took a breath and cast the spell.

"It's taken hold," Pip said softly.

"Ten minutes and counting," Seb added, matching Pip's tone.

Gerry relaxed, and as she did, she felt her thoughts settle. The first thing that came to her mind surprised her: Seb. It occurred to her suddenly and strongly that she really ought to hire Seb as a permanent fixture at her shop. He was doing so well. She loved getting to know her younger brother better and she adored being able to teach him new things. All of her worries about keeping him from Laurence melted away and she knew with certainty that she ought to trust Seb and Laurence to tell her when they needed time together. She smiled at this decision that she didn't know she'd needed to make and let out a slow breath.

"Five minutes left," Seb said.

She gently tucked her thoughts about Seb away and was pleased with how cooperative her mind was. The next thing that came to mind was Charles, which also surprised her. She noted, with interest, that under the influence of the spell, her first thoughts with Charles weren't ones of irritation, but fondness. She knew Charles was trying to help, no matter how frustrating his meddling could be. Gerry could see that from his point of view, she was on the verge of ruining her own happiness and that he was desperately trying to keep that from happening. Now, without the buzz of everything else distracting her, she remembered some of the letters Gavin had written to her from London. He shared that Charles did not have much family of his own. Bertie had told Gavin that Charles always went out of his way to make everyone he loved happy. Charles was, she realized, doing his best.

"Two minutes remaining," Seb said.

Gerry's mind froze. Two minutes? How had eight minutes passed by so quickly? She hadn't had time to think about what she planned. What was she going to do? She straightened her back and attempted to calm her mind again. Perhaps she didn't need to worry quite so much about the situation with Mr. Thorne. Perhaps she ought to simply let things take their course, just as she'd always planned to do, meddling friends and relations notwithstanding.

Even before Seb said, "Time," she could feel the usual noise in her head rise up to its usual pitch. Her mind was jumbled with thoughts about the shop, about her family, about the spell, about what Pip and Seb had observed.

Pip reached a hand out to help her up. Gerry took it and stood, wiping her skirt of dust.

"Well?" Seb said eagerly.

She glanced at Pip. He smiled. "It felt very strong, very balanced." He paused. "Interestingly enough, it didn't exactly feel steady. It felt like...a lake or a stream. Sometimes there would be a rippling feeling to it and then it would even out into calm. It fell apart right before Seb called time. So your estimate was spot on."

She nodded. "Thank you." Seb was hurriedly taking down all of Pip's observations. "It worked," she said, grinning at them. "My mind felt...quiet. The thoughts came easily and without distractions."

"What did you think about?" Seb said, looking curious.

Her smile broadened. "First and foremost: how would you like to work here? Permanently? Officially?"

Seb nearly fell off his stool in surprise. "Really? Do you mean it, Gerry?"

"Yes," she said, laughing. "I mean it. You've done wonderfully well here. I couldn't have done this without you. I love teaching you how to build spells and I'd be delighted to teach you both anything you want."

"Can I work out front?" he said, surprising her.

"Of course," she said. "I didn't realize you wanted to."

He looked self-conscious. "Well, it didn't seem right to be out front when I wasn't really working here."

She tousled his hair. "Don't be such a goose. You should have asked me!"

He laughed and pulled away. "I just did!" Then he surprised her again by hopping off the stool and pulling her into a hug. "Thank you. What should I do about Bertie?"

"If you want to keep working with him, then do it. We'll have you here any day you wish to come."

Seb looked as though he couldn't believe what he was hearing. "Did you really decide all that during the spell or are you having me on?"

"You were the first thing that came to mind."

He grinned. "What else?"

She cleared her throat. "Well, I didn't have time to think about everything I wanted to. Ten minutes isn't very long, all things considered. And it's...an oddly fatiguing spell."

"Might have something to do with casting the magic on your own person," Pip said.

"You're probably right. We can ask Bertie."

Seb scribbled the note down. "Anything else?"

She shook her head. "I'd like to try it again to test its reusability, but I think that's enough for one night."

As they cleaned up the spell and put everything away, Gerry thought about how nice it would be to tell Mr. Thorne about her success. She immediately rejected the notion as silly. After all, she had no call to go all the way to his house just to tell him about a spell she'd designed. But the more she considered it, the more she realized she wanted to. By the time their aprons were off and they were heading out the door, she had made up her mind.

"Go on home without me," she said. "I think I'm going to make a call on my way home."

Pip only smiled knowingly, but Seb grinned and said, "I rather think you should call on Mr. Thorne and tell him the big news."

Gerry blushed, worrying again that it was a silly thing to do.

Pip put an arm around Seb's shoulders and said, "We'll tell Charles and Gavin for you."

She nodded, encouraged by Pip's evident approval of the plan. Then again, Seb had approved too. She strode off to the Thornes' house.

Chapter 69
Basil

Basil was sitting with the Dukex of Molbury and Mr. Charles Kentworthy as they helped him go over his father's ledger. The dukex was providing helpful suggestions about certain symbols and abbreviations, Mr. Kentworthy was offering advice and commentary on some of the expenses, and Basil was taking copious notes. They all looked up in surprise when the butler knocked on the door and informed them that Miss Hartford had come to call.

"Really?" Mr. Kentworthy said in obvious amusement. "How delightful. Perhaps the dukex and I ought to step outside for a moment—"

The dukex stayed him with their hand on his arm. "Not at all, Charles. We shall stay right here."

Basil swallowed and nodded to the butler. "Do show her in."

To say Miss Hartford was surprised that he had company would have put it lightly. She stepped into the room and immediately froze, color rising in her cheeks. "Oh!" she said. "Forgive me. I did not know you had—"

"No, please," Basil said quickly. "Please stay. The dukex and Mr. Kentworthy have been kind enough to help me understand my father's paperwork. I can't make heads or tails of it myself," he added with a self-deprecating smile.

"I don't wish to interrupt."

"Well, if the shop is closed," Mr. Kentworthy said, "then your arrival is really quite timely, darling. I'm afraid we got rather carried away in our project. Why don't Julian and I wait in the other—"

"We will stay right here," the dukex said again.

Basil had a feeling that it wasn't the time to inform his guest that he had already talked to Miss Hartford alone in the study. So instead he held out a chair for her.

She took a seat with evident discomfiture. "It was really nothing," she said. "I merely came by to tell you that the spell I've been working on is complete."

Basil gaped. "You finished it?"

"Yes, we still have some things to work out, I imagine. But I was able to cast it tonight with Pip and Seb's help."

"That's marvelous!" Basil said. He dearly wanted to take her into his arms, kiss her, and tell her she was a genius, but he resisted the urge to do so and settled on simply saying, "You are incredible."

She gave him one of her twinkling smiles (they were his favorite) and said, "Thank you. It is very kind of you to say. I...erm...I wanted to tell you since you inspired the idea, after all."

"I'm glad you did. I'm honored to be among the first to know."

She blushed, glanced behind him at his other guests. "Well, anyway, that was all I came here to say."

She clearly intended to get up and leave and, as usual, he could only think about how he might extend their conversation further. "Do you think, perhaps, I might be able to cast it? I'm sure it is far beyond my skill level, of course," he added hurriedly. "So, I suppose that was a foolish—"

"No, no, not at all," she said, putting her hand over his. "I am sure you could do it. I...I don't have it ready for spell bags yet. But I can send you the instructions. It ought to be done with another spellcaster present anyway." She glanced again at their small audience who, thankfully, had remained quiet during the conversation. "So, I'm sure if you took it to Bertie or Laurence, they could not only assist but provide the ingredients."

He would have liked to ask for *her* assistance, but he suspected the dukex would not approve of that notion. "That would be...perfect then. Thank you."

She nodded, smiling up at him. "Well, I really ought to go now."

"I can take you home, Gerry," Mr. Kentworthy said.

"You took your horse, Charles," the dukex said. "I shall escort Geraldine home."

Mr. Kentworthy appeared to be on the brink of arguing, so Basil said, "I can take your horse home later, Mr. Kentworthy. Or you can come collect it tomorrow."

Mr. Kentworthy gave him a dazzling smile. "How kind of you, Mr. Thorne." He glanced at Miss Hartford. "As a matter of fact, why don't you join us for dinner tonight? We can celebrate Gerry's success together."

"Oh," Miss Hartford said, blushing. "That is very considerate of you, Charles. But we couldn't do that without Bertie."

"We'll send a note for Bertie," Mr. Kentworthy said. "He'll be over in a trice. I guarantee it."

"I could stop by the viscount's estate on my way," Basil said, laughing.

Miss Hartford sighed, "This is feeling like musical chairs. It really isn't necessary."

The dukex chuckled. "Quite right, Geraldine. Charles can ride home and inform his staff that he shall be hosting three additional guests tonight. Perhaps you should say four, Charles, in case Miss Munro wishes to join. Mr. Thorne shall ride with Geraldine and I, and we will collect Bertram on our way."

Basil thought Mr. Kentworthy would protest but, to his surprise, the gentleman smiled and said, "Ingenious, my dear. That will suit admirably."

They sent for the carriage to be readied and Mr. Kentworthy's horse to be brought to the door while Basil informed Mary and Modesty of his change of plans. He was relieved when Mary did not recommend he take any of the children with him. Modesty eagerly agreed to join the party.

"I'll come in your carriage," she told him. "I need to change into something more appropriate." Then she shooed him out of the room, instructing him to lavish Miss Hartford with compliments of her genius.

By the time he rejoined his guests, Mr. Kentworthy had left. They all climbed into the carriage (Basil was grateful when the dukex allowed him to help Miss Hartford inside) and went to collect the viscount.

He was worried the conversation in the carriage would be awkward, considering the dukex was well aware of his interest in Miss Hartford (then again, who among his acquaintances wasn't aware by now?), but the dukex took control of the conversation, asking Miss Hartford about her day. They neatly avoided the topic of her spell, pointing out that Lord Finlington would want to be present for that subject. Miss Hartford obligingly talked about her work and Basil was delighted to hear a report on her daily life. He blissfully imagined that he might someday draw out such conversation from her, learning about the intricacies of shop life, gossip about the other villagers, which spells were currently the most popular. Basil sat quietly in the carriage as the dukex asked questions and gave little commentaries and he gratefully absorbed it all.

When they arrived at the viscount's home, the dukex instructed Miss Hartford to fetch Lord Finlington. Basil hurriedly stepped out to help her down and then glanced at the dukex questioningly after Miss Hartford went inside.

"She knows the house very well," they explained. "She will be able to find him more quickly than you could." They did not need to explain why they didn't go inside.

Basil nodded and got back in.

"I like how you are both settling in with each other's families," the dukex remarked into the quiet.

"Pardon?" Basil said.

They smiled. "Charles invited you as if it were the most natural thing in the world. It is very helpful when courting someone that you get along well with their family. Not as critical as getting along with the person you are courting, of course. Still, it helps."

"I'm not exactly courting her, Your Grace."

They gave him a wry look. "Oh, no?"

"We are simply friends. At the moment."

"And what is keeping you from pursuing what you both quite evidently want, if I may ask?"

"What do you mean we both—"

They sighed. "Really, child. She walked all the way to your house after a long day of work to tell you she had created a new spell that you inspired. She hadn't even told her family the news yet."

Basil registered this. "Oh."

The dukex tsked. "Young people these days. It's a wonder any of you manage to get married at all."

Basil chuckled. "I apologize, Your Grace."

"Well, never mind that, poppet. Just consider what I asked you and do get a move on. Geraldine is very beautiful and clever and has a healthy regard for herself, but anyone would start to doubt their own charms if left in too much suspense."

"You think she may...doubt my interest?"

"I think she may be entirely unaware of it. You might want to consider being a bit more obvious."

Basil laughed in surprise. "Very well. Thank you, Your Grace."

"Only take care you are more obvious in the right company," they added hastily. "But I trust you to not be foolish in that regard."

Before Basil could respond, the carriage door was opened and Lord Finlington was helping Miss Hartford inside.

"Good evening, m'dears," he said cheerfully as he sat beside Basil. "What a delightful occasion this is." The carriage had barely begun to move when the viscount said, "Now, I know you will be explaining it all at dinner, darling, but I simply must know everything about the spell. Spare me no details."

Miss Hartford laughed. "I think Gavin is the only one at home who would be remotely interested." Then she launched into a report of her experiment.

Basil was fascinated to be an observer of a conversation with the lady. The viscount clearly knew a great deal about magic, despite his earlier comments of it being a hobby he merely dabbled in. His questions grew technical and complex and Basil was awed by Miss Hartford's ready answers. He followed along as well as he could but was mostly content to simply listen and watch, admiring the way Miss Hartford's eyes lit up when she talked about her craft.

He took the opportunity to consider the dukex's advice. He was certainly not ready to propose to the lady, but perhaps it really was time to indicate his interest to her.

Chapter 70
Charles

Charles was practically giddy as he rode home ahead of the others. Gerry and Mr. Thorne were so perfect for each other, Charles really had to do very little work at all. It was, he thought, very considerate of them. Imagine Gerry walking all the way to Mr. Thorne's house to tell him about a spell. She had looked exhausted, poor darling, and considering the fact that she had worked a full day and experimented afterwards, it was hardly surprising. And now he was about to make her socialize. Ah well.

He got home to find Seb practically hopping in excitement. "There you are! Where have you been?"

"I was visiting Mr. Thorne."

Seb grinned. "Really? Was Gerry there?"

Charles laughed and threw his arm around his brother-in-law's shoulders. "She was, and very surprised to see me."

Seb looked puzzled. "Why isn't she here yet?" His eyes widened. "Did you really leave her there with him?"

Charles laughed again as they walked through the house. "They're coming here for dinner."

"What, all of them? The little ones too?"

"Oh, really, Charles," Gavin said as they approached. "You couldn't have given me any warning?"

"Not the little ones. Just Mr. Thorne, Miss Munro, Julian, and Bertie."

Gavin rolled his eyes. "That is a relief, but all the same: why didn't you warn me?"

"It was only just decided, darling. Shall I go and tell the cook?"

"No, I'll do it," Gavin said in a huff.

Charles sought out John and Veronica, figuring it was the least he could do to help Gavin. Veronica, predictably, complained about the last-minute change in plans. John, however, appeared to be pleased. Charles couldn't help but feel a surge of pride and fondness for John—his approval of the guests suggested he was capable of having good taste in company. Whether this was a recently acquired taste or one he buried when he married Veronica remained to be seen. Nevertheless, it was a start. Pip joined them and slid easily into the conversation, quietly asking John about his day. Pip was also pleased to hear about the guests, although this was hardly surprising.

When the first carriage arrived, Charles wondered if Miss Munro had uncharacteristically chosen not to socialize as she was not among its passengers.

"Modesty is on her way," Mr. Thorne explained. "She said she needed to change into something more appropriate."

Charles hid a smile. From what he had seen of her, Miss Munro was always dressed to the height of fashion and could have easily come in whatever she'd been wearing considering it was such an informal party of friends. He suspected she was providing more opportunities for Mr. Thorne and Gerry to talk and he approved of the tactic. He thought back to what the lady had said upon her arrival, about preferring to let people underestimate her. He realized he likely had done just that, assuming her brash manner left no room for subtle ingenuity.

They did not have to wait long as Miss Munro arrived a scant quarter of an hour after the others. She burst into the room and exclaimed how thrilled she was to be there and what an honor it was to dine in the presence of genius.

Gerry smiled at the compliment. "It is very kind of you to say, Modesty."

"I am not saying it to be kind, my dear. It is a fact." She tucked her arm around Gerry's as they went into the dining room. "I do not say it lightly, you know. I've been to any number of spell shops and I've never seen so many original spells in one place."

Gerry looked up in surprise. "Really?"

"Yes! You are a remarkable spellmaster. It's no wonder your shop is so popular."

Gerry looked at Bertie, who nodded in reply. "She isn't wrong, m'dear. Adjusting spells to suit what ingredients one has on hand is one thing; inventing new spells as you do is somewhat unusual."

"You told me Mr. Fenshaw said you represented a new generation of spellmasters," Pip said. Gerry blushed.

"Hear, hear," Charles said. "I think it's past time we celebrated Gerry in this manner."

"Can we make it a new tradition?" Seb said.

"Seems overly extravagant, if you ask me," Veronica said with a sniff.

"Not at all, Mrs. Hartford," Julian said. "Extravagance is to flaunt one's wealth or waste resources unnecessarily. A small dinner party between friends and family can hardly fall under that definition. Now, poppet," they said, turning to Gerry. "Why don't you explain to everyone what your spell is for and how you came up with it? It seems an appropriate topic, given the circumstances."

Gerry did, explaining how she had thought of the idea from a comment made by Mr. Thorne and how Seb had helped with the research portion. Then she described the experimentation process with Seb taking notes and Pip sensing the magic. Bertie and Miss Munro contributed to the conversation by peppering Gerry with questions.

"One of the first things she said when she was done," Seb said, "was to offer me a permanent job at the spell shop!"

"My word," Miss Munro said. "Magic must run in your family. Are you all so remarkably talented?"

Seb blushed. "I wouldn't go so far as to say that. I just help with the research."

"Don't be a goose wit, Seb," Gerry said. "You're very talented."

"Indeed you are, m'dear," Bertie said. "You have very good control and a significant amount of power."

Seb looked pleased.

"And dear Gavin is too," Bertie continued. "Extraordinary ability to master spells within one try. I remember the first time I saw him cast—it was in London, wasn't it, my sweet?—and he executed a very advanced piece perfectly."

Gavin was blushing now. He gave a nervous little cough. "Yes, well, except for my tendency to get myself ill—"

"Oh, pishposh, Gavin," Gerry said. "That was one time."

"And it wasn't from lack of talent," Bertie said. "Only improper handling of a rather dangerous ingredient. Entirely different matter."

"Extraordinary," Miss Munro said. "What a fascinating family. Are you a powerful spellcaster as well, Mr. Hartford?"

Now it was John's turn to blush. "I rather think not," he said, fiddling with a serviette. He glanced at his wife. "I don't do magic very often anymore."

"Magical talent is highly overrated, in my opinion," Veronica said primly.

Miss Munro chuckled. "Forgive me, Mrs. Hartford, but only people who don't have a great deal of magical talent say that."

"What of your family, Mr. Thorne?" Julian said.

"My family, Your Grace?"

"Yes, does magic run in your blood?"

"Some," he said. "Nothing like the Hartfords, I'm sure."

"Oh, I don't know," Gerry said. "You've come a long way with the spells I've given you. I've been offering you more difficult ones without saying anything and you're still mastering them."

He looked incredulous. "Have you really?"

She grinned.

Miss Munro threw back her head and laughed. "How I adore you, Miss Hartford! That is exactly the way Basil needs to learn things. He will never admit when he's doing well. One has to sneak it up on him."

"As to your family," Bertie said, "I spoke to your father when I first moved to the neighborhood. I gathered that he was very proficient."

"He came into the shop quite often," Gerry said.

Pip nodded. "He was particularly fond of the quieting spell." He smiled wryly. "Which I can imagine came in handy."

"And that one is not easy," Gerry said. "Not to mention Sophia seems to be doing quite well. The spells she picks out are of a good level for someone her age."

Mr. Thorne looked embarrassed. "I remember you telling me that," he said quietly. "Silly of me to forget it. I imagine the younger ones are too little to determine their talents as yet."

"Perhaps," Bertie said. "But there are several tests we can do to gauge their power. A topic for a later time, perhaps. When you're a bit more settled."

Mr. Thorne looked thoughtful. "What are you thinking, my dear?" Charles asked.

The gentleman gave a small smile. "I was only thinking that it didn't occur to me that things like tests for magical ability and schooling in general would fall under my purview, but I daresay it does. It's easy to see that dowries and social Seasons will be my responsibility and I'm still learning how to handle the day-to-day challenges, but there are so many small things...that aren't quite so small, I suppose."

"It's really very simple," Veronica said. "You just need to send them all to schools. My husband and his siblings all went to Oxford. You probably ought to look into boarding schools like Eton as well. Goodness knows with that many children, it would do you some good to get them out from underfoot."

"I regret to say, Mrs. Hartford, that I have no intention of sending them to boarding schools. I lived most of my life in such institutions and it was miserable. They are not underfoot, so I don't mind the challenge. It's merely something I hadn't thought of."

"What?" Veronica said. "Will you have them all educated at home?"

"Why not?" Gerry said. "At-home tutors are sometimes more effective than schools. And the Thornes are surrounded by friends who want to help them."

"I learned more here than I did at Oxford," Seb said.

Mr. Thorne was looking at Gerry with an unreadable expression. "It's very kind of you to say so, Miss Hartford."

"It's the truth," she said.

His smile was soft.

"Well," said Laury from the doorway. "This is quite a merry party to come home to."

Everyone looked up in surprise. Seb bolted out of his seat to greet his fiancé. They kissed, blithely ignoring Veronica's protests about propriety. Then Laury pulled Seb to his side, sliding an arm around his waist. "What's the occasion?"

"We're celebrating Gerry's most recent spell-building success," Charles said, coming over to greet him. "When did you get in town?"

"About an hour ago. I came back for the ball."

Charles had another chair brought to the table and Laury took a seat next to Seb.

"Now," Laury said. "Did Charles say you built a new spell? Tell me everything."

Chapter 71
Basil

Shortly after Basil's dinner at the Kentworthys', Miss Hartford sent him a copy of the spell she had designed, some advice on the casting of it, and a small note encouraging him to visit her if he needed help. He had several pieces of paper in her handwriting at this point, but the small missive and attached spell felt far more personal and valuable than the others. He spent an embarrassing amount of time reading it and rereading it, thinking about how she had written it just for him and not for some unknown future customer.

He was relieved that by the night of the ball, Mary had been in mourning for six full months and could attend, although she wouldn't be dancing for the remainder of the mourning period. Considering the fact that Lord Finlington had also invited the children to attend, he was particularly grateful for his stepmother's presence.

The night of the ball, Basil dressed in his finest suit and helped Mary and Modesty herd the children into two separate carriages. Mary, Sophia, Lucy, Martin, and Grace took one carriage, while Basil, Modesty, Levinia, and the twins took the other. After they arrived, there was a similar amount of confusion in getting everyone out of the carriages, but the viscount's staff assisted and soon Basil was leading his family into the house.

He entered the ballroom and was greeted immediately by the viscount and the dukex. Lord Finlington welcomed all of the children, assuring Basil that he was delighted they came and that they were welcome to explore the house if they were bored with the festivities. Basil wasn't entirely sure about that, considering the elegance of the event. But he thanked his host, kissed the dukex's knuckles, and went inside. Modesty encouraged the twins to take advantage of the viscount's offer, took Lucy out of Basil's arms, and gave him a small shove.

"Go ask your charming spellmaster to dance," she said.

"You see her already?"

"She's breathtaking in a salmon-colored gown. Quite a feat, really, with her hair. I daresay it has a great deal to do with having the confidence to pull it off. But she might be self-conscious all the same, especially with that dreadful sister-in-law, so make sure you tell her she looks lovely."

He saw where she was pointing and felt his breath catch. Miss Hartford did indeed look beautiful, but then she always did. She was standing with the Kentworthys and Mr. Standish. Basil felt unsure about asking the lady to dance so early in the evening, especially in front of an audience.

"You need to make your interest known," Modesty whispered. "Asking her for the first dance is a very polite and practical way to do it."

"It won't be presumptuous?"

She sighed. "It would be if you hadn't spent so much time visiting with her and talking with her and getting to know her family and learning about her work and—"

"All right, all right. I'll go." He squared his shoulders and walked across the room, trying not to look like he was focused on a target.

Mr. Charles Kentworthy saw him first, which was a relief, because he smiled broadly and even gave Basil a wink as he approached.

Miss Hartford saw him and smiled. "Good evening, Mr. Thorne."

He bowed, feeling awkward. "Miss Hartford. You look... lovely."

She gave him a twinkling smile. "Thank you," she said and leaned forward. "Veronica said I have no business wearing this color, but I thought it was pretty, so I ignored her."

"I'm glad you did," he said, thankful that Modesty had advised him to start with a compliment. "May I have the pleasure of this dance?"

Her smile widened. "Yes, you may," she said softly.

He led her onto the dance floor along with the other couples. He was vaguely aware of the Kentworthys, the Hearsts, and the Ladies Windham among those dancing. But when the music started and he took her in his arms, he noticed nothing else.

The color of her dress brought out the beautiful dark

brown of her eyes and made her cheeks glow becomingly. Up close, he could see small copper tendrils curling around her face. She fit in his arms perfectly. She could have leaned forward and laid her cheek on his chest or rested her head on his shoulder: a perfect height. He wished she would. He could see the exact shape of her lips and the way the ends curved up slightly with good humor. They were keeping a proper distance, but he wished he could press her against him and feel the warmth of her body. He never wanted the dance to end. When he looked into her eyes, noticing tiny amber flecks within the brown, he thought she might be thinking the same thing.

It occurred to him he ought to make some effort at conversation. "You dance beautifully," he said.

"Thank you," she said, her smile soft. "You do as well. Do you enjoy dancing?"

"Very much. It has been some time since I had the pleasure." He hesitated. "I hope it would not be presumptuous to ask for a second opportunity to stand up with you?"

She blushed and bit her lip. "I would like that."

"Would you like to dance the second set or wait?"

"Well..." she said in a musing tone. "We're already on the dance floor..."

He grinned. "Perfect."

Chapter 72
Gerry

Gerry thought that Mr. Thorne looked far too appealing in formal attire, and far too sweet and earnest when he asked her to dance. He studied her face like she was an oil painting he needed to memorize. She liked the way she felt in his arms, admiring his strength and grace. His thumb stroked idly where it rested on her back—did he realize he was doing it?

She had always enjoyed dancing, moving in time with the music and taking advantage of the opportunity for conversation without chaperones hovering. She used dancing as a means to indulge in fancies of what it might be like to kiss her partner or be held closer. These fancies did not always end favorably; some people lost their appeal at close proximity. Mr. Thorne, however, did not. She could easily imagine going up on tiptoe to press her lips to his. She could even imagine the way he might smile afterwards. She could practically feel his arms pulling her closer at the very thought.

She was grateful when he proposed another dance,

even though she knew her friends and family would tease her and exchange conspiratorial glances. She anticipated the scolding she would get from Veronica. Despite this, she was thrilled when she and Mr. Thorne kept their places for the next set.

"Did you have any difficulty in bringing your family?" she asked.

"No more difficulty than usual. It has helped to have Modesty and Mary present to help with the...er... herding."

She laughed. "You are not giving yourself enough credit—as usual—you are marvelously good with the children."

"Thank you." His voice was as soft as his smile as he looked down at her. "You always say the nicest things."

"I don't say anything I don't mean."

"I know."

Gerry met his gaze, feeling uniquely drawn in by it. She thought back to when Gavin had written of his first London ball and how Charles had danced with him three times. She had known for some time that Charles was in love with her brother, even though Gavin had doubts, but the ball had confirmed her hopes that Charles's friendship was, in fact, a sort of courtship, a prelude to a proposal. She had spent many a ball afterwards wishing for that sort of certainty. Now, here she was, dancing with a gentleman she liked very much, who her friends and family liked as well, standing up for a second time.

But she did not feel the certainty she expected and, for once, she understood how Gavin could doubt what she thought was obvious. It wasn't that she doubted Mr.

Thorne liked her or that she liked him. The way he looked at her confirmed it and she was fairly sure she was looking at him in much the same way. Still, she doubted if it was enough to enjoy dancing twice, to enjoy his company and conversation, to find him attractive. Was that what it was like to be in love? She had always expected more...*something*, something she couldn't quite lay a finger on.

"I've long said you were a quick learner," she said, attempting to rekindle the conversation after the lull caused by her own tumultuous thoughts. "You've only been here for a few months and look how far you've come. It seems only yesterday you were in my shop wanting advice on how to talk to your siblings."

He chuckled. "It feels like yesterday and it also feels like I've been here all my life."

"Not in a bad way, I hope?"

"Not at all. I..." He tapered off and was silent for a couple of steps. "I cannot imagine a life outside of Tutting-on-Cress now. It feels like home. Or at least, it has felt more like home than any place I've ever lived."

Gerry grinned at him. "Tutting-on-Cress is special like that."

"It is. Although I suspect the magic dwells in the inhabitants. It would be just another country village without my family, and Laurence, and Lord Finlington, and your family, a-and you." She felt her face heat at his words. Before she could come up with an adequate response, he continued, "Not to say it isn't charming, of course. But I'm coming to learn that home is made up of the people one is fondest of. I felt terribly unmoored until I moved to Bath to live closer to Modesty. And even then—well, something always felt missing." His gaze was steady as he said, "But I think I'm finding what I was looking for."

It took everything Gerry had not to cause a ridiculous scandal by kissing him right then and there. Instead she breathed out slowly and looked away from his earnest expression. "I'm glad to hear it."

The set ended sooner than she would have liked. Unlike Charles, Mr. Thorne did not ask for a third dance; she suspected he was too proper for such a thing. She was rather grateful for it as she did not think she would have turned him down and it would have all but confirmed an attachment.

He led her back to her party. "You dance very well, darling," Charles said to him.

"Thank you," Mr. Thorne replied. He looked as if he was going to say more, but instead he gave a small smile, bowed politely, and said, "I suppose I'd better see if Modesty or my stepmother need any help with the children," and walked away.

"That's a pity," Charles said. "I was about to say what a fine couple you two make."

Gerry rolled her eyes. "Thank heaven for small mercies."

He chuckled. "Well, since our lovely friend did leave so precipitously, I do have the opportunity to observe that you both looked as if the world had faded away around you."

"It...um...felt that way."

"Marvelous," he whispered.

Gavin cleared his throat. "I am sure you will be angry with me, and I cannot blame you, but I feel bound to point out that you once informed me two dances was a particular mark of interest."

"Actually, I said three dances," she said.

"Yes," he said, "but the dukex informed me later that two would have been a more *proper* mark of interest. So I think that sentiment still holds."

Gerry did not want to admit that he was correct.

John and Veronica joined them, and Gerry prepared herself for criticism. To her surprise, John said, "You and Mr. Thorne look very well together, Geraldine."

"Thank you?"

Veronica sniffed. "I'm not sure how you shall handle that horde of children."

"I'm sure I don't know what you mean," Gerry said.

John frowned. "Has Mr. Thorne not made his intentions known to you?"

"We are merely friends, John."

He raised an eyebrow but did not reply.

Charles said, "I understand what you are thinking, John, but I rather think a couple of dances is perfectly natural, even if there is no official courtship."

Gerry did not appreciate the subject of the conversation. "Would you kindly not speak of this right now?"

"Don't be silly," Veronica said. "This is the first opportunity you've had since you left London and stepped down in such a disgraceful way. If that gentleman is taking even the slightest bit of interest in you, the least you can do is encourage him."

"Veronica," Gavin said, "Do keep your voice down. People will hear you."

Veronica rolled her eyes. "I'm sure it's common knowledge. Why else would her friends be foisting so many single gentlemen upon her? They might be more circumspect in their approach, but I'm sure they're all thinking the same thing."

"I seem to recall my friends telling you in no uncertain terms that they were not thinking the same thing."

"Nevertheless, Mr. Thorne is a man of property, and he will certainly give you some amount of respectability, which you truly do need."

"Oh, really, Veronica," Gavin said.

"I suppose I should commend you for capturing his attention. Goodness knows he's distracted with that brood." She considered for a moment. "You will have to give up your shop, of course."

Gerry bristled. "I am in no mind to put aside my shop, Veronica."

"You must consider your future husband," Veronica said. "No firstborn in their right mind would marry someone who is gone all the time. How would you mind your responsibilities of keeping house? How would you take care of the children? Perform spousal duties? It's all very well to have a silly hobby in your youth. But you are past such idleness."

"I feel certain," Charles said, "that anyone who courted Gerry would recognize how well she does her job."

"Yes," Veronica pressed, "but to keep it after

marrying suggests *eccentricity*." She said the word as if it gave her a bad taste. "Hardly becoming in a nextborn of quality."

Gerry wanted to scream, but she also wondered if, perhaps, Veronica was on to something. Was this why Mr. Thorne had never been particularly marked in his attentions? Was he worried about the same things Veronica had mentioned? Was this what had been holding her back all along? She had known taking a career in trade would include some sacrifices; she had seen friends abandon her, had lost contact with dozens of acquaintances—did it mean she would have to sacrifice him too?

The dukex approached their party. "It is good to see you dancing again, Geraldine," they said with a fond smile. "You always look so happy on the dance floor."

She attempted to return the smile but found she couldn't.

"Surely the dukex will agree with me," Veronica said. "Your Grace, is it not the best course of action for Geraldine to give up her shop when she marries Mr. Thorne?"

"I rather think that decision would best be made by the two people in question," they replied calmly. "What I think doesn't signify."

"Ah, so you *do* think so!"

"I was not aware a marriage was imminent. Did I miss an announcement?"

"No," Gerry said through gritted teeth. "There has been no proposal and no announcement."

"But he clearly likes you," John said. "Anyone can

recognize his interest. See? He's already coming back to our party."

Gerry turned and saw with dismay that John was right. Mr. Thorne was not only approaching their party but was practically upon them. How much had he heard? The thought of him overhearing the horrid conversation was appalling. Without stopping to think, Gerry excused herself and fled the ballroom, filled with embarrassment.

Chapter 73
Charles

Mr. Thorne approached, looking worried. "Is Miss Hartford unwell?"

Charles opened his mouth to assure the gentleman that she was, but Julian beat him to it. "Not at all, child. She was feeling overheated by the number of people in the room and stepped away for some air. I am sure she would appreciate some company."

Mr. Thorne gave a small smile and said, "Thank you, Your Grace. In that case, I'll be on my way."

As soon as he left, Veronica said, "They will need a chaperone. I'd better—"

"I will keep an eye on them," Julian said. "Trust me, Mrs. Hartford, I would not have encouraged him to seek her out if I was worried." They bowed and walked away in the direction Mr. Thorne had taken.

Charles immediately turned to Veronica. "That was badly done."

She looked up at him in shock. "What? Suggesting a chaperone? I know you are overly relaxed in your responsibilities of guardianship, Kentworthy, but I am not."

"I did not mean that," Charles said. "Although to suggest that the Dukex of Molbury was mistaken in the propriety of a situation was not only laughable but insulting. I meant that it was badly done to say such things to Gerry."

"I was only speaking the truth."

"No," Charles said as calmly as he could. "You were speaking with malice. To suggest that Gerry would have to choose between love and the career she has worked so hard for proves that you hardly know her and suggests that you want her to be unhappy."

"Well, I'm sure John will agree that his sister ought to think less of her own happiness and more about propriety and her future."

"She has nothing to worry about for her future," Gavin said. "If she were to never get married, Charles and I would happily house her forever."

"Precisely," Charles said. "Although I'm very much hoping that won't be the case because Gerry and Mr. Thorne would be perfect together. And if you have ruined this, I shall be very displeased."

Veronica cut her husband a glance. "Are you going to stand there and let me be spoken to that way?"

John looked pained. "Veronica," he said quietly, "I would like my siblings to be secure and well cared for. Mr. Thorne can certainly provide that and, clearly, so can Kentworthy. It's not the life I would have wished for her, but she is happy here and safe and...and that's all that really matters in the end." He blushed and glanced at Charles. "And I daresay Kentworthy is better at arranging that than I am."

Veronica's face went red. "Better?"

"He...he has taken care of my other siblings very competently. As long as my family is happy and safe... that is all that truly concerns me."

Veronica glared at him.

"Perhaps we ought to partake in the refreshments," John offered tentatively. He held out his arm for his wife. Her scowl deepened and she turned away from his arm and stormed off, thankfully in the opposite direction from where Gerry and Mr. Thorne had gone.

"That, however, was very well done," Charles said. "Thank you, darling."

John pinched the bridge of his nose. "Your standards are embarrassingly low, Kentworthy." He let out a long breath and looked in the direction his wife had taken. "I fear we have long overstayed our welcome. It was inevitable, really. We shall...we shall leave in the morning."

"John—" Gavin said.

John walked away before Gavin could finish his sentence.

Gavin sighed. "Imagine putting such nonsense in Gerry's head. I know we never take stock in Veronica's opinions, but I'm quite sure I saw Gerry start to believe it."

"I've never been so angry with her," Charles admitted.

"Do you really think she's ruined everything?" Gavin said.

"I'm hoping that Mr. Thorne is able to patch things up. He is remarkably intuitive, that one. So I'm still optimistic."

"One can but hope," Gavin said. "Perhaps..."

Charles turned to him. "Yes?"

"Well," Gavin said hesitantly. "Gerry did seem frightfully embarrassed when we pointed out that they'd danced two dances together. Perhaps we could...erm... help her out a bit by..."

"Distracting the gossips and dancing a few more times?" Charles said. "I'd be delighted."

Gavin's mouth quirked. "I was going to suggest twice more, but you know so much more about these affairs than I do."

Charles grinned as he took Gavin's hand. "Oh, I think we'll have to dance almost the entire evening to be really effective."

"The things I do for my sister."

Chapter 74
Sophia

Sophia watched as Miss Hartford strode away from her party and down the hall. Then she watched as Basil followed.

"Come on," Bel hissed. "We need to see if he makes a declaration. And don't do anything stupid," she added to Eli. "You'll ruin everything if you jump out of the bushes and start chattering again."

Eli nodded, looking annoyed and chastened. Sophia followed the twins as they stole to the garden. She felt sneaky doing such a thing, but she reasoned that if she weren't there to keep an eye on them, one of them might do something rash. When they finally reached the lamplit garden and crept behind a hedgerow, it was not to find Basil with Miss Hartford, but rather Lord Finlington with Mr. Standish.

The two gentlemen were not locked together in ardor; they were sitting together on a bench. Mr. Standish was resting his head on the viscount's shoulder and the viscount had draped his arm loosely around the younger man. They spoke so softly, Sophia could not hear the conversation, but she had no doubt she was witnessing a conversation between two lovers. She was sure Levinia would be disappointed by the lack of passion, but Sophia noted a tender expression in both men's faces and it made her feel a little lonely. She was distracted by hearing Bel hiss something. Sophia turned to see Eli run back into the house.

Bel rolled her eyes. "Idiot."

Sophia tugged on her sister's arm and they both trudged back inside. They were greeted by Miss Munro, who was standing at the door as if waiting for them.

"They did not go to the garden," Miss Munro said.

"How do you know that we—" Bel began.

Miss Munro raised an eyebrow and Bel abruptly stopped mid-question. "I'm quite sure they went to the library. And I'm even more sure that to follow them would be disastrous. If you want your brother to work up the courage to propose or admit that he's completely smitten with Miss Hartford, then you would do better to leave them alone."

"Do you really think he might?" Sophia said.

Miss Munro smiled. "I really think that I've never seen dear Basil so taken with anyone. Now, Bel, darling, be so good as to eavesdrop subtly on the other partygoers and report back to me about whether Mr. Bowden is a well-liked member of his community."

Bel gave a salute and ran off. Miss Munro tucked her hand around Sophia's arm and led her to a sofa. "And you and I shall observe from here."

"Are you...erm...going to pursue Mr. Bowden then?" Sophia tried not to sound disappointed.

Miss Munro smiled and patted Sophia's hands which were folded in her lap. Sophia felt her face go warm at the gesture. "No, not really. From what I've observed, he's a fortune hunter and very dull."

"How can you tell?"

"He only talks to ladies wearing the best jewels, despite the fact that some dresses—like the one Miss Hopkins is wearing—indicate not only wealth but taste. So he's not only a fortune hunter, but a foolish one at that. I can tell he's dull because no one seems to enjoy his conversation. So not a good marriage prospect. But it will keep her busy. And I do like gossip."

Sophia attempted to look at ease. "What else have you observed, if you don't mind my asking? I'm going to be a writer, you see, and it would be good for me to learn these things."

Miss Munro gave her a wry smile. "Well, darling, that is a very good skill to hone. Let's start with them."

"The Ladies Windham?"

"Yes. Lady Caroline Windham is a tremendous flirt. Do you see how she's touching that other woman's arm? It's intentional. She's expressing interest."

Sophia gasped. "But she's married."

"Yes, I know. And her wife has not only noted Lady Caroline's behavior, but has not lost her cheerful demeanor. She is either very good at pretending or she likes to observe it."

"Why would she like it?"

Miss Munro shrugged. "She might simply be an

indulgent spouse. Or she might enjoy seeing her wife with other women."

"Some people like that?"

"It's a certain taste. Lady Maria does not appear to be possessive at all, which suggests to me that she truly is unbothered. See how she draws the other lady into the conversation. She is encouraging the behavior."

Sophia was a little scandalized. "What else?"

"Well, let's look at the Kentworthys. This is their second dance together. They are very evidently in love, which is probably the primary reason for multiple dances."

"There could be other reasons?"

"Your brother danced twice with Miss Hartford. That is proof of his interest in her. When she returned to her friends, she was blushing even after Basil walked away. I suspect her friends were giving her some good-natured teasing. Then Mr. and Mrs. Hartford joined. There was an argument, although I don't know what was said. Miss Hartford saw Basil approaching and ran off."

"Oh," Sophia said. "We just saw them both leave the ballroom. We thought they'd gone to the garden."

"No, they didn't go into the garden. But I wouldn't worry about it. I had a better vantage point of the hall," Miss Munro said. "And I've been doing this sort of thing longer than you have."

"You know who went to the garden?"

"Yes, I was pleased. They seem very well suited for each other."

"I'm surprised that you spend your evening simply observing."

"Oh?"

She felt her face get hot. "Well...I would have expected you to...erm...socialize more." She couldn't very well say she expected Miss Munro to be the life of the party, though that's what she was thinking.

Miss Munro chuckled. "I alternate. I discovered when Basil took me to call on others that too many mistook me for his intended. I do not wish to encourage that line of gossip, so I thought it might be prudent to stay here. If I socialize too much, it will look like I'm trying to get to know my neighbors, rather than getting to know Basil's neighbors."

"Oh. That makes sense, I suppose. But you were so excited to meet everyone," she added sadly. "It seems a shame that you can't."

Miss Munro squeezed her hand. "Don't fret about me, sweet Sophy. I shall certainly come visit after Basil has married his lady love. Besides, it is quite companionable sitting with you. Who else should we observe?"

Sophia felt a thrill at the lady's words. Her heart sped up when Miss Munro didn't remove her hand over Sophia's. She wanted to lean into the other woman's warmth. Instead, she looked around the ballroom and said, "What do you think of Laury and Mr. Sebastian?"

Miss Munro lit up. "Excellent choice, darling. Let's watch."

Chapter 75
Basil

Basil watched in dismay as Miss Hartford left the group and walked to the other side of the ballroom. It took very little encouragement for him to follow. He followed her as she left into the busy hall. He followed even when the crowd thinned and she slipped through a pair of tall double doors.

Once inside the dark room, he hesitated. He discovered that he had followed her into the library. This was not only impolite, but also imprudent and possibly unwanted. His impulse had been to offer comfort, not additional frustration. He wavered on the threshold, but decided the gentlemanly thing to do was leave, and turned to go.

"You can stay," he heard her say from above.

He turned and saw her on the second floor, silhouetted against a window. Tentatively, he walked up the staircase. She was standing in an alcove, her back against the wall and looking outside. She didn't turn to greet him as he approached. The lanterns and moon from outside cast a gentle glow on her face and he stood, transfixed, by the sight of her. Quite frankly, he was often stunned by her beauty, but he so rarely had liberty to indulge the desire to stare. Now they were free of shop customers, friends, or family. She had given him permission to stay and he was taking her silence as permission to gaze his fill.

Finally, she turned and gave him a long look. "I'm sorry I left before you could join us. I didn't mean to be impolite."

"There's no need to apologize," he said. "I'm sorry the conversation was upsetting to you."

She sighed and looked out the window again. "I wish things could be different. That is...I wish...I wish things weren't so confusing."

"Are they?"

She nodded her head glumly. "Sometimes, it feels exactly as it should, but other times...well, perhaps it was foolishness on my part. Only, I've long hoped..." She paused and glanced at him. "Well, perhaps it would be too much to ask, after all."

Basil felt as if he had entered in the middle of a conversation. He had no idea what she was talking about and he desperately wanted to know. After some deliberating, he decided to simply ask, "It would?"

"I won't give up my shop," she said, as if it settled the matter.

This actually confused him even more because he couldn't remember a time when that had been suggested. "Has someone said you ought to? I thought your family was supportive of your career."

"They are," she said. "Even John has come around, oddly enough. But, well, a...a husband is...that is, a wife in trade would..." She looked away and firmly out the window. "When I made the choice to run the shop, I always knew I'd be sacrificing...I didn't think that I would also...anyway, I'm still figuring out how I feel. I rather wish everyone else would understand that."

Basil rather wished Miss Hartford would finish her sentences. He couldn't make out what she was trying to tell him. He stepped closer to her, settling himself against the opposite wall in the alcove. He looked out the window, as if seeing what she was seeing would help clear things up. It didn't, but it was a pretty sight. The viscount's garden was lit with lanterns. He could see the shadows of a couple standing farther back in the garden, too out of sight to determine faces. He felt a little wistful. The garden in the moonlight was a very romantic spot. Then again, the library in the dark with the moonlight shining in was also a romantic spot, assuming he could understand what his companion was trying to tell him.

He tried piecing together the fragments of what she'd said. She was concerned about being a wife in trade? She was sacrificing something in keeping the shop. But what had that to do with marriage?

He said, tentatively, "You're worried that your career might be incompatible with marriage?"

She let out a breath, as if relieved that he had figured it out. "Yes."

Basil was relieved too. If that was her only concern, he could certainly help with that. Only he wasn't entirely sure he was ready to propose quite yet. He tried to put himself in Miss Hartford's shoes. If she had been telling her family and friends for some time that she couldn't marry (and from the sounds of it, this was exactly what she'd been telling them), it would be a dashed difficult thing for her to stride out of the library and announce her engagement. The actual proposal would have to come later. Nothing for it.

He took a deep breath and tackled the first aspect of the situation. "Miss Hartford, anyone who knows you and has seen how good you are at what you do, would never suggest you give up your shop."

She gave him a warm smile. "Thank you, Mr. Thorne."

He relaxed against the wall at the sight of her smile. "I hope you'll forgive me for saying that I find you... extraordinary."

Her smile widened. "I think I can find it in my heart to forgive you for that."

"Thank you." He hesitated. "I'm grateful you let me stay and keep you company."

"I always enjoy your company. It is rather vexing, really."

His heart quickened. She enjoyed his company? "Is it? I'm so sorry."

She laughed. "It is. Because my family is extremely meddlesome. I rather wish they would simply...But they're not entirely wrong, of course. I mean, you're so pleasant and—" She glanced up at him and bit her lip. "Well, I rather wish you weren't quite so perfect sometimes. It is vexing because Charles has a tendency toward smugness when he's right about things."

A curl came loose from her updo and fell to the side of her face. Basil wanted to touch her, be near her. She had just said he was perfect, which made him think she wouldn't entirely mind his touch. Slowly, gently, he tucked the curl behind her ear. She smiled at him, so he didn't move his hand away, allowing it to settle against her cheek. She leaned into his hand a little.

"You see what I mean?" she said quietly. "Infuriatingly perfect."

He leaned closer and she slid her hand across his coat lapel. "I apologize for the inconvenience," he said. "I'll do my best to rectify the problem."

"Please do."

Then she gripped his lapel and pulled him down for a kiss. Basil eased his other arm around her waist and she settled against him. He had imagined what holding her would be like, but the reality far exceeded his dreams. His heart felt light and he tried to memorize the taste of her lips, the smell of her perfume, and the feel of her body pressed against his—he wanted to hold onto the moment forever. They fit so well together, almost as if they had been made to be in each other's embrace. Basil deepened the kiss and felt her sigh in satisfaction. He decided, quite suddenly, that he would do just about anything to make Miss Hartford sigh in satisfaction forever.

He was very aware that they were in a dark library and unchaperoned, so he kept his hand on her cheek and kept the arm around her waist light, taking care not to muss her hair or wrinkle her gown. She pulled away and said in a teasing tone, "If that's your way of not being perfect, Basil, I'm afraid you are going about it all wrong."

He grinned and kissed her cheek, a thrill coursing through him at the sound of his name on her tongue. "Forgive me. I've never been a quick learner."

"Nonsense," she said, tilting her head to give him better access to the side of her face. "I've taught you, myself. You're very clever."

He was pleased by the compliment and the gesture. He pressed light kisses across her face. "It's very kind of you to say. But I rather think the credit goes more to your instruction. If my tutors had been half as beautiful and fascinating as you, I'm sure I'd have been an excellent pupil."

"You think I'm beautiful?" she said, pulling away to look at him.

He didn't bother hiding his surprise. "Were you in any doubt?"

"And fascinating?" she said, delighted.

"I am in awe of you," he said simply.

"Damn," she muttered, and pulled his lapel to kiss him again.

Chapter 76
Gerry

On the one hand, Gerry wished Basil was not quite so good a kisser. She wished he had been clumsier in how he'd handled the conversation, wished he didn't look so impossibly handsome in the moonlight, wished he'd been less of a gentleman—anything, really, to help her say that he wasn't for her or to feel that Charles had less reason to be smug. She wished she didn't want him so much. But on the other hand, he was kissing her both tenderly and deeply, as if he loved her, and so she also wished the kiss would slide everything into place and make her feel certain.

He said he was in awe of her, that she was fascinating and beautiful. He was holding her carefully, his touch light. She could tell by the way he kissed that he was quite capable of passion. It was, frankly, infuriating. She almost wanted him to give into the passion: perhaps that was what she needed to be sure of her own feelings.

However, it occurred to her that despite Basil's care,

they were kissing in a dark and empty library unchaperoned and that if they were caught it would put paid to any of her stalwart stances on staying single. Perhaps it was just as well that he wasn't giving in to passion. So she pulled away, reluctantly. Basil seemed to sense her change in mood, for he didn't return to light kisses on her cheek. It was both disappointing, because she'd enjoyed them, and vexing that he had, once again, proven himself a worthy choice.

She sighed. "We should go back."

"Probably for the best." He carefully pulled his arm from around her waist, but he did brush his thumb across her cheek affectionately before dropping his other hand from her face. "Would you like me to leave first or you?"

Gerry considered for a moment. "I think there are multiple entrances. So if we each take a separate one, it might not matter."

He turned and looked around the room. He pointed to a door on the opposite side of the second level. "Do you know where that one goes?"

"I think it goes to the residential section of the house. But I believe there's a door downstairs that lets out near the garden."

He gave her a small smile. "How fortuitous. I just noticed how lovely the garden was in the moonlight."

She nodded, feeling sad that he had been gallant enough to volunteer for the longer route. He really was making this difficult for her. "Thank you."

He reached up and tucked an errant curl behind her ear. She laughed. "I really should pin it better."

"I wish you wouldn't," he said. Then he bowed and walked quietly down the stairs.

She heard the door directly below her open and close and then saw him walk into the garden. She took a deep breath, let it out, and made her way back into the ballroom. She was relieved that the room was so crowded. She was sure she was flushed and stepping into the midst of the crowd gave her a good excuse. Naturally, Bertie hired an excellent staff of spellcasters who kept cooling spells throughout the space, but there were always sections in any ballroom that tended to be stuffy. Gerry wandered aimlessly, unwilling to engage in conversation and let go of the moment she'd shared with Basil—Mr. Thorne.

A servant cleared his throat next to her. When she turned, he said, "Miss Hartford, Their Grace requested to speak to you."

Gerry felt a small frisson of panic in her chest, but swiftly quelled it. She nodded and followed the servant to where the dukex was sitting on a settee in the corner of the room. They thanked the servant and patted the cushion beside them in a wordless command. Gerry sat.

They didn't say anything for several minutes, long enough for Gerry to start panicking again. Finally, they said, "I told the servants nearly half an hour ago that I'd like to speak with you. Whatever you were doing, I commend you for being swift and tidy about it. Barely a wrinkle." They passed her their fan. "You're flushed, child. I take it you enjoyed yourself."

Gerry sighed and began fanning herself. "That seems like a dangerous question."

They chuckled. "It is. However, Mr. Thorne has not reentered the room, so I suppose I can also commend you for a cleverly orchestrated exit."

"How do you know I didn't simply take a walk somewhere?"

They raised an eyebrow. "Give Bertram's staff better credit. They would have found you much sooner if that had been the case."

Gerry decided it was useless to deny it. "So, what now?"

"Thankfully, you were not gone long enough to cause real concern. No one discovered you, I assume?"

She shook her head.

"Very good. And you are not disheveled, remarkably, I might add, and—" They curled a finger under her chin and tilted her face. "Yes, the blush is decreasing. So what happens next is rather up to you."

Gerry sighed in relief. "Thank you."

They released her chin. "Don't thank me yet. You still have a choice, but I do not think you are making it an easy decision to make."

"He is not making it an easy decision, you mean."

They chuckled. "Actually, if I had a guess, I'd say he was making it very evident."

She huffed. "Hardly. I don't care what Veronica says, I will not give up my shop. And you know as well as I do that in standing firm to that decision, I will most assuredly be considered an eccentric and no one will want to marry me then." She was annoyed with how sad she sounded.

"And what are you now, child, if not an eccentric?"

They tutted at her shocked expression. "Has Mr. Thorne given you any indication that he thinks less of you because of your career?"

"No," she said quietly.

They raised their eyebrows.

She continued, "He actually seemed pleased when I told him my family supports me."

"Has he said anything slighting of you as a person in trade? Ever made you feel less than in word or look?"

She shook her head. "He..." she faltered. The conversation in the library still felt too intimate to share. She glanced up at Julian and then away. She swallowed. "Quite the opposite, in fact."

"Then, consider this as an option, if you please: he might want to marry you—not regardless of your career but rather including it."

She looked up at them in confusion.

They sighed, cupped her chin, and said gently, "From what I've seen of Mr. Thorne, he is a good, generous, kindhearted, and sensitive person. If he would take issue with eccentricity, he has a great deal of trouble on his hands because most of the Thorne children, if not all, are likely to grow up to be very eccentric."

Gerry laughed.

"And," they continued, "I think we can both agree that the young man has been nothing but encouraging to his siblings in embracing their uniqueness. He has already proven to be more gracious and generous than society demands of him—he would have been lauded as generous if he had merely given his family money before sending them away. He would have been praised for leaving them to the stay in the house alone—but instead he stayed and took over as guardian, not only taking responsibility for dowries and allowances but helping raise the children too. He has all but legally adopted them, and practically without a second thought, despite his self-doubt and lack of self-assurance."

They smiled. "I agree that you will be hard put to find someone who will marry you as a shopkeeper while also not depending on you financially. But I think you have found that someone, improbable though it may be." They released their hold on her chin and settled back in their seat.

Gerry was grateful; it gave her time to think. Was it really that simple? She supposed she shouldn't have been so surprised. Julian had been the most adamant that she think of all aspects about stepping down in society, and had pointed out most of them to her. If Julian thought marriage was still a possibility despite Veronica's arguments to the contrary...

She looked up at them, "Do you really think he wouldn't mind?"

They gave her a warm smile. "I really do. And keep in mind, poppet, that he still hasn't asked you—at least, I assume he hasn't—but you could certainly make sure you are both of the same mind before accepting or rejecting any marriage proposal."

"He hasn't asked me," she admitted. "It's probably presumptuous to assume he will."

They chuckled. "Say rather a logical estimation. Have you given thought to our other conversation?"

"Yes, and I still haven't come to any conclusions."

"Well, did you take my advice and analyze the way you feel around him?"

She nodded.

"And?"

"Nothing's changed, not really," she said quietly. "I even wrote to Nell to see if she had any advice on the matter as someone who is not romantically inclined. She said her friendship with Patience is more valuable to her than anything she might experience in a romance. She urged me to determine if my friendship with him would be enough to make me happy. I still feel very fond of him and I still like his company. But I cannot say with certainty that I am in love with him. I should like to be certain before I enter into anything as permanent as marriage."

"An understandable sentiment, I think, but do keep in mind that nothing in this world is certain. If you like the gentleman's company, find him attractive, and could imagine these feelings to continue for years to come, that might be enough." They paused. "How was the kiss, by the way?"

She blushed and was relieved she still had Julian's fan in her hand.

They watched her fan herself. "That good, eh?"

Chapter 77
Basil

Basil needed time to think. The kiss with Miss Hartford made him even more muddled than before. He skirted the garden, careful to avoid the couple he'd seen from the library window, and found himself at a door leading to the conservatory. He realized he'd known of his destination without really acknowledging it, but he didn't entirely know why he wanted to go there. It just felt like the right place to think.

He was grateful to find the room dark and empty. The lights from the garden shone through the windows, bathing the whole space in a dim glow. He made his way around the plants to the bench on the other side of the room.

He sat down and sighed. The bald and horrible truth was that he was completely and wholly in love with Miss Hartford. He was all but ready to propose. There was still a niggling doubt in his head that it wasn't the right time to get married, not while he was still sorting out his place in the family and learning how to take care of his siblings. But Mary didn't think the timing was poor, and he would have been surprised if the children objected to the notion. So why was he stalling? Well, besides the fact that Miss Hartford seemed to think marriage was not a possibility for her.

That started another chain of thoughts. He had not entirely followed her line of thinking. She feared she'd have to get rid of the shop if she married, but he couldn't work out why or how that was ever a consideration. Did she expect to step completely into the role of nextborn spouse and run the house? In his mind, that problem was quite simple. Mary was already doing a marvelous job of that and had been doing it for years. If Miss Hartford preferred to keep her shop rather than take over running the house, Basil thought the solution remarkably convenient for everyone.

He chewed idly on a thumbnail, stewing over his predicament. The fact of the matter was, he couldn't make any decisions about whether or not marriage with Miss Hartford was an option because Miss Hartford's opinion was still unknown. As much as he wanted to propose as soon as possible, he feared that she might reject him. What could he say to change her mind without outright stating his intentions? He was not sure what he should do. And he was not entirely sure sitting in a dark conservatory in the middle of a ball was quite the best place to decide such things.

He heard a small rustle of leaves in the corner behind him. He turned, wondering if Lord Finlington had a pet that had heretofore been unseen, when he also heard a small sniffle.

"Who's there?" he said.

"Just me."

Basil frowned. "Elias? What are you doing back there?"

"Nothing."

"Well, come out, will you?"

Elias crawled out from behind a large potted plant. Basil couldn't see the boy's face very well in the dim light, but his posture indicated he was miserable.

"Are you all right?"

Elias shrugged. "I don't want to talk about it."

Basil put one hand on Elias's shoulder and leaned down to squint into his brother's face. Elias had been crying. Basil was pretty sure he was precisely the wrong person to help with this situation, but the twins had a habit of disappearing on him; he didn't want to lose track of Elias while searching for his mother. So, he pulled Elias to sit next to him on the bench. Then Elias did a truly remarkable thing: he curled forward onto Basil's chest, gripped his waistcoat, and sobbed.

Basil was at a complete loss, but he wrapped his arms around his brother's back and held him tightly. He did what the school matron used to do when he skinned his knees at Eton, and rubbed Elias's back and murmured useless condolences like "It's all right" and "I'm here now."

Elias cried for several minutes and then finally seemed to exhaust his supply of tears and simply slumped in Basil's arms.

"Are you sure you don't want to talk about it?"

"You won't understand. No one ever understands."

"I can try."

Elias sighed but didn't move. "No one is ever going to fall in love with me."

Basil tried to hide his shock from such a pronouncement. "Why do you think that?"

"I'm not pretty enough or clever enough or talented enough."

"Are you barmy?" Basil said. "You have genius ideas for your ship, you play the piano beautifully, and—"

"The ideas are all Bel's. I'll never be good enough at the piano to be interesting. Certainly not as good as Gracie. I'll never be the best at anything."

Basil tried to think of an appropriate response. "I hardly think that's true. Besides, you're young yet. You have plenty of time to—"

"No matter what I do, I'll always be second best to someone else."

"And what does this have to do with your marriage prospects?"

Elias shook his head into Basil's shirt. "Don't want to talk about it."

Basil resisted the urge to sigh. He half wished someone would walk into the room, someone who had a better idea of how to handle such a crisis.

Elias crumpled a bit. "I miss Papa."

Basil smoothed Elias's hair. "Tell me about him."

Elias shifted so he was leaning into Basil's side rather than his chest. "He used to take me riding all the time. Just me." Elias sniffed. "And he used to leave books on my bed. He did that with everybody, I think. But it was still nice."

Basil felt sad. "Yes, I can imagine it was. I didn't know you could ride."

He felt Elias nod. "Father told me I was an excellent horseman."

"It must run in the family," Basil replied. "I love riding too."

"Do you really?" Elias said, leaning back to look up at him.

Basil pulled out a handkerchief and wiped the boy's cheeks. "I really do. Tomorrow we'll go out riding together. Just us. All right?"

"Do you mean it, Basil?"

"Of course I do."

Elias hugged Basil's chest. "I'm so glad you've come to live with us. I hope you'll stay with us forever."

Basil smiled. "I don't plan to go anywhere."

They sat like that for so long Elias fell asleep. Basil was relieved, to be honest. He scooped his brother into his arms so Elias's head rested on his shoulder, and carried him out to the hallway, hoping to find someone he recognized. He ran into Lord Finlington and Mr. Standish, coming in from outside. The two men seemed to pull away from each other when they saw Basil.

"The first casualty of the night, I presume?" the viscount said, grinning at him.

Basil smiled back. "I'm afraid so. Would you be so kind as to tell my stepmother? I think we'd better take the children home now."

"I'll go," Mr. Standish offered, and stepped away into the ballroom.

The viscount circled Basil to see Elias's face. "Dead asleep, sweet thing."

"Bit of an exciting night, I think."

Lord Finlington nodded. "In many ways, I suspect. Pip and I were enjoying a chat in the garden. We both heard some footsteps in the bushes. I believe we had a small audience."

"Ah," Basil said. "I apologize if—"

Lord Finlington held a hand up, smiling. "Neither of us minded, my dear fellow. But..." He paused and glanced at the sleeping form on Basil's shoulder. "I rather suspect there may have been some disappointment from one or two of the audience members. Perhaps a slightly fractured heart."

"Oh dear," Basil said, thinking back to how he had found Elias. "Yes, you may be right. Thank you for telling me."

Lord Finlington gave him a wink. "Not at all, my sweet. I hope the information might be useful in your attempt to mend said heart."

"It certainly does explain a few things. But I confess I have no idea how to help. I'm sure his mother or...his father would do a better job of it."

"Oh, I think you're more than up to the task," Lord Finlington said.

Mr. Standish reappeared at that juncture, carrying Martin on his shoulder in the same way Basil was carrying Elias. Mary was holding Lucy in her arms. Modesty held Grace's hand. All of the children looked exhausted. The carriages were called, and Mr. Standish and Lord Finlington helped get everyone settled inside.

Mary attempted to encourage Basil to stay and continue enjoying the festivities, but he was, truthfully, ready to go home.

"Would you be so kind as to explain our departure to...er...our friends?" he asked his host.

"Glad to, darling," Lord Finlington replied with a knowing smile.

Basil took his family home. After they got the children settled in their beds, Mary pulled him aside. "Did you not have a pleasant time, dear? You seem very subdued."

"Just tired." She gave him a look that suggested she didn't believe that one bit, so he tried again. "I...fear I have fallen in love with Miss Hartford."

She smiled. "Well, of course you have. But why should you be afraid?"

He looked down at his hands. "I have no idea if she returns my affections."

She sighed and took his hands in hers. "I've seen the way she looks at you. It is fairly obvious that she does return them."

"But—I'm not sure if she wishes to marry."

"Have you asked her?"

"No, but she said something tonight that...well, it doesn't seem like the right time."

She gave him a long look and then squeezed his hands. "Your father often said the same thing when I told him to send for you or invite you to stay."

He stared. "H-he did?"

"Of course he did," she said softly. "He was so afraid you were not ready, that coming home would bring back too many painful memories, that he had waited too long —oh, he had a hundred excuses. In the end, they were only excuses because he was afraid to do what he truly wanted." She gave him a sad smile and reached up to brush some hair out of his face. "You're so like him. Just as kind, just as patient, just as generous." She cupped his cheek. "But this is one area where I would very much like you to set yourself apart from him. Do think about it, dear."

Basil felt tears pricking his eyes, and before he knew it, Mary had pulled his head down to her shoulder. He carefully wrapped his arms behind her back. "I don't know what I should do if she were to refuse me," he whispered.

She rubbed his back gently. "You'd let us take care of you, for once. And besides, I don't know why her refusal is such a foregone conclusion. She danced two dances with you."

He laughed, the sound muffled in the ruffles on Mary's dress and pulled himself out of the embrace. "You make it sound so easy."

"There is nothing easy about love. But it is worth the risk."

"Even..." He hesitated. "Even with such a loss as yours?"

She smiled. "I would choose him a hundred times over, if it meant sharing the precious time we had."

Chapter 78
Charles

Early the next morning, when most of the household was still asleep after their late night at the ball, the John Hartfords left. Charles got up early to see them off. He walked John, Veronica, their servants, and their son out to the waiting carriages. He bade his nephew farewell first and saw that he was settled comfortably with the servants.

"Thank you for having us," Veronica said archly, and climbed into the carriage without waiting for a response.

John turned to him, hesitant. "Thank you," he said. "I'm not sure I did—"

Charles put his hand on his shoulder. "You did very well, darling," he said quietly, so Veronica wouldn't hear. "I'm proud of you."

John pressed his lips together. "Give my regards to my siblings, if you would."

"Of course," Charles said. "You know they would have said goodbye if—"

John shook his head. "The journey is long enough

without delaying it until everyone is out of bed. Besides, I'm well aware that they—"

Charles squeezed John's shoulder. "They would have come to say goodbye."

John rolled his eyes. "I'm not sure I'm in the mood to hear empty words of how I'll be missed. But I do... appreciate your...help. This..." He glanced back at the carriage and then said in a low voice, "This was the most I've talked to my siblings since before Sebastian was born."

Charles pulled John into a brief hug. He felt John tense in the embrace, so he quickly pulled away with both hands on John's shoulders. "Write to me," he said. "I want to hear how your son is doing and how you are doing as often as you're willing to tell me. All right?"

"I'm not very good at letters, I'm afraid. Veronica usually writes most of them on my behalf."

"You'll learn," Charles said. "I would prefer subpar letters from you than better written ones from your wife."

John pressed his lips together again. "Very well."

"And I'll send you reports of how everyone is doing here."

John's mouth quirked ever so slightly. "Thank you. I would like that."

"And I'll tell you when Mr. Thorne finally asks Gerry to marry him."

John gave a brief but genuine smile. "Please do."

"Oh, do hurry up, John," Veronica said.

Charles clapped his shoulder. "Have a safe trip. Give your parents my regards."

John nodded and stepped into the carriage. Charles watched them drive off, feeling a strange mixture of relief that Veronica was finally gone and pain at the thought that he could have helped John more if he'd stayed a bit longer. He sighed and went into the house. He walked up the stairs and into his bedroom, stripped off his clothes, and carefully climbed back into bed next to his husband.

Gavin shifted and blinked at him. "Are you up already?" he said sleepily.

Charles pressed a soft kiss to his lips. "John and Veronica left. I was just seeing them off."

Gavin frowned. "They left? Without saying goodbye?"

Charles nodded and brushed some curls off of Gavin's forehead. "I tried to convince them otherwise. Veronica was most adamant."

Gavin rolled his eyes. "Of course she was." He was silent for a moment. "Never thought I'd be sorry to see my brother go. I can't say I'll miss him exactly, but it did feel strangely like...progress."

"I know," Charles said. "I would have liked him and his son to stay longer. Perhaps another time."

"Perhaps." Gavin yawned. "I rather think I owe you a victory prize, don't I?"

Charles grinned. "Yes, I believe so. But we can wait until you're more awake. Go back to sleep."

"Very generous," Gavin mumbled.

Chapter 79
Gerry

Gerry was grateful that Bertie had thrown his ball on a Saturday so she could have the next day to rest. She needed a day to sort through her thoughts. Her mind whirled after the ball: dancing with Mr. Thorne, the dreadful conversation with Veronica, kissing Mr. Thorne in the library, and her conversation with the dukex afterwards. Then Mr. Thorne left without a word and Gerry wondered if she had done something wrong. She disliked being so uncertain.

When she finally went downstairs for breakfast, she was greeted with the news that John and Veronica had left. "Thank goodness," she said. "I thought they'd never leave."

To her surprise, Charles, Gavin, and Pip did not echo her sentiments.

Seb yawned and said, "I'll be glad if I never see Veronica again."

At that, everyone else nodded. This made Gerry even more thoughtful. Did they miss John? Did *she* miss John?

She'd never experienced missing him before. She couldn't be sure how she felt about him now. It was another confusing thing to sort through.

"Did everyone have a good time last night?" she asked.

"Oh, yes," Charles said lightly. "Did you, my dear?"

Gerry paused. Did she have a good time? She weighed the enjoyable parts of the evening against the horrid ones. Finally, she said, "Yes, I did."

Charles beamed. "Excellent."

"Would it be all right if I went and saw Laury today?" Seb asked her.

"Why are you asking for my permission?" she said.

"I wasn't sure if you needed me for any spell work or anything."

She laughed. "No, take the day off. Take the rest of the days off until he goes to London again."

He grinned. "Oh, good. Thank you." He ate his food quickly and left.

"One might wonder if he was hoping for that answer," Gavin said.

"And what will you do with your morning, darling?" Charles said to Pip.

Pip looked embarrassed. "Well, I thought I might go and visit Bertie. You know I usually do on Sundays."

"Yes, of course," Charles said. "Do send him our love."

Pip nodded and finished his breakfast with slightly less haste than Seb and then left as well.

"You know," Gerry remarked into the silence, "for as nosy and meddlesome as you are, Charles, I'm very surprised you've gone so long without pushing them together."

Charles laughed. "Not to worry, darling. They're next."

"Incorrigible," Gavin said.

"And what are you doing today, darling?" Charles said, grinning at her. "Do you, perchance, have another teatime visit with your friends?"

She rolled her eyes. "Not today, thankfully. But I'm sure I'll find something to occupy my time. Thank you for your concern."

He chuckled. "Well, if you find yourself needing any advice, you know you only have to ask." He gave her a wink and then walked out of the room.

Gavin gave her an unreadable look.

"What?" she said.

"Are you all right?"

"Why wouldn't I be?"

"Veronica said some horrid things last night."

"Oh, that."

"I hope you know that Charles had words with her afterwards."

"Did he?"

"Of course he did. Even John agreed that her opinion was unfounded. Well, in so many words."

She blinked. "I never would have expected that."

Gavin drummed his fingers on the table, looking thoughtful. "Neither would I. It's strange. I almost wish he could have stayed for longer. I was glad to see her go, of course. But he said some things last night that made me wonder if...well, if he might be worthy of another chance. Would you like some company or do you want to be alone with your thoughts?"

She chuckled. "The latter, I think. Thank you."

He stood. "I know Charles was teasing, but you really can come to either of us if you need advice." She looked up at him in surprise. He gave her a small smile. "You're easily the cleverest person in our family. But even clever people need advice sometimes. I certainly needed it when I was in London, so I would be glad to return the favor. And I promise not to tease you if you do."

She returned his smile. "Thank you."

He nodded and left. Gerry finished her breakfast and went to her room. She found her notes and instructions for the focus spell and held them in her hand, wishing she could use them. She really could have used Seb or Pip's help today after all for she definitely needed some time to really think. She sighed and tucked the papers into her pocket. Perhaps she didn't need a spell to think clearly. Perhaps she just needed some peace and quiet. With Veronica gone, she might actually have it. She made her way to the garden and strolled slowly down the path.

Why was she so muddled on the subject of Mr. Thorne? In the light of day, she realized that Veronica's words the night before had been a great deal of nonsense. When she had hinted at them to Mr. Thorne, he clearly had no idea what she was talking about. Besides, the dukex had given her well-reasoned advice on that matter. So perhaps her worries about the shop could be set aside as quickly as they had appeared. She mentally did so, wishing she had the clarity of the spell to make those thoughts melt away.

Next, she supposed, was the matter of romance. She had always had a very particular idea of what romance might look like and it was infuriating that her friends and family had kept her from the courtship she had always dreamed about. It had all felt too orchestrated, too intentional. She wanted what her brothers had enjoyed: a gentle friendship that blossomed into something more. That had always seemed perfect.

Instead, everyone was speculating about an imminent proposal. She wasn't even sure she was in love with Mr. Thorne. They were friends, but surely that was not the proper grounds for a good marriage. She had expected passion and to be swept off her feet. She had expected to know that it felt right. She had expected the path to be clear.

She stuck her hand in her pocket and felt the pages for the spell between her fingers. Was it foolish to expect magic to tell her the answers to her problems? Gavin had found his way without the spell's benefit. So had Seb. Pip seemed to know exactly what he wanted, for all that he was taking his time. She didn't like feeling foolish.

She thought about what Gavin said at breakfast: even clever people needed advice sometimes. She knew perfectly well what Charles would say if she went to him, and her friends' opinions on the matter were perfectly clear. It occurred to her that she had never spoken to Gavin about Mr. Thorne. She stopped short in the garden. When had she stopped going to Gavin for advice? They used to tell each other everything. He knew her better than most. She remembered his promise not to tease her if she did need help.

With that in mind, she went in search of him. She found him in his study, reading a poetry book.

"You know," she said as she walked in, "I've often wondered how you can enjoy the same poetry over and over."

He gave her a sardonic look. "This is a new one. Well, sort of new. Bertie loaned it to me a while ago, but I haven't had time to give it proper attention with John and Veronica here."

"Bertie loaned you a book of poetry?"

"Cynthia Lacey Randolph. She's combining poetry and magic. It's fascinating. There are nearly two dozen spells in here."

"Really? That actually sounds interesting."

He rolled his eyes and closed the book. "High praise indeed. Did you need me?"

"Well," she hedged. "I thought I might take you up on your offer from this morning."

He set the book aside and folded his hands on his desk. She was relieved he hadn't looked sarcastic or even smiled knowingly. Then she was irritated with herself all over again for overlooking her brother for so long.

She sat down in the chair across from him. "I always expected to fall in love before I got married."

He raised an eyebrow. "Are you not in love now?"

"Well, it certainly doesn't feel the way I thought it would."

"What did you expect?"

She gestured vaguely. "I don't know. Excitement, I suppose. Or certainty. I thought it would be an overpowering feeling I couldn't ignore. Instead I feel uncertain and confused. I wanted what you had with Charles. I knew it was love before you even danced with him, well before he proposed. I expected that."

Gavin frowned. "Gerry, you knew it was love before I danced with him. I did not. You might recall that you pointed it out to me and I specifically asked you not to pursue the subject."

She sat back in her seat. She'd forgotten that. "So what did falling in love feel like for you?"

"I didn't know it was love for a long time. At first, it was a vague notion that he was handsome. I liked that I could talk to him and that he genuinely seemed to want to listen. I enjoyed his company. I... looked forward to seeing him. I felt comfortable and safe around him. I did recognize when I was growing fond of him, but it frightened me because I didn't think he felt the same way in return. So I did my best to ignore it." He gave a small smile. "Silly, really. It wasn't overpowering. It was gradual. When he left, I missed him. When I feared I might never kiss him again, it was all I wanted to do. The prospect of a life with anyone else sounded...miserable and empty." He shrugged. "It wasn't fireworks and it wasn't clear. It took me months to come to the conclusion."

She leaned her cheek on her hand. "It still sounds as though you were sure."

"Eventually," he said. He paused. "Do you believe Seb to be in love?"

"Of course."

"He wasn't sure, even after Laurence proposed to him. He spent days being a miserable sod, fretting about what to do."

"I'd forgotten that."

"What makes this feel less than perfect to you?" he said. "Because from where I stand, you two seem perfect for each other."

"That's just it! Everyone keeps telling me how perfect we are together, what a lovely couple we make. It feels so orchestrated, so contrived, so forced. I want love to come naturally."

He rolled his eyes. "Gerry, the reason everyone keeps saying that is because he lights up the moment he sets eyes on you *every time*."

"He does?"

"Yes!" he said, exasperated. "And you blush in a quintessentially Hartford manner every time he enters the room. When you smile, he looks like a man in a desert who's just spotted an oasis."

She scoffed. "He does not."

"Have you ever known me to exaggerate things like this?"

"No..." she admitted.

He sighed. "You're one of my favorite people in the entire world. I would never encourage you to marry someone who wasn't worthy of you. Mr. Thorne seems to be one of the few people who might actually deserve you. I've seen the way you are together. At Charles' dinner party, you talked to each other as if no one else was present. At the ball, you looked as though you were in your own world." He paused. "If you don't wish for marriage, I will completely understand. And if you don't want to be married to Mr. Thorne, however perfect he may *seem*, I will stand by your decision."

"I *do* want to be married."

"Why?"

She frowned. "Why?"

"Yes, why does the notion of marriage appeal to you?"

She shrugged. "I want to have someone to come home to. I want someone who's...mine?"

He smiled encouragingly. "And what sort of person would that be?"

"Someone who's patient and kind. Someone who doesn't mind that I talk about magic all the time. Maybe even someone who enjoys talking about magic as much as I do. Someone who isn't bothered by my working in the shop. Someone who gets along with my family. Someone who wants children, and who likes children, and —" She broke off and was silent for a long moment. Gavin didn't rush her. He didn't need to tell her that she had just described Mr. Thorne. She heaved a sigh. "Someone who kisses me the way I want to be kissed and holds me like I'm precious," she said quietly.

"Can you imagine yourself being married to Mr. Thorne?"

"Of course I can."

"And...does that feel promising or...disappointing?"

"It sounds rather lovely," she admitted. "I like him

very much. I enjoy his company. I'm always pleased to see him. You all seem to like him a great deal, which is very important, and he likes you too, which is even more important. I like his family. I like that he lives in Tutting-on-Cress..."

"But?"

"But I keep waiting for lightning to strike. I keep waiting to feel an irresistible pull. Is enjoying someone's company enough for a happy marriage? Is looking forward to seeing them sufficient? I always wanted passion. I'm worried that...I'm worried that friendship, even really good friendship, won't be enough. Julian says I shouldn't wait for a feeling that may never come."

Gavin looked thoughtful. "As I said, it wasn't lightning for me, nor fireworks. The feeling of love crept up on me. Friendship came first. Now, I cannot imagine loving anyone the way I love Charles. There is—" He broke off and his face reddened. "—passion. But underneath that is the friendship we formed in London. For me—for us— it has been the foundation upon which everything else was built. I could not tell you if friendship is enough for a happy marriage, but I can say that friendship was a sufficient start."

Gerry was very irritated that she was beginning to cry when faced with her brother's reasoning. She sniffed. "Really?"

He stood, circled the desk, crouched in front of her and took her hands. "Mr. Thorne is kind and good. He is patient. He is sensible and generous. Whatever Veronica may think, he's not the sort of person who would quibble about you working every day."

"Julian said something similar."

Gavin let out a long breath. "I know you don't like everyone pushing you two together, and I can most certainly understand that. But if you weren't being pushed together, would you consider him as a potential husband? If he asked you to marry him, would you be tempted?"

She thought of how much she had liked him the first time they'd met, the way he focused when she taught him spells, the way he'd watched her when she was in his study, the way he kissed her in the library. "Yes," she said at last. "I would."

"Do I need to tell you that you practically described Mr. Thorne when you described your ideal husband?"

"No, but go ahead," she said, rolling her eyes.

"The man has visited your shop so many times to learn about magic. I remember when he came over after your spell was complete and it was clear as day that he knows nothing about magic and could barely follow the conversation. Yet, he still asked questions and gave you his full attention. I think you could talk of nothing but magic all day, every day, and he would listen like it was essential to his being—not because he gives a fig about magic, but because he wants to know as much about you as possible."

"Do you really think so?"

"Yes," he said gently. "I really do. I cannot tell you if you are in love with him. But at the risk of sounding like you several years ago, it is very plain to me that he loves you and that you, at least, care for him in return."

"But is that enough to build a whole life on that?"

"I cannot tell you that. But I can tell you that, for me, it has been enough to see that Charles smiles every time he sees me, that I could talk about poetry for hours and he would never tell me to stop, that he loves my family, that he respects me, that I can be honest with him, and that I will always miss him when we are apart. I'm not sure what you are looking for or waiting for. I would never tell you to settle for anything less than complete and total happiness. But if you can imagine yourself being happy with Mr. Thorne, then that is enough, regardless of what you thought it *might* be like."

She leaned forward and kissed his cheek. "Thank you." He handed her a handkerchief and she wiped her face. "I had hoped that focus spell might help me work it all out, but I can't cast it alone, and then I felt foolish for even needing magic for this sort of thing."

He rolled his eyes and stood up. "Sometimes I think you forget that I can cast magic perfectly well, despite the fact that I have none of your ambitions or Seb's restlessness."

"Oh," she said. "You're right. I could have asked you."

He gave her a wry smile. "I'll help you if you'd like, but I don't think you actually need it."

She laughed. "I think you might be right."

His smile turned fond. "Good."

Chapter 80
Basil

When Basil awoke the morning after the ball, he was immediately flooded with memories: the sight of Miss Hartford, dancing with Miss Hartford, kissing Miss Hartford, and, finally, Elias crying in the conservatory. It didn't take him long to come to the conclusion that as muddled as he was about Miss Hartford, he knew where to start with Elias. Granted, he had little idea of what to do after he started, but he vaguely remembered his promise to take Elias riding, and that seemed as good a place to start as any. He hoped the rest would become clear.

"We're really going out riding?" Elias asked when they met in the stables.

"Didn't I tell you we would?"

Elias hugged Basil. Then he stepped back, looking embarrassed. "I'm sorry about last night. You must think me so very—"

Basil crouched and put a hand on his brother's shoulders. "I think I haven't done a very good job of giving any of you my undivided attention, but I'm going to do better. All right?"

Elias nodded. "Thank you," he said timidly.

Basil smiled and ruffled his hair. "Where would you like to go?"

"Could we visit Laury?"

"Of course. That sounds like a wonderful idea."

The stable master helped Elias onto the horse. Once he saw his brother safely seated, Basil swung onto his own horse and led the way out of the stables.

"You set the pace," he said.

Elias smiled and coaxed his horse into a trot. Basil was pleased to observe that he was a confident and capable rider. He said as much and Elias gave him a wide grin in response. They went at an easy pace that allowed for conversation. Basil did his best to tease out questions about what Elias liked to read, what his favorite meals were, what he was learning to play on the piano. He guided the conversation back to the topic of their father and listened as Elias told stories and provided small details about a man Basil never had the chance to know. His father did all the voices when he read out loud, he ate apples from the bottom of the fruit, he always made time for each of his children even when he started to feel poorly.

At length, they arrived at Copperage Farm. Basil worried they had arrived far too early for visiting, but was hailed from across the garden by Laurence himself. Basil dismounted and helped Elias down.

Laurence pulled Elias into a hug. "This is a wonderful surprise," he said.

"I hope it's not too early," Basil said.

"Not at all. We've always been early risers." Laurence looked down at Elias. "Have you had breakfast yet?"

Elias shook his head. "We went for a morning ride first."

"Hm. Well, lucky for you, we have a delicious spread this morning. Go inside and surprise my parents. We'll be along in a moment."

Elias nodded eagerly and ran into the house.

"I suppose we ought to have gone after breakfast," Basil said. "I'm afraid that didn't occur to me."

Laurence chuckled and took the reins of Elias's horse. "Quite all right. He's perfectly fine. With children, though, you have to plan around food or else they turn into frightful grumps."

"Duly noted."

Laurence led the way to the stables and got the horses settled. "Did you come here at Elias's request or did you need advice?"

"It was at his request but...er...I'm sure I could use some advice."

Laurence grinned. "You looked very well dancing with Gerry, you know."

"So I've been told."

"Is there a reason you haven't proposed?"

Basil sighed. "I haven't been sure of her interest and I wasn't sure if it was the right time."

Laurence raised an eyebrow. "You do look at her face when you talk to her, don't you?"

"What?"

Laurence huffed. "I think her interest is rather apparent."

"Oh," Basil said. "Well, that's...um...good. To be honest, I suppose I do recognize that she is...interested... but I'm still unsure if it's the right time."

"Are you waiting for a sign?"

"I'm not sure."

"Well, if you want my advice..."

"I do."

Laurence stopped walking and turned to face him. "You're in love with her, aren't you?"

Basil nodded.

"Then tell her. If she truly isn't interested, which I doubt, then waiting won't change much. You already know each other's character well enough by now, I think, to determine if you're well suited. If she is interested and the timing truly isn't right, then she'll tell you. You'll be able to decide together when the right time would be."

"Oh," Basil said. "Do you really think it's that simple?"

"Yes!" Laurence said, laughing.

Feeling encouraged, Basil allowed himself to be led into the cottage for breakfast. He considered Laurence's advice as they ate, as he and Elias rode back home, and after he'd tucked himself away in his study. He pulled the spell out of his pocket and unfolded it, reading the instructions and brushing his thumb over the handwriting.

Miss Hartford had designed the spell with him in mind. That meant something, didn't it? The dances at the ball, the kiss in the library...it was evident that she returned some amount of affection. But would it be enough? What would he do if she refused him? Modesty had laughed off the proposal, explained why it wouldn't work, kissed his cheek, and carried on as if nothing had happened. It had been embarrassing, but he had seen her reasoning and accepted it. Their friendship hadn't changed. He had a feeling that wouldn't happen with Miss Hartford. If she refused him, he would be...devastated. In such a small community, they were sure to see each other often. His life in Tutting-on-Cress felt so new and fragile, he hated to ruin it with misguided haste.

He heard a knock on the door and then Modesty poked her head in. "Where did you run off to this morning?"

"I took Elias out for a morning ride. Come in and keep me company?"

She closed the door and sat down. "Have you proposed to her yet?"

He shook his head.

"Good heavens, darling. You kissed her in the library. It was either terrible and now you feel like a cad, or it was wonderful and you're being an idiot. Which one was it?"

"How did you know that?"

She raised an eyebrow.

He sighed. "The latter."

"Good."

"Well," he said irritably. "I'm glad you're pleased."

"I am. You being an idiot is a far simpler problem to fix than you being a cad. And I had a very good view of the hallway. Be more subtle next time you follow a person out of a ballroom."

"Subtle heart never won fair lady," he murmured.

She laughed. "There! You see I was right! I don't think anyone else noticed, except a few of the children. And the dukex. I doubt much gets past them."

"Well, the dukex was the one who encouraged me to follow her actually...but I don't think they expected me to...erm..."

"Kiss her? I saw them talking to her after she returned. Considering the fact that you weren't dragged to the vicar, I can only presume you're safe from scandal."

He breathed a sigh of relief.

"So why haven't you proposed?"

"I've been waiting for the right opportunity. Laurence did tell me this morning that I should simply admit my feelings to her, regardless of my fears about the timing."

"Well, as your first best friend, I can tell you that your second best friend is right." She leaned forward in her seat. "What exactly are you afraid of?"

He swallowed. "I'm not sure I can take it if she turns me down."

Her face fell. "Oh, my dear." She stood and hurried to the other side of the desk, wrapping her arms around his shoulders.

He buried his face in her neck. "It won't be like it was with you. We won't be able to laugh about it and carry on like it was nothing."

She rubbed soothing hands down his back. "I know," she said. "It's much more frightening when you're in love.

There's so much more to lose." She pulled back and framed his face with both hands. "You can't guard your heart forever, Basil, trying to keep it from breaking. You did that with your father and look where it left you." She wiped her thumb across his cheek, catching a tear. "I didn't realize this fear was holding you back. Take some time to work up the courage. But don't wait forever, darling. It would be a disservice to you both."

"I know. I...I will."

She dropped her hands. "Good. And I'll stay here until you do. If the worst happens, I'll be here to help you patch your heart back together."

He gave a watery chuckle. "Thank you."

She glanced at his desk. "Is this another one of her spells?"

"Her most recent design."

"The one she designed for you?"

"It wasn't exactly for—"

"Oh, don't be pedantic, silly. Everyone knows it was with you in mind. May I?"

He nodded.

She picked it up and looked it over carefully. "Were you going to cast it?"

"It needs two people. Well, she advised having a second person on hand. I certainly didn't intend to ignore her advice."

"Certainly not," she said wryly. "Do you want me to help you?"

"We don't have the ingredients. And I'd feel foolish going to her shop for them."

"That makes no sense, darling. It's what her shop is

there for. Nevertheless, you're in a fragile state so I won't press the matter." She tapped the paper, looking thoughtful. "I imagine Lord Finlington has the ingredients we need. Why don't we call on him?"

"Remember what you were just saying about my fragile state?"

She tutted. "He's your friend."

"I'm not sure we're that—"

"He is your friend and he threw that ball specifically to get you two to dance together."

"What? What makes you think so?"

"Because Charles Kentworthy is anything but subtle. He and Lord Finlington are friends and it is exactly the sort of thing I would have done in their place. Almost everybody in this county seems to be conspiring to get you two together. It's really a wonder of this age that you're both still single."

He gave a small smile. "Well, you're right on that count."

"I'm right on every count, don't be ridiculous. Now, dry your face, send for the carriage, and we can call on the viscount for tea. We'll tell him what a marvelous time we had last night and then we'll ask him very politely if we can use some of his ingredients so you can cast a spell in order to plan your proposal properly. Besides, from what I gathered, he was very intrigued by the spell himself, so he'll probably be pleased by the opportunity to observe."

Basil inclined his head in acknowledgement. "You might be right."

"I'm always right. When will you learn? Now, up, up,

let's get going. Tell yourself you're doing him a favor. That should motivate you."

He laughed and stood. "I'm glad you're here."

"I know you are. Let's go."

When they walked out of the study, Mary seemed to understand immediately what was on his mind. She kissed his cheek, gave that same cheek a pat, and told him not to hurry back as the whole family was still exhausted from the late night. It took shockingly little time to call for the carriage and travel to Lord Finlington's home, considering how anxious Basil was about the whole thing. He was relieved that Modesty took over when they arrived.

"My dear Lord Finlington," she said as they were shown in. "We simply had to come and tell you what a marvelous time we had last night. It was a triumph, my dear! A sheer triumph!"

Lord Finlington laughed and seemed completely unfazed when Modesty kissed his cheeks. "Thank you, my sweet. It is good to see you both so soon. How nice of you to come and tell me in person."

"Yes, well, it does make for a very good excuse to come visit a person the day after they've thrown a ball, doesn't it?"

Basil was less relieved that Modesty had decided to take over.

The viscount grinned. "Yes, it does. Do come in, m'dears, and tell me the real reason you've come."

Modesty took Basil's arm and led him forward. "Well, dear Basil is in quite a state because he has a proposal to make—which I'm sure you know—but thankfully he has a charming spell that Miss Hartford designed and—remind me again, Basil, who put the idea for this spell in her head?—we thought you might be able to lend a hand in the small matter of ingredients. Not to mention some academic curiosity on your part as to how the spell works."

Lord Finlington, to Basil's great relief, looked delighted. "What a clever notion, darling. I'd be happy to assist. Do come into my study." He led the way into the room.

Basil was surprised to see Mr. Standish was already there. "Good morning, Mr. Thorne," he said politely.

"Good morning, Mr. Standish. I do hope we aren't interrupting your visit."

The young man shook his head. "Not at all. It's always good to see you."

"They're here to cast Gerry's new spell," the viscount explained.

"Ah, excellent. I'll sit here in case you have any questions," Mr. Standish said.

"Where is your cousin?" Basil asked.

The viscount chuckled. "My cousin took their breakfast in bed this morning. They usually do, particularly after a late night. I'm sure they will come and join us before long. Now, you have the spell?"

Basil handed it over. Lord Finlington read it and began pulling items off the shelves. "I've been frightfully curious about it," he admitted. "I hope you won't mind if I observe while you work."

"Not at all," Basil said. "I'm not very good at spellcasting, really, so I may need your assistance."

"That's not what I hear," the gentleman replied. "Gerry says you've learned a good number of spells since you've come to town." He glanced up at Basil. "She's not one for false compliments, you know."

"Oh," Basil said. He had a feeling Lord Finlington was referring to more than his spellcasting abilities.

"Just give me a moment to weigh a few of these, my sweet, and then everything will be ready."

Basil watched as the viscount prepared everything and then stepped back with satisfaction. "There," he said. "Fortunately, I just cleared the space for some experimenting of my own, so the room is yours." With that, he leaned against his desk and looked expectantly at Basil.

Basil picked up the spell and carefully began placing objects. He felt very self-conscious to have Modesty, Mr. Standish, and Lord Finlington watching him. The viscount surprised him by occasionally offering small words of encouragement or advice: "A bit to the left with that one, I think," or "Perhaps a touch more centered? That's it."

Basil chalked the sigil and looked up to the viscount, who nodded encouragingly. "You're doing very well, darling. Go on."

He started to hold his hand over the spell to cast, as he had done on previous spells, but Lord Finlington gently caught his elbow. "You'll want to be in the circle, m'dear. Step carefully now. There you go."

Basil sat down cautiously and cast the spell. All at once, he felt his thoughts still and settle. He breathed in deeply, willing himself to feel calm, and breathed out slowly. He thought of Miss Hartford, how beautiful she looked at the ball, how well she had fit in his arms, how sweet she had been to kiss. He thought of their conversations and how happy he would be to spend the rest of his life hearing about her shop, her spell projects, and her family. It all felt so simple, he wondered why he had been so muddled.

He tried to imagine himself proposing and found that it too was astonishingly simple. He had, he realized, come very close to proposing the previous night. And she had responded to his honesty with a kiss.

Perhaps Laurence and Modesty were right after all. He was just thinking that of course they were right and it had been silly to doubt them when the spell's magic abruptly dropped and he felt his mind begin to crowd with the usual distractions, doubts, and fears.

He looked up at his friends.

Lord Finlington looked thoughtful. "You have very good control," he remarked. "And a good amount of strength to your spellcasting. You'll undoubtedly get even better the more you practice."

"How could you tell that, my lord?"

"I have my ways, m'dear. We'll have to see to it your siblings have sufficient training. I imagine at least some of them will have immense talent and it will be best to catch that early."

Basil nodded.

"The spell itself was neatly cast—well done, darling —but it dropped very suddenly."

"Yes, I felt it drop."

The viscount raised his eyebrows. "Did you?"

"Well, I should say, rather, that my mind felt very clear when I cast it, but it felt a good deal less...well, less clear very suddenly."

Lord Finlington nodded. "I see. Does Gerry have plans to fix that, petal?" he said, turning to Mr. Standish.

"Yes, she does. She also wants to extend the length of the spell and check for recastability."

"Excellent. She's very thorough. I've always liked that about her."

"Did it help?" Mr. Standish said to Basil.

"I think so."

"You know what you're going to say to her?" Modesty said.

"I have an idea."

"Enough to be going on with," Lord Finlington said, reaching a hand down to help Basil up. "Would you like some tea?"

"That would be lovely," Modesty said. "Unless you want to go and propose to her right now?"

Basil laughed. "No, I think tea first. My mind is made up, but I still need to work up the courage."

Lord Finlington smiled. "Well, that's half the battle."

Chapter 81
Sophia

The family meeting was inevitable. There was a lot to discuss after the ball.

As predicted, Levinia started off the meeting speaking eloquently on how beautiful Basil and Miss Hartford had been together and did everyone see how he looked at her, et cetera. She launched into a monologue on how romantic it was to find the viscount and Mr. Standish in the moonlit garden. Sophia was grateful to her sister for ticking most of her agenda notes so effectively, although she did wish Levinia could be a bit more succinct.

"Right," Sophia said when Levinia paused for breath. "Before we go any further: Eli, are you all right?"

"Yes. I'm sorry for running off like that. I had to sort myself out."

"Did you?"

"A little. Basil helped."

"You mean when you two disappeared this morning?"

He glanced at Bel, who was fastidiously not looking at him, and nodded.

Sophia said, "I'm glad he helped. I think we should make it clear right now that we will not be jealous of each other for spending time alone with Basil. All right? He's doing his best. If you need to talk to him, just ask him. He's not unreasonable."

Eli nodded, more enthusiastically this time. "Yes. That's why this morning happened, really. I was telling him about how Papa used to take me riding."

"Good," Sophia said. "So I don't want to hear any complaining about it from anyone."

Bel heaved a sigh. "Oh, all right."

"Now, the next thing we need to decide is what to do next. I think—"

"Do you know why Basil never came to visit?" Eli said suddenly. When they all turned to look at him, he gave a shrug. "I've always wondered. Do you think he didn't want to see us? Is it because we're only related by half-blood?"

"I can't imagine that's the reason," Sophia said, although now that the question had been brought up, she realized she wanted to know the answer to it.

Levinia opened her mouth and closed it.

"He probably didn't want to be bothered with a whole bunch of children," Bel said in a bitter tone.

"You think we're a bother to him?" Grace asked.

"We aren't, are we?" Martin said.

"Of course we aren't," Sophia said.

"Yes, we are," Bel said. "We're always in the way. We talk all the time."

"He'll have to see to our dowries and expenses and everything," Eli said. "And our commission for the navy," he added hastily.

"Weighed down by responsibilities," Levinia said sadly.

"What should we do?" Grace said, looking worried.

"I don't know," Sophia said. "Perhaps we could try to be more—"

"What are you all doing out of bed?"

They all turned to see Basil standing next to them in his banyan and slippers. He looked weary—but not in the way of someone who has been woken from sleep, Sophia thought. He looked as if he hadn't been sleeping at all.

"Family meeting," Martin said.

Basil's eyebrows rose. "Oh? And do they always happen at this time of night?"

Martin nodded.

Basil looked at each of them in turn. "Is everything all right?"

Lucy slid down from her seat and proceeded to do what she always did if Basil stood still for too long: she asked to be picked up. He did, almost mechanically.

Sophia glanced at Bel, who shrugged. She said, "We hold family meetings after...after our parents have gone to bed. It gives us time to discuss things without any adults present. And ensures everyone is here and that we won't be interrupted."

"I see," he said. "You've been having these meetings for a while?"

"Years," Levinia intoned. "It's a sacred tradition."

Basil smiled. "Understood. Well, perhaps I ought to leave you all to it then?"

Impulsively, Sophia made a decision. "No, you can join us."

He looked startled. "Are you sure? You said 'without any adults present.'"

"Well," she said. "I'm going to be an adult soon. And I expect I'll still be invited to the meetings. So there's no reason you can't be."

"Besides," Grace said. "The topic was you."

Basil's eyes widened. "You're quite sure you want me to be here for that? I may be a bit biased on that particular topic."

Sophia laughed. "Yes, you should join."

They scooted over to give him room in the center of the bench. He sat down and shifted Lucy to his lap. She curled against him and leaned her head on his chest.

"It's rather late for the little ones," he remarked, smoothing Lucy's hair. "Don't they ever fall asleep mid-meeting?"

"Oh, all the time," Levinia said.

He chuckled. "So what is first on the agenda? That is, what can I contribute to the discussion?"

Sophia hesitated. Now that Basil was there and sitting next to them, she had no idea what to say.

Then Eli said, "Why did you never come visit us?"

"Oh," Basil said. "It had nothing to do with...no, that's not what you asked. Let me think." He sat silently for a long moment. "I suppose the best way I can describe it is: I was afraid."

"Afraid of what?" Grace said.

Martin wedged himself behind Basil's back and looped his arms around Basil's neck, as if that might help their older brother in whatever fears he was about to indulge.

Basil gave another small smile and reached up to cover Martin's hands with one of his own. "I suppose I'd better start from the beginning. When my mother died, my—our father was...devastated. He barely talked or came out of his study. I was incredibly lonely for months, only ever having nurses and servants to talk to. By the time I went to Eton, it was almost a relief to be leaving home. When I did come back to visit, at the beginning, it was evident that seeing me was painful to him. I was like a visible reminder of what he had lost. So, I stopped visiting as much."

He sighed. "Being at school was lonely too. I didn't have many friends. I'm not a particularly talkative person, by nature, you know. And I'm not interesting enough to engage people. But it was easier being at school and lonely than being at home and lonely, and guilty on top of it. Then your mother married my— married Father. I came to see them a couple of times at the start of their marriage. I held you when you were a baby," he said with a smile at Sophia. "But I felt very much like an outsider, a visiting relative. I didn't belong. So I stopped coming altogether."

He rubbed his cheek against the top of Lucy's head. "I suppose I never visited because I was afraid of causing Father pain when he had finally found happiness again. And I was afraid that I didn't really fit in with his new family. And I was afraid of coming and not being..."

He faltered a moment. Grace leaned against his side. Basil continued, "Of not being wanted, or needed. And I confess I thought Father didn't care much for me. I've come to realize I was wrong. That will always be one of my biggest regrets. But at the time, it was still just a fear and I didn't want to come and prove that fear right. So I stayed away." He looked around at them all. "I'm so sorry."

Eli leaned against his other side and said, "You know now that you're wanted, don't you?"

Basil smiled. "I'm coming to that realization, yes. Although I confess I still don't quite know how I fit into this family. I'm still figuring that out."

Sophia was stunned. How did Basil not know? Had they not been showing him all along?

"Oh, Basil," Levinia sniffed. "That is so tragic. To live so many years alone, without a friend in the world."

Basil reached up and rubbed a tear off her cheek with his thumb. "It wasn't so very bad. I made some friends. I just didn't have any close friends until Modesty."

"How did you meet her?" Sophia said.

He considered for a moment. "We met at a dinner party held by one of my classmates. She's about seven or so years younger than I am, but she was my classmate's cousin, so she had been invited."

"And you fell in love with her?" Sophia said.

"I loved Modesty—I still love her. But I was never in love with her, exactly. She had become one of the few steadfast presences in my life. So I think I proposed more out of fondness than anything else. She was quite right to reject me. I must say I'm rather glad now that she did. I'm not sure I would have been able to stay here if I'd had a wife to return to."

"And now you can propose to Miss Hartford," Levinia said, clasping her hands together.

"What?" Basil said, startled.

"That was another topic on the agenda," Sophia admitted. "We think you ought to marry Miss Hartford."

"Really?" he said with a small smile.

"You do like her, don't you?" Grace said.

"Yes, I do," he admitted.

"You're in love with her?" Eli said.

Basil hesitated and then said, "Yes, I am."

They all breathed out in relief.

"Thank God," Bel said.

Basil chuckled. "I'm glad you approve."

"Of course we approve," Eli said. "She's wonderful."

"We've only been trying to get you two together for months," Bel said.

"Have you really?"

"It's so romantic," Levinia said. "You two will be the most beautiful couple in Tutting-on-Cress."

"Thank you," he said. "I'm very glad to have everyone's support. Although I should warn you that I have not yet proposed."

"Why not?" Martin said.

"Well..." Basil paused. "I'm not entirely sure she'll say yes."

"Of course she will," Sophia said. "She's in love with you too."

He tilted his head. "I do think she likes me. But that still doesn't mean...Miss Hartford has some concerns about marriage. And I'd hate to—"

"No," Bel said, and stood in front of him, hands on

hips. "You're doing it again. You just told us how you didn't come to visit because you were afraid. You spent years not coming to see us because you were afraid of being hurt, so instead you stayed away, feeling a little bit hurt over and over again, rather than face the possibility of being very hurt."

Basil blinked at her. "Go on."

"And I should add that while you were trying to protect yourself from hurt and trying to protect Father from hurt, we were all a little hurt that you didn't come to visit us."

"I'm so sorry."

She shook her head. "And now you're about to do the same thing. You're about to avoid proposing to Miss Hartford, even though you want to, because you're afraid she'll say no and you'll be hurt. So instead, you're going to stay away and be a little hurt until it's too late. And meanwhile you might be hurting her too, making her think you don't like her well enough."

Basil swallowed. "Well, I can't exactly argue with that."

"Then you'll do it?" Sophia said.

Basil took a deep breath. "I'll do it. Give me a week or so, though. All right? There is such a thing as bad timing."

Bel nodded. "One week."

"Thank you, Captain," Basil said with a quirk of a smile. Bel grinned.

"And we'll help you," Sophia said. "If you need it."

"Thank you," he said. "I'll let you know."

"No, Basil," Eli said. "We really will help you. You're not alone anymore, all right?"

Basil smiled down at Eli. "All right. Thank you." He let out a long breath. "Well, is that the extent of the meeting? I think Lucy's ready to adjourn."

Lucy had fallen asleep on his lap.

"There's one more thing," Sophia said. "To call a family meeting, turn the shepherdess in the dining room to face the fireplace. That's the signal."

"The one your mother hates?"

Sophia nodded.

Basil chuckled. "Very good."

"Any member of the family can call a family meeting," Sophia said carefully.

Basil gave her a warm smile. "Thank you."

Levinia launched herself at Basil for a hug. Grace, Eli, and Martin followed suit, already in prime positions for an embrace. Sophia reached carefully around Lucy to give her older brother a hug too. She noticed that Basil held a hand out for Bel, who was not overly fond of hugging, which she clasped—as close to an embrace as Bel ever gave. Sophia thought she felt Basil relax, as if their words assuring him he belonged hadn't really resonated until that moment.

Chapter 82
Gerry

Laurence left for London two days after the ball and Gerry found herself relieved that Seb had distractions at the ready. He spent half his week at the shop and half his week with Bertie. Any time he was at the shop, he worked with a notable intensity, as if hoping to forget that his fiancé was miles away.

"Did he say when he would return?" she ventured.

Seb huffed. "Not for a few months. He said it likely wouldn't be until September."

"Oh dear." Then she had him follow Pip around and learn how to sell products. This seemed to help, as Pip had a soothing influence on everyone, and provided Seb an appropriate amount of distraction. But it did leave Gerry alone with her own thoughts, which was not terribly convenient.

Ever since her talk with Gavin, Gerry had turned the matter of Mr. Thorne over in her mind. She began to more deliberately imagine a life with Mr. Thorne, and found the idea becoming more and more appealing. When she imagined herself with anyone else, she had difficulty dreaming up anyone who made her feel happier than Mr. Thorne. She kept equipping her fantasy husband with Mr. Thorne's tenderness, his gentle manner, his curiosity, and his smile. She gave up that exercise and started imagining herself with Mr. Thorne, which turned out to be a very enjoyable prospect. She found it easy to imagine coming home to him each night, helping him raise his siblings, having him be a father to their own future children.

One afternoon as she was stocking spells, she paused in the act of replenishing Personal Quick-Dry Spells. She held a bag in her hand, remembering Mr. Thorne's first purchase and the way he had twiddled the strings between his fingers. The memory made her pulse quicken. She smiled and stared at the bag in wonder. Was this what love felt like? A small rush of excitement and pleasure at the thought of someone else? She hung the bag up quickly and busied herself with another task. But she couldn't take her mind off of it. Could love sneak up on a person like that? Gavin had made it sound like it could.

"Are you all right?" Seb asked as she weighed rose petals. "You look rather funny."

"Oh, thank you kindly."

"You know what I mean."

She hesitated. "How did it feel when you fell in love with Laury?"

He gave her a sly grin. "Thinking about love, are we?"

"It was a serious question, Seb."

577

He dug his hands into his pockets and looked pensive. "I don't know," he said at last.

She sighed. "Very helpful."

"What do you want to know?" he said plaintively.

She braced her hands on the counter. "Did it come to you in a flash or did it come on gradually?"

"Gradually," he answered promptly.

"So how did you know when it was love?"

"I..." He frowned. "I don't know. I liked his company. I looked forward to seeing him. He proposed and told me what sort of life he wanted. I liked the way that life sounded and I wanted to be a part of it."

"That's it?"

"What else would there be? I know I found him attractive. When I told him I needed time before getting married, he was very patient and understanding. He made my fears feel manageable. He made me feel...safe. Happy. And I found that being happy with him forever sounded very nice."

Gerry sat with that for a long moment.

"Maybe you should go ask Basil what it felt like when he fell in love," Seb said cheekily, before ducking out of the room.

She leaned her chin on her hand. The thought of Basil being in love made her heart do strange things. She continued to think about love and grow accustomed to the sensation for several days, feeling her steps get lighter and her anxieties drifting the more she thought about it. She was working herself into a very pleasant mood until she received an invitation from Rose.

"Oh, no," she said upon reading it one morning at breakfast.

"What's the matter?" Gavin said.

"Rose has invited me to tea again."

"Really?" Charles said. "I'd have thought those would have stopped after the ball."

Gerry had privately hoped so too, but she knew better than to say so.

"Would you like me to come with you?" Charles offered.

"Perhaps," she said. "And I'll tell Rose that this absolutely must be the last such invitation."

"A very sound plan, darling."

On Sunday afternoon, Gerry walked to Hearst Cottage, resolved to face the lion's den by herself. She found comfort along the way by reasoning that this would be a prime opportunity to really test her love for Mr. Thorne. She would have a real comparison, rather than depending on her own imagination.

However, when she walked into Hearst Cottage, it was not some random and unappealing suitor sitting amongst her friends: it was Basil Thorne.

Chapter 83
Basil

Basil had spent days trying to decide the best approach for proposing to Miss Hartford. He had considered and rejected the idea of going to her shop, calling on her at home, or inviting her to visit. When he had received Mrs. Hearst's invitation to tea, he hoped it was a sign. He decided that if Miss Hartford was there, he would offer to escort her home afterward. Modesty would take the carriage and he would walk with Miss Hartford and ask her when they were alone. If she said yes, he would be able to take her all the way home and talk to the Kentworthys about writing to her parents. If she said no, well, they could part on the path and walk their separate ways. Maybe he could even spend the rest of Mary's mourning period hidden away at home.

When Miss Hartford stepped into the sitting room, she blushed bright red and stopped on the threshold.

"There you are, Gerry," Mrs. Rose Hearst said.

Mrs. Julia Hearst hurried forward. "Are you all right, dear?"

Miss Hartford nodded and said very unconvincingly, "Yes, I'm quite all right, thank you." She sat down and resolutely did not look at him.

Basil was at a loss. Had she changed her mind toward him since the ball? Perhaps the kiss in the library had made her realize she wasn't in love with him and that she actually didn't even like him. His heart began to break before he'd even had the chance to offer it up. Modesty must have suspected his thoughts, for she put a hand on his arm and gave it a squeeze. Perhaps proposing wasn't such a good idea after all.

The tension in the room was palpable.

"Gerry," Mrs. Canterbury said in a valiant attempt at cheeriness. "Mr. Thorne was just telling us about a romance he's reading. What was the name of it again?"

"*The Dragon's Breath Bouquet*," Basil said, doing his best to keep his voice even. "Levinia recommended it. She...er...we hope to start a sort of book club if I like it. Well, I suppose we could do that even if I don't...like it... Sophia thought some of you might enjoy the discussion... and perhaps Mr. Charles Kentworthy."

"That's a wonderful idea," Mrs. Julia Hearst said warmly. "I'm sure I should like that."

He gave her a small smile. "She thought you might." He glanced at Miss Hartford. "I probably should have suggested it an age ago. Levinia was reading it...well, I can't even remember when...but I've been so busy, you see. It was...um...it was difficult to find the time."

"And are you enjoying it?" Lady Maria Windham said, giving him an encouraging smile.

"It's difficult to say. Things look pretty dire at the

moment. I'm not sure at all if the hero will wed the heroine. I'm afraid I have no interest in tragedies. I couldn't disappoint Levinia, though, so I'm hoping rather than believing it will all turn out all right."

"At the risk of spoiling it for you," Miss Hartford said, "*The Dragon's Breath Bouquet* does end happily."

Basil was startled by her tone. She sounded like she was trying not to cry. What on earth was going on? Could it be that she still cared for him? "Thank you," he said tentatively. "That does put me at ease."

"I'm glad."

"Do they...erm...end up together?"

She gave him a small smile. "I think you'll have to finish it to find out."

Basil felt his heart lighten again. She'd smiled at him! It wasn't one of her twinkling smiles, but it was...well it was enough to give him hope again.

But then Miss Hartford set down the teacup she'd only just been given and said, "Forgive me. I really don't feel well. I have to go." She stood and headed for the door. Basil wanted to tell her to stop, but he didn't quite dare.

"I think it's going to rain," Lady Maria Windham said.

"It will not rain," Miss Hartford said.

"How do you know that?" Mrs. Rose Hearst said.

"It doesn't matter. I see more distinctly through the rain."

"That doesn't make any sense!" Mrs. Rose Hearst said.

Miss Hartford turned on her heel suddenly and said,

"Rose, I want this to be the last of these visits. Do you understand?"

Her cousin nodded, clearly chagrined. "Yes, Gerry. Of course."

"But, Gerry, wait," Lady Caroline Windham said. "You're getting it all wrong—"

But Miss Hartford had already left.

"Oh, dear," Lady Maria Windham said.

"That's not how that was supposed to go," Mrs. Canterbury said.

Mrs. Julia Hearst cleared her throat. "I think it's safe to say we misjudged that particular part of the plan."

"What plan? What is going on?" Basil said.

Mrs. Rose Hearst took a deep breath. "We've been having Gerry over to tea for months so she can meet different suitors."

"Oh."

"And...er," Mrs. Canterbury said, "we've made it a sort of theme that all of the suitors were actually quite unsuitable."

"Oh."

"We don't think you are," Mrs. Rose Hearst said hurriedly. "You were supposed to be the last of these. We were leading up to the inevitable conclusion so Gerry could see that you were the right man all along."

"Well, that's a relief, I think," he said.

"Unfortunately," Mrs. Julia Hearst said, "Gerry evidently did not realize that was the plan. We really ought to have prepared her for it."

"Oh, darling, stop looking so stunned," Modesty said.

"Go and run after her. Their plan can still work. I'm sure none of the other suitors did that."

Mrs. Canterbury clapped her hands. "Oh, yes, do!"

"Quite right," Lady Caroline Windham said. "Get a move on, Mr. Thorne."

"She's a very good walker," Mrs. Julia Hearst said, laughing.

Modesty took his teacup and gave him a shove.

Basil opened the door and was already running before he realized that it was, in fact, raining.

Chapter 84
Gerry

Gerry felt very dramatic striding through the rain, torn between mild amusement by how appropriately it matched her mood and what an utter nuisance it was to be wet when also irritated.

She had finally gotten around to the idea of being in love with the gentleman. Hadn't that been what everyone was after? Couldn't they leave her and Mr. Thorne in peace to come to the conclusion that had largely been deemed inevitable? Did she really need to be prodded all the way to the altar? It was too insufferable, really.

She absently started thinking about whether or not she could bespell her clothes to repel water and was feeling mildly encouraged that she was already thinking of other spells she could design, when she heard her name being called.

Mr. Thorne had followed her.

"Gerry, please stop."

She tried to quell the thrill that rose up in her at the sound of him saying her name and turned to face him.

"They explained everything," he said. "Well, they explained enough, anyway. I'm sure they didn't explain everything, but they hardly needed to. I wasn't meant to be another unsuitable option."

"I'm sorry?" she said, confused.

He stepped forward. "I understand that you've had to put up with a great many unsuitable suitors the past few months. Apparently, I was meant to be the...grand finale, you could say. I was supposed to be the...I don't know... right one?"

"Those ninnyhammers!" she exclaimed. "Those goosewits! My God, I'll give them a piece of my mind when I see them next. Of all the outrageous, ridiculous plans!"

He smiled, which felt very much like the sun coming out. But she was still angry. "Doesn't it bother you that they were scheming such nonsense? Everyone, it seems, has been meddling in our affairs: my family, your family, my friends, your friends. It is the outside of enough."

He blinked in some confusion and Gerry was distracted by how impossibly dashing he looked in the rain. Raindrops caught on his eyelashes and to the ends of his hair. She was very resolutely not looking at what the rain was doing to his white shirt. She was relieved there was a coat over most of it.

"Not really, no," he said at last. "I must admit it explains why I have been enjoying myself so much the past few months."

Now it was her turn to blink in surprise.

He gave a small smile. "I enjoy your company," he said, as if it was the simplest thing in the world. Then he shook his head. "Everything I said at the ball is still true. I am in awe of you. I think you are the most intelligent, beautiful, charming, and interesting person I've ever met. I cannot imagine a better existence than to spend the rest of my life in awe."

Gerry held her breath, willing herself not to cry. It was all too perfect. He was too perfect. She wanted to throw her arms around him and proclaim her love, but there were enough niggling worries bubbling to the surface. She remembered what the dukex had told her at the ball, that she could verify his opinion on the matter of her shop before accepting any proposal.

She took a steadying breath and said, "And everything I said at the ball is still true too. I will not give up my shop for anyone. I am far too busy to keep house and be a proper nextborn spouse to you. And you have too many things you are working through. It would be too much for both of us to even contemplate marriage right now."

He cocked his head. "I remember you saying that. But I don't remember ever saying I thought you should give up the shop. Why would I?"

"Because it would be your responsibility to handle our financial affairs and it would be my responsibility to run the house."

"And what would Mary do? I don't intend to make her leave, and she has been running the house for years. It seems to me," he went on, "that the situation is rather perfect. Mary would be free to continue running the house as she sees fit—although I'm sure between the two of you, you could work out a solution that you both like—and you could continue working at the shop without having to worry about the menus and the laundry schedules and whatnot."

Gerry held her breath. Was it really that simple? She had to be sure. "That wouldn't bother you?"

"Why would it?"

"You wouldn't mind having a wife in trade, who goes to work every day and leaves you alone at the house?"

He laughed. "I don't mind having a friend in trade, so what difference would it make? And you can hardly describe me as being alone right now. I'm hardly ever alone these days." He seemed to think through his next words. "As for the rest, I confess I do have a great many things to work through. I don't know how to take care of my siblings or how to take my place as head of the family. I am at a loss of what to do most of the time... but I think I would be more at ease with you by my side. You...you make everything seem easier."

"Even when I'm arguing with you?" she said, raising an eyebrow.

He smiled. "Yes, even then." He took a tentative step forward. "I won't pretend that marriage would be easy. I am juggling seven siblings right now. You are managing a business. I don't understand half of what you do; I hardly understand what I'm having to do these days. I can't promise you a life free of challenges or interruptions." He cocked his head. "But I also don't think you'd want that."

"You're right. I don't want that." She considered for a moment and then said, "What could you promise?"

His smile broadened. "I can promise to love you, to be in love with you. And I can promise to always wait for you when you come home from work. I can promise to always be impressed by your spell-building. I can probably promise a loud and busy household for a good many years. I can promise you friendship."

He was promising, Gerry realized, everything she ever wanted. After years of wanting a friendship to blossom into love, she had found it, despite all of the meddling and the doubts. She also realized that as she'd been thinking this, she'd left him completely in suspense.

So she stepped closer and put a hand on his cheek. "That seems to be enough to be going on with," she said.

He slid a hand carefully around her waist. "If you need time to think it over, or if you want to make it a long engagement—"

She smiled. "Well, we ought to at least wait until Laurence comes back from London."

"And when will that be?"

"September."

"Sounds perfect."

"Good." Then she clasped his lapel and went on tiptoes. He obligingly leaned down to kiss her. She wrapped her arm around his neck and felt his fingers sink into her hair. He deepened the kiss with a surety that pleased her, and Gerry allowed herself to be swept up in the moment, being held in his arms. The rain didn't bother her anymore.

Basil gently pulled away. "I should take you back," he said. "Before they start to worry."

She chuckled. "Let's be honest. They'll be more worried if we go back too soon."

He smiled again. "Do you think so?"

"Oh, I'm very confident."

"In that case..." He pulled her in for another kiss, and she relished it. When he pulled away again, he whispered, "I love you, Gerry."

She smiled against his lips. "Oh, Basil. I've wanted to hear someone say that for a very long time."

"I love you," he whispered again, kissing the corner of her mouth. And then he repeated it softly, gently, as he kissed along her cheek, her temple, her jaw, and her neck.

Gerry didn't think she'd ever grow tired of hearing it.

"Will you marry me?" he said. He gave a self-deprecating smile. "I think we already established it, but I don't want there to be any confusion as to my intent—"

"Yes," she said. "I'll marry you."

"Oh, good," he breathed. He paused. "We needn't go on a honeymoon, if it means closing the shop. I know how much it means to you."

And because he understood, she said, "Actually, I think a honeymoon sounds lovely. The shop will keep for a week. And...I don't think I've mentioned it yet, but...I love you too."

He smiled again and took her into his arms and kissed her for a very long time.

* * *

The End

Note from the Author

Dear Reader,

I've been wanting to tell Gerry's story ever since I finished telling Gavin's. But her journey wound up being surprisingly challenging to write. No love interest felt good enough for her and all the plots I came up with felt too contrived. At one point, I even had a love triangle going on even though I hate love triangles. So I finally had to take a big step back and start over.

Basil came about when I tried to think of a good reason for yet another single person to move into Tutting-on-Cress. When I thought of him moving there because he'd inherited some property, he began to take shape. As such, he is somewhat inspired by the horrible half-brother in Sense and Sensibility. I wanted to explore what would have happened if John Dashwood had not been The Worst.

I hope to someday tell the story of each of the Thorne children, although I can't promise any set dates as I keep adding more projects to my to-do list. All I can say is that several of the books are already partially written.

This novel is an ode to forming relationships on your own terms, understanding yourself later in life, and found family. I hope you enjoyed Gerry's story as much as I enjoyed writing it.

As always, thank you for coming along on this journey!

Affectionately,

Sarah Wallace

Acknowledgments

As ever, this book came to life thanks to my own found family. To Ashley, thank you for being one of the first and last people to read my stories. To my alpha and beta readers, Alexis, Kayla, Katie, Anna, Lauren, Meg, Shannon, Leslie, and Maeve thank you for all of your valuable feedback! To my editor, thank you for all of your valuable feedback and for sticking with me throughout this series!

And to my incredible readers, thank you for continuing to read my stories! I couldn't do this without any of you!

Editor: Mackenzie Walton
Proofreader: Ashley Scout
Sensitivity Reader: Salt & Sage Books
Front cover photo by Annie Spratt via Unsplash
Back cover photo by Katherine Hanlon via Unsplash
Author photos by Toni Tillman

About the Author

 Sarah Wallace lives in Florida with their cat, more books than she has time to read, a large collection of classic movies, and an apartment full of plants that are surviving against all odds. They only read books that end happily.

Also by Sarah Wallace

Meddle & Mend: A Regency Fantasy Series

Letters to Half Moon Street - Read Gavin's story

One Good Turn - Read Nell's story

The Education of Pip - Read Pip's story

Dear Bartleby - Read Seb's story

The Glamour Spell of Rose Talbot - *Meddle & Mend* Prequel - Free to all newsletter subscribers!

Fae & Human Relations: A Regency Fantasy Series by Sarah Wallace & S.O. Callahan

Breeze Spells and Bridegrooms - A new series by cozy fantasy authors Wallace and Callahan - Read a sneak peek now!

Sign up for my newsletter!

Are you signed up for my newsletter? Join now at sarahwallacewriter.com to be in the know!

Newsletter subscribers are the first to see book covers, receive the first chapter of new releases a month before release date, get sneak peeks at preorder campaign art, and a free novelette! I've also been known to send deleted scenes or scenes in alternate POV and I plan to do more of that!

Preview for Breeze
Spells and Bridegrooms

Torquil's Tribune

Greetings fair folk and haphazard humans,

For those just now returning to London, welcome back.

Did you miss me?

The summer months are always horrifically dull for this humble writer. So little gossip to share. So little havoc to wreak. We are excessively relieved to see people return to the city. Whose lives shall be changed this Season? Who will fall in love? Who will flirt with scandal? We are, as ever, eager to find out.

It would appear that the Council for Fae & Human Magical Relations is preparing to convene soon, a whole month before the Season begins. To what do we owe the pleasure of a group of blustery and generally useless politicians to our fair city?

Well, the trend of human children receiving low scores on their Hastings Exam has started to reach a crisis point. Low scores have always been a potential result of the magical testing process, but high scores are becoming increasingly rare. As more and more humans with low Hastings scores reach adulthood, we are seeing the strain on society.

This strain is not caused by those with low scores but rather the way the world treats them. We are seeing more humans rejected for employment opportunities, or reaching the age of majority without a single marriage proposal. As human children are increasingly less likely to receive the desired score, this presents a troublesome insight into our future.

Will the Council find a solution? This writer considers it unlikely. But who knows? Perhaps a hero will emerge from the midst. It hasn't happened since King Arthur's reign but, as they say, nothing is impossible where magic is concerned.

Your esteemed editor,
Torquil Pimpernel-Smith

The Spellmaster Of Tutting-On-Cress

Roger

Roger Barnes attempted to surreptitiously dab at the beads of sweat gathering on his forehead. The Council's chambers were notoriously hot, even in the waiting area. Some blamed it on the heated debates between councilmembers, but Roger privately believed it had more to do with the placement of the wing. It really did get the most atrocious amount of sunlight. Convening in late summer did not help. Roger had a brief wistfulness for his family's country estate, wind gliding over the pond as he read by a tree. He shook his head and reined in his thoughts. Now was not the time for wistfulness.

He took his notes out of his pocket, reading them for what felt like the hundredth time. The paper was crumpled from so much handling. He didn't need to read the notes; they were memorized already. But he tended to get flustered when he was nervous, agitated, or generally upset. Quite frankly, flustered was practically Roger's natural state. He folded the paper, his hands shaking. He put it back in his pocket, decided he ought to have it handy just in case, and pulled it out again. He tapped the paper against his thigh, decided that wasn't doing the crumpled state any favors, put it back in his pocket, and clenched his hands together.

He could hardly believe he was doing this again. Was he really foolish enough to approach the Council for a third time? When an aide appeared at the door and beckoned him in, he concluded that, apparently, he was foolish enough to do just that.

He felt six pairs of eyes follow his progress into the

603

room. He had always believed that an even number of members was an absurd way to assemble a council responsible for big decisions, but no one cared much about his opinions on the subject. In this case, his reasons for approaching were so important that Roger felt overwhelmed by it all. He walked up to the little stand and placed his wrinkled notes down, smoothing out the edges. He looked up and found his father sitting at the end of the table, the lowest-ranking human councilmember, and the only person in the group that did not thoroughly intimidate Roger.

"Well, Mr. Barnes," Councilmember Williams said, his gruff voice making Roger feel even smaller, "to what do we owe the pleasure this time?"

He tried to hide his wince. He glanced at his father, who gave him an encouraging smile. He cleared his throat, "Thank you, sir. I am grateful for the opportunity to approach this august company again." He could tell his voice sounded monotone as he read out the words, but monotone was preferable to stuttering, so he kept going. "I understand that the Council is working to find a solution to the...Hastings score...situation and I-I would like to offer a suggestion."

Councilmember Cricket glanced at Roger's father. "Yes," she mused. "I suppose you would have opinions about that."

"I hope it is different from your last suggestion," Councilmember Gibbs sniffed. "Your last one left much to be desired."

His last suggestion—to raise the testing age to eighteen—had been squashed in record time. It was a pity. He'd really believed in that one. However, he had been significantly less prepared when he'd approached the Council before. His reasoning behind changing the testing age had not been well argued. Perhaps now that the situation was more dire, the Council would be more willing to hear his solution—particularly when his notes were better organized.

"To be fair," Councilmember Applewood put in, "the previous suggestion was not a bad one. But I'm still concerned about keeping families in suspense about inheritance for so long. It would be very taxing, particularly for the children involved."

"Not to mention, valuable time would be wasted that could be spent training heirs in what they need to know," Councilmember Williams added.

"There is little need to go over the subject again," Councilmember Wrenwhistle said coolly. "I take it Mr. Barnes has a different solution in mind this time."

"Y-yes," he stammered. "My proposal is to move away from the Hastings Examination rubric altogether."

There was, predictably, a small clamor at that, mostly from the human side, although there were a couple of fae members who were chattering too. He thought they seemed approving. Councilmember Applewood was looking at him pensively, a smile playing upon her lips. Roger felt a small bit of hope at that expression.

Councilmember Wrenwhistle raised her hand to silence the rest. "That is certainly a bold suggestion. I am curious to hear your reasons and what you suggest as an alternative."

"Well," he said. "My reasons are fairly simple, I think. As you know, the success rate for the Hastings Exams are extremely low. Some families see children with no passing rates at all, even from powerful bloodlines. My belief is that the exam is too narrow in its observations to be properly conclusive. My proposal..." he shifted his notes so the second page was on top, "is to have a more nuanced approach to testing. We only test human children on one spell. If we were to broaden the scope of the examination, we could test multiple strengths at once. I do not have a new model fully drafted yet, but I believe testing for...er...spell force, as we currently do, but also control, attention to detail, and...creativity, would be beneficial."

Councilmember Williams scoffed. "Creativity? What, are we going to have students offer up poems to their examiners?"

"N-no, sir. But it would be good to see students apply principles of basic theory to multiple spells. Sort of a theoretical examination on top of a practical one."

"Roger," his father said, his tone mild, "what do you propose for the fae examinations? I agree that the Hastings Exam may be out of date, but it is the most standard form of testing we have and has the benefit of being the most closely aligned to the fae test, the Sciurus Exam. Both rubrics must be comparable."

"I admit, sir, that I do not have sufficient expertise on fae magic," Roger said. "I would cede to the Council on that part, although I do agree that it is an important part of the issue."

"It hardly matters what the testing rubrics are,"

Councilmember Cricket sneered. "We do not treat our children like outcasts when they don't do well. I think that is the most critical issue at hand."

His father looked like he wanted to agree but Gibbs was quick to say that the fae had issues of their own, thank you very much. Then Cricket argued that whatever issues the fae had, they at least protected their own, which could not be said for humankind.

Roger felt himself wilt a little. This was more or less what happened the first time. He had made a proposal that started a debate, then he had been unceremoniously sent out. It wasn't quite as bad as the second time, when he suggested the testing age be altered. That time he had practically been laughed out of the room. He supposed if he had to choose, watching the Council descend into its usual chaos was somewhat preferable.

Wrenwhistle raised her hand again. The arguing died down, primarily because the fae were pointedly respectful to their Head of Council and the humans couldn't very well argue against silence. When the bickering stopped, she was silent for a long moment before saying, "Your proposal has merit, Mr. Barnes." Roger felt hope kindle in his chest. "But," she went on, quickly extinguishing that brief feeling, "a vague idea is not sufficient. We will give you a fortnight to come up with a detailed proposal, a workable testing rubric. I agree that a comparable model for testing fae magic is necessary, although I appreciate your restraint in overstepping beyond your expertise." Roger thought this was said with some sarcasm but he tried to pretend it wasn't. "So for now we will give you an opportunity to present to us a real solution. Something we can act upon. If your rubric is accepted, we will assign a fae to work with you on a comparable rubric for fae magic. Are we in agreement, Councilmember Williams?"

Williams gave Roger a long look. Finally, he nodded. "I believe that will suffice."

"Thank you, Mr. Barnes."

Roger knew a dismissal when he heard one and wasted no time in leaving. Once outside the room, he allowed himself to process his warring emotions. On one hand, they actually listened to him and hadn't laughed at him outright! That was certainly progress. On the other hand...he had not figured on developing the testing rubric himself. He had ideas, but with his Hastings score, he didn't have much hope that those ideas would be taken seriously. However, his mind was already starting to churn. He strode down the hall, lost in thought.

The Spellmaster Of Tutting-On-Cress

Wyn

At one point in time, Wyn supposed, the grandeur of the
Parliament buildings along the Thames had been quite
impressive. Countless spires stretched from the
rooftops, tall enough to pierce the dreary, unwelcoming
clouds that often collected overhead. Inside, the ogive
arches helped draw attention to the stained-glass
windows and intricate stonework on the walls and high
ceilings. It was easy to let your jaw go slack at such a
spectacle if you were not accustomed to it.

Wyn had been visiting his grandmother in the
Council's chambers his entire life, effectively numbing
him to the beauty of the architecture. Even the
meticulously manicured grounds that surrounded him on
his brisk walk along the cobbled path had long since
faded into familiarity.

He followed his older brother Emrys up the steps,
who touched his fingers to the brim of his hat as he
greeted the doorkeepers by name.

"*Ugh,*" Emrys moaned as they passed through the
vestibule, quick to voice what both men were thinking.
"Could it possibly be any hotter?" Even the echoing of
their footsteps in the long hallway seemed muffled by
the stifling air inside the building.

Wyn struggled to ignore the way the damp fabric of
his cravat was sticking to his neck. His discomfort wasn't
enough to make him regret wearing his thick, wavy hair
long enough to reach his shoulders, though. It was a

decision he'd made just recently, opting to let it grow out of the more fashionable cut that most men were wearing. His mother could protest many of his decisions, but this would not be one of them.

He took a deep breath and let it out in an impatient sigh.

"I just hope Grandmother makes this quick," he muttered, still trailing behind Emrys toward the chambers. There was an invitation to the first event of the Season with his name on it sitting atop his dressing table. He would wear something far less stuffy than his high boots and heavy coat. With any luck, the evening would dissolve into a more private situation that required no clothing at all.

"When has she ever been known to do that?" Emrys asked with a faint chuckle. "Although, maybe if I show her the way my new clothes are being ruined with sweat stains, she'll take pity and grant us leave."

As they approached the final corner in the maze of window-lit hallways, someone called Emrys' name. Both men turned to look over their shoulders and discovered the familiar smile of Keelan Cricket, one of Emrys' closest friends and the son of another councilmember.

"Go ahead, I'll catch up with you in a moment." Emrys left no room for argument as he pivoted and took off in the direction they'd just come. Wyn rolled his eyes, knowing that was the exact opposite of the truth, and turned the corner—directly into someone else.

"Watch it," Wyn hissed, taking a steadying step backward, trying his best to maintain appearances in case his brother or anyone else had seen. Upon realizing who had run into him, his annoyance flared. Of course it would be Barnes getting in his way.

"Apologies," the shorter man mumbled, his hands doing a ridiculous little dance, as though he couldn't decide between reaching for the scraps of paper he'd dropped on the floor or fixing his spectacles that had fallen askew after crashing into Wyn's chest.

Wyn crossed his arms and watched as Roger bent to pick up the papers from where they had fluttered to their feet. His mouth curled into a faint smirk.

"Had to draw yourself a map to find the exit, did you?"

Roger righted himself with a puff of an exhale and quickly folded his papers away into a pocket, fixing his spectacles with an indignant glare. Wyn's gaze slid down to the man's shoes and back up again. Barnes had never known how to dress for his plump figure, nor find a suitable color palette to match the light brown of his skin. Such a pity.

"I've been here just as many times as you, Wyndham," Roger said. Wyn bristled instantly at the casual use of his name. "I know my way around—"

"You will call me Mr. Wrenwhistle," Wyn ground out with a slow emphasis on each word, his jaw tight. The man was a year older than he was, but the fact remained that he wouldn't tolerate the disrespect of being addressed by his first name in public, especially by the likes of Roger Barnes. They might've known each other since they were children, but that did not make them friends.

He felt it then, the familiar tingling, and Wyn knew his

magic was seconds away from begging to be set free. It was an issue he'd dealt with for as long as he could remember. Returning to London was most stressful for a fae who struggled with being surrounded by disorder. For Wyn, his melancholy was exacerbated by the stress, resulting in his magic demanding to be felt as his emotions flared.

Wyn drew in a deep, silent breath and held it, eyes sliding shut. He focused on what he could feel. The growing ache in his chest from holding the sweltering air in his lungs. The perspiration clinging in some unmentionable places. The cool, smooth metal of the rings on his fingers. He exhaled as these thoughts filtered through his mind, quelling the surge of emotion that had dared to unwind him right there in the hall.

"Are you...feeling quite the thing?"

The sound of Roger's voice, laced with just enough concern to sound sarcastic, washed away every speck of control Wyn had just regained.

"Do get out of my way," he said brusquely, stepping around Roger and continuing down the corridor.

The heels of Wyn's boots clacked harder than necessary all the way to the final door that separated him from the Council's chambers. He slammed through it with a flourish, coat whipping about his hips as he went. Without needing to read the nameplates hanging outside the offices, Wyn approached his grandmother's and let himself in.

Iris Wrenwhistle lifted her gaze from the papers on her desk, a pleasant look of surprise on her face despite the fact that she'd been the one to request his presence. This was the way she always regarded her grandchildren. She treated every interaction with them like a small gift.

"There you are, darling," she said with a warmth that helped wash away the last of Wyn's twist of frustration. "Where is your brother?"

"Chatting up a friend," he replied. The chair by the window had always been his favorite. He plunked into it like a sullen teenager and crossed his arms over his chest, eyes cast to the floor.

"Ah, yes. It's good to be back in London with everyone, is it not? A little early, but we've got important work to do."

I hate it here, he wanted to tell her. *I hate it more than anything.*

Wyn wanted to be back in the country where he could enjoy the fresh air and sunshine and nights under the stars without the constant bustling and noise of high society. Somewhere he was not continually reminded that, despite his magical aptitude, he was inferior in the eyes of others thanks to the score he'd been given when he was just a child.

"It's good to be back," he agreed, though the lie burned hot on his tongue.

* * *

Want to read more of Breeze Spells and Bridegrooms? Buy it now!

9 781964 556123